To my Dad, Donald Wagner

MALLWORLD, INCORPORATED

BY

JEFFERY ZAVADIL

ISBN: 978-1-54399-666-1 (softcover)
ISBN: 978-1-54399-667-8 (ebook)

TABLE OF CONTENTS

Preface...1

Chapter 1:   Emptiness in Fullness.................................. 7

Chapter 2:   Rebound of a Mind.................................... 47

Chapter 3:   Taking Flight 65

Chapter 4:   We Deserve a Better World.......................96

Chapter 5:   Beginning Democracy 130

Chapter 6:   First Awakenings.....................................151

Chapter 7:   Citadels of Democracy 186

Chapter 8:   Valiant Campaign.................................... 203

Appendix 1:   Classical Republicanism 243

Appendix 2:   Democratic Socialism.............................260

Appendix 3:   Deliberative Democracy.........................271

PREFACE

Science fiction, including dystopia and utopia, can inflame the imagination with visions of different social worlds—but, of course, such stories usually tell us more about contemporary society than any future ones. *Mallworld, Incorporated*, the first book in a trilogy, begins as a dystopia that is not much different from market society today, although, like a magnifying mirror that reveals flaws more clearly, it amplifies some aspects of the contemporary world in order to highlight problems. Modern society is thoroughly commercial, so the idea of the shopping mall as its master metaphor is, I think, fitting and accurate. While most political theory is non-fiction, writing mine as fiction enabled me to depict that metaphor more effectively. Even though we have seen many real-world malls shut down in recent years due to mismanagement and online shopping, "Mallworld" as a metaphor refers to a *way of life*, not only to the physical buildings of retail outlets. Last year, plans for the largest mall ever to be built in the United States were approved in Florida—a massive structure that will contain an amusement park, water park with a beach, ski hill, artificial lake with sea lions and submarines, luxury apartments, and all the retail shopping one could want. Its name? "American Dream." Similar large malls have been built in China, the Middle East, and elsewhere. Clearly, the definition of the good life established by globalized capitalism is that of ostentatious consumption and entertainment.

But, like any metaphor, "society is a shopping mall" fails to capture the entirety of a complex phenomenon. Alarmingly, modern society is too often like Skid Row or a concentration camp, and of course for the homeless, migrants, and many Othered people those are not merely metaphors. They are, rather, what capitalism turns to when the main social control devices of its grand shopping-plaza civilization—consumerism and spectacle—start to break down. Coercion is always available to the elite when bread and circuses fail.

By the end of this trilogy, however, dystopia will turn into utopia, and one purpose of the series is to trace a path to get there. We have been mired for a long time in the material circumstances of consumer capitalism, and blinded by its conservative and neoliberal ideologies. The resulting failure of society to adapt and progress is now causing parallel global crises of democracy and the natural environment. Another advantage to writing political theory as science fiction was that it not only allowed me to describe the principles of the interconnective republic and coexaltation, but to illustrate, through narrative, *how* they might be brought into practice. The "transition problem" has been a perennial question in socialist theory for over a century: "How can a socialist society be brought about when capitalism is so all-pervasive that it shapes the very individuality of its subjects?" I undertook this work to try my hand at answering that question, because I think it is the most important one of our era. While my own version of a realistic utopia will be described in the third book, the series as a whole is written to show one way to get from a sick, suicidal society to a healthy, flourishing one. Here I should caution the reader: I did not find any magical solution to the transition problem. Rather, I concluded that a more democratic world tomorrow requires us to be more democratic here, today. It's going to take all of us, pitching in.

One shortcoming of much utopian and science fiction is an obsession with technological invention and a neglect of the social aspects of progress. Our problems will not be solved by technology, however, for technology has been one of their main causes. The area where we desperately need improvement is *the social*, in our practices, norms, and institutions. I find the possibility of such social progress to be the most fulfilling thing to read and write about. Dear reader, make no mistake: social progress *is* possible, and we *must not* listen to the voices of cynicism and despair who say that things can never change. The climate crisis is not insurmountable: just a few months ago researchers announced that simply planting a trillion trees will go very far (although not all the way) toward ameliorating climate change. That is a decidedly low-tech solution, and it is eminently doable if we have the political will. Other solutions for our many problems likewise exist. However, we need to catch up *socially and politically* to the level of our technology. Until we do, we will only make more problems with our machines than we solve. Unfortunately, capitalism invests in new gadgets because it can profit from them, but it can't invest in social progress because that would be the end of it. Market forces can't do the job of saving the world; we have to do it politically and democratically.

The stakes couldn't be higher for humanity: democracy, justice, quality of life, healthy social relations, and environmental survival depend on it.

+ + +

Readers should be aware that, while this is a dystopian novel, it is not genre science fiction meant to entertain; nor is it a tale of young adults resisting the system. It is political theory, albeit written as fiction. It contains substantive discussions of political philosophy that are somewhat lengthy (although limited to several pages, as I wanted to avoid Ayn Rand-like screeds of a hundred pages). If you find that frustrating, or don't want to put effort into reading those passages, then this might not be the book for you. I just want to be honest with prospective readers up front, in order to avoid disappointed expectations.

Unusually for fiction, this book also includes three appendices at the end, each of which is a background excursus on some aspect of democratic political theory as I understand it. Some readers will be familiar with classical republicanism, democratic socialism, and deliberative democracy, but others will not, so these sections are there for those who may want an introduction. They are, of course, my own interpretations of these theories, with which other political theorists may disagree in whole or in part.

My approach to political theory is eclectic, multiperspectival, and synthetic, although certainly not onmiperspectival. I have ideological influences from the socialist, republican, liberal, environmentalist, deliberative, communitarian, postmodern, Frankfurt school, feminist, and multicultural traditions, and consider myself resolutely opposed to fascism, neoliberalism, and libertarianism; indeed I think the latter two ideologies create a path that runs straight to fascism through oligarchy. The majority of the ideas in *Mallworld, Incorporated* are drawn from my many influences, although I think I can modestly claim some sparks of originality too. Thinkers who have influenced me include Aristotle, Epictetus, Cicero, Marcus Aurelius, Machiavelli, Ferguson, Rousseau, Kant, Jefferson, Madison, Thoreau, Marx, Nietzsche, Edward Bellamy, Eduard Bernstein, Emma Goldman, Durkheim, Huxley, Orwell, Adorno, Marcuse, Albert Ellis, Martin Luther King, Guy DeBord, Rawls, Walzer, Habermas, Lakoff, Wendell Berry, Carol Gould, Susan Moller Okin, Bernard Manin, and Naomi Klein, who I think is the most perceptive political analyst active today.

I would like to thank Senator Bernie Sanders for making democratic socialism an acceptable part of American political discourse for the first time since Eugene Debs. His leadership is inspirational. I would also like to express admiration for the new generation of democratic socialists, led most prominently by Representative Alexandria Ocasio-Cortez, as well as the Democratic Socialists of America and the Justice Democrats, for picking up the torch. Some readers may assume that the character of Samantha Gomprez in this novel is based on AOC, but that is not the case; I decided already in 2010 to include a strong woman as a labor leader, and in drafts the character had evolved into a Latina by January 2017, before AOC's run for congress. It is heartening to see a democratic socialist of her class and background become a national political leader in reality, and not merely on the page.

I must acknowledge a delightful sci-fi book with a similar name, *Mallworld*, by S.P. Somtow, the American-Thai artist and musician, which was first published in 1981. It had been out of print for many years and I was not aware of it when I originally chose in 2009 to call my project by the same title. An expanded edition of Somtow's *Mallworld* was published in 2013. When I discovered another work already existed with my intended name, I altered the title of this work to *Mallworld, Incorporated* out of respect for the earlier book. Somtow's *Mallworld* is imaginative, fun, and adventurous in the spirit of the *Hitchhikers Guide to the Galaxy*, and I recommend it. But the present book is very different. *Mallworld* is about a giant shopping mall in space, after the Earth's solar system has been cut off from the rest of the universe by advanced aliens; *Mallworld, Incorporated*, on the other hand, is social science fiction about a giant shopping mall on post-climate-collapse Earth, and explores the possibilities for political change. The concepts of malls and their settings are thus entirely different, and there are no other similarities in the stories. S.P. Somtow has lived a wonderfully creative life, and we all should aspire to develop our talents as he has.

I want to express my deep gratitude to the following people for reviewing parts of the manuscript and helping improve the story: Jim Williams, Terry Ball, Kate Bracht, Summer Liu, Scott Stebelman, Andre van Eeden, Deborah Kaminski, Dorian Maffei, Aemilia Phillips, Sarah Bolling, and Laura Strachan. Special thanks go to Jon Shifrin, my friend and fellow traveler in learning the world of publishing, without whom I would've been lost. Any errors that remain in the book are my responsibility.

Stephan Martinère's beautiful cover painting is everything I imagined. I am grateful that he thought enough of my project to paint for it, and for his utmost professionalism in accommodating requests for changes as the cover developed.

I would also like to thank the organizers, panelists, and participants at the San Francisco Writers Conference, the Washington Writers Conference, and the Muse and the Marketplace in Boston, from whom I learned so much about bringing one's vision to the public, in particular Mark Coker, David Landan, and Steve Saffel. And many thanks to Matthew Idler and the staff at BookBaby for their editing, advertising, and publishing expertise.

I owe a special debt to Jennifer Rodriguez, who counseled me many years ago to try writing fiction, as an alternative to the analytical writing I did in my day job. Without that advice I wouldn't have started this project. And last but not least, all my love and gratitude to my partner Angie Ahmadi, whose advice, encouragement, and support along the way improved the book, boosted my spirits, and kept me going.

Finally, I thank you, dear reader, and hope you find this book valuable enough to continue reading the trilogy. If you do like it, please let others in your communities know, both in the real world and online.

Bound forward, bound together,
Jeffery

Jeffery Zavadil, PhD
Alexandria, VA
November 2019

CHAPTER 1:
EMPTINESS IN FULLNESS

Only scrubgrass and dust lay before him, and the colossal Mall loomed behind him. Scrubgrass and dust as far as the eye could see, although even runty little tufts of grass wouldn't grow in the lakebed. Lake Michigan had been poisoned by pollutants before drying up, he knew, and you couldn't get anything to grow there now, not even weeds. Not that much would grow anywhere Outside anymore.

Which is why I'm stuck in this moonscape, Jime thought as he turned back toward the algae paddy that he ran. If we had real farms like the ancients maybe I wouldn't be managing this shit-plantation.

I should've just bought up to my minimum Shopping Quota last year like everyone else, he thought. Still, it wasn't fair. Mall Management shouldn't have assigned me to months of algaecultural purgatory outside the walls of Mallworld, with no spectas, no restaurants, no stores—nothing but algae farms and assembly plants. And scrubgrass and dust. Jime resented it. He had been such a star in business school that everyone called him "Prime Time Jime"—but his career had fizzled as he drifted between mid-level Manger jobs. And look where he was now. At least his Time Out was finally nearing its end and he would be back Inside soon. He couldn't wait to buy himself something nice.

Jime walked back to the dark red algae paddy, which lay in the shadow of the immense Mall, breathing hard at the effort it took to haul himself across just a few hundred yards. He hadn't lost any weight during his reassignment, despite seven months of deprivation; his brown, baggy, off-the-rack suit could only do so much to hide his girth. He shambled past the company jetcopter he was learning to fly as part of his supervisory duties. Looking toward the algae pools, he barely noticed the bent-backed workeys who were laboring to stir the blood-colored slime. Jime turned and eyed the long line of the Mallwall, really the many walls of the Mall's millions of interconnected buildings, which stretched so far it vanished into the horizon. He spotted a mange-rat scurrying along the wall's base, dodging in and out of various pipes and mechanisms. Manges were a kind of rodent that survived off the trash and scrub Outside, and here on the edge of civilization they were everywhere. A few weeks back the workeys had been abuzz because one of them had gotten locked out of the dorms overnight and was eaten by manges. The dumbass should've made it back in before they locked up for the night, Jime thought; what do you expect rats to eat anyway, since there's practically nothing outdoors but you? He felt that workeys were dumb and filthy and smelly, and mostly just lazy. If they would only move their asses and do some real work then they could be Managers too, instead of breaking their backs stirring the red goo. The mange-rat scampered toward him along the wall.

As Jime lumbered back toward his office at the base of the Mallwall, he took in the immense enclosure looming above him and stretching as far as he could see in both directions. The ancients would be proud of the people today and the gargantuan Mall they had built. Mallworld extended from here, the Northgate section of the Milwaukee Annex, down through the Chicago–Gary Rotary where Mall Central was, and across the Ohiodomes to Penn Pastures. It thus encompassed the Southern Great Lakes Corporate Regional Zone—although with the lakes sucked dry, Jime didn't know why it was still called that. Over seven billion shoppers lived and worked in the belly of the Mall, with its stores and kiosks and waterparks and office towers, all covered by roofs and domes of concrete or algaeplastic, all perfectly climate controlled, and filled with pleasant music, pleasant scents, and pleasant shoppers—everywhere. I should be Inside, Jime thought, not out here with the wretched workeys. He looked down and saw the mange disappear into a dark hole in the wall, presumably to fatten itself and then shelter in some dreary nest it had found Inside.

Inside: where Jime could go shopping to buy new food and clothes and plastiplants and hologames, and be part of the latest thing again. He missed strutting the mallways—the corridors and walkways of the Mall—with their colorful sim-skies and constant buzz of human commotion. He loved how different sections were set up to imitate different places: ancient streets, foreign cities, tropical islands. Shopping and entertainment had been stolen from him during his Time Out, and all he could think of right now were the fantastic pork ribs in New Tropicana. When he got back Inside in two weeks, those ribs would be one of the first things he'd buy.

He looked back toward the cracked and dusty lakebed.

You can't make dinner out of scrubgrass and dust, he thought.

+ + +

On billions of holoscreens across Mallworld an advertisement was projected. In it, an attractive, perky mom in her thirties bounces down a hallway of her home, holding the hand of one of her children while others run screaming through the house. "Come on kids! Time for breakfast!"

As they enter the kitchen, handsome dad is already there, standing by the counter sipping his coffee. He says, "Before you rush off to school, don't forget to eat your Cake!" As he serves his children a tray of the artificially sweetened confectionary food product, wrapped in brightly colored plastic packages, an announcer says, "Cake: made of the freshest algae-ingredients, for the best in simulated sweetness and nutrition." The children scarf down the Cake without thinking.

The camera zooms in on attractive mom, who declares, "It's convenient, too, for home, work, and school!" She winks at the camera as she tosses more plastic packages of Cake into her children's' schoolbags, which the kids grab as they run pell-mell out the door, yelling and screaming at the top of their lungs.

The announcer proclaims: "Cake: it tastes as good as it makes you feel!"

+   +   +

The sights, the sounds, the smells Inside enchanted Jime just as before. After long deprivation his senses were, in fact, overwhelmed, but he knew he would readjust quickly. Now Jime could once again switch off his thinking and let sensations grab him and carry him away. No matter where he turned his gaze, a screen intruded into his field of vision, usually displaying flashy holographic images of advertisements, while loud announcements of sales and staccato bursts of muzak blared over loudspeakers. His attention was drawn to new stimuli with every passing second as he walked down a standard mallway: the cold gleaming whiteness of a molded plastic bench; the gaudy neon sign of an art store; the perfume that a saleswoman sprayed on passersby, causing others to steer clear of her kiosk; the obnoxious man in a pastel smock shouting at shoppers to enjoy some relaxation in his meditation center. All of it competed to make irresistible demands on the senses of the shoppers strolling by. They, too, were competing for attention: those who were thin enough to look somewhat like models in advertisements flaunted their bodies, displaying lots of skin or showing off taut muscles under tight clothes; meanwhile, the more typically overweight shoppers wore garments cut to make them look thinner and taller than they were. It was all too much. Yet Jime was so stimulated that his arms and legs tingled with excitement.

Jime set foot onto the massive paved square of Piazza Plaza just as an explosion of light in pink, purple, orange, and red blotted out the bluish-white of the sim-sky above. The public square, filled with thousands of shoppers, was built in Italian Renaissance style and surrounded by a mosaic of simulated quattrocento building facades. At the moment it was bathed in a light show that had erupted from its central fountain. There, a specta was being enacted by a troupe of auto-actors. It was a re-creation of a heretic being burned at the stake. Jime stopped and watched for a minute, and, glad to be back Inside, smiled at the show. You'd never see a mechanical *auto-da-fé* Outside, that was for sure, he thought. Flames engulfed the screaming victim, who wasn't a real person but was a mechaniman. As its fake skin and hair burned, howls of delight from the crowd filled the square.

The specta was fake, and Jime knew it. The crowd knew it on some level too, Jime thought, although most of them were perhaps not keen enough to act*ually* see its fakeness, unlike educated people like him. The robotic performer would, after all, return to repeat the spectacle in thirty minutes. Jime was glad that the world didn't have real oppression like this anymore, even if the simulation of it was mildly amusing to some. The specta itself wasn't all that impressive in its production qualities, but Jime liked having all this history around him. It was reassuring. The show was in the tradition of the Great Synergy, a public relations campaign of a few generations earlier when the Mall was first built, which had used modern advertising techniques to weaken the hold that differences like race, religion, and nationality had on people's minds. A technocratic triumph, it brought an end to identity conflict, and Jime was grateful for it. Such spectas reminded people of how good the world was now compared to the past. Religious, ideological, and racial discord, it was commonly known, had proven to be largely a product of discontent. Ever since the building of the Mall, shoppers had an abundance of consumer goods and entertaining diversions to choose from. With everyone fat and happy, there was no protest or heresy, no scapegoating of out-groups, and therefore no need anymore for anyone to be tortured or burned.

Jime wandered around Piazza Plaza, taking it all in. Draped in one of his baggy tan suits, he saw that everyone else was wearing blues and grays and realized he was woefully behind this month's fashion. He meandered over to a bazaar of market-stalls off to one side. At the entrance a mechaniman version of Mallworld's CEO, Ronald Ryan, greeted shoppers. The automaton was handsome, with dark hair and angular features and, like the upper-class Executive he was, dressed in an expensive business suit.

"Welcome, Mallworld shoppers!" the plastic Executive said, grinning a mechanical grin and stiffly waving hello. "Indulge yourself, you deserve it! Mallworld: living the good life, in the moment."

"Hello, CEO Ryan!" said Jime.

"Hello …" the robot searched its surveillance recognition banks, "… Jime Galilei! Welcome to the Piazza Plaza bazaar. Please enjoy your shopping experience."

"What's today's trending, must-have purchase?"

"The Mallmart mini-bazaar has the latest in fashions, electronics, and entertainment every day. We hope your shopping experience is enjoyable and convenient!"

"It's good to be home, Mr. Ryan. Thanks for making this such a great place to live!" Jime said with a broad grin.

"Welcome, Jime! We value all our shoppers. We hope your shopping experience is enjoyable and convenient!"

Jime felt relieved beyond belief to be free of the dull deprivation he had endured Outside—life couldn't be more convenient or entertaining Inside. He of course felt very much at home, for he was, in fact, in the place where he had been born and grown up, and the loss of his native habitat had been disorienting. Nonetheless, after seven months away, it was an adjustment to be back Inside.

Jime walked to a nearby souvenir kiosk and browsed through the selection. Although nothing looked appealing, he bought a marbled algaeplastic replica of a Florentine villa—his first new purchase. He had to use up his store credits, after all, or he'd be exiled back Outside again! As he bought the model, Jime squinted at the salespartner, or "saley," who manned the kiosk's sales station. The man wore the standard saley attire: a polo shirt and a cloth apron in the color of his franchise, in this case orange. Jime noticed how pudgy he was underneath the apron. After seven months of looking at emaciated workeys Outside, Jime thought this cashier looked very round, and he wondered if he looked that unhealthy himself. He knew he needed to lose a few pounds, but jeez. Turning to look at the crowd, he saw that most of the people in the square weighed too much, and, quickly comparing himself to them, he thought maybe he had, after all, lost some weight while away from all this.

"Nice show, huh?" asked the saley.

"Huh? Oh, yeah, but I like the gladiator fights over in Great Rome better; more action," Jime said. He turned up his nose and only looked sideways at the obese man.

"Yeah, those fights are good. They're different every time. Selling here, I gotta sit through the same stupid show twenty times a day, and it gets boring after a while. You get used to it, I guess."

"Does the crowd always scream like that?"

"Every time. The show's *supposed* to make them scream."

"I like the big shows at the Colosseum, where they reenact whole battles."

"Did you know they're doing ship battles now?"

"Oh, I saw that on the holonet."

"Yeah, the Romans used to fill up their stadium with water, I guess, and, uh, do fake navy battles, so they're doing that here now too. They do a really good pirate show—cannons and swashbucklers and everything."

"That's not Roman!"

"Who cares? It's cool."

Stupid idiot, thought Jime as he walked off with his plastic villa. He wandered back to the fountain to watch the rest of the show; the mechaniman's body was fully consumed by flames now, and a man in robes said priestly things in a solemn voice while the crowd chattered in approval and satisfaction. They had gotten their daily stress out of their systems.

Next, Jime got on a tube shuttle, bumping elbows with other passengers boarding the metro car. He was scheduled to meet a friend from whom he had purchased time on Affinity.mal, the companionship app, and they were going to one of Jime's favorite restaurants in the New Tropicana resort dome. There, he would get his ribs. It was good to not have to walk anywhere for a while—he had done *sooo* much walking Outside. The shuttle car left Piazza Plaza and passed through the next plaza over, Old Moscow's Potemkin Square, and as his shuttle sped by Jime stared out the window at the colorful onion domes of the replica of St. Basil's Cathedral. Then the car entered a long residential section of apartment buildings and close-packed condominiums, at first passing through stretches of mostly gray and dreary middle-income zones. But the brightness, size, and value of the housing units increased as the car approached the upscale New Tropicana.

It was one of the most pleasant and desirable parts of Mallworld, a great vacation dome a dozen kilometers across that replicated an ancient tropical jungle. As the car shot out into the dome, it traveled in a transparent tube that formed an arc up through the air and across the expanse, then branched off to take passenger shuttles in several different directions. Jime's tube took him up and out over the Amazonia, which, despite being artificial, looked to his eyes exactly like the once-great South American river must have looked two or three generations before the Mall was built. Without Mallworld's ersatz environments, he thought with a proud smile, no experience at all of the historical Amazon River would be possible anymore. As Jime admired the green of the plastiplant jungle, he saw tropical mechanibirds taking wing from hidden roosts among the trees. In the distance he spotted New Tropicana's immense tiered ziggurat rising from the mists, larger than any historical Aztec structure had ever been, while behind it, kilometers away, towered a slightly larger volcano, which gave the dome's wealthy residents and visitors a spectacular show of exploding lava and steam every night.

Jime turned and looked around the interior of the shuttle car. It had the average pleasantness common to areas of the Mall that were frequented by middle- and working-class people: algaeplastic seats, colorful carpeting, animated advertising posters sprayed on the walls, all of it slightly worn from regular use and benign neglect. The riders were office workers, or cubeys, and retail saleys who, on the whole, ignored each other—most were watching holovideos or playing games on their phones. If someone died a quiet natural death in their midst they wouldn't even notice. Jime sat and listened to music on his headphones. He saw one attractive woman in sunglasses, seated with a tilted head, looking intently at the handbag of the woman standing next to her. She reached into her own handbag, slowly pulled something out, and lifted it up; it was her phone, and, taking pains to keep her actions hidden, she took a picture of the other woman's purse, making sure to get the designer label into the shot.

Most shoppers used the mass transportation provided by the Mall Metro monopoly. Those who could afford automobiles, however, could drive everywhere, just as the ancients had done, on a well-kept, convenient system of highway tunnels that snaked through the interior of the Mall. The highways linked the richest communities with each other and with Mallworld's centers of commerce, influence, and power. Cars and highway tolls were expensive enough that few could afford them, however, and there weren't any trucks on the highways, since goods were shipped around the Mall in a pneumatic tube system. Thus the highways were nearly always empty, and the wealthy were able to zip back and forth, unimpeded by traffic jams.

Jime's shuttle car approached a station that was located on the grounds of a spa and hotel at the base of the Aztec pyramid. As the car descended Jime spotted a boat cruising along the river, a simulated safari ride on the hunt for mechanimals. He saw a swimming pool with shoppers relaxing in lounge chairs, enjoying drinks and delicacies while watching holovision, or "HV." Nearby, on a sandy sim-beach, sunbathers lay under the bright sim-sky.

The shuttle slowed along the ground before entering the station, and Jime spotted an HV crew nearby filming a group of rifle-bearing safari hunters. They had corned a Fat Pig near the pyramid wall. The person was so obese that Jime guessed he wasn't a mechaniman. He was naked and sweating, and he had obviously been fleeing the hunters. The Fat Pig's terror was evident in his posture, and he raised his hands in a futile attempt to stop the inevitable bullets. Just before the shuttle entered the station and Jime lost view, a shot caught him, and his head snapped back in a spray of red. *Oh!* Jime recoiled in shock but quickly realized what had happened. He must have been a contestant on "Wheel of Fate" or another holovision reality show—one of those people who had agreed to a year of decadent consumption before facing The Wheel. A year of the best hotels, restaurants, and brothels, and at the end you spin The Wheel: spin well and you go home with a fat cash prize, spin badly and you're the Fat Pig, plumped up to be exploited for HV ratings as you're led to the slaughter.

Tough luck for that guy, Jime thought.

+ + +

"How are those ribs, Jime?"

"The best thing I've had in months. Look, they fall right off the bone! I missed this soooo much when I was Outside."

"Are they pork or beef?"

"Pork. How's your fish?"

"A little dry, but good enough. Never had piranha before. I saw a show on HV that said that a school of piranha could strip a cow or a pig to the bones in seconds."

"Well just be glad that you're eating your food, rather than it eating you, ha!"

Jime's Affinity friend wore a plain and inoffensive business jacket, plain dress shirt, plain pants, and plain shoes; his hair was conventionally cut; he could switch places with any of a billion cubeys and no one would notice. The restaurant they were in was called the Texas Slaughterhouse, and was built to look like an Old West barn and corral. It seemed out of place in the middle of this tropical paradise, its rough pioneer structure surrounded by plastic palm trees. The building, like all buildings, was manufactured from extruded algaeplastic, but it had been fashioned to look like it was constructed by frontier settlers out of unfinished timbers and corrugated tin. On the walls hung plastic tokens of the Old West: replicas of old-fashioned rifles and six-shooters, lassos and branding irons, saddles and spurs, the horns of great steers. The waiters wore ten-gallon hats and the waitresses cowgirl vests and chaps. The whole atmosphere evoked macho cowboy dominance and masculinity, and it was meant to make customers feel as if they were ranchers eating the meat of animals they themselves had raised and butchered in the dust and danger of the ancient frontier. Yet the consumers in the restaurant, most having come from the resort nearby, gorged themselves in complete climate-controlled comfort, their beefy bodies clothed in Hawaiian shirts, sarongs, and other beachwear.

Jime reveled in his first good meal in months and spent the time chatting with his friend. They mostly talked about the latest sports and celebrity news. Immediately upon sitting down, Jime had ordered appetizers: a double-size portion of fried cheese, the buffalo-wing donut sliders, and a 128-ounce soda. As his main course, he greedily finished off a large platter of ribs dripping with red barbecue sauce. When Jime's second rack of ribs arrived, it didn't have enough sauce and came with the wrong kind of potato. Annoyed, he summoned the waiter.

"I don't want this, therefore it is unacceptable. Look at these ribs, they're inedible. And I thought I was getting twisty fries. Take it back and make it right."

"Yes, sir," the cowboy said with a bow. "I'll take care of that right away. Unfortunately, we're out of the twisty fries now. May I get you a double-order of regular fries instead?"

Jime sighed in exasperation. "Yes, I suppose." After the waiter scurried off, he said, "Well, there goes his tip!" His friend laughed. "See, free markets work great," Jime said. "It's only rational: you don't bring me twisty fries, and you lose pay."

"It fixes the problem every time," said his friend. "Like markets always do!"

"It's hard to imagine how bad the world was before libertarian capitalism made us all free, without market distortions from government and labor unions."

"Get ahead on your own individual merits—you snooze, you lose. That's what I always say."

They continued talking while Jime feasted with the abandon of a person who was actually starving. Despite his girth he hadn't, after all, stuffed his face for seven months.

His friend asked, "Have you seen any new spectas since you got in?"

"You haven't asked me about Outside yet."

"Because it must've been boring. Aren't you glad to be back in? There was a great HV show about workeys eating their own kids! Did you see that?"

"No, I haven't been back in long enough."

"No, not the show, I mean when you were Outside, did you see it for real? JNN had some workeys, dirtier than shit, cutting the flesh off their kids' butts to cook for dinner. It was so gross. The kids were drugged when they did it, but it was still repulsive, them on HV eating butt stew! It was disgusting! Awful! I watched the whole show. Do they really do that? They're just filthy."

"I never saw that happen."

"But they showed it live. That's not what they eat?"

The waiter delivered Jime's reorder, and he tore off a hunk of meat with his teeth. "They're not like that; they're dumb but they eat normal, processed food in cafeterias, and usually energy bars at work. We've set up very efficient systems for feeding them," he said with his mouth full, gesticulating with the rib bone. "You know the media, they take people's worst fears and preconceived notions and make it out like the regular thing."

"Oh. I see. Anyway, did you see any spectas yet or what?"

"Just the regular ones on the streets, nothing big yet. I think I'll go to the sea battle tomorrow at the Colosseum—not something you'd like."

"You dripped some sauce on your chin."

"Oh, thanks." Jime wiped the red liquid from his face. "How's your job at Significorp? Did you get your promotion yet?"

"Yeah, but it still sucks. You know how it is. Too much overwork. It took forever to get that promotion—all the extra hours, which I didn't get paid for, all the ass-kissing. I was doing the actual work of the position for almost a year before they finally promoted me. So now it's more responsibility and even longer hours, without much more pay, really. Helps with the new condo bills though."

"That sounds like a lot of overwork," Jime frowned, sympathetic. "But that's better than no job at all."

"It sure is a lot of overwork, isn't it? Too much." His face dropped and he frowned. "You've always got to scramble. Still, I'd hate to go back to my early days of interning and temp work, jumping from job to job, not knowing when your next paycheck will come."

"Working on anything special now?"

"As if! You know how I used to complain that my job was pointless bullshit, just making holo ad signs for lettuce or whatever? You think that you'd be doing more significant things when you're a Manager, you think that you're going to be in charge. But no! Now I go to big important meetings, but that just means I get to see how stupid decisions get made—on top of already seeing how shitty the salespartners are. I tell Management the right way to do things every time, but nobody listens, and everyone else does the dumbest stuff, from top to bottom. It's always so hard. They never do it right, and no one ever listens to someone like me who knows what they're doing. It's so unfair! But whaddya gonna do? Let the workeys decide? Ha!"

Jime set down his fork and pushed his plate away; he used to be able to eat two racks of ribs, but this time he couldn't even get halfway through the second. There was no way he would be able to have any Cake. "Someday you'll be an Executive in Mall Management and you'll get to make the big decisions!"

"Yeah, right! I'd fix the whole Mall and then somebody else would come along and mess it up. At least I'd be making a fortune then." He pointed at Jime's plate. "Are you gonna finish that?" Jime shook his head and offered it up. "Maybe in a few years I can make Sectional Management and then it'll all be good. Those guys have it easy. Just gotta keep climbing the ladder."

"And for fun you've been going to spectas?" Jime asked.

"When I can. It's my only release, really, to see a big show or explosions or something. I get all pent up during the week, and then on the weekends I let it out."

"Well." Jime dabbed his mouth with his napkin. He had paid for another couple of hours of his friend's time. "Dinner was great; are you ready to buy some stuff?"

"I bet *you* are, after having been Outside for months!"

On billions of holoscreens an advertisement is projected:

"Duhn-da-da-DA!" Excited, happy music heralds something fun. An announcer says, "This Sunday, it's the 75th Annual Shopper's Choice Awards!" The screen shows dozens of glamorous celebrities in tuxedos and evening gowns parading down a red carpet, camera lights flashing, as they enter the annual awards show for the best in entertainment. The announcer happily yells, "Take a break from your work routine and join the biggest stars for the most important event of the year!"

The camera shows legions of fans crowding against the barricades that separate the Very Important People—entertainers, troubadours, comedians—from the regular saleys and cubeys who pay them and make them famous. Yet the working people are waving and seeking autographs, thoughtless in their adoration and mesmerized in their devotion to the stars. One fan, wearing poor clothes and a saley's apron, and missing several teeth, looks directly into the camera with a frenzied visage and screams, "I love you!"

The announcer asks, "Who will win the Best Specta award?" The camera shows last year's winner for best entertainer, a handsome actor who had played the role of Mallworld's Chief Medical Insurance Executive in a hospital drama. He is smiling and holding up his Specta Star, a gold-chromed algaeplastic statue consisting of a man and a woman locked in an embrace, triumphantly holding aloft a star that was the head of a comet; they are clothed only in the comet's tail, wrapping around them in spirals.

"Kick your feet up and join the leading celebrities to watch the winners for Best Holofilm, Best Arena Show, Best Reality Show, Best Home Specta, and more!" An incredibly beautiful woman actor, widely branded as "fierce" and as having "spunk," yet rumored to have a major drug habit and to have sent her three children to orphanages, blows a kiss at the camera and smiles. The crowd cheers. "The 75th Annual Shopper's Choice Awards, brought to you by the Specta Corporation. Entertainment is our business!"

+ + +

Jime and his Affinity friend went to one of New Tropicana's massive, bustling open markets, where crowds of shoppers wended their way through countless booths and tables of knickknacks, clothes, and jewelry. Merchants loudly hawked their goods or lured customers in with free samples.

This particular market was a kilometer square, and it was one of the smaller ones. But as they shopped Jime wasn't satisfied with anything he saw and couldn't figure out what to buy, and his indecision only increased as they went round and round the market in circles. After a frustrating, fruitless hour they left to look elsewhere and walked down a nearby street of shops.

"How about this antique store, Jime?"

"Looks fine, I guess. I need to spend my Shopping Quota or it's back Outside!" Jime held open the plastiwood door for his friend—the place was so faux-antique that the door wasn't even automatic.

"Well, we gotta shop to keep the economy going. It's your duty to society, you know."

"So CEO Ryan says on JNN all the time."

They browsed for a few moments, and Jime found something interesting. "Hey, look at these old eyeglasses. They're really dark. I know that before they invented contact lenses, shoppers used to wear spectacles, but these are too dark to look through."

The saley behind the counter, a tall, stiffly proper man wearing the usual saley apron, explained. "They're called 'sunglasses,' and the ancients wore them Outside before the domes were built, to keep the bright light of the sun out of their eyes. If you were out in it too long you would go blind, you see."

"Hmm," Jime turned the glasses over in his hands, peering at the plastic. "I could've used these out there—the sun does get pretty bright, and they tell you during orientation not to look directly at it. It doesn't blind you if you don't look at it, though."

"You were Outside?" the saley asked, his nose turned up.

"Yeah, corporate job thing. It sucked."

The attendant frowned. "I'll stay Inside myself, thank you very much. Would you like to see more?"

They said yes, and the salespartner showed them a variety of sunglasses, eyeglasses, watches, and other ancient jewelry—all of it real, they were assured, and all of it from the dark ages before Mallworld was built. Jime selected a pair of sunglasses with gold frames and bronze lenses, as well as an old watch that ran on solar power and a few rings and other baubles, simply in order to spend some store credits.

The store had many other antiques, from ugly brass lamps to old computing equipment, some of it still marginally functional. One square-shaped light was labeled "sun lamp," and the saley told Jime that its bulb emitted the same wavelengths of light as the natural sun—but he couldn't imagine why anyone would need such a device.

In the rear of the store, against the walls, were a half-dozen bookshelves stuffed with colorful paperbacks, magazines, and children's books.

"Look at these—real books. I haven't seen one in years." Jime gingerly picked one up and examined the cover, which displayed a portrait of a beautiful woman; it was a book about photography. Another showed a fancy chocolate cake; it was a cookbook. Jime shuffled through a dozen murder mysteries, romance novels, sci-fi adventures, and personal memoirs. There was even a textbook on political theory in the stack.

His friend looked over his shoulder. "I held a book on a school museum trip once. That one with the buildings on the front looks interesting. What's it called?"

Jime picked it up. "*Intentional Ecommunities: Alternatives in Connected Living,* by Ari Muireau."

"Swipe your credit card and open it."

"You don't have to pay each time to read an old-fashioned book." Jime cracked the cover. "Ah, let's see . . . there are pictures. Kids. Trees. What's this?" Jime's brow furrowed as he thumbed through the book. It held picture after picture of people working, playing, even singing, always with some structure or row of small buildings in the background.

"Are those . . . *houses*?" his friend asked. In the Mall, few people lived in detached homes because the enclosed space required a higher residential density. Most shoppers lived in extended blocks of duplex or triplex condominiums or in apartment buildings—or in barracks-like dorms, Jime knew now, if they were workeys Outside.

"Yes, it looks like these shoppers lived in houses," Jime said. "I've seen pics of ancient mansions, and in high school history we learned about suburbs, which had stand-alone homes that individuals or families lived in." Jime turned some pages—clumsily, since he was not used to doing so. "But wait, that's only the first few pages. In the back of the book the homes all become connected."

"Probably early condo prototypes. Hmm, interesting history. What does it say?"

Jime turned back to the first page and skimmed through the introduction. It was hard to read while holding the book and physically turning pages; he was used to text scrolling across a computer screen automatically, the computer tracking your eyes as you read. The book jiggled unsteadily in his hands, and he couldn't keep his eyes on the words, so he set it down on a nearby table and bent over to read it.

"Introduction: The Great Community.

"Human beings are *social animals*: we are organic creatures who naturally live together, interconnected and interdependent. Let's examine the two terms of that phrase. We are *social* and need human fellowship, but life in the 21st century creates divisions between us. We are *animals* and need communion with nature, but life in the 21st century creates divisions between us and Mother Earth. Divisions, and subdivisions, if you will, cause a host of social and environmental ills that have destroyed our common spirit and are destroying the planet. Capitalism divides us into classes of wealthy and working, leisured and laboring, included and excluded, powerful and powerless; modernity alienates us from each other, creating and re-creating poverty and sickness, insanity and depression, violence and crime, loneliness and boredom. Capitalism's profit-seeking and consumption are relentless and unlimited, and therefore drive resource depletion and climate change. Unless we create a truly new way of life, human beings will scour the planet's surface of living things, destroying the rich natural ecosystems that we depend on for air, food, and water—that is, for life.

"Ironically, while we do this in an attempt to lead comfortable lives of consumption and entertainment, we make ourselves miserable in the process. It would be one thing to cause social and environmental destruction if we became happier; that would be bad but would have a certain utilitarian rationality to it. But as we use up the Earth we become *less* happy, not more—in an absurd downward spiral, we deplete ever more of our beautiful Earth in a vain attempt to fill our emotional voids through consumption. In the end we will make the surface of the planet a wasteland of weeds and desert, its resources exhausted. At that point humanity will have destroyed itself as well, except for perhaps a lucky few who avoid the mass death that will inevitably follow. It will be tens of millions of years before the Earth, through evolution and other natural processes, recreates an ecosphere as rich and diverse as the one that existed on our planet until very recently. But it is not too late. This is a fate that we can avoid if we find the personal and political will to do so.

"This book offers a way to avoid that fate. It shows how to find the will to create for ourselves and our posterity a new, just, sustainable way of life. If done responsibly, with purpose, and soon, then this new way of life does not mean an existence of subsistence or deprivation. It doesn't even mean giving up much comfort, although it does require us to live at a higher level of attention and awareness. In fact, once we have overcome our inertia and fear of change, creating this new way of life will be an adventure the likes of which humanity has never experienced, leading to more fulfillment, happier relationships, stronger communities, and greater human creativity. The longer we procrastinate, however, the harder it will be to start, the more work we will have to do, and the longer we will have to wait to experience the rewards.

"Our current way of life is rooted in the political philosophy known as *liberalism*, which in its healthiest forms emphasizes the rights and development of the individual, and in its least healthy and bloated forms goes too far, isolating the individual from social connections and setting people apart from one another in indifference and competition. Liberalism, first developed in the 17th and 18th centuries, was *the* classic modern political philosophy. Following the basic principles of 'liberty, equality, and solidarity,' it gave rise to representative democracy during revolutions in America, France, and elsewhere. Liberalism rested on the pillars of human rights, representative government, and separation of the public and private spheres. Proponents believed that the rights to life, liberty, and pursuit of individual interest or happiness were rights universal to all persons, and codified them as civil rights that included freedoms of speech, press, assembly, religion, association, and occupation, and the rights to vote and petition the government. While proponents of liberalism assumed the democratic sovereignty of the people, they sought to constrain democracy from impulsive or uninformed decisions by limiting the people's choice to the election of representatives, who would do the actual work of governing because they were believed to be more knowledgeable and wiser than the people themselves. Furthermore, proponents of liberalism sought to protect fundamental rights from the politicking of regular law- and policy making with a known, settled constitutional law interpreted by an independent judiciary.

"At first, liberalism also included nearly unlimited individual rights to property and freedom of contract, thus affiliating itself with capitalism. That, however, resulted in horrific conditions and extreme poverty during the industrial revolution of the 19th century. Consequently, some liberals saw a need to regulate some kinds of property and to institute social programs to lessen inequality. They became known as 'reform' or 'welfare' liberals, being concerned with people's welfare or well-being, while those liberals who supported uncontrolled property rights were called 'classical' liberals or sometimes 'conservatives,' especially in the United States, since they sought to *conserve* the traditional liberal privileges of property. Eventually in America these factions became known simply as 'liberals' and 'conservatives,' respectively. But they are both branches of the same original liberal political ideology and agree on the fundamental aim of individual freedom; they just differ on the means to realize it. They certainly are closer to each other than either is to, say, totalitarian fascism or communism.

"Liberalism contains much of value and should not be rejected outright. In setting out to promote the security and happiness of the individual person, liberalism was an advance on what came before, and it bequeathed humanity invaluable political ideas and practices regarding the dispersal of power, protection of rights, representation of interests, and public discourse; these beneficial features should be built upon and taken to the next level, not thrown overboard. But, as many critics have pointed out, liberalism sometimes goes too far in its individualism, positing a human subject that is a self-interested, acultural, isolated monad, rather than a person enmeshed throughout life in a web of social relations. Here it will be helpful to distinguish between *individuality* and *individualism*. *Individualism*, the idea that each person should promote their own narrow self-interest, aloof from or in competition with others, is an ideology, not a natural state. Despite its claims to the contrary, individualism diminishes individual personality rather than helping it grow because it promotes self-aggrandizement rather than self-development. It stunts humans' lifelong education as social animals and, I will argue, benefits the powerful by separating and isolating those who might oppose them. *Individuality*, on the other hand, recognizes that an individual can do well and be free only as an individual living within, and connected to, a healthy community, society, and planet, which provide the social and natural environments that make the development of individual talents and capabilities possible. But such human flourishing and development are not in the interests of the powers that be, who demand docile workers and compliant consumers.

"The new way of living that I propose in this book, therefore, is based on closer, stronger, more respectful, more civil, and even more loving and caring human *interconnection*. Although this new way of life would strengthen cooperation in society, it still respects individual freedom. Indeed, by rejecting individualism it would *enhance* individuality by creating a net of support for individuals to flourish and become who they were meant to be. We will not be able to solve our problems and develop a better way of life until we reject the view that human beings are singular individuals who should pursue their own interests and, instead, adopt a morality that recognizes, respects, and reinvigorates our interconnectedness and shared interests.

"Some might ask, 'Why imagine a new way of life when we can't change anything anyway? Today's capitalism is the best we can do, because of human nature, and our social and political systems are slow to change.' This is the old question of the *transition problem* in progressive politics. It was first asked by socialists: 'How can society move from capitalism to socialism, when capitalism is so all-encompassing?' It is a question not only of overcoming alienation to build strong and healthy communities, but of overcoming entrenched centers of power, especially economic power, to create an economy that works for individuals, communities, and society at large. The transition problem is a perplexing one that has not yet been solved. To find solutions we must explore alternative political theories, and we must challenge our conventional wisdom and conventional language about politics. In short, this is not a book for entertainment but one that asks the reader to read with some effort, to exercise their brain. The stakes couldn't be higher: for billions of people, democracy, healthy social relations, quality of life, and the environment depend on a successful transition to a better way of life."

Jime stopped reading. "It's utopian fiction," he said to his friend. "It might be an amusing read. I think I'll buy it."

+ + +

On billions of holoscreens across Mallworld an advertisement is projected:

Low, ominous musical notes pound like the heartbeat of someone waiting for a storm to hit. *DUH-duh. DUH-duh. DUH-duh.* The camera pans across the empty squares and buildings of the predawn quiet of Mallworld, cutting with each beat to show empty mallways, empty food courts, and empty stores, their shelves fully stocked.

The camera comes to rest on the face of a beautiful, elegant woman. "I need to get to the sale at Bergendale's Sixth Avenue … but it's Black Friday," she says, eyes wide in fear.

The camera cuts to the round, mustachioed face of Mall Security Guard and action hero Jonn McKnight, who, glaring into the camera, says to the woman, "Ma'am, please come with me."

Da-da-da, DUHN. Still following the beat of intense, pounding music, the image cuts quickly from scene to scene: Jonn McKnight, in his Mallcop uniform, faces a mob of frenzied Black Friday shoppers rioting through a Mallmart, blood and gore flying everywhere. He barks a command: "Please form a calm and orderly line!"

Da-da-da, DUHN. Jonn McKnight swings on a rope across upper-level terraces of a tall, wide mallway, fountains and shoppers far below, his arm wrapped around the beautiful woman.

Da-da-da, DUHN. Jonn McKnight tasers a bearded hipster to the floor, who writhes in electroshock pain: "Sir, I'm going to have to ask you to leave the premises."

Da-da-da, DUHN. Finally, Jonn McKnight and the woman stand in a large square, which, like a battle zone, is filled with bloody bodies. They are directly across from Bergendale's, its glowing sign flickering in the darkness. From adjoining corridors, a riotous horde of bloodthirsty shoppers charges in. Jonn McKnight pulls out his pistol, looks into the camera, and says, "Let's power shop."

Da-da-da, DUHN.

The screen goes black as the movie title, made of letters of steel, swings into view: *Black Friday VI: Kill to Shop.*

+ + +

The crowd at the Colosseum was a giant beast, and it roared when a volley of cannon fire blasted from an ancient sailing ship, an opening barrage of flame and smoke that heralded the start of the evening's entertainment. A moment later, across the water-filled arena, choreographed splashes and the scripted cracking of plastic ship timbers announced the arrival of cannon balls—all simulated, of course. A pause, then another barrage, this time from a dozen ships. Mechaniman "sailors" scurried across the decks, and the crowd could make out their shouts and grunts between cannon volleys. As timbers split and rigging tore, a few fake sailors fell into the water, where the fins of mechanisharks circled, waiting for the right moment in the drama to consume their prey.

The ships were replicas of seventeenth-century galleons and frigates, but they floated, anachronistically, in the center of an ancient Roman coliseum. It was a faux arena of a massive size never actually seen in the ancient world. Fighting on one side of the naval skirmish were pirates, and on the other the navy of the country that had once been called England. Jime couldn't help but think with bemusement how the ancient arena in Rome was fortunate to never have been invaded by hordes of cutlass-wielding pirates. Many shoppers wore costumes to these events, so the crowd reflected the incongruity of the ships in the arena and displayed the contrast between the spectacle and the daily lives and personalities of the spectators. Some in the audience were dressed in ancient togas and sandals, others in stylized versions of seventeenth-century pirate regalia, while many had come in their regular clothing. Despite their different costumes, everyone in the crowd cheered in unison when something exciting happened, such as the explosive volley that knocked down the mast of one ship.

The million-strong crowd busied itself with feasting and drinking. Jime himself was overindulging in order to properly eat up his Shopping Quota. He had paid for an expensive seat in the first rows, close enough to the action to see the expressions on the actors' faces. And he had purchased an expensive bone-white toga with a senatorial purple stripe, complete with tunic and sandals, because he wanted to be seen as a noble Roman senator. The price of the costume certainly made him feel like one. He sat anonymously among the crowd. He folded the algaeplastic table in front of him down and ordered plate after plate and drink after drink from the aproned waiters who were paid to both encourage and indulge gluttony. He ate a Pizza Trough and a Superburger, with mega twisty fries and nachos, while drinking from a Big Bucket of soda. Then he topped it off with an extra-large piece of Cake. From time to time he dropped some food or spilled some drink into his lap, cursing himself at the thought of having to get his new white costume specially cleaned—but then again, he would probably just throw it out and get a new one next time anyway.

One of the ships rammed another, which, per the script, split it in two. Jime was splashed by water from a cannon shot that sprayed the front rows where he sat. The crowd roared. Jime jumped up and roared with them, dumping liquid cheese all over himself. When he sat down again he realized that the excessive noise and activity was making his head hurt. He also felt bloated and queasy. It had been seven months since he had eaten this much in one sitting. His body wasn't used to it, and his discomfort seemed strange to him; why should he feel bad doing an activity—eating—that was so natural and so necessary for health and survival?

Except during the regular spasms of shouting and jumping that the specta was designed to produce, everyone in the crowd just sat there, passively, overeating and absorbing the show—also an effect the specta was designed to produce. They consumed both calories and sensations thought-lessly, mindlessly, like a hungry animal scarfing down its dinner. The spec-tacle overwhelmed the senses and burned off the nervous energy of daily life, which for most of the spectators, as working people, was a paradoxical combination of endless striving and frustrating stagnation. Something Jime had read from the utopian book came to mind: a new way of life requires us "to live at a higher level of attention and awareness." As he looked around, it occurred to him that no one in this mob was operating at even close to that level, even though their senses were totally captured by the specta. His stomach groaned. Another cheer went up, and his moment of thoughtful reflection was broken, his attention forced back to the show.

By this time the pirates had won the battle and were taking prisoners. Many mechanimen were clasped in algaeplastic irons or lashed to the deck, whipped and taunted by their buccaneering captors. The pirate captain of the last standing ship stepped forward to the rail and spoke, his voice amplified so the audience could hear:

"Today, my fellow buccaneers, we achieved a great victory and won many spoils! We have conquered, and will have endless treasure!"

The fake pirates cheered.

"Already the sharks have gathered to drag the dead down to the cursed deeps." The captain paused and waved his hand in a downward motion, and the crowd could see the monstrous, man-eating mechanifish patrolling the water. "Now we will show these English servants of king and country who it is that rules the sea. Bring out the governor!"

A Fat Pig dressed as an English noble, complete in waistcoat and pow-dered wig, was dragged kicking and screaming from below decks. As he was hauled to the plank, he managed to struggle free. He made a break for it, waddling rapidly across the deck; but he was surrounded by guards immediately, and where was he to go, anyway? Diving into the shark-in-fested water was no escape, for that meant the very execution he desper-ately hoped to avoid. He lunged this way and that, as fast as his corpulent body would allow. But the mechanical pirates closed in around him; his shoulders slumped in resignation, and he allowed himself to be detained. The cameras captured it all. He was promptly hustled to edge of the ship. The mechanisharks roiled the water below. As he faced the plank his head turned to one side, and by chance he looked at Jime. Their eyes met, and Jime gasped. He was shocked at how wide and red the man's eyes were, full of a fear and despair that transferred to Jime in a way that would not have been possible if he were sitting at home watching on holovision. Jime's heart sank, his breath caught in his lungs, his stomach churned, a hole opened in his chest. In that moment a thought came to his mind: no year of luxury was proper payment for the terror in those eyes. Jime felt, rather than saw, the roiling of the water, and believed that he could smell the bloodlust of the sharks, even as his gaze fixated on the game-show contestant. In that moment he felt the same fear the Fat Pig did.

The pirate captain read a list of reasons why the man was being made to walk the plank, and even though the crowd had become deathly silent, Jime didn't hear a word of it. The man was prodded with a sword in his back, and he took tentative steps out onto the plank. The pirate crew jeered and laughed; a drum rolled.

In an instant the plank was withdrawn. A splash and a scream, followed by a tremendous roar from the crowd. As the water foamed and grew deep red, all of Jime's empathic fear roiled up from his belly. He doubled over and threw up nearly everything he had eaten.

This distracted those sitting near him, who stared in disgust for a moment, but then quickly turned back to cheering.

Jime managed to stumble to a restroom before getting sick again, and he ended up retching there for almost an hour. By the time he emerged the spectators had cleared out of the Colosseum. Only workey janitors remained, the sounds of their cleansing echoing from the vacant stands. The sense of kenopsia the empty stadium emanated was overwhelming, and Jime felt all his emotions drain away. He found an exit, then shambled through the cobbled streets of Great Rome to the nearest people-mover station, choking back bile along the way. Once inside a shuttle car, he slumped in a seat, propped his head against the window, and stayed that way as the car passed through three sections of Mallworld. He saw none of the scenery that passed by. Jime did notice, barely, a young couple sitting across from him, snickering at his costume and whispering about his filthy appearance and the stink of vomit.

As Jime held his pounding head, his mind kept alternating between feeling ashamed at how he looked and feeling just plain empty. Why had he done this to himself? This was supposed to be fun, but he felt awful. He had filled himself to bursting, and not just with food. He had gone to one of the biggest extravaganzas in one of the biggest venues in Mallworld, and he had thrown himself into it fully. Yet he felt as desolate as he ever had, as though he had vomited up his heart along with his stomach. All he had wanted to do when he was Outside was to get back Inside to enjoy life, and all he had done since was eat and drink and buy. Jime's mind kept insisting that there must be something more than this—this sitting, doing nothing but consuming things—even consuming the humiliation and death of another person!

No wonder he had vomited. He had imbibed poison today.

Somewhat to his own surprise, Jime remembered to get off at the right stop near his place in Sol Condominium Community Homes, which was named after the Latin word for the sun. The Sol complex consisted of row after row of old, shabby, algaewood-clad low-rise condos, only five or six stories tall. The streets were covered roof-to-roof rather than by a dome, which made the overhead ceiling low and claustrophobic. This was aggravated by the fact that the sim-sky here was active only in places, keeping the section dimly lit for most of the day and giving the subdivision a feeling of perpetual dusk. The condos weren't exactly run-down, but they weren't well-kept either: the algaewood panels needed paint, and the untended plastigrass and shrubs were a faded, sickly yellow-green covered with a thin layer of dust. As Jime stumbled past the large sign at the front of the complex, he noticed that some graffiti artist had painted periods between the letters of the name. It now read "S.O.L. Condominium Community Homes." Got that right, he thought.

Jime, still queasy, reached his building and with an effort climbed the stairs to his dreary second-floor condo. He pulled out his store credit card, tapped the lock reader to pay the fee to open his door, entered, and immediately passed out on the couch.

His sleep was restless, disturbed by nightmares of being chased and eaten by a mob of shoppers in togas and pirate hats, all of them with shark-toothed mouths.

+ + +

On billions of holoscreens an advertisement is projected:

An attractive but otherwise ordinary couple in their late thirties is shown hiking up a forested hill, laughing together. The scene cuts to an older couple in a park flying a kite, the park's dome visible in the sky above. A deep voice asks, "Has life got you down?"

The woman holding the kite string looks at the camera and says, "Sometimes we all need a little help with routine."

Cut to the man climbing the hill: "Life's ups and downs can be hard to handle."

The scene cuts to a Manager in a construction hat on a building site, workeys busy around him. He looks at the camera and says, "Work can be tough, but don't let it you slow down."

Another woman, shown working in a plastiflorist shop, says, "Whether working or shopping, you've got to keep going."

The man flying the kite appears again and says, "One daily pill treats my symptoms. Why wouldn't you take it?"

The woman hiking the hill appears and says, "Sometimes the easy solution is the right solution."

The deep-voiced announcer continues to speak as all these people are shown carrying out their activities with vim and vigor. "Theriac is authorized to treat depression, stress, social anxiety, heartburn, joint pain, muscle pain, insomnia, acid reflux, irritable bowel syndrome, flatulence, and restless leg syndrome. Active ingredients include snake oil and opioids. Do not drink alcohol in excess with Theriac. Do not take Theriac if you are allergic to peanuts, wheat, or biosolids. Side effects may include numbness, blurred vision and in some cases loss of vision, memory loss, drowsiness, loss of alertness, apathy and loss of energy, incontinence, loss of muscle mass, and lack of assertiveness. Theriac may cause heart failure. The risk of suicide increases when taking Theriac. The risk of suicide also increases when stopping Theriac.

"Ask your doctor if Theriac is right for you. Theriac: the closest thing to a cure-all."

Jime awoke groaning, with a crushing headache and a full bladder. He slowly lifted himself from his bed and stumbled, eyes half closed, to the bathroom, where he swiped his store credit card on the toilet's reader. The lid lifted and he relieved himself. He was grateful not to throw up again. He grabbed some hangover pills from the medicine cabinet and made his way to his small kitchenette, where he put a mug under the coffee maker, swiped his card, and hit "strong." In a moment the coffee was done, and in another moment he had washed down three of the pills with his first swallow.

He lurched over to the sofa and collapsed onto it, waiting for the pills to take effect. Jime knew the headache would soon be gone, but he would probably be depressed for the rest of the day. The pills didn't cure that part of a hangover. He closed his eyes for a few minutes. A little bit of sim-sun was leaking through a window from one of the half-lit ceiling panels outside.

Jime had a big-screen slab holovision set on his wall. Like all HVs, it was made of clear algaeplastic, and three-dimensional images were projected in high definition upon its transparent internal volume. Although Jime's rectangular HV was mounted on the wall, other shoppers had large cubes, globes, or domes that sat on the floors or hung from the ceilings of their homes. HVs of all shapes were ubiquitous in shops and passageways throughout Mallworld, and even personal phones and tablets had holographic capabilities. All these screens were connected to the holonet, an all-purpose, three-dimensional interactive communication, information, shopping, and entertainment network which combined the functions that television, the internet, and social media once had in the ancient, pre-Mall days. Indeed, even though everyone lived in a giant shopping mall, most purchases were actually made on the holonet; but then, Mallworld embodied a lifestyle, not merely a shopping opportunity.

After his head had cleared a bit, Jime grabbed the HV remote and inserted his card. He clicked through channels, searching for a home specta or HV show to grab his attention. He found news about Central Office rules cracking down on teenage loitering: boring. The business report on the Jackal News Network: yawn. A shopping channel. A history show about the building of the Mall. Another shopping channel. A sci-fi movie about a Mall on the moon. Another shopping channel. *Retail Space*, a sitcom. Another shopping channel. Yet another shopping channel. A romantic comedy. Another shopping channel. All dull, all worthless; Specta Cable took his money every month but never put anything good on HV. At some point Jime got up and got some breakfast to fill his empty, and now thankfully settled, stomach. As he ate he kept channel surfing for something good to watch, but he found nothing to fill the void that lingered from the previous night. No matter what was on HV, it did not satisfy. Jime flipped through the channels and eventually ran into a specta critic's report about the naval battle. He quickly turned off the HV. No need to see that again.

Bored, Jime looked around the dim beige of his condo, and a weight of debilitating dissatisfaction fell upon him. He didn't feel like going out, and he didn't feel like staying in; he wanted to do something, but at the same time didn't want to do anything. It was a complete contrast from the intensity of the previous night's events. He looked down at the coffee table. The Intentional Ecommunities book was sitting there. He picked it up, laid back on the couch, opened it, held it unsteadily, and began to read.

"Subdivided," the chapter was entitled.

"Let us begin by examining the current state of our neighborhoods (they cannot properly be called communities) in order to understand how they divide and subdivide us, both from each other and from nature. The 'American Dream' of a large detached home on an extended lot, inhabited by a single family or even a single individual, is probably rooted in old pastoral habits of thought and action. The typical suburban lot, with its swath of grass and greenery, presents a simulated farm in miniature, almost like Marie Antionette's faux farm at Versailles: it has flower and vegetable gardens, pet animals, sheds and garages, fields of grass for children to run in, and a central house. But the owners, for the most part, wouldn't know how to farm if their lives depended on it. This residential model is a nostalgic attempt to recreate the calm, quiet life of the country gentleman, to provide a safe and tranquil home for people who are otherwise constantly subjected to the tumultuous competition of capitalism. Yet housing large numbers of people this way requires huge amounts of physical space and natural resources, and it separates people both from each other and from nature. Meanwhile, the pastoral simulation fools people with the illusion that they are living in a friendly, traditional, close-knit community. In the mid-twentieth century people sought to escape from the cramped alienation of industrial cities, but they only found a new, uncrowded alienation in the suburbs.

"The consequences of social alienation are well enough known that they needn't be explored here in detail, but they include increased crime, substance abuse, physical and psychological illness, aggression, political conflict, and an environment in which broad-minded education becomes devalued and anti-intellectualism reigns. Alienating communities are certainly not the only cause of the social isolation that plagues modern society; there are many other causes, including economic competition, prejudice and bigotry, untempered individualism, objectifying consumerism, and spectator entertainment. But divisive communities are one major cause, and the one I want to address here."

Lots of verbiage here, Jime thought—typical of intellectuals who wrote books but never achieved anything. Very arrogant. So what if shoppers wanted to live that way? It was their choice, and no one had the right to tell them what to do. It irritated him so much that he kept on reading.

"Consider that many people wake up in the morning, go into a garage attached to their house, get in a car, hit a button to lift the garage door, and then drive to work, repeating the process in reverse on the way home. They never speak with their neighbors, never breathe the open air of their own neighborhood. Built to be convenient for cars, subdivisions are actively hostile to pedestrians—that is, to people. The arrangement of space makes spontaneously bumping into your neighbors and getting to know them exceedingly difficult. It's far easier to talk with neighbors when you run into them while walking to the corner store than it is while driving to a distant strip mall in a hermetically sealed vehicle, where the only convenient form of communication is the car horn."

More arrogance, Jime thought, and totalitarian arrogance too. Shoppers could've *chosen* to walk if they really wanted to. But they *chose* to use their cars. Even if it was the easier choice to make because there were more roads than sidewalks, they still chose it. They were in control of their actions. Weren't they?

Besides, Jime thought, alienation doesn't appear in Mallworld, since it only had a few suburban domes for the rich. Most neighborhoods now were medium- to high-density condominiums, everyone sequestered in their own individual unit, everyone riding the Metro, conveniently immersed in their phones. Obviously alienation couldn't be a problem here. Could it?

"Another crucial factor is to consider what this way of life does to *us*, to our character. The suburban arrangements of space, use of resources, and patterns of social relationships create a social system. What kind of people does this system create? That is, what are the people like who are born, socialized, and educated in such a society? How do their conditions limit their options and put boundaries on their choices? How do those conditions shape their daily habits and mold their personalities? Is it desirable to actually be the kind of people that a consumer society makes out of us?"

Jime smirked at this. We can always choose to be whatever we want to be. Can't we?

"Our widespread, consumerist idea of 'freedom of choice,' which holds that people make choices simply based on their 'preferences,' doesn't account for the facts that our preferences come from who we are; that we *are* what we habitually *do*; and that what we habitually *do* is mostly a response to the conditions and circumstances that surround us. If you live in a world that makes it easier to drive than walk, you will probably get out of the habit of walking and into the habit of driving. Eventually using your car will become second nature. At this point you are a 'driver.' If you live in a world that makes it easier to eat unhealthy, fattening food than a healthy diet, you will probably tend to overeat and perhaps become chronically obese; even people who maintain a balanced diet and a healthy weight have to work harder at it in such a world. If your conditions demand that you go to a job every day to make or sell something, you will, every day for hours, repeatedly make or sell; when that is second nature, you are a 'worker.' 'Freedom of choice' is a thin and inadequate theory of freedom that doesn't actually explain what freedom is because it doesn't ask where people acquire their preferences in the first place. It doesn't matter if people have a choice of red or blue or black dresses or neckties if, prior to that choice, they are constantly bombarded with advertising that socializes them to believe they must have the latest fashion to be professionally respected or sexually desired. In order for us actually to be free, the advertiser's idea that 'clothes make the person' must be critically examined. Our consumerist idea of freedom doesn't ask where *the reasons* for our choices come from, nor whether those reasons themselves are freely chosen or merely a matter of habituation. If someone else has habituated you to choose certain things uncritically, then you are not truly choosing them yourself, and you are not truly free.

"That is why it is necessary for individuals to critically reflect on the beliefs with which they have been raised and the habits they have acquired, and for groups of people to democratically and deliberatively examine the habits and practices they have adopted. Humans cannot avoid having habits, but we also must take care to examine them critically and change them when necessary. People *can* learn to challenge long-standing habits and make choices for good, well-thought *reasons*. Indeed, the thing most worth being habituated to is the habit of critical deliberation.

"What kind of character, then, is created in a high-consumption world? We start with the fact that the primary activity is consuming—people are always using, eating, wearing, or otherwise consuming objects and services, and they have purchased these objects and services in commercial transactions. It wasn't always this way, and it doesn't always have to be this way in the future. By way of comparison to today, think about how things were done before modern industrialization. It used to be that people made, by their own hands, most of the things they consumed—food, clothes, homes, implements, and even entertainment. They did not buy them as commodities on the market. Going to the market was a special occasion, occurring only on market days, and was done to acquire the occasional luxury good or necessity that could not be fashioned at home. Of course, that was a subsistence existence, done at a primitive level of physical technology, and few of us would trade our advanced commercial society for a crude, unhealthy agrarian one. But it is useful to contrast a different way of life with our own, first to see how people's minds are affected by different daily activities and experiences, and second to avoid thinking that our own way of life is natural and inevitable. For most of human history, people did *not* live in commercial consumerist societies; such societies are neither natural nor universal.

"In our present society, we constantly create objects that are designed for some *use*. That is, our objects are treated as *instruments*, as opposed to being, say, things we relate to as sacred or sentimental articles, or as natural things existing in their own right and not for human consumption. As has often been observed, consumer capitalism treats nature as consisting of 'natural resources' to be instrumentally used and transformed into things for human ends. Capitalism, intrinsically, cannot recognize that the natural environment is not merely a resource or instrument to be used up but is the very ground and context in which all human activity occurs, and on which the very survival of humanity depends. If nature dies, we will all die. Nature must be treated with care, respect, and stewardship, not as a resource—but that's something capitalism is fundamentally incapable of doing.

"As mentioned, in capitalism the objects we use are commodities that we have *bought* in commercial transactions, whether they be our clothes, lunches, homes, the electricity that powers our lights and computers, or what have you. And the actions of other people, everything from haircuts to medicine to sex, are also treated as instrumental services to be bought and used. From constantly reinforced daily habits of buying and using, eventually *everything* comes to be treated as an object to be consumed— including human beings. People come to relate to other people as things, as mere objects, and not as people. Indeed, they can even come to relate to *themselves* as things to be consumed and used up. All of this leads to uncaring neglect of nature, of objects, of others, and of the self—neglect that comes from a life focused on using things up as objects of consumption. In sum, a consumer society creates characters that are habituated to using other people and things instrumentally, while neglecting any aspect of them that might contain inherent dignity. A consumer society creates *consumers*.

"The physical separation and lack of shared public space in suburban life reinforce our alienating consumer habits and further habituate people to be separated from one another; people take on the character of isolated social particles and lose nearly all sense of community. It is difficult for such people, as a group, to summon up the civic spirit necessary to come together, make deliberative, democratic decisions about their values and their lives, and then take collective action to guard their freedoms, solve common problems, and improve their conditions and themselves. A few individuals may, under struggle, manage to sustain strong civic and moral character, but sadly the social, collective mass as a whole will not."

No, no, Jime thought, human nature is fixed: self-interested and self-centered. It's not just consumers who lack civic spirit; everyone does. Humans will never change. Right?

"But other ways of life are possible, ways of life that allow space for values other than commercial values and that still maintain high standards of living and technology. Commercial values should not be dominant in society but should be subordinate to other, higher values—at most, a means to their realization. We should ask ourselves: what different kinds of personal character might develop in a way of life focused not on consumption but on creating, building, maintaining, and caring? On giving to others, to one's community, and to society, through shared effort? On creative living through artistic expression, scholarly comprehension, technical construction, or scientific discovery?

"The solution I offer here involves replacing consumerism with community in order to form healthier shared identities. Let the basic interaction of our society become the handshake rather than the handing over of money; let the basic model of daily life become democratic discourse rather than commercial transaction. New forms of *intentional community*, from cohousing to eco-villages, seek to redress the alienating imbalance between the private and the public, and therefore to bring people back together. In such communities, people come to know their neighbors. They share a beer on the front porch, help carry each other's groceries, watch after each other's children. Privacy is still respected, to be sure, but there is a rebalancing that promotes the public spaces and activities that create and sustain close bonds and connections between people—the heart of any real, living community. This respect for the public sphere is achieved in part simply by rearranging physical areas to create public space, and in part through new democratic practices that cultivate civic spirit. These two things, public space and civic spirit, are mutually reinforcing: spirit creates a vision that redesigns communities, while the design of intentional communities reinforces the spirit of communal dedication and service that keeps those communities self-sustaining."

Sounds nice, but stupid and naive, Jime thought. Just look at the pirate show last night, and how the crowd treated the Fat Pig. Humans are selfish, and a society based on consuming and entertainment is the best we can do. Isn't it?

"Co-housing communities prioritize space and spirit by returning public space and activities to the center of daily life. First, in a tradeoff for expanded public space, members accept smaller private homes. Rather than detached 2,000–3,000 square foot McMansions, people live in 900–1,200 square foot homes with smaller yards, sometimes clustered together and sometimes attached. This keeps spaces closer together, on a more human scale. Rather than wide streets with individual driveways and garages, pedestrian walkways predominate, and parking is located off to one side of the community. With smaller lots and clustered homes, more space can be devoted to public/communal playgrounds, gardens, sports fields, or just the preservation of a copse of trees.

"Perhaps the most important feature of intentional communities, one that exemplifies space and spirit, is the common house. This is a larger central building with a hall, cooking facilities, and possibly other rooms like offices, playrooms, a TV lounge, perhaps a laundry, gym, or tool shop, and maybe even a small communal general store. In most co-housing communities, people make a point of sharing community meals in the common hall four to five nights a week. When breaking bread with their neighbors, they have informal discussions about everything from their personal affairs to community concerns to the politics and culture of the wider society. Everyone is on 'cooking duty' once or twice a month, so everyone contributes to the shared satisfaction of the community by giving their time. Intentional communities are run democratically, and weekly or monthly public meetings are held in the common house. Since the community is relatively small, with 15 to 25 families, everyone can have an impact on decisions that affect them. Participation in community affairs therefore tends to be high because members feel empowered about common decisions. Additionally, everyone usually has an extra responsibility, such as maintaining the landscaping or signing out the tools from the common tool shed. Members also informally provide each other shared social services such as child and elderly care, home and auto maintenance and repair, teaching, home health care, landscaping, and pooled community finance. It is through sharing the burdens of these duties that people build reciprocity and mutual trust, for they become willing to do their part for the community, knowing that others will too. This is in stark contrast with consumerism, in which the only duty is to take, take, take as much as possible, which only builds a climate of mutual exploitation and distrust. Who trusts those who are always out to take as much as they can get?

"One of the best effects of the common house is that it facilitates the community members' own self-entertainment through artistic creation that is not bought, sold, and used as a mere commodity. Rather than being passive spectators of television, they hold community holiday celebrations, actively play games and sports together, put on their own musical performances, read from poems or novels they have written, and so on, all while growing closer and becoming mutually supportive. Such shared creativity and celebration helps build a neighborhood with a communal spirit where people know and trust each other. Instead of yelling and screaming at a concert or sporting event as an anonymous member of a mob, imagine an evening of helping the community's children put on a show, listening to the community's musicians sing, and then taking your turn by being part of a dramatic play. Art is the highest form of human expression; it is what makes life worth living and shouldn't be reduced to mere show business to be used and consumed. In expressing your creativity mutually and actively, in shared trust and fellowship with the members of your community, you would elevate each other to a higher and more meaningful level of life."

Jime slammed the book shut.

He sat there for a minute in thought.

He wondered, how could I have that?

He realized that he had to make some changes. He was not exercising all his human abilities; in fact, he was neglecting the best of them. He needed closer friends. He needed to create something. He needed to get healthy. He needed to live in a community.

Which meant that he needed to get out of Mallworld, because there was no way that was going to happen here.

He got up and paced around his gray room and decided that he needed right then and there to go for a walk. Maybe see some trees or something. He wondered where the nearest real ones were. He put on some clothes, went downstairs, and started walking around the neighborhood. He saw only ugly plastiplants. There were no people strolling and laughing together, no children playing, no music practice. He mainly saw shoppers shuffling from one place to another alone, frowning with their heads down, aimless and weary, barely noticing each other in the dimness.

He took a deep breath. Time to get going, he thought.

CHAPTER 2:
REBOUND OF A MIND

J ime's feet pounded the treadmill, and beads of sweat began to form on his forehead.

Exercising was already coming more easily than it had when he began a few weeks ago. The first day had been easier than he had expected because he had a lot of enthusiasm for the change he was embarking on; the second day wasn't so bad either. But the period immediately after that was hard. He had to remain intensely focused on each moment and on each action that he took at the gym, letting himself just be, just act, just flow through time, moving in parallel with the discomfort of change, rather than trying to evade or escape it through nervous tics and movements. Mallworld's culture of immediate gratification had left him with a low level of frustration tolerance, and he knew he needed to work on that as he started his new path. He found that rather than fight feelings of discomfort it was better to fully feel them, remembering that *he* in toto was not the feeling, but that he was only the being who felt it. He kept telling himself, "Be patient with yourself as you move through time; move in parallel with the discomfort." Within moments the discomfort and anxiety he felt about change would disappear, and he could carry on with the actions needed to make positive changes in his life, whether it was physical exercise at the gym or the mental exercise of reading a challenging book. Since business school his ambition had been to be a Manager, and he had achieved it; thus he had experience with self-improvement and understood the value of it.

Now, only a few weeks into his new routine, exercise was becoming normal and even welcome, and he knew the worst of the physical and mental discomfort was over and he could move forward with increasing ease and confidence. He was already seeing positive results in a noticeably slimmer waistline and a feeling of being lighter on his feet—both literally and figuratively.

Jime's chest expanded and contracted as he breathed deeply in a steady rhythm.

Jime reflected on other changes that he had been making in his life. His improving physical fitness had led to improved energy and mental awareness, and he was able to accomplish more in his daily life. He cleaned and repainted his apartment and bought some ancient, and pricey, furniture made of real wood, which had a warmth and feel that plastic just couldn't replicate. He also went back to the antique store to buy the sun lamp to brighten up his place. His apartment had become almost livable, although it was only a tiny island of relative brightness in the gloomy, dim sea of his neighborhood. He now thought of it as a way station until he could somehow create a real home, somewhere. He bought an app to help control his diet: it counted calories, making him aware of how much he was eating, and planned out meals that gave him the proper nutrients. He was reading and exercising now, so he had less time for HV and spectas—but he didn't miss them. Since he had a purpose and didn't feel empty anymore, he didn't need to fill himself up with nutritionless calories and empty entertainment.

The treadmill accelerated, and Jime kept pace, a drop of sweat rolling down the side of his face.

Jime found, unfortunately, that he got less satisfaction out of spending time with his friends, since he no longer shared their interests in overeating, partying, spectas, or otherwise overindulging the senses. He consumed in the sense that he supplied himself with what he needed, of course, in terms of food and drink and replacing worn clothes. But he wasn't trying to fill an empty hole or distract himself from discomfort by buying things.

He didn't go to restaurants as much anymore, partly because of his diet and partly because he didn't get much out of the conversations with his friends. After an initial discussion of his months Outside, which quickly bored everyone, discussion would spin in a circle around things that Jime now saw as shallow and empty—HV programs, sports, celebrities, clothes, shoes. Jime had gotten rid of his big-screen holovision set, and one friend who found out he wasn't watching HV asked, "Where do you shop for your news now?" In short, his friendships were no longer fulfilling, and all his acquaintances seemed like identical, nameless, empty vessels. He hadn't logged into Affinity in weeks. He wasn't judging his friends; indeed, he wished them growth and happiness. But he was now different from them, and he had to deal with that fact. Unlike them, he just didn't want to consume much anymore.

Thus, Jime's new outlook had led to two problems. First, he had less in common with other shoppers—with other *people*, he mentally corrected himself, as he was trying to adopt the older, noncommercial term. He could try to make new friends, but nearly everyone in Mallworld was the same as the friends he already had. This was not an easily solved problem. Second, despite redecorating, he wasn't consuming enough credits and eventually would be in danger of another Time Out. As a practical matter, eventually he might have to buy something very expensive to make up for his new lack of spending, despite having no need to overconsume.

Jime was breathing heavily now and not minding it. Sweat rolled down his face and he reached for his towel.

The most important change he felt was that the ecovillage book had fired both his curiosity and imagination. Jime had always taken it for granted that the commercial market society of Mallworld was the best way to live. Even though, historically, communitarianism had never gone viral, the fact that some people had once actually organized their lives differently, while still being modern and rational, was an epiphany to him. He now had a vision of a different, better way of life, and he felt inspired to attain it. His mind had opened to new possibilities just from reading, and he felt driven to understand this different way of life. He considered himself lucky to have encountered a book that challenged his conformity and widened his horizons; he was like anyone else in Mallworld, he thought, but had stumbled across new ideas that were changing his life.

Jime read how a real community spirit had taken root and grown in the cohousing communities before the Mall: shared meals and celebrations in the common house meant that people got to know each other, while weekly democratic meetings meant that they learned about different problems, got in the habit of taking other peoples' needs and perspectives into account, and became skilled at compromising to resolve conflicts and solve common problems. Simply clustering homes more closely together and connecting them with walkable pathways, rather than setting them apart on large lots and dividing them by wide roads, meant that people would bump into each other often. The emphasis on the value of common spaces seemed to Jime like it would create a stronger community in which people developed real, deep friendships with their neighbors, while the deliberative, democratic way of doing community business meant that everyone had actual input into group decisions about their day-to-day lives. Both of these things—respect for the commons and communal democracy—contrasted sharply with his current society's neglect of public things and self-centered overemphasis on private property. Most Mallworlders were aloof or even passively hostile toward their neighbors, if they knew them at all, and neighborhood governance was done by condominium owners' associations chosen in sham elections in which few people bothered to vote. Communitarianism seemed warm, welcoming, and edifying in comparison.

Jime spent most of his off-hours, when not at the gym, on the holonet. But he wasn't using it as most people did, and as he previously had—shopping, playing games, having shallow conversations on social media. For most people, virtual life was just a copy of consumerist real life; Mallworld as a way of life existed online as much as it did offline. Instead, Jime was now researching different historical archives for books, articles, essays, and studies about intentional communities, and thus using the holonet to acquire knowledge, exercising his mind just as he was his body. Unfortunately, there wasn't much information, and investigative leads that seemed promising frequently wound up as dead ends. There had once been social media groups about intentional communities, but they had been defunct for decades. Yet Jime persisted and learned much about different aspects of the old communitarian movement.

First, it was obvious that it had somehow failed, because Mallworld existed and ecovillages did not. But was that failure some inherent weakness in the idea, or had it been overpowered by an external force? Next, he learned that there had been many different experiments in communities. Some had built from scratch, usually out of recycled materials and in environmentally sustainable ways. Others had refurbished older construction. The people living in a row of townhouses in a city, for example, might decide to tear down the fences in their backyards and make the resulting open space communal; they might not be able to set aside space for a common house, but they would hold frequent potluck dinners, rotating which house held them. Even some suburban neighborhoods had retrofitted themselves by creating shared backyard space and sometimes even buying a vacant house to turn into the common house. Some communities created community gardens, and some practiced sustainable agriculture to increase self-reliance in food.

Jime also learned about objections at the time to the communitarian movement. Some critics thought it was motivated by sentimental nostalgia and thus was not a rational response to social and environmental problems. Jime thought this was too dismissive: while most communitarians obviously had believed that the erosion of community bonds was a loss, they had not sought to live in the past but had wanted to *rebuild* strong communities for a better future. Other critics feared that strong communities would impose a singular moral doctrine on their members, which Jime thought was a reasonable objection and should be prevented; communities should not become cults that mandate a religion, creed, or ideology in order to belong. Rather, Jime thought, the value of community is found in the practical social education members get in building and maintaining healthy relations with others. Among people that revere freedom, that education should include respecting other members' different identities, perspectives, and beliefs. Finally, some academics dismissed communitarianism as impractical except on a small, experimental scale: since communities were by definition small units, intentional communities didn't seem to be transferable to large, complex societies. But Jime didn't understand this: why couldn't changes in neighborhood design be extended to most or all of the neighborhoods in a larger society? After all, the "suburb" was also a small unit of community design, but it had spread widely across the society of the time. Why couldn't the same happen for the intentional community, if it was supported with favorable laws and policies, as suburban development had been? Thus, it was a mystery to Jime why this healthier way of life had not taken hold.

Jime reached a comfortable stride on the treadmill now, his face and shirt covered in sweat.

One entry in particular had intrigued him, a blog article written almost fifty years earlier by an anthropologist. She had described a small community near the Mall that had been forcibly broken up to make room for Mall expansion. The anthropologist explained that it was occupied by workeys, although Jime thought that they weren't really "workeys" yet, since they weren't doing any work for Mallworld but lived on their own in their village. The anthropologist was more or less sympathetic to the villagers; she described them as literate, happy, and healthy, with a vibrant local culture. She certainly did not see them as brutish savages. She described their shared meals, self-created entertainments, and mutual caring and support. But she also displayed a Mallworlder's prejudices by scoffing at their lack of luxuries and spectas, by saying that they didn't have a "winning attitude," and by asserting that the villagers would be better off having jobs in the Mall, rather than living independently as they did.

The anthropologist singled out one villager as an example. He was a leader in the community but was fairly young, only about twenty-five years old. He could conceivably still be alive, Jime thought, although if he had been forced to become a workey that was unlikely. Workeys lived hard lives and died young.

Maybe, Jime thought as the treadmill entered its cool-down phase, maybe he shouldn't buy that expensive thing to spend up to his credit limit. Maybe, instead, he should make his way back Outside again.

+ + +

On billions of holoscreens an advertisement is projected:

Da da ta-DA! an electronic trumpet blasts. "Nothing's better for a hungry stomach than an endless supply of pizza!" an announcer shouts. The camera pans over a seemingly infinite table of pizza pies, garlic bread, and cheese sticks, eventually zooming in on a steaming hot pizza piled a foot high with every conceivable ingredient, all covered in melted cheese. "Try Pizza Trough's new Super Deluxe Mega Mountain Pizza with everything!"

The camera zooms out again to show that the pizza table is actually a moving conveyor belt in a colossal restaurant kitchen. The conveyor belt dumps pizzas into large boxlike receptacles in the shape of inverted trapezoids. A smiling, scantily clad waitress bounces over, grabs one from the end of the line, and whisks it away into the dining room. "And now at Pizza Trough, get our Supersize Trough for only 999 store credits!" the announcer yells. The waitress hefts the trough onto a dining table, where thin, athletic, hungry diners dig in with their bare hands and, laughing and smiling, shovel pizza into their mouths. "Pizza Trough: fun food that tastes great when you wanna stuff your face!"

+ + +

Jime stirred the pot of soup he was making. He lifted the spoon to taste it, smiled at its aromatic herbal flavor, and decided to let it simmer a bit longer. The most common way that Mallworld shoppers prepared meals at home was exceedingly artificial: while many condos still had small kitchenettes for storing and cooking snack foods, usually people ate complete, automatically prepared meals that were ordered from vending machines in condominium hallways, then taken back to individual units for private consumption. It was a cash cow for the Gramma's Homemade VendoMeals Corporation. Jime had, as much as possible, stopped eating the way that most shoppers did and was now cooking much of his own food. He was avoiding junk food like Cake and, with a little effort and attention, able to eat a healthier diet.

Fresh ingredients were hard to come by since real plants and animals were extremely rare and expensive. Most food was manufactured from algae and extruded to look and taste like the real thing—although Jime wondered how anyone but the wealthiest could know how accurate it was, since for decades natural food had not been widely available to make a comparison. Still, with some research he was able to identify more-or-less healthy ingredients and recipes so he could make more nutritious meals. They tasted better, too.

When the soup was finished, he took a bowl to his real-wood table, turned on his sunlamp, and sat down to enjoy his dinner with a good book. Jime had found that reading about philosophy, politics, and history was a much better mental diet than HV had been, which was junk food for the mind as much as Cake was for the body. Jime's reading on communitarianism had led him to explore other, related schools of political theory, and he was going through a process of questioning his received beliefs. He had, since his business school years, thought of social arrangements in a technocratic way: people and resources were things to be managed, usually in order to achieve organization, efficiency, and a stable and productive order. Those goals were ostensibly neutral and objective. Private property and deregulated markets were the best economic arrangements since every individual, by pursuing their self-interest, created an economy of potentially unlimited growth, he had believed.

But he was currently digesting an ancient school of political and moral thought called *classical republicanism*, the primary concept of which was the public good, not self-interest. Thus it had nothing in common with the Republican political party of the Old United States, other than the name. Rather, he thought of the Roman republic of antiquity. The civic republican tradition in political thought had begun in ancient Greece and Rome, flourished during the Renaissance, was very influential during the Enlightenment and the founding of the O.U.S., and enjoyed a revival in the late 20th century. Contributors to the tradition included Aristotle, Polybius, Cicero, Machiavelli, Adam Ferguson, Rousseau, Jefferson, and Madison.[1]

Classical republicanism, Jime learned, is oriented around five concepts. First, it takes the idea of the *public good* seriously—that people have shared, common interests distinct from their individual self-interest. Second is the notion of *civic virtue*, the idea that citizens must attend to the public good rather than their own self-interest, at least sometimes. This virtue is not flimsy sympathy or altruism, but strong political excellence: citizens must become informed about and participate actively in politics, put effort into working for the good of all, vigilantly guard their liberties, and firmly quash any power-hungry individuals or groups that want to rule the republic for themselves. Civic virtue is necessary in order to prevent *corruption* of the republic, which is not only about bribery but occurs when self-interest, faction, or class dominance cause the republic to be governed in the interest of a part, rather than for the public good. Corruption inevitably undermines the people's *liberty*, which republicans define as participating in making the laws and rules by which the polity is governed, and it leads to *tyranny*, the arbitrary rule by one person or faction over the public at large. Jime learned that there was always some group—usually economic, military, or ideological elites—eager to fill the vacuum left by apathetic citizens and capture power for themselves. Notably, classical republicanism's concept of civic virtue contrasted with modern liberal capitalism's notion of self-interest. Whereas liberalism had a tendency to reduce human

---

1   For the full lesson in classical republicanism that Jime read, see Appendix 1.

motivation to self-interest, republicanism's central idea was that people could attend to group and social interests, and that they could learn to do so consistently and regularly. Republican citizens *must* do so, in fact, because republican liberty is an active practice, not a passive state. Citizens who failed to be politically active were not simply being apathetic; they weakened the collective self-government of all. Thus liberty did not mean simply possessing freedom from interference or domination; republican liberty meant actively participating in the politics and governance of the republic in order to maintain and even strengthen healthy social and political interconnections.

To ward off corruption and tyranny, republicans over the centuries had proposed solutions of constitutional design that included the rule of law, a mixed government in which both elites and the common people had a share of governing, a distribution of powers among different offices, limited terms of office, citizen assemblies, short-term militias rather than standing armies, and the education and cultivation of good political habits among the youth.

One republican idea that piqued Jime's interest was the Old United States founder Thomas Jefferson's proposal for a "ward system." In the ward system, local communities and neighborhoods, with small populations of several dozens of people, would have responsibility for local affairs: they would run a primary school, maintain local roads, supply a constable, and so on. They would meet to discuss and decide about local issues, and therefore they would, through regular practice, learn how to take others' points of view and interests into account, to compromise, and to attend to their local collective good. The wards would be "little republics," Jefferson said, believing they could be the schools of the then-young American democracy.[2] Jime thought that the institution of communitarian neighborhoods could serve a similar purpose.

2   Thomas Jefferson, "To Samuel Kercheval, Monticello, September 5, 1816," in *Jefferson: Political Writings*, ed. Appleby and Ball, eds. (Cambridge: Cambridge University Press, 1999).

Jime learned that many republicans over the centuries had also argued for *moderation* of both wealth inequality and consumption in order to maintain a republic. Aristotle had pointed out that a city with great inequality was a house divided: the experiences and interests of the wealthy and the poor were so different that an unequal society would become, in essence, two cities within the same walls, and those two cities would be at war with one another—a colorful way of describing factional civil conflict. It would be better, Aristotle thought, to arrange things so the polity is dominated by a middle class in which most people have a moderate level of wealth, so that the citizenry generally has similar experiences, develops similar outlooks, and shares common interests.[3]

This republican case for economic moderation is a civic one based on political considerations of preventing the wealthy class from usurping the self-government of the common people and thus destroying the republic as a healthy set of moral and political relations. This made it different from religious sumptuary laws, such as bans on dancing or skimpy clothing for supposedly being sinful. Sumptuary laws imposed limits on consumption based on sectarian religious or moral beliefs, an entirely different set of reasons from the civic case for moderation. Moreover, republican moderation clearly contrasts with the liberal notion of unlimited freedom of consumer choice in acquiring property: for republicans, wealth hoarding and consumption choices that undermine the polity's structure can legitimately be restricted or prohibited based on their threat to the polity, notwithstanding the dogmas of market ideology. If the mere existence of concentrations of wealth threatens the health of the republic, those concentrations can rightfully be ended by the government in order to preserve the public good. There is no right to property where the property in question threatens the existence of the republic. This could potentially justify a maximum income, Jime thought, and a maximum limit on accumulated wealth, as well as limitations on owning companies.

---

3   Aristotle, *Politics*, Book 4, chapters 11–12, Bekker no. 1295b ff., trans. C. D. C. Reeve, (Indianapolis: Hackett, 1998).

An additional, more modern consideration occurred to Jime. In modern consumer societies, moderation was not simply a matter of personal virtue and self-discipline, or of individual choice; rather, immoderation and overconsumption were products of the advertising system of capitalism. Although immoderation manifested as individual behavior, overconsumption did not happen primarily from an individual lack of self-control over desires; it was created by the psychological effects of advertising, which was designed to promote unlimited consumption—and which was exceedingly efficient at it. Therefore, thought Jime, advertising must somehow be resisted, controlled, or changed in order to achieve, for the public good, the helpful civic benefits of moderation of consumption.

Jime decided he needed a change of scenery, so he grabbed his tablet, left his apartment, and headed to his favorite place for reading and thinking, a café called Percolate a few blocks from Piazza Plaza. As he walked, he reflected on how appealing he found civic republicanism to be. It put into words his feeling that he needed to be part of something bigger than himself, part of a healthy community in which people actively engaged in a shared public life and treated each other with respect as equal citizens, rather than as mere instruments to satisfy each other's consumption desires. At the same time republicanism was very down-to-earth: its appeal to belong to something greater was not based on religious or metaphysical essentialism, nor on nationalist or ethnocentric fanaticism, but simply on basic, general material and social facts about community and society. Thus it could give meaning and purpose to this earthly human life in a way that religions and idealist philosophies could not: republicanism need not evoke the imagined commands of mythical gods, races, or nationalities to give significance to life but had the potential to create purpose directly from healthy social relations.

+ + +

On billions of holoscreens an advertisement is projected:

The high-pitched *plinkety-plink* of banjo music plays, and a gangly man in an oversized cowboy hat and large mustache dances on screen, his knees kicking high.

"YEE-HAW! Wayne Westwood here, at the Texas Slaughterhouse!" He pulls out two oversized, golden six-shooters and fires them off into the sky—they make the buzz-saw sound of fully automatic machine guns. "Come for the barbecue, stay for the good old shoot-'em-up values!"

Several half-clad waitresses in cowboy hats and boots, cut-off jean shorts, and camouflage halter tops square dance into the picture, carrying large platters piled high with buffalo wings. Wayne Westwood yells, "Texas Slaughterhouse—where Mallworld finds hope, where wings take dream!"

The scene cuts to Wayne Westwood riding a spinning mechanical rodeo horse, shooting his blazing guns left and right; cows and pigs are cut down by bullets, blood spraying everywhere. The camera cuts to a family sitting at a Texas Slaughterhouse table, pigging out on barbecued ribs, their faces covered in red sauce.

Wayne Westwood appears and yells, "Texas Slaughterhouse … so Mallworld can put food on its families! YEE HAW!"

+ + +

At Percolate, Jime sipped tea and watched people go by. Some were dressed to the nines in colorful suits and sleek dresses, bejeweled with shiny baubles, hair and makeup in the latest style—which changed every month. All of it was incredibly expensive and meant to impress. And while that expense, Jime thought, was far above the actual cost of producing the outfits, it achieved nothing much of import—it only won fleeting approval through superficial appearances. Conversely, he saw others dressed as complete slobs, not attending to their appearance at all. Class distinctions were displayed right on the surface, in peoples' apparel. Both the well and poorly dressed were carrying bags full of commodities, however, engaged in the most common activity of his society other than work: shopping.

Jime saw a team of workeys across the way hauling heavy office furniture into a building and up a stairwell; they were sweating and cursing at the work, and at one point a bulky cabinet fell on one of the workey's hands, badly injuring it. He saw cubeys in office suits and saleys in aprons hustling by to do their business. All around him was a landscape of clangorous commercialism: nearly every ground-level building façade was a storefront, while animated signs and gaudy spray-posters vied everywhere for his attention and his money, making his field of vision a clashing kaleidoscope of color. Everyone was in a hurry to buy or sell in an environment that created the optimal conditions to do both, in a society that socialized its people almost solely for those activities.

Both Outside and Inside the Mall, people did not become all that they could become. Workeys Outside and saleys Inside had it too hard and never *could* reach their full potential, while the consuming classes Inside had it too easy and never *would* reach their full potential.

It was easy to see how a life of endless toil prevents human flourishing, Jime thought. Overwork requires monotonous, burdensome, servile, or dangerous activity; exhausts people's energy; causes stress and mental illness; ruins health; lessens time for mutually supportive social relations; increases crime and antisocial behavior; intensifies social conflict; and cuts participation in volunteer and political activity. Overwork is personally and socially debilitating, and a society that accepts it weakens itself. To be sure, working at a reasonable level to carry one's weight in society is the responsible thing to do, although ideally, everyone should have an occupation, profession, or vocation that matches their talents and aptitudes and that they find fulfilling, such that it doesn't even feel like work. But whether that is possible or not, the hours, pace, and intensity of work should never be so much as to degrade a person's physical or mental health or to prevent an active social and family life.

It was harder, however, to understand how the unchecked license of consumers to indulge themselves is also debilitating. Wasn't getting all the pleasure you wanted the very definition of the good life?

The answer was a definite "no." First, overindulgence can make a person as physically unhealthy as deprivation or overwork can, just in a different way. For example, overindulging in alcohol does not lead to the good life, and moderation is clearly better. Jime felt so much better now that he had lost the excess weight from his body and gotten fit through exercise. Most people awash in the overconsumption environment Inside were overweight and under-exercised. High-consumption societies had first developed a crisis of mass obesity in the twentieth century and a parallel crisis of narcotics abuse. While poverty and starvation are obviously unhealthy states that sometimes kill people, overconsumption also makes people generally unhealthy and produces its own set of ailments and early deaths, from osteoarthritis to diabetes to heart disease to some cancers. Furthermore, being habituated to overconsumption creates mental illness and dysfunction—short attentions spans, lack of frustration tolerance, status anxiety, narcissism, and sociopathy.

Thus, both extremes of poverty and wealth, of overwork and overconsumption, lessen human flourishing by creating poor physical and mental health. They also keep people incapacitated as overworked producers, passive overconsumers, or both—and in any event, under elite control. In neither case are people really free, psychologically, socially, or ultimately politically. Some in Mallworld were enslaved by overwork; others were enslaved by overconsumption.

Jime concluded that a moderate level of challenge and difficulty would be best for human growth and flourishing. People did best when they faced moderate challenges in achieving their life goals: too much resistance was crushing; too little created passivity and ennui. But Jime also saw the need to err on the side of lesser resistance than greater: people who were beaten down distinctly had it worse than people who had things too easy. You could change your actions more easily than your circumstances.

Jime realized that this moderation would be impossible in a society of unequal classes in which some people systematically exploited others. It would only be possible in a society of equals who spent sufficient time and effort giving each other mutual support and security. Equality would require two things. First, it would require conditions of moderate prosperity for everyone, instead of endless toil by some to support endless indulgence by others. And second, it would need the mutual generation of real social and communal spirit. Jime felt that such social spirit would have to be developed in an ecovillage or a similar "ward" or intentional community, where the habits of character needed to overcome self-interest and self-centeredness, and to cultivate civic-mindedness, could be learned and practiced as a part of daily life.

Jime sipped his tea and recalled what he had read in *Intentional Ecommunities*: in past societies, markets, money, and exchange played only a limited role in most people's lives. In commercial societies, on the other hand, people buy and sell things constantly, to the point where there is almost nothing in life that is not a commodity. People pay money for housing, food, clothes, personal possessions and tools, communications, information, the energy they used, other people's labor, physical and mental health care, entertainment, water, sometimes sex, and even friendship. And they sell things, too—mostly their own labor for wages or salaries. How could this constant buying and selling of everything not affect their habits of thought, their interpretations and perceptions of the world, their consciousness—in a word, their characters?

The constant commodification of everything was fused in the shaping of character with the incentives and norms of competitive markets. Markets *require* that people, to survive and succeed, compete against one another, and market society teaches them to embrace aggressive competition rather than prioritize fair cooperation. Mallworld's commercial society promoted self-interest, acquisitiveness, and profit-maximizing greed. Furthermore, all this commodification and competition got people into the habit of treating *everything* as a good to be consumed—even other people, at least implicitly. Consumerism taught that others exist for our convenience, creating an ingrained sense of entitlement in which people constantly treat others as means to service their desires and whims. It encouraged an instrumental rationality in which consumers thought of other people (service workers, for example) as only tools or instruments, rather than as full-fledged human beings deserving of respect; in the worst cases, it propagated a selfish, narcissistic self-orientation that was amoral and thus randomly cruel. Consumerism corroded any sense of fairness based on mutual equality, respect, and reciprocity.

Commercial society's drive to immediately satisfy desires without delaying gratification or exercising effort and creativity, furthermore, fueled a race to the bottom in culture and education, making the society as a whole thoroughly anti-intellectual. Money-making and overconsumption shoved out learning and knowledge, creating instead a willful ignorance that stupefied people and thwarted critical philosophic questioning. Short-term thinking and immediate gratification stifled long-term planning, self-disciplined pursuit of goals, and looking at the big picture. Overconsumption bred a passivity that was at odds with an active life of personal development and participation in public affairs—meaning that it deterred the realization of both personal and political liberty. And in discouraging freedom, it nurtured servitude. The immediate gratification and passivity of consumerist society created herds of people willing to go along with almost anything, even violence to some of their own number, as long as their desires were met without much effort.

The most important lesson Jime had learned from republicanism was that liberty is an active concept that requires choosing, doing, and exercising, in real-life practice. It is not a passive state of being. Therefore, it requires positive empowerment of the human capacities, both individual and social, necessary to exercise and maintain liberty over time. To actualize their collective liberty and individual autonomy, people had to engage in self-government in practice, and they had to cultivate the habits and qualities of character that promoted that exercise of freedom. But given the degree of self-interest inculcated by commercial society and the predominance of commercial habits of competitiveness, aggressiveness, economic subservience, consumption, distraction by spectas, media disinformation, and disrespect of education, Jime feared that a commercialized people could never govern themselves well. "Consumer choice," the selection of consumption goods, was not an active exercise of freedom in which humans exercised their creative powers and capacities, but was merely a form of passive absorption, albeit with options.

Jime looked up from his tablet, and everywhere around him he saw advertising holoscreens, flashing commercial signage, bright lights, and loud colors, all vying to bypass reason and directly hit the senses with the message, "buy, Buy, BUY *THIS*! NOW!" There was nothing in this commercial society that habituated people to attend to the needs of others or to the needs of everyone considered collectively—that is, to the public good.

Jime tasted his tea, realized the cup had grown cold, and grimaced. He gazed around one last time at the people walking by, all of them concerned with shopping, eating, drinking, and being entertained, but seemingly none of them concerned with the state of their society. Not long ago Jime had been just like them, and it was only by accident that he had escaped that stupor. There's no way, he concluded, that the Mallworlders he saw all around him, so habituated to passive consumption and pursuit of self-interest, would be capable of exercising the civic virtues or of actually governing themselves. Surely they must, deep down, want to be a part of something bigger than themselves, to contribute to society, to have a purpose more significant than their next specta or purchase. But Jime had no hope of activating that in them. How could a people so accustomed to self-interest look to the common good? How could a people incapable of governing their own desires govern themselves democratically?

Jime concluded that he would never find a healthy community here.

CHAPTER 3:
TAKING FLIGHT

J ime flew the jetcopter along the Mallwall at a steady pace, and from his seat in the sky was able to get a good view of both the Mall itself and the non-Mall parts of the world. Jime had learned only basic jetcopter flying during his last stint Outside. It was mostly computer controlled and thus not tremendously difficult, but he hadn't yet learned how to land, so once they arrived at their destination he would have to transfer control back to the pilot who was with him.

From the air Jime could see how gargantuan a beast Mallworld actually was, and the sight was overwhelming. When he looked right he saw the sparse scrub of the desiccated nature that surrounded the Mall, and when he looked left his entire field of vision was filled with millions of buildings, towers, domes, and roofed-over market squares, connected by a vast network of covered streets. The structures of the Mall were made of algaeplast concrete and colorful tinted glass, which glinted in the sunlight and painted a stark contrast with the patchy browns and greens of the surrounding terrain. At night the domes and buildings glowed with haunting twilight colors. Jime could see several of Mallworld's massive, multi-kilometer domes, the largest of which were as tall as twentieth-century skyscrapers and, like New Tropicana, might enclose a simulated jungle, desert, mountainscape, or even a faux-historical city. In the distance, he could see the domineering tower of Mall Central, not a dome but a conoid, pointed glass spire that stabbed the sky, with a great, glowing corporate logo that read "Mallworld,

Inc." It contained the Central Office skyscraper itself, as well as an office park of large gardens, pools, and corporate office buildings. It was the headquarters of Mall Management and the tallest of the hermetically sealed structures.

The Mall, when viewed in its entire magnitude, overpowered the mind: covering several former American states, it stretched all the way to the horizon and beyond—Jime could see the sun reflecting from its off-white surfaces a few hundred kilometers away. He knew that if he were in orbit around the planet it would be plain to see, a giant concrete cyst on the surface of a scoured planet. When Inside, one's perspective was limited to a single isolated corridor or dome, but from this higher, wider perspective, Jime became aware of the structures of the Mall as connected parts of a colossal, organic whole—although if it was an organism it was a mutant: the structures were all jumbled together in a kluge of intersecting lines and clashing forms, lacking in proportion or order. It was obvious that Mallworld was an unnatural thing that did not belong on this earth.

Jime's new sense of awareness caused him to turn away from Mallworld and look to the green of nature, which still made its wounded presence felt despite humanity's worst destructive efforts. While much of the planet's surface now consisted of lacerated and abraded earth pocked by ancient ruins and scrubby weeds, occasionally an oasis of tenacious fauna was visible. Nature's powers of recovery, it seemed, were more resilient than even humanity's worst powers of destruction. Jime knew that in the future, after the human species extinguished itself through consumerism and exited the evolutionary stage (taking most other species with it), nature would eventually recover, and the surface of the planet would once again teem with life. This recovery, however, would take tens of millions of years, just as it took tens of millions of years for humans to emerge after the dinosaurs died out. It was a timescale so long that it was only an abstraction. To put hope in a recovery of that scale would be misanthropic. Looking at the tiny pockets of green around the Mall that clung to life and grew despite human over-consumption, Jime wondered if there was enough natural material and energy left in the world to make it green again on any timescale meaningful to human beings.

Jime had been Outside again for almost a month, and he had already made progress in his personal mission: to get all the information that he could about living workeys who had once inhabited real communities at some point in their lives. Having changed his circumstances, he felt like he was moving forward with purpose.

Jime was again managing workpartners, but he had arranged to get a different job this time, one as an inspector/investigator. Most workeys died before fifty, whether from accidents or exhaustion. Occasionally a workey was rumored to live long enough, through perseverance and no small amount of luck, to receive a sort of informal retirement: an older person no longer capable of work would be hidden away in the back rooms of a barracks, and other workeys would pick up the slack to cover for the retiree's assignment. Sometimes such a retiree would be reported as dead, and a fake cremation might even be staged. That was harder to pull off, however, and it also entailed losing the "dead" person's ration card, so everyone else's rations would have to be stretched until the elder really did pass away. Thus, most workeys tried to keep laboring as long as physically possible in order not to burden others. In any event, retirement for any workey was rare and reserved for elders who simply could physically no longer work. Part of Jime's new job, in addition to regular inspections of barracks, was to root out such cases. Then the elder workpartner would be put back to work, under strict supervision. Most died within weeks. Jime felt guilty about this—he found himself struggling with it emotionally as he never would have before—but he had an ulterior motive: he was looking for elders who might once have lived in a village. He rationalized his actions by telling himself that these investigations would have been done by someone else anyway, so the workeys he caught would be found no matter what; and at least he had a moral reason for taking this job, because he was getting information necessary to resist the whole system. Sometimes you have no choice but to work within the constraints of a system before you are able to escape from it.

Eventually Jime uncovered rumors about an elder within jetcopter distance of his posting who had possibly once lived in a village, so he requisitioned the aircraft and pilot to go there as soon as he could.

When not busting retirees, Jime spent much of his time inspecting barracks for safety and hygiene, all the while surreptitiously observing the lives of the workeys. He got to see how they interacted, how they conducted their family relationships and friendships, what they did when not working. He began to notice things he hadn't before, when he had seen workeys merely as a means to doing his job as a manager or simply ignored them as part of the landscape. With lives so full of labor and so lacking in free time, many were defeated by toil, and they were certainly unable to form any sort of collective resistance to their oppressive conditions. There were, however, many acts of kindness and mutual help. One day he watched a mother with three children in tow helping another, younger woman carry laundry to the wash machine in the barracks; the whole family helped carry or drag bags and bundles of dirty clothes. One young workey man, obviously drunk, interrupted and started pestering and grabbing at the younger woman, but soon other residents of the barracks intervened to keep things civil. Jime had witnessed many such examples of mutual assistance in the last month.

Jime thus gained a new appreciation for the workeys: he was now seeing them, really seeing them, as fully human, not as the dirty, disgusting, cannibal caricatures created by Mall HV culture, fit only for use as work animals. He began to admire the communal spirit they were able to maintain despite living in conditions of never-ending work, discipline, and deprivation. He realized that Mallworlders thought of workeys in the same dehumanized way that Americans had once thought of black people—as a lower grade of person. As he rehumanized them in his mind, his feeling toward them shifted from contempt for their persons to compassion for their circumstances, and he wondered what they could achieve if their quality of life improved.

The jetcopter was approaching their destination, so Jime transferred the controls back to the pilot. They started to descend, and his mind turned back to the task he had set himself: to find a living example of a villager.

Wearing his new sunglasses, Jime stood under the bright Outside sky and took a moment to inhale the atmosphere. Inside, the air normally smelled like ozone and electricity—that is, when one's nose wasn't assaulted by some pungent artificial odor emitted by a plastiplant. In shopping centers, corporate offices, and wealthy residences the plastic foliage was designed to imitate natural aromas, although, like sense experience in capitalism generally, the smells were both magnified and made more pleasant than what nature would have offered. But of course, few people recalled what the natural scents were anymore. Otherwise, the air Inside was often stale in its lack of oxygen and could make one sleepy, except in shopping areas and arenas, where a higher oxygen content was injected to agitate and excite shoppers. Outside, however, Jime found that the air was often dusty but somehow . . . fresh. When he was near a rare thicket of scrub or other vegetation it was even fresher, as well as wetter and cooler. It had taken a few weeks for Jime to notice this difference—he had grown up within the overwhelming sense experience of the Mall, so at first it was hard to notice subtle differences outdoors such as microclimate changes, but he was getting better at it with time.

The earth just smelled *good*. He inhaled deeply and felt more comfortable in his own skin with every breath.

Jime now saw more nuance with his eyes too. On sunny days like this he was grateful to have his sunglasses, not only because they reduced the glare but also because they made it easier to take in the sky and the horizon. While there was little that was beautiful anymore in the accursed, used-up wasteland, the clouds were a natural wonder, white and gray against the vivid blue of the sky. Most days now Jime never wanted to go back into the Mall, with its gaudy, clownish, pink and lavender sim-skies.

The interrogation of the retiree was not going well. At the moment, the elder sat silently, with her arms crossed, refusing to speak. She was old and weathered by time, her wrinkles unhidden by layers of makeup, her head crowned in a shocking undyed white that no Insider would accept as a color for their own hair. Underneath her gray workey's uniform, her body was bent from years of hard physical labor. Jime had been questioning her for several hours, and everything he'd tried had failed to penetrate the taciturn wall that had descended around her soon after the interview began. Earlier that morning Jime had read from her file that her name was Phoenicia, but he hadn't found out much else since.

"Who's been helping you hide from Management?" Jime asked for the fifth or sixth time. He was personally most interested in the social aspects of her retirement; how and why people helped her, what the social connections were. He was trying to understand community better and to open up a line of questioning that would, he hoped, lead to a discussion of her youth in a real community—and maybe to its location.

The elder didn't see it that way. This idiot, she thought, wants me to tell him who helped me so he can punish them, too. Phoenicia felt a sense of resignation; she was old and nearing the end, and she didn't feel that her life was valuable enough to get anyone else in trouble in order to make it last just a bit longer. Let them take it. The thought of being beaten or tortured scared her, but she also felt that it was a blessing that her old body wouldn't last long before giving out.

"Someone had to help you. I'm only trying to find out why."

Phoenicia sat quietly staring at him, saying nothing, and hoping that her fear didn't show. Jime was frustrated, but he knew that he had to get through to this person if he ever wanted to find a village, so he couldn't quit. He had to keep trying. His head dropped wearily into his hands.

"You are tired, Manager," Phoenicia said, leaning back while she glared at him with a frown. "I won't tell you who helped me, just so you can give them extra work. So why not let me go?"

Jime sighed. After hours of interrogation, he was, in fact, fatigued. "Alright, let's take a break. I'll have food brought in for you." He got up and walked out of the interrogation room and gave instructions to one of the workeys in the hallway to bring a meal.

In the room next door, some Sub-Managers were watching the questioning on holovideo. Jime wearily looked at them, and they looked back at him with frustrated impatience.

"Why are you coddling her?" one asked in aggravation. "The only thing that works with these lazy fucks is getting tough. You gotta yell and scream and slap her around."

"Don't you know that you're the boss? You gotta act like one," another spat with barely concealed contempt. Jime couldn't tell if the antipathy was for him or for Phoenicia. "You can't tell people what to do if it looks like you're weak. You can't reason with these people!"

Jime felt self-conscious. These Sub-Managers believed him to be gutless, and he didn't have their respect. They saw him as a little pansy, and this made him nervous. They already hesitated to follow his orders and instructions, and soon they wouldn't be willing to do so at all.

"Why don't you just kiss her?" an anonymous someone let fly from the back of the room.

Another part of Jime awoke, a part that was quietly confident, not brutishly domineering, and it not only intuited a good course of action, it believed in it.

"Who said that?" He demanded. Having touched his inner strength, Jime found his voice more confident than he thought possible. He went with it and demanded again. "Well? Who said it? No one will admit it? Listen and hear me well. I reject your approach as short-sighted. You get more flies with honey than vinegar. I will get through to her, and you *will* patiently wait for me to do so, even if it takes longer than you personally think it should. You will wait."

"She's a lazy-ass fucking workey!" said one man near the front.

"She's still a person."

"Phhht. No, she's not."

"Listen to yourself!" Jime barked. He stared at the man with eyes of ice. "She might be a workey, but she's still a human being, and a living thing that feels." The volume of his voice rose. "And she's an old lady, dammit!" Jime glared. "I'm not going to beat her, and *neither are you*. You *will* be patient. That is an order." Jime stared the other man down until his gaze dropped. He welled up with confidence.

Jime looked over at his briefcase. He had one more tactic to try. It had better work or his failure would be reported back to the Central Office and cause him all sorts of complications.

+   +   +

Now that she had eaten, Phoenicia was even surer of her ability to resist Jime's questions. But she feared that the questioning would end soon and the interrogation would shift to more coercive methods. She knew that Managers didn't like too much blood and gore, but they could cause any amount of pain if it didn't make them feel queasy. They wouldn't cut or maim, but could get around their natural sympathy by using electrical tortures, water tortures, noise and temperature tortures, visual tortures. She was terrified but also determined to stand firm.

The door opened and she flinched. Jime stomped in, dragged a chair over, and sat down.

On the table between them, he placed a book.

"Have you ever seen any buildings like these?" he asked, pointing at the cover. Phoenicia leaned in for a closer look, her curiosity getting the best of her. She squinted for a moment, not recognizing what she saw at first; then she reached out, touched the cover, and slid the book toward herself. Her mouth fell open, and she sighed in recognition. She opened the book to see more.

"I used to live in a place like this," she whispered.

"When?"

She glanced up at him. "When I was a girl. A long time ago." She slowly turned the book's pages. Her eyes grew sadder as she gazed at pictures of wood-clad homes nestled amongst trees, with people chatting and laughing, arms wrapped around neighbors' shoulders or holding the hands of children. "I grew up in a neighborhood like that, until I was eleven. My mother used to hug me just like that woman is hugging that little girl." She stared long and wistfully at the page.

Jime held his next question for a quiet moment while she looked at the book, and then, with a soft voice, asked, "How big was your house?"

Phoenicia looked up, a little surprised to have her reverie broken, as if for that moment she had been in the room alone, rather than with a security interrogator. "Not big at all. It was my parents, my brother, and me, and we had two bedrooms, a living room, a loft that we played in, and a kitchen with a dining table. But we mostly ate and played in the Hall."

"The Hall?"

"There was a big building that was used as a common house. Everyone ate dinner there most days, and it had a TV room, I remember, and a playroom, and some offices that the grownups used. A workroom too. My mother and father used to go there; Dad would do woodwork while Mom would paint and make pottery. She let me paint too—I loved to paint pictures. I would paint green forests under blue skies, sometimes with a yellow sun and gray clouds."

Phoenicia paused, and withdrew back into herself. She looked straight at Jime. "Why did you ask me about this book?"

Jime was on edge, knowing that the Sub-Managers were watching in the next room. He swallowed before he spoke. "I had reason to suspect that you lived in one of these communities, and I'm glad that I was right; I'm looking for one."

"If you find one you will destroy it." She crossed her arms and glared at him.

"It's my job to root out dens of escaped workeys," Jime said. Then he leaned in, conspiratorially, and whispered quietly enough that the microphones wouldn't hear clearly. "If I find one I won't destroy it. I'm going to live in it, and I'll take you with me."

Both stared silently at each other across the table for a moment.

Jime leaned back and spoke in a normal voice again. "What happened to your village?"

"Mall Management took over everything. First men in suits came and argued with the grownups. They always smiled and said everything would be the best, the greatest. They were going to expand the Mall onto our land, but of course we didn't want to move into the Mall. So they started offering us different things, like free vacations in the domes, free baseball tickets and things. Some people took them. Then they came with Mall Security Guards, and the arguments got worse and there was shouting. Some of our people left. Eventually they got one of our people to sign the land over to them. Everyone in the village owned it in common, so the Mall said that if one person signed a lease, they signed it for all. We said no, that meant that we all had to sign it. But they didn't agree, and soon they said we had to start paying rent. On our own land! Since we raised our own food and built most of our own things, we had no Mall store credits to use for rent, so we didn't pay. Then one day they told us we had forty-eight hours to pack and leave. We didn't, and the bulldozers came, and they destroyed the whole village. Then, instead of living happily as we had, my parents had to take jobs as workeys."

Phoenicia sighed and frowned and looked down at Jime's book, but she stared right through it as she drew a finger along its edge, lost in memory. She sighed again, closed the book, composed herself, and looked up at Jime.

Jime asked the important question. "Do you know where the villagers who left went? Did they tell you where, mention any places?"

"They said they were going to a place up north near Eau Claire, by Chippewa Falls, in a ravine with a river, I remember. They called it Lindis. It was only one of many villages, but it was the closest one with available space. All I remember is that after a lot of yelling and arguing, some families took the village vehicles and drove there. They took what supplies and belongings they could with them. They said it was going to be a long drive."

"That sounds like what I'm looking for," Jime said loud enough for the microphones to hear. Then he leaned and talked quietly to Phoenicia for a little longer. When Jime walked back out through the control room the other Managers there looked at him suspiciously, so he glared back at them and curtly issued some routine orders—he knew his best chance to keep them quiet was to keep them cowed, hesitant, and busy, so he acted like he owned the place. Then he left to look for a map.

+ + +

The pilot stretched and yawned as he walked down the tunnel toward his jetcopter pad; the door at the end was open a crack, and the Outside's morning light and chill air trickled in. He was a tall man, and his stiff, outstretched arms almost spanned the width of the passage. He frowned. Despite having a job that required him to be Outside on a regular basis—only in the biggest domes of the Mall could you fly a jetcopter—he never liked the alternating schedule that took him into the open air every other month, away from football games and holomovies. After he finished his current job of shuttling the Manager on his little errands, he'd finally head back Inside tomorrow for a month of beach time.

He strode Outside into the bright morning sun and squinted. The copter would need a maintenance check, as it had a bad motivator that was cutting its low-speed lift by about 14 percent. He turned left toward the helipad, his brain expecting to see the looming bulk of the copter. His eyes saw only empty space. His steps slowed, and his eyes blinked involuntarily. Wait. What? The copter wasn't there. Where did it go?

He kept walking toward the empty helipad that should be filled with jetcopter but wasn't. His arms stretched out again and his jaw went slack with bewilderment. After a moment it set in that there was a very expensive piece of equipment missing, and he was responsible for it. His arms fell to his side, he spun around, and he ran back into the tunnel.

+ + +

Jime banked the jetcopter to the left to put it on a northwesterly course, the sun rising in the east and the gray and glass roofs of various Mall sections, dotted with the occasional air filter or other piece of climate control machinery, speeding past below. It had not been hard to abscond with an unguarded jetcopter at daybreak, before the morning shift had arrived for work. Jime felt fairly comfortable flying the copter, but he wondered how he was going to land the damn thing.

As the jetcopter approached the northern limit of the Mallwall, Jime looked up from the controls and saw the rising sunlight gleaming off the last domes and buildings of Mallworld; beyond that, nature stretched to the horizon. It was a wasted nature, to be sure, but nature nonetheless. He looked back over his shoulder as he left the Mall behind. He intended never to return.

"How are you going to find Lindis?" Phoenicia asked him. It had also not been hard to persuade the lone guard on the night shift to release her from the locked room where she was being held. Jime had convinced the guard that she was going to guide him, as part of his investigation, to the location of a cell of shirking workers. That was also his plan in case Mall

Management sent someone after them, although it would be easier if they ignored the missing jetcopter for a few days—which was plausible given the usual corporate red tape. If that happened, he would find a way to camouflage, dismantle, or destroy the aircraft and hide his trail. He had brought enough food and supplies to last him and Phoenicia for several days, if needed.

He turned to answer her question. "We know the general location of the village from what you told me, and I downloaded an old map of the local area. Once we're there we'll fly around until we find it."

"There are maps of villages? I'm sorry but I never got to go to school for long. I've only seen maps of the Mall with pipes and conduits."

"It won't show the village, but it shows the terrain around Eau Claire and Chippewa Falls. We can find the village from there by flying along the local ravines. The map I have is pretty accurate."

"How do they make maps that good?"

"They don't anymore, but they used to. There was a satellite network that mapped everywhere Outside very accurately . . ."

"Satellite network?"

"You know what a spaceship is?"

"Oh yes."

"Same thing. Spaceships flew around the earth and took pictures of the surface, and then they used the pictures to make very good maps. But those satellites fell out of the sky or stopped working years ago as people retreated into the Mall and forgot the rest of the world. So with a little searching, I found an old map. There aren't any current, up-to-date ones."

"I see," Phoenicia murmured in understanding. She smiled and said, "I'm very happy that you are giving me the chance to go back to live in a village, Manager." Her voice was weighted with long years of overwork and exhaustion, but Jime could hear hope coming through as well.

"It's really exciting, isn't it?" He said giddily, turning his head to look right at her.

"Yes, it is," she said, humoring him. She changed the subject. "This machine moves smooth, Manager, not like the worktrucks. You drive it well."

"You haven't seen me land it yet. You might want to wait before you compliment me."

Jime accelerated, and they flew in silence for a while. As they left Mallworld behind, he noticed that things gradually grew greener as they got farther from the Mall. Not by much: just patches of green grass that appeared on land not completely poisoned by chemicals or totally sucked of nutrients and topsoil. Most places were still rocky, dusty, and barren. The Mall had appropriated most of the fresh water for hundreds of kilometers around itself, draining even the Great Lakes, which, combined with climate change, had turned the region from lush farmland and forest into parched wasteland.

The remnants of long-abandoned human structures dotted the low, dusty hills of the landscape. The ruins were the remains of pre-Mallworld experiments in hermetically sealed urban planning, carried out to protect people from the harsh storms and extreme temperatures of a warming world: before people in North America had consolidated themselves into the Mall, other attempts had been made to cover the existing urban areas, sever them from the natural world, and keep their internal environments comfortable. On the horizon rose the ruins of these now-empty cities, their coverdomes collapsed, exposing the spiky skeletons of now-rusting mid-twenty-first-century buildings. It was a landscape of creative destruction, of limited resources spent only to be abandoned when supplanted by new technology. Most had failed because they couldn't compete on the real estate market with the rapidly expanding Mall.

Although some shopping malls had closed in the early twenty-first century during a market correction caused by online shopping, a great many stayed open, and the shopping mall remained an enduring feature of American life. It could hardly be otherwise, when the whole economy and society had become a vast edifice of consumerism. The shopping mall *as an experience* was archetypical of consumer society, combining advertising-driven desire with purchasing and entertainment in a package of convenience, overstimulation, and pleasure. Online shopping was even more convenient, but it couldn't replace the totality of the experience; indeed, even as the retail contraction had proceeded, shopping malls consolidated and expanded their entertainment, restaurant, theme park, and spa offerings to draw in shoppers, while in cities, open-air downtown pedestrian zones emerged that were basically outdoor shopping malls. Thus gigantic megamalls continued to be built in America, Asia, and elsewhere. Mallworld itself began as a shopping and residential megacenter in Chicago, inspired by earlier attempts at large-scale malls such as the Mall of America, the Dubai Mall, and the New Century Global Center in China. Its launch was fortuitously timed to benefit from innovations in engineering and social control that made rapid Mall expansion and consolidation possible. Initially Mallworld had succeeded through aggressive marketing by Mall Management, but eventually it gained so much momentum that people had little choice but to join, if they could.

Amidst the seas of dust and scrub, alongside the broken domes of abandoned cities, Jime also saw the dead remnants of even older suburbs, towns, factories, and farms, succumbing to the slow decay of time. Lakes and rivulets of a deep purplish-red ooze, usually called "red sludge," ran like veins of blood across the earth. Jime knew it was the toxic by-product of algae processing. In some places the landscape still showed the crisscross outlines of the ancient industrial agriculture that once covered nearly the whole of North America, displacing its arboreal forests. But industrial agriculture had become increasingly uneconomical as the region's water resources declined, and eventually megafarms also had to compete with the more efficient food production brought by the invention of algae cultivation, which genetically sped up natural growth processes by several orders of magnitude. Algae farming could churn out massive amounts of organic raw material for food and plastics in days or even hours, unconstrained by the limits of nature's seasons. Outside agriculture finally disappeared when Mallworld monopolized the region's last water resources, including the Great Lakes.

After a couple hours of flying, Jime and Phonecia started to pass out of the drained zone, and small streams and sporadic patches of green foliage appeared. These grew most abundantly around water, and as they flew onward these oases became progressively more lush, first filled with grasses, then shrubs, and then even stubby trees. The air got cooler and foggier as they flew northward, too. Jime swooped lower over one green zone to get a closer look; were those trees arranged in a grid? He couldn't be sure as they sped past, but he didn't think it worthwhile to turn back for a second look to see if there might be an active community there. They were only an hour away from Eau Claire, and Jime was eager to press on—and to start a new phase of his life.

Then an electronic beep sounded from the control panel, and the radar screen popped up on his display.

"What's that?" Phoenicia asked.

"Two other jetcopters, about fifty klicks away." Jime turned to the control panel and flipped some switches. "Mall Security. I expected them to come after us, but I hoped that it would take longer than this."

"What do we do now?"

"We talk our way out of it and delay as long as we can."

A voice came over the radio. "Jetcopter 1225-1921, this is Mallworld Security. You have taken a copter without authorization for your travel."

"Roger, Mallworld Security. This is James Galilei, External Oversight Investigator," Jime said. "I have reason to believe that there is a subversive cell of escaped workpartners a hundred kilometers north-northwest of our current location, and I am conducting an investigation to confirm or deny the information."

"We have no record of a flight request, no flight plan on file, and no copy of your credentials. We're going to have to escort you back to the Mall until we get this sorted out."

"I've flown over two hundred kilometers, Security Guard, and I'm not turning back now. If I do, the workeys are likely to disperse. As an Oversight Investigator, I'm authorized to use Mall property in the interests of an ongoing investigation."

"Roger, 1225-1921. You still have to put your credentials and pilot's certification on file, and file a flight plan. For insurance purposes."

"I had a lead, and it required immediate investigation. I'll file all the paperwork tomorrow and we'll backdate it. I'm authorized to do that, if necessary. It's not like it would be the first time that was done."

There was silence for a moment, and then a "stand by." After a minute the Security Guard came back on. "We're going to have to check back with Management for further instructions. We're going to hang back to make radio contact with the Mall, but keep you on radar. Stay above 1000 meters so I can keep a lock on you."

"Roger, and out." Jime clicked the radio off; he was a little surprised that his scheme was working. Once they neared Eau Claire, he would have to fly lower to search for the village by eye, so he had no intention of staying above 1000 meters. He would have to gradually decrease altitude until he was under the radar.

The clumps of forest on the ground had grown thicker and bigger, but Jime knew that they weren't as full and healthy as they had been many decades ago; he had been to the Mall's Grizzly Mountain Dome to ski and so had some idea of what a pine forest should look like. He saw a flock of birds take flight as the jetcopter approached, startled by the rotor noise. Real birds! Jime smiled. Soon he could see outlines of the ruins of the town of Eau Claire, right at the coordinates where they were supposed to be, and it wasn't hard for Jime to find the ravine to the north. He slowed and flew down into it, telling Phoenicia to keep her eyes peeled for any structures. The ravine was green and lush, thicker with trees and plants than any of the oases they had seen so far. After flying slowly through the canyon for about twenty minutes, Jime spotted a thick square of trees aligned as a grid. It was definitely an orchard, and obviously man-made. It was dense and verdant and looked like flourishing agriculture to Jime. Amongst the trees he spotted the roofs of homes and outbuildings. From what he could see, it was a fairly large village of about a hundred buildings, all of them set amongst the forest such that Jime and Phoenicia couldn't see the ground beneath. Phoenicia saw a dog running through the brush, and Jime could see the painted metal of vehicles.

"I think we've found it!" He hadn't felt this excited since he was a young boy waiting to open holiday presents.

"Well, then, this is it!" Phoenicia declared. "Stop this machine, and we will go greet them."

"No, if I land here, Security will track us right to the village. I'm going to try to land several kilometers from here, and we'll have to backtrack on foot. Landing somewhere back at Eau Claire is probably best."

+   +   +

Jime and Phoenicia limped away from a smoldering building, which now contained a bent jetcopter frame, while smoke rose behind them into the gray sky.

"That wasn't too bad," Jime said, limping. He was favoring his left leg, the right having several bruises.

"I take back what I said about you driving smooth," Phoenicia said, holding her back with both hands.

Jime had landed the copter slowly but very roughly, aiming for the glass storefront of a building on the edge of Eau Claire, because he thought it would break the jetcopter's momentum. He was right. The copter body was damaged and the rotors bent, grounding it, although it was not beyond repair; meanwhile both human occupants had been protected by the usual harnesses and airbags and, while bruised and sore, they had avoided major injuries. Jime, however, wanted to leave no evidence that the jetcopter's passengers had survived, so he decided to short-circuit its large battery pack in order to start a fire and completely destroy it. The smoke and flame would also attract Mall Security, misdirecting them. Meanwhile, Jime and Phoenicia snuck off in the direction of the village.

Both of them were energized by the prospect of finding Lindis. Jime shouldered his pack, and despite their bruises, they marched with purpose through kilometers of scrub toward their future home. Dusk was falling by the time they got to the ravine, and the temperature was dropping quickly. Rather than risk a nighttime descent into the crevasse, they set up camp in the open air with a field stove and warming electro-blankets. These were essential: although the average post–climate change temperature of the planet was five degrees Celsius warmer than it had been for millennia, in the near-desert landscape, Outside temperatures ranged wildly from scorching hot during the day to freezing cold at night. They planned to make their way down the ravine and into the village in the morning.

"Manager . . ." Phoenicia said while laying out her bedding.

"You should call me Jime, please," Jime interjected.

"I'm not used to that."

"The people that we're going to meet don't have Managers, and they believe that everyone is equal. At least, I hope that's still the case. They might not even use titles at all. So we both should get on a first-name basis, Phoenicia," he smiled.

"I will try . . . Jime." She thought for a moment. "That was how it was when I was growing up. Everyone respected each other. But people were also closer. More familiar."

"Maybe that's how equality works. Since everyone is seen as basically equal, you get mutual respect and greater closeness, too. Did anyone boss other people around, that you remember?"

Phoenicia thought for a moment. "No, not that I recall. Some people tried, of course, because some people have mean personalities. But since everyone else was equal to them they were kept under control, and I think they tried to control themselves better, too. What I do remember is that most people were very warm and caring. I have clear memories of that, and strong feelings from them. I felt loved as a child, and not just because my parents loved me, but because everyone did."

"That sounds beautiful. That sounds like a wonderful way to grow up. It's an experience that almost no one in Mallworld ever has; my memories of being a kid are of busy, indifferent parents and uncaring teacheys at school. I think it's probably made me cold and indifferent too, less caring."

"More selfish?"

Jime paused. "Yes, probably, now that I think about it."

Phoenicia smiled and wrapped both hands around her knees. "Whenever I have had difficulty with how my life has gone, I am able to go back in my mind to the times of growing up and remember the feeling, and it makes me strong. And then I remember to care for others who are in need, the way that I was loved as a child."

"I probably don't have a reserve of caring like that," Jime said with furrowed brows. "Mallworld's greed makes us callous, heartless, even domineering. You were given a beautiful gift as a girl, Phoenicia."

"Oh, I think you have care in you. Maybe you just have to learn to bring it out in yourself, though. Since your parents didn't do it for you."

Jime silently pondered that. Phoenicia climbed under her electro-blanket. She said, "I think that tomorrow, I will feel young again." She rolled over.

Jime stayed up a while to think about times when people had shown him care and attention, and then he too lay down to rest. Warm in his blanket, tired from physical exertion, and hopeful for the morning, he fell into a deep, satisfied sleep.

+   +   +

Jime awoke to cool morning air, yellow sunlight coming through slatted window-blinds, and the sound of birds chirping outside. He was lying in a soft bed. He felt rested and content; his eyes opened and focused as he rapidly came to a full and natural alertness, the way one does from a deep, healthy sleep. The bedroom that he found himself in was small and tranquil, with floors of natural stone and walls of golden wood, the flow of its beautiful grain not covered by paint as though it were an embarrassing disfigurement. The bed that he occupied was low and dressed in warm cotton and wool blankets, and the room was furnished with a desk, a padded chair, and a long low chest of drawers. He heard the sounds of talking and cooking from another room. He got out of the bed and crept through a hallway toward the sounds; he felt anxious in anticipation of the unknown, but was smiling. As he turned into the kitchen, there was a family seated at a dining table that was set for breakfast. There were two parents smiling and three happy children drinking juice and laughing. Phoenicia stood next to the stove, twisting its knobs.

"I can't get a fire started in this fog, the wood is too wet," she said, her voice trembling as if she was hypothermic.

"What?" Jime asked, bewildered.

"I got cold and tried to make a fire. The mist has made the wood too wet to light. Wake up and start your electric heater."

Jime felt a hand gripping his shoulder and shaking him. His sticky eyes opened, he felt the wet morning chill penetrate his bones, and he shuddered. He sat up with a jerk; he must have kicked off his blanket in the night, and he was so cold that he scrambled on all fours to the camp heater and slammed the "on" button in a panic; then he curled into a ball and shivered until the device started radiating heat.

They ate some rations, drank some coffee, and washed up a little. It was still dark, but the sun was rising and starting to warm them; by midday it would be searing hot. When they felt ready, they struck camp and prepared for the climb down to Lindis. Jime checked his map. They walked a short distance to the edge of the ravine and began to pick a path down it. Jime was both nervous and excited, eager to meet the villagers. The slope was not precipitous, but it was steep enough to force them to go slowly and deliberately, especially in the fog, which down in the valley was burning off slowly as the sun rose. They had to backtrack more than once, and their legs soon ached with the effort of picking a careful path to the bottom. Each of them slipped and fell, with Jime aggravating his crash injuries; despite his relative youth and recent physical exercise, it seemed that Phoenicia was made of tougher stuff.

The fog clung thick to the bottom of the ravine, so Jime used his digital map to guide them to Lindis. As they approached in the burgeoning daylight, they could see the dark outlines of buildings among the trees. Since it was early morning, Jime wondered if there would be anyone up yet to greet them. He heard no human activity, but he did hear a few dogs barking at each other—and as the sun rose a rooster called out.

Jime looked at Phoenicia. "How many chickens do you think they keep? Enough to feed the whole village?" he asked. He wondered what real chicken tasted like. He had only ever had the simulated kind made from algae in Mallworld. He wondered what real eggs tasted like too.

"I don't know. Quite a few, I'm sure," Phoenicia answered.

As they walked into the village, Jime looked through the mist and dim light at the silent homes; they were low to the ground with horizontal lines that melded with the earth. The buildings were made of honest, unadorned natural materials—wood and cut stone, with a minimum of paint, varnish, or other synthetic applications, and roofs made of copper sheathing. Jime knew from his research that there were certain kinds of wood that resisted weathering and vermin, and he presumed that's what he was looking at.

Jime thought about the daily routine of people who lived in such homes. He imagined families snuggled under warm covers, breathing air that smelled of pine and cedar and redwood. He imagined a father making the family breakfast, and a mother waking a son with a kiss to the face. He thought of people tending their gardens, hanging sheets in the open air to dry, carrying in wood, doing chores for the village, going to the common house for the community dinner and staying for the community meeting, with its discussion and voting. Jime sighed, and behind his reverie he heard birds chirping and chickens clucking.

And then he sensed danger, and gasped as a large, brown, toothy blur shot into his field of vision. He heard Phoenicia gasp too. It stopped, facing them, ten paces away. They both froze—Jime heard Phoenicia's quick fearful breathing before he heard his own. The animal glared at them in the early morning light; it growled, and then it barked once, loud and sharp.

"Nice doggie," Jime said in as calm and confident a voice as he could muster. He elongated his words: "Gooooooood puppy dog."

The dog relaxed and sat down. It barked again in a friendlier tone. It tilted its head in curiosity, and its tongue fell from its mouth and wagged in the misty air. It decided they were not a threat and sauntered over to one of the houses, disappearing into a hole in the wall where some boards had been knocked out.

They composed themselves, and Jime wondered aloud, "Why would the owners of that house keep a hole like that in it just to let the dog in? Doesn't that let the heat out?" He looked more closely at the house—it was near the edge of the village, just three houses in. He noticed some cobwebs in the eaves and dirt on the windows—one of which was cracked and broken. The sun had now risen, yet the house remained dark inside, with no morning bustle.

They proceeded slowly, and as the sun burned off the fog they looked around and saw building after building, home after home, broken and run down, dirty and unkempt. Next to one house a rusty truck lay immobilized on four flattened tires, its weather-beaten shell coated in a layer of dirt deposited by countless rains. Next to that was a small power digger in somewhat better shape, as it was still partially covered by a tarpaulin. Jime looked about the landscape and could piece together the patterns of flowers and hedges that had once lined the sides of the walkway, but which were now overgrown. Then a chicken ran clucking across an unkempt yard—definitely not confined to coop or cage.

They walked dejectedly for long silent minutes through the dead bones of the community. Jime's fantasy that he could find a community Outside was dying, and his body sagged like a plant starved of water and sunlight.

Phoenicia broke the silence first with a whisper. "What happened here?"

"God. I don't know."

"You're an investigator, right? Maybe you should go into a house and investigate."

Jime agreed. They walked to the nearest house and tried the door; it was unlocked. Jime cautiously opened it and they crept inside, eyes wide. It was a small home with mostly wooden walls and floors, though a few surfaces were plastered; a fireplace of stone connected to stone walls that wrapped around the core of the interior. As they shut the door behind them, Jime realized that he was surrounded by interior walls of natural building materials, which he had never seen before, not once, except in last night's dream. There was no plastic in the structure, nothing laced with artificial chemicals. He breathed the air, took in the smells, felt himself surrounded by warm wood, standing on solid stone, and he realized that *this* feeling of being inside was very different from that of being "Inside."

They walked into the living room, and the first thing they saw was a large, almost black-colored rug, upon which sat a long-dead human skeleton, propped up against a sofa, its skull drooping as though its chin had once rested on its chest. A knife lay on the carpet beside it. Jime realized that the dark coloration of the rug came from blood that had run from this person's body, probably from the wrists.

The skeleton, like the rest of the living room, was covered in dust and cobwebs. Jime scanned the room. One wall consisted of glass doors that let in the morning light, but they were now so dirty with neglect that a brown film blocked the view outside. He then spotted some papers and books on a small table near the skeleton and, thinking they might contain clues to what had occurred, walked over and shuffled through them. He found a diary, some printed photos, and a ledger, on top of which was a handwritten note. It said:

"I have lost everyone. They're all dead. Tonight I stayed home sick from dinner but they all died. There is no one left, and I can't stand living without them.

"Francis Little"

Jime pondered this as he looked through the photographs. They showed a man in his mid-thirties with friends and loved ones, all the pictures apparently taken in Lindis when it was still a living community. In some of them, however, the figures looked to be growing thin and gaunt, as if sick or malnourished.

"He committed suicide, but it looks like he lived happily before that," Jime said softly. "Somehow all the rest of the people died. It doesn't say why."

Phoenicia had been reading the diary. "At the end of his book, he writes about going hungry. He says one of his jobs was to keep records of the village food and farming. Is that in the other book?"

Jime flipped through the ledger; it told a story of declining food yields and calorie counts. "They were running out of food, starving. But why was he the last one? It sounds like the rest all died at once, but not him. Why? We'll have to do some more investigating."

They searched the rest of the house, finding no more clues, and then left and searched a few more. Until their food production began to fall, the people of Lindis appeared to have been prosperous. Their homes were filled with books and musical instruments and painting supplies; they still had mechanical and electrical devices, although rather than disposable devices destined for annual replacement in a cycle of planned obsolescence, they appeared to use durable versions that were maintained and repaired well. In addition to the houses there were some sheds with tools, including power shovels, auto-tillers, and an automated mechanishop to assist in small-scale manufacturing. Phoenicia and Jime found a carport protecting several trucks and jeeps, too. The people of Lindis had their needs met and more, but they weren't decadent.

Finally, there was the common house. They both dreaded what they knew was inside.

The building had obviously once been very handsome, two stories with an observatory or cupola of some sort on top. It was larger than the village homes but not overwhelmingly so, perhaps the size of four or five of them. Jime and Phoenicia walked up the front stairs and through a wide wooden entry door, which passed into an atrium where coats and jackets hung limply on one wall. Jime noticed a bulletin board with schedules for various activities and some pictures of people. They looked happy, smiling and laughing, sitting at tables together, some playing music or sports. The people in the latest pictures, however, were thinning noticeably. One picture of a thin man with a gray beard and a thin woman with short brown hair caught his attention; they had taken a selfie together and were smiling with their arms around each other's shoulders.

Next Jime peered through a doorway that opened off the atrium to the left; it led down a corridor containing several other doors. He then turned right and looked through another doorway that opened into a large hall. It was filled with death.

The great hall of the community was the size of a restaurant dining room or large barroom. It held long dining tables with benches and chairs to seat community members together, and a few smaller tables too, both round and square, that could accommodate four or five people each. The tables had been knocked askew, however, and many of the chairs upturned in a long-past violent spasm of distress. The room was now the community's morgue. The skeletal remains of the people of Lindis were there, hunched over in their seats or sprawled on the floor. Altogether there were about a hundred people in the dining hall, and a few more in the adjoining kitchen.

"What the hell happened?" Jime exclaimed.

"Something made them sick. Some poison." Phoenicia said.

"Yes, but how and why? Was it bacteria in the food, or did someone actually poison them, or what?" Jime said. "We should look in the kitchen."

The cooking area of the kitchen was open to the dining hall, separated by a counter and an island, and the dishwashing equipment was in another, adjacent room. They looked through both spaces for clues of chemical or other poisoning and found some soap bottles and organic cleaning supplies, but nothing that would be lethal to a whole roomful of people. Phonecia found a recipe book in the kitchen, but a quick scan showed that it only referred to natural ingredients, none of them obviously poisonous.

They decided to search the rest of the building. They discovered a half dozen smaller rooms down the corridor opposite the dining hall. The first was a craft room, and the next a small general store that appeared to have disbursed baked goods, candy, herbs and medicines, and so on; it apparently worked on an honor system, whereby someone who took something recorded their "purchase" in a logbook and then voluntarily left something else or deposited a chit into a basket indicating an IOU. Some of the goods were mass-manufactured, and Jime wondered how the community had gotten them; had there been a black market connection with somebody in the Mall? The other rooms down the hallway included a children's playroom, a storage room, a library with old books—Jime spotted several copies of *Intentional Ecommunities*—and an office with a couple of desks.

Jime entered the office while Phoenicia kept exploring. On top of one desk was a tablet computer, and Jime knew that it would contain clues to the cause of this massacre, if anything in the building would. He tried to start it, but it had no power, so he plugged it into his e-map to energize it. It started right up. He searched "food," "recipes," "crops," "farming," and similar terms; after an hour or so he had pieced together what had happened.

Jime walked back into the macabre great hall and edged his way around the outer wall to a bank of large windows opposite the entrance. The windows once must have offered a view out of the back of the common house, but they were now obscured by a film of dust and dirt. He turned the window-crank with some effort, a layer of dirt cracking as he forced the stuck frame open. He poked his face out of the window; the morning fog had cleared, and it was growing warmer outside. He looked down and saw a small, rudimentary algae paddy. The algae had long ago turned blood-red and overrun the sides of the paddy, creating a self-sustaining toxic marsh. According to a contract that Jime had read on the tablet, the paddy had been built with technology lent by Mallworld, Inc. The agreement had given the village a design for the algae paddy, but Jime had noted that there was no clause giving Lindis a red sludge processor. The community, struggling to survive in an environment that was increasingly sucked dry by the Mall, couldn't grow enough food through traditional or organic farming, so as a last resort Lindis had turned to the industrial solution. But without the proper controls to remove the worst of the harmful elements, the villagers' attempt to survive by turning to the Mall had resulted in their own poisoning.

+ + +

Jime and Phoenicia sat slumped at a wooden table in a kitchen of one of the homes. Although the electric stoves no longer worked anywhere in the village, they had found a house with a fireplace, started a small, sullen fire, and warmed some soup and coffee from Jime's rations. Phoenicia listened as Jime described what had happened to the village.

"So they had to grow algae?"

"Yes."

"But they didn't know that they needed to filter it?"

"No, they didn't."

"And they were poisoned?"

"Within twenty minutes of eating."

There was a long moment of silence before Phoenicia spoke again.

"So the Mall killed them."

Looking at each other, they both frowned but tried to keep their composure. Then they cracked at the same time, and tears flowed. They reached across the table and held each other's hands. In the village of Lindis capitalism had imposed the same ultimatum that it had across the entire surface of the earth: commercialism or death. Accept merchant values, market power, and commodification, or be deprived of the means of life. In this case it had systemically and deviously massacred all the people of what had been a happy community whose members supported and cared for one another. It had done so simply because they had dared to live together independently of the Mall's capitalism, had dared to make high-value human relationships their final end while keeping lower-value consumption goods as only a means to that end.

But without an independent economic base, Lindis couldn't defend itself. Community alone couldn't stand before the pervasive power of capitalism, because community functioned at the level of culture, not the level of economics, where material power exerts its force and tries to extend itself over everything. A healthy way of life and an uplifting identity had been completely wiped out because the Mall would not be satiated until it owned everything and everyone.

Jime and Phoenicia knew that no one else in Mallworld would be able to understand their sorrow. They were comforted that the other was there.

"Well," Jime eventually said, wiping his face on his sleeve. "I guess the only thing to do now is go back. The Mall has conquered everything." His face fell. "There's nowhere else to go!"

He fell silent for a long time. Then he said, "There should be a salvage crew back at the jetcopter. If we get back there today we can turn ourselves in. I'll get another Time Out and you'll have to go back to work, but at least we'll get back to civilization."

"The Mall is not civilization. It is a fat murdering beast."

"True."

"I'm staying here." Phoenicia declared it with finality.

"No, you can't."

"These people. They need a proper burial, and there is a power-digger."

"But you'll starve. And you'll be all alone."

"I am old, Jime, and I am not going back to the Mall to spend my last days breaking my back in work. Leave your camping food, and I will forage and catch chickens for a while. But I am going to die soon anyway, and I would rather do it here among the memory of these people than in a barracks back there. This reminds me of my home when I was a girl. I feel as if I've come full circle."

+   +   +

Jime stood alone at the bottom of the ravine and stared up at the steep wall, knowing that he had to find some way to climb out of the hole he was in. He was made half of despair and half of anger. He was hopelessly trapped by the Mall's all-encompassing web, which in its ungoverned drive to exploit and consume did not tolerate that anything be left truly outside it, and he was furious at the murderous greed that led it to violate nature, human personality, and justice. His jaw clenched. He reached out and grabbed the roots of a bush up the slope and began to climb.

The Mall had killed his dream of deep and meaningful human connection by killing Lindis and all communities like it. No, that wasn't all, he seethed: in its quest to replace real interpersonal satisfaction with empty commercialism, it had smothered *all* satisfying human relationships. He realized that capitalism was a cult of death: those it did not kill outright through structural violence it ensnared in an inescapable living death, a half-life of shallow, alienating, unfulfilling consumerism. While it promised abundance, it was, to the roots, a system of deprivation: material deprivation for those Outside, psychological deprivation for those Inside. And both could be lethal. He was imprisoned in an all-encompassing system that starved people of healthy relationships and made them selfish, shallow, and callously cruel.

Jime topped the cliff and stood there panting. His shoulders shrugged and he bent over. What could he do now? How could he escape the totalizing Mall?

How could anyone?

How could everyone?

CHAPTER 4:
WE DESERVE A BETTER WORLD

"Where should I drop off the container?" the deliveryman said, his arm resting on the handle of the power dolly he had used to haul in a meter-and-a-half square shipping crate.

"It goes here, where my old cubicle was." Samantha's monotone hid her frustration; her supervisor, Mr. Ellitson, was standing right there, so she couldn't show her real feelings. Sam, dressed as a consummate professional in her favorite business suit, stood with her arms crossed. She had worked at this Significorp district processing center for years, had risen to become a line supervisor, and had witnessed many thoughtless alterations in the company's business practices, but she was particularly angry about this latest change. Things always seemed to go downhill. This time, rather than replace the old, run-down cubicles in her office with new, better, more comfortable ones, management was installing the latest in office workspace efficiency: Automated Work Cubicle Replacement Devices, or AWCRDs, which were derisively called "Awkwards" by office associates. Soon after that slur had become popular, Awkwards began to be advertised as "cubisizers" to induce popular acceptance by creating a mental association with popular exercise equipment like the Absizer and Buttsizer machines.

"Try it out, Sam, and let us know what you think," Mr. Ellitson said with a vacuous smile, as if having the Awkwards in the office was going to be an improvement. Ellitson looked the part of a typical business-school empty suit: hair slicked back, suspenders over a striped shirt with white collar, expensive holowatch. This was because he *was* a typical business-school empty suit, smarmy to those above him and domineering to those below, all to compensate for the existential fact of his life, which was his across-the-board mediocrity. Installing the newest, shiniest technology would certainly give an appearance of progress and efficiency to his annual Manager's evaluation. The deliveryman finished unloading the Awkward, pulled the crate and dolly out of the way, reached over, and hit the start button.

The contraption unfolded into a complete, self-contained, automated work-enhancement embrasure. A combination desk, chair, and exoskeleton, with armatures for the worker to insert limbs, it was a *mecha* for the office workspace. It was made of gaudy pink and orange algaeplastic, which some tasteless marketing philistine obviously thought was eye-catching. It sat there whirring and buzzing, and a soothing, saccharine music played softly from its background speakers.

"Well, go ahead, Sam," Ellitson said, gesturing eagerly toward the device. With resignation, Sam looked at the glossy colored plastic of the machine and listened to the tranquilizing muzak. After a moment she sighed, and then reluctantly climbed into the chair. She was tall and had to hunch to squeeze in. A corner of her skirt caught in a joint between two armatures, tearing a few stitches of the seam, and she frowned. The machine jumped to life and a restraint wrapped around her torso, while the armatures automatically clamped around her wrists and ankles. Her well-pressed suit coat was completely wrinkled—she liked this outfit best because its tan color complemented her brown hair and eyes. And now, she fumed, it was ruined. With a sudden whipping motion the whole mechanism snapped her into the optimal posture for workplace productivity enhancement. She felt pains in her back, neck, and legs from being jerked into such an unnatural position.

The Awkward's built-in helmet slid onto her head, and its transparent computer visor slapped down over her face. A blindingly bright screen lit up right in her eyes, forcing her to squint. When her eyes adjusted to the light, the monitor displayed the standard cascade of error messages and advertising pop-ups that workplace computers usually showed, and she knew that she would have to take ten minutes to click them off one-by-one. On the desktop in front of her a power keyboard flipped into place, and the armatures pulled her arms forward until her hands were clamped into mechanical rapid-typing gloves designed to maximize data entry speed. They pinched her fingers. Cynical frustration flashed across her face: how was she supposed to be more productive while in pain? These cubisizers were going to be an even worse disaster than last year's software "upgrade," which only put everyone through months of reprogramming and aggravation.

Ellitson was reading from the machine's user manual now. "'The AWCRD's robotic features,'" he said, pronouncing each letter in the acronym, "'can enhance an associate's productivity by at least 30 percent by speeding up typing, filing, and other tasks. Its cyber-helmet makes sure an associate's attention is always focused on the display. A built-in helmet-phone eliminates the need to pause a task while taking a call, allowing data entry to proceed simultaneously while answering the phone.' Pretty neat stuff, eh?"

Right at that moment a brief electric shock burst through Sam's system. Her muscles seized up and she screamed "Ouch!" and then, "What the hell?"

"Oh, that's just part of the system startup test," the delivery man said.

"What?" Sam said in anger and panic. "Is there a short circuit or something?"

"No," Ellitson said. "It has a built-in taser to jolt a lazy cubey into action. We all sometimes need help to stay on task!" he said with an unctuous grin.

"That was just the system check. You have to do something every thirty seconds or it will zap you again."

Sam's eyes grew wide and she immediately started typing. Then a strong, sickly sweet fruit odor hit her nostrils, and she scrunched her nose. "What's that smell?" she asked.

"Air freshener with low-level amphetamines to keep you alert and productive."

"It's giving me a headache. How will that make me productive?"

Ellitson didn't look up from the tech manual. "The AWCRD even contains integrated waste elimination tubes to end the need for bathroom breaks!"

Sam groaned. "It makes me feel like a mechaniman," she said. Her back and head were hurting, and she had stopped typing to think for a moment and get her bearings. But then the Awkward zapped her again. "God dammit!" She hated that.

Ellitson read, "'The AWCRD enhances efficiency, frees up management time, and takes up half the space of a regular cubicle, allowing twice as many associates per square meter of office space.' And you know, it even has a slot for you to personalize with a picture of family or a loved one! What a wonderful invention!" he ejaculated.

+ + +

On billions of holoscreens an advertisement is projected:

A confident young woman with a clipboard directs several people carrying boxes into a modern, sleek office. The boxes are labeled with a corporate logo: "Significorp." A voiceover says, "For the important things in life, you need a company you can trust." The woman passes the clipboard, also labeled "Significorp," to a man dressed as a Manager, who then discusses it with another woman attired in a sharp, Executive business suit; they nod at each other knowingly, and they smile.

Cut to a restaurant storefront, where the restaurateur accepts a delivery of a large envelope from a courier; he looks at it and sees that it is from Significorp, nods with a smile, and shakes the courier's hand. The voiceover says, "Put your trust in us."

The scene then cuts to a sleek and modern living room, where an attractive family sees the Significorp logo appear on the large holoscreen mounted on their wall. "Whoever you are, wherever you go, throughout life . . . we're always with you."

Cut to a street scene with confident, well-dressed people striding past a glass building façade with the Significorp logo on prominent display. The voiceover says, "Significorp: importance is our business."

+ + +

The book club sat around plastic tables in one of the many food courts that dotted Mallworld, bathed in a gaudy rainbow of neon light. Like most things in the Mall, the tables, chairs, and other furniture were made of algaeplastic, as were the floor tiles, wall coverings, service counters, plastiplants, trays, plates, cutlery, napkins, clothing—almost everything in sight. The plastic here, as in most commercial spaces, was a garish rainbow of bright reds, oranges, greens, and blues. Mallworld Institute of Technology's Marlborough School of Medicine, via a grant from the Algaeplastic Consortium, had studied the psychological and physiological health consequences of living amidst all this plastic, and famously had found no ill effects.

It was Sam's office book club, and everyone was in business casual attire: collared shirts, dress pants or skirts, and dress shoes. While they ate their lunches, the group listened over the soothing, syrupy background music to a lecture being given by a thin, fit man standing behind a temporary podium set on one of the tables. He had both hands on the lectern as he spoke, one on each side. He was well-groomed and dressed in a sharp, crisp tailored shirt and blazer. They were meeting after most of the day's lunch crowds had already dispersed, but there were still a few other saleys and cubeys around on late lunch breaks. While lunchtime gatherings among workgroups were not unusual, most of the time they consisted of a boss talking at subordinates about office rules or pay structures, or perhaps a group of coworkers celebrating a birthday or retirement. But today the speaker was an expert on ancient society who was discussing a book called *Intentional Ecommunities*. He had been talking for about half an hour, and, because he had actually been Outside and had some adventures there, people were paying close attention. He was now discussing how changes could be made Inside the Mall in order to make it better for people.

"... and life in Mallworld is empty and unfulfilling, because people have been convinced to spend their lives trying to fill themselves up through consumption," Jime Galilei said. "But consumption cannot truly fill you up. The emotional voids that most people have cannot actually be cured by the Mall. In fact, I would argue, our system of hyper-consumerism magnifies and multiplies those voids in order to get people to constantly consume more and more, so as to maximize profit and keep people passive and under control. Ancient myths of religion have been supplanted by the myth of consumerism: that we can lead fulfilling, meaningful, happy lives by buying lots of gadgets, bigger condos, more and fancier food, and seeing more exciting shows and spectas. The whole way of life within the Mall is set up to make us try to satisfy ourselves this way, but it's a fool's errand. The system creates desires that can *never* be satisfied, like dangling a carrot in front of a horse; it's *designed* to create a perpetual state of dissatisfaction. It uses advertising, status anxiety, peer pressure, socialization, debt, social structures, and other techniques to maximize the *pursuit* of desire in order to maximize sales and profits—but not to actually *satisfy* desire, for to do that would be the end of profit. By creating voids that can never be filled, it also creates existential emptiness, despair, cynicism, and nihilism. Consumerism tries to fool us into thinking that consumption leads to the good life, but it actually denies us active lives in which we express our creative potentials and exalt each other's existence as rational, social beings.

"As it maximizes consumption, as it produces and consumes, capitalism is also heedless about how it treats human lives and the life of the planet. It is willing to use up some people for the consumption of others. It has used up the earth's resources too, which is why we all live inside the Mall: because the Outside has been scoured clean."

At this point one of Sam's co-associates, Sandra, snuck in late and sat down at a table. She was the office's administrative assistant. She quietly mouthed hello, and then leaned in and whispered in Sam's ear, "Aren't the new cubisizers terrible? We should talk about it after the book club; we have to *do something* about them." Sam nodded and turned back to Jime's lecture.

"Happiness is not that hard, actually, although most people think it is," Jime was saying. "Happiness is doing what you love and being with people whom you love. The things that can really fill us up and make us happy are healthy human relationships and fulfilling creative efforts that expresses our talents, and, for most of us, make a contribution to a greater good. The 'good life' does not consist of having lots of money and spending it on big mansions, mind-blowing spectas, fancy clothes, exotic vacations, and toys and baubles. Rather, a good life, a life lived well, is a rich, full life of meaningful relationships, creative expression, fulfilling experiences, and significant accomplishments toward one's goals. This all needs to be supported by a moderate level of material prosperity in which one's physical needs are securely met, of course, but overconsumerism actually detracts from a well-lived life.

"While a few people may find fulfillment or even transcendence through solitary contemplation, as monks and hermits sometimes do, for most people happiness requires healthy human relationships. A good life is thus a social life, in which we support and elevate each other, validating each other's personhood and fundamental human dignity with an uplifting spirit. Because such a life must be created and maintained together with others, I call this kind of life a 'coexalted' life. The good life is a life of mutual coexaltation in which we not only become our best genuine selves, but we support others as they do the same, and exultantly celebrate and maintain this mutual elevation.

"I submit that history shows one main path by which most people find fulfillment, and it's not ancient religion, nationalism, or consumerism. It is community, friendship, and fellowship, directly. I'm talking about a community for which the main purpose is maintaining healthy community relationships themselves, and otherwise allowing members to choose their own purposes and visions of the good life. Those other kinds of human association—religious, nationalist, commercial—sometimes create community, but only indirectly, as a side effect of their own, doctrinal purposes. When they do so they make people happier, but the communities they create sustain themselves by keeping other people out, or even by making other people enemies. And, usually, they can only support their singular, intolerant doctrines with social and even physical coercion. Thus, in the end they create more division, oppression, and conflict than harmony.

"Rather than today's consumerism, we need healthy community, where mutually respectful relationships can grow and flourish. We are a long way away from building healthy communities here in Mallworld, and we have to build wider social and economic support for them one step at a time.

"One of the most noncommunal things that we can do is to treat other people's lives as a resource to be used up for our own consumption, as though other people were mere algae. We do that most obviously with regard to our entertainments, such as the HV reality-show lotteries like *Wheel of Fate* that actually kill players, whom we degradingly call Fat Pigs. They die simply for losing the spin of a wheel—a murder that is by no means justified *even if* the victims have been fattened by unrestrained hyper-consumption for a while first. Nor is it justified if they have chosen to participate. No one deserves to die for the entertainment of others, no matter what bargain they've made, and no bargain is legitimate that commits someone to risk all they have, even life itself, in a quest for mere consumer goods. Humans cooperate socially to *reduce* the uncertainties and contingencies of life, not to maximize the gamble by risking everything on the spin of a wheel. Our top moral priority should be to immediately end our systems of death so that we can begin to walk a path to coexalted living in life-affirming communities. We must put an end to exploitative spectacles and consumer lotteries that kill."

Jime leaned forward and emphasized: "*Neither the goal of making communities nor the goal of making social change can be achieved by an individual alone.* These things by their nature cannot be done by people acting in isolation. They can only be done by groups. To make a community, by definition, people have to work together: it's not a community if it's only one. The same is true of social change: while we can make personal changes to our lives on our own, social change by definition can only be done together. If you want to address the problem of obesity, for example, there are two ways to do it. To lose weight as an individual, you can personally diet and exercise—and that works for some strong-willed individuals. But the roots of our obesity *crisis* are economic and social factors that overwhelm most people's willpower—overeating is constantly promoted in Mallworld through advertising, oversized portions, tax subsidies for Burger Palace and other fast-food restaurants, and so on. These things are *designed* to overcome people's willpower. So if you want to solve obesity as a social disease, you have to find ways to get a lot of people to do it *together*, to change public policy. Policy is needed to help most people lose weight—you might give free consultations with doctors and time off work for exercise, regulate portion sizes, find ways to stop the constant promotion of overeating, and promote and subsidize healthy eating instead. Blaming it on individual responsibility won't work, and is insulting and offensive to those afflicted by obesity. And that is only one example. We have many social problems that can only be solved through political action and social and legal change.

"In short, the rediscovery of *Intentional Ecommunities* and my time Outside both showed me that I couldn't escape from Mallworld; I couldn't escape from my own society. Instead I had to work *within* it in order to change it for the better. And that's what I'm doing now: talking to people to try to show them that this way of life is an unhappy, destructive one that divides us from each other; and to convince them that we can work together to change things. Transforming society requires political and social organizing and is long, slow, patient work.

"With that I'll end my talk and take a few questions, if you have any."

"OK, Mr. Galilei, so you think that smaller, stronger communities are needed, but how do we get there?" someone asked.

"The first step is to acknowledge your social interconnections. Even though we are individuals, Mallworld makes us forget that we are *connected* individuals. We are always, every day, interacting with each other, and we always affect each other, and so we are all linked together. The problems that we face are a result of larger social relationships that have become dysfunctional. So the first step is to get as many individuals as possible to understand that, if we are to change things for the better, no individual can do it alone, but we all have to do it together. Or at least, a large enough group of people has to do it. Once you've realized this, the next step is to persuade others of the same thing, and to persuade them that the kind of change we need involves building stronger connections. Stronger connections mean stronger communities. Once we get a core group persuaded of that, we build it up until we get a critical mass of people so large that we have enough power to change the world."

Another questioner said, "So do you practice what you preach?"

"Yes, I am trying. The issue that I'm focused on most right now is ending the death lottery. I speak against it wherever I go, and I have holonet pages on the usual social media sites, where membership and traffic are growing. I've organized an association with monthly meetings to discuss the issue and criticize the ideas behind the lottery that keep it going. And then we are getting out and speaking to others as often as we can, to try to persuade as many people as possible of how bad the lottery is. Eventually I hope to turn that group into something that can take broader political action. One exciting development is that I've been in contact with a famous holonet personality, and this person is going to make a public statement in favor of ending the death lottery. I can't say who it is yet, but I'm very hopeful this will get us some attention and backing."

"If we go to your netsite is there contact info? Maybe I can help."

"Why yes, you can contact me there, thank you. And if anyone wants to talk about it afterward I can stay for a while."

After a few more questions, mostly about Jime's adventures Outside, the talk wrapped up. A few people stuck around to chat, while others shuffled back to work.

Sam approached Jime, despite feeling a little nervous. "Hello. My name is Samantha Gomprez, and I have a question," she said.

"Hi," Jime replied, looking her in the eye as he shook her hand and grinning a welcoming grin. He had a way of relating to people that combined intelligence, understanding, and assurance, a personal style he had developed during his Management years.

"You said that communities are for mutual support and security. But do all communities have to be people living in the same neighborhood?"

"What do you mean?"

"Well, I have problems at work. Can a community be people who work together but don't live near each other?"

Jime thought for a moment. "Oh yes, I think so. My anti-lottery group, for instance, is just an association. But associations can be a kind of community, even though they aren't geographic. Geographic communities literally bring people together physically, and they must learn to support and elevate each other by virtue of their proximity: the members of a geographic community are already together in physical space, and they should learn to coexalt each other so they can be together in a healthy way in social space, too.

"But for nongeographic voluntary associations, I think it depends on the basis of the cooperation. If it's an association based on contracts and commercial interests, then it's not going to develop much of a common spirit, because it's based on self-interest, not a genuine group interest—the participants in that case only work together transactionally and opportunistically, to advance their individual goals of self-promotion. But if an association is based on mutual love for an activity, a shared project, a common philosophy, or group solidarity in the face of oppression, then I think it can develop that communal spirit. I'm sure that you can find ways to unite your work community, and to sustain that unity over time, to have the benefits of community in the workplace. What exactly is the problem that you have there?"

"The management keeps making the work environment worse for us."

"Sounds like you have a shared experience of being abused around which your communal spirit can form. Maybe if you and all your coworkers stand united, you can first think together about ways to put a stop to it, and when you've thought it through and come up with a plan, you can act together to do so. That's what labor unions in the ancient world used to do. Why don't you try to persuade your coworkers to cooperate with you to stop the management from going too far?"

"Who, me?" Sam said in surprise.

"If you don't start, who will?"

"But I'm not like you, I don't do public speaking very well."

"I haven't been doing it that long myself. It's like anything else, it takes practice. I still get nervous about doing it, every time."

"Really? You don't seem nervous."

"I think a lot of public speakers feel more nervous than they look." Jime smiled. "Just remember: you know your coworkers, you don't have to be afraid of them. You'll only be *talking* to them—you talk to them every day, right? Just get them together and do your best, that's all. You and your coworkers deserve it. You deserve a better life."

Sam then asked for some writings about worker communities, and Jime referred her to some books he had read on labor unions and workers cooperatives.

"Thank you, Jime," Sam said. "Good luck working with your spokesperson on the lottery issue." She didn't think that the spectacle deaths were that big a deal, really, but she could see Jime's point. She hadn't thought about it much before. As she walked away, one of Jime's remarks stuck in her mind as something that couldn't be right. It was true that she was afraid to talk in front of a group. But she also didn't actually believe, deep down, that they *should* have a better life. After all, they were only cubeys; why did they deserve better than what they had?

+ + +

On billions of holoscreens an advertisement is projected:

A beleaguered, exhausted cubey, clothes askew and hair a mess, lifts the data-visor on his Awkward helmet with a sigh, looks up, and spots a holo-poster on the wall nearby. It shows an animated picture of a sunlit beach. The camera zooms in on his face and he smiles as he is mentally transported to a tropical paradise; he runs along a shore of white sand, past beautiful, happy beachgoers in skimpy swimwear. The words "Tropicana Dome" scroll across the screen.

The image cuts to him standing on a snow-covered white ski slope, shoving off with his ski poles and zooming down the mountain with a yelp, while the screen reads "Grizzly Mountain."

Next he is shown seated at a table on a terrace in a Provençal countryside, dining *al fresco* amidst cypresses, acacias, and grapevines. The screen says "Mediterranea." He clinks wine glasses with a beautiful companion, looks into the camera, and smiles.

Finally, he is shown returning to the office from his vacation with a broad smile and an energetic bounce in his step, and he virtually jumps back into his Awkward. A sultry voiceover says: "Heaven, Inc. Resort Domes: it's just like being in paradise." The refreshed and reinvigorated cubey happily goes back to work.

+ + +

At the food court a few days later, Sam's co-associate Galton, a midlevel data communications specialist, was finishing his lunch: a Burger Palace Double Pounder Deluxe Angus Beef Donut Burger, with Megasize french fries, a Jumbo Cake, and a Gigamax Cola. Galton was as large as his lunch and was ordinary in every other way. He had earned average grades in school, had a stale career, worked in a dreary office, and lived alone in a rental unit, where he mostly watched HV.

Before going back to the office Galton wanted to finish the chapter of the book he was reading, a novel called *Anthem* by the ancient writer Ayn Rand. It was the story of a heroized architect who triumphs over the perceived mediocrity, bureaucracy, and inconveniences of society in order to express his artistic vision. Galton identified closely with the main character; he always felt stifled by his Managers and other cubeys, and he felt with certainty that he could run things better than they did. If only he was in charge, bureaucracy would disappear, things would be run right, and the people who truly deserved it would be rewarded. Galton loved Rand's exaltation of the individual and her opinion that selfishness was a virtue, and he wholeheartedly agreed with her message that the creative "producers" of the world should receive untold riches and had the right to push the parasitic "takers" out of their way; he was often quite angry at the takers all around him who were constantly depriving him of his just rewards. He saw their incompetence and indolence every day in his office, and he knew that someday he, or someone like him, would be in charge and do something to fix it.

Galton undoubtedly would've been happier, and would become a better person, if he acknowledged he was just a regular guy and set out to cultivate the talents he had and participate with other people in activities he found meaningful. But he kept reading Ayn Rand instead.

When he finished, Galton stood up to go back to the office, tugging at the waistband of his khaki trousers as he rose to pull them up around his portly belly. His necktie was tied too short, which only accentuated his round stomach, but he either didn't notice or didn't care. He burped; he felt very full, as he did every day from eating his big lunch. His brain buzzed with the momentary high that comes from eating lots of grease and sugar. He knew that he would soon start feeling sleepy from the big meal.

Back at the office Galton's eyes were already drooping as he plugged himself into his Awkward. He accepted the machine as an example of capitalist ingenuity, even though he disliked it—it made his back hurt and gave him headaches. Because of that, he was now so tired and uncomfortable at the end of the workday that all he could do in the evenings was to try to rest and recover for the next day. The thought crossed his mind that if work was going to do that to his body, it would only be fair if he got paid extra for his lost hours of free time. Ha! Like that would ever happen! The stupid bureaucrats and politicians would stand in the way. The Awkward's helmet, with its integrated computer visor, slid down over his head, and his eyes began to hurt. Well, he thought, he chose to work here at Significorp and could always get a job at a company that didn't use Awkwards, if he could find one. This was a free market, after all.

The plastic arms of the Awkward clamped down on his arms of flesh, jerking them forward and shoving his hands into the auto-typing gloves, which tightened around his fingers with a whir. This time it felt like they tightened a little more than before, making his hands hurt even worse than usual. Oh well, it was all part of the job, he thought. It would take weeks to get a repair order completed for something so minor, so it was easier to just live with it. Galton began typing right away in order to avoid being zapped—something that he, unlike his coworkers, appreciated as a market incentive. Things went smoothly for a few minutes, but then the Awkward suddenly jerked Galton's right arm straight outward, palm down, and then angled it forward and up over his head! He felt a jolt of muscle pain from the sudden, involuntary motion, and his arm was stuck in the air in an awkward and uncomfortable position. Galton pulled and twisted, trying to get the machine to return to its normal operating mode. After he'd tugged for thirty seconds, the machine zapped him for not typing. Galton yelped, and then started to panic. A few seconds later, however, the Awkward returned to its regular position, lowering his arm so that he could start typing again, its gears happily whirring.

Galton got right back into a rhythm, and then his visor bugged out and started flashing different programs and images randomly across his screen. Then the Awkward jerked and bounced uncontrollably, lifting his arm right back up where it had been, then dropping it down again only to lift the other arm, which it then promptly dropped. It stopped moving altogether for a moment before suddenly blaring out an alarm and jerking and jumping again. The machine began flailing Galton's limbs all about, and he started to scream over the loud siren: "Help me! Help me!" Other associates came running and frantically tried to stop the Awkward chaos. One tried to reach in to hit the ejector seat button, but his hand kept getting batted away, painfully, as the machine spun and twisted. Another pulled his phone out and called for help. A third grabbed a side chair and she bashed Galton's Awkward, but the chair's thin algaeplastic immediately splintered against the machine's thicker exoskeleton. Nothing seemed like it could stop the crazed, automatic work maximizer; its systems had gone mad.

Then, just as suddenly as it started, the Awkward stopped. It ceased flailing about and settled back into its normal operating position, quietly humming. Galton's eyes were wide. But when he realized the cubisizer had calmed down, so did he, and a look of relief crossed his face.

The Awkward gave him another zap, and he screamed, "Dammit! Stop already, jeez!"

Then the cubisizer suddenly folded itself into its meter-and-a-half square shipping and delivery configuration, there was a loud crunch, and Galton screamed again.

+ + +

That night after work, shocked and angry, Sam wandered to Mall Street, where the Mallworld Central Bank building was. It was a large plastimarble building in a large plastimarble square, grand and imposing. The Bank itself was built in a neoclassical style of white plastistone blocks and white fluted columns, which supported a great golden dome at the top. It was fortress-like: there were no visible exterior windows, and the oversized entrance consisted of imposing metal doors. Bankers in expensive suits hustled to and fro across the expansive plaza, which held a plastimarble water fountain in its center comprising large, water-spouting statues of famous businesspeople from history, all depicted in relaxed poses of rest and recreation, as if on a resort beach.

Sam was there on purpose. Fuming about what had happened with the Awkward, she sat down on a marble bench and pulled out her tablet. She had come here, to the front of the Mall's biggest bank, and was going to read one of the books about labor movements that Jime had recommended at the lunch. It was a book on democratic socialism. She needed to do something, and somehow, psychologically, it felt like an act of defiance to read this particular book in this particular place. She raised her tablet so that the title of the book, *Democracy and Socialism*, was visible to any stockbroker who happened to walk by; then she aimed it at the Central Bank like a weapon, flipped the bank the bird, and started reading.

What Sam had read so far presented a vision of a just and democratic economic order, and it had fueled her sense of righteous anger at how she and other workers were treated under capitalism. *Democratic* socialism wasn't the communism of the totalitarian regimes of the twentieth century, in which the entire economy was run by a central bureaucracy whose dictates were enforced by a police state. Rather, the basic principle of democratic socialism was that democracy, the rule of the common people, must be extended from the political sphere to the economic sphere.

Fundamentally, democratic socialism meant transforming the basic productive economic unit of society from the privately owned corporation into the worker-controlled firm, known as a *workers cooperative*, or *co-op* for short. In co-ops, workers have the right to run business democratically, either by making production plans and policy directly or by choosing their supervisors, managers, and higher administrators in free and fair elections. Workers, as a group, get to vote for their bosses and have the final say over policy. This aspect of democratic socialism is not primarily about equalizing wealth but about equalizing power. Granting workers the right of democratic control over their economic enterprises would put them in control of one of the most important and enduring aspects of modern human life: their individual work lives and careers. Giving workers the right of final say over business operations would prevent the systematic abuse and exploitation of working people that capitalism had always practiced. It would also, Sam read, halt the parasitic and destructive capitalist practice of something called *capital flight* or *capital strike*—when companies use the threat of moving or closing down enterprises, and the consequent loss of jobs, to extort tax benefits, subsidies, and other privileges from governments, labor unions, and workers. No group of workers, if they had the democratic power, would agree to move their own jobs to another city, region, or country. Although workers' control is primarily about democratization of economic power, it would also tend to reduce economic inequality, because with the power to determine their own compensation and that of managers and executives, workers would be able to reduce capitalism's irrationally unequal pay differences: real-life workers' cooperatives of the ancient pre-Mall days, such as the Mondragon corporation, limited pay ratios between workers and executives to between 5-to-1 and 9-to-1, vastly less than the levels of 200-to-1 or 300-to-1 seen in privately owned capitalist firms in the O.U.S.

To be truly democratic, workers co-ops would need to have access to capital from sources other than private capitalist investors, so banks owned by workers, communities, and the public would be essential. And democratic socialists also often called for democratic administrative councils at the local, regional, and societal levels to help set the rules for economic activity, coordinate the allocation of resources, and make necessary collective economic decisions; this, the book said, is sometimes called *participatory economics*, or *parecon* for short.

Lastly, Sam read how democratic socialists also pressed for *social democracy*, which is somewhat different despite the similarity of names. Social democracy is the traditional "welfare state," the government programs and social insurance that enhance human welfare in the unequal capitalist system, such as the right to universal health care, public pensions, workers' compensation for on-the-job injury and wage loss, public education, income subsidies for the poor, and so on. Additionally, social democrats advocated for the public provision of infrastructure such as roads, bridges, ports, utilities, communications services, schools, and hospitals. These programs were funded by progressive taxation, which taxes richer people at higher rates than poorer people in order to reduce inequality. Social democracy was primarily about equalizing wealth, but also had the effect of equalizing power: by reducing economic inequality, it helped to prevent oligarchy and preserve democracy. History showed that social democracy was necessary in the technological world to prevent the dire poverty and misery of industrialization and to build and sustain a healthy, strong middle class.[4]

Democratic socialism was a political and economic philosophy Sam could believe in. She had always believed in political democracy, even though she knew most condo association elections were badly

---

4   To see the fuller description of democratic socialism that Samantha read, see Appendix 2.

administered and lacked in public participation. But she took it as given that democracy was the best workable form of government, an ideal to strive for. After all, everyone should have a say in decisions that affect them. It was not hard for her to see that there ought to be democracy in economics, too, because economics impacted peoples' lives as much as politics, so everyone should participate in making decisions about how it goes.

Sam looked up and glared at the looming fortress of the Central Bank. She thought about Galton's accident and knew that as long as the capitalist system was in place, people would continue to be abused, harmed, and even killed in order to make profits for the rich. Something ought to be done about it. She snapped her tablet shut, stood up, and walked off.

+ + +

The next day, the cubeys met again at the food court, agitated and upset. Galton was not very popular among them, but he did have a few friends, and more importantly, they *all* had to use the Awkwards or be terminated. What had happened to him could happen to any of them.

"Well, what are we going to do now?" asked Sam, worry in her tone.

"Someone should say something," said a deep-voiced man named Sidney. "We can't work in those things." Sid was in his early 40s, tall, lanky, and bald, and wore a collared blue shirt but no coat. The office's long-term trends analyst, he had a graduate degree in the social sciences, was bookish and serious, and was respected for his intelligence. Despite his authoritative basso, his personality was not a particularly scintillating or captivating, and he knew it—although he was likeable once you got to know him.

"But who will say it? And why bother? We can't do anything about it," a data processor called Nate said in a quiet, faltering tone. Sam felt the same fear that was in his voice.

"You all can do what you want," said a cocky young coworker named Nic who worked in public relations. "My contract is getting upgraded to Advertising Sub-Managing Affiliate soon anyway. With a promotion I won't be working in an Awkward anymore." He was over-dressed in a fitted suit with a gleaming salmon-colored plastisilk tie, a gleaming coral-colored plastisilk pocket kerchief, a pink algaeplastic boutonnière, and gleaming jewelry—a watch, bracelet, tie bar, and signet ring. His dark hair was slicked to one side in a dashing swoop.

"The very first thing that we have to do is to sign Galt's get-well card. Here, let me pass it around." Sandra, the office admin specialist, pulled a holocard from her bag and digitally signed it with a finger, passing it to the next person.

"We *have to* put a stop to this, or one of us will get killed!" Sam chirped, agitated.

"But *there is nothing we can do*." Nic shook his head. "This is objective reality. You can't change things. It's not economically possible."

"By which you mean we're only cubeys, and they're Management. They're the bosses, they're in charge, and they call the shots," said Sid.

"When you get your own company then *you* can call the shots."

"No, Nic, we can object, we can put pressure on them, we can even go on strike," said Sam.

"Ha!" scoffed Nic. "Strike! None of you can afford it, you won't last it out."

Nate mumbled, "I don't think a strike is a good idea either. We might get fired. And Ellitson just wouldn't like a strike."

"Well, maybe we can still do *something*," Sid said. "If we stick together, then I'm sure that we can convince them to make changes."

Sam wanted to agree with Sidney, but she was nervous about speaking in front of the group. And nervous about maybe getting fired if they went against their Manager. And she was not very optimistic they could actually win. They *were* only office associates, not Management. Someone passed the holocard to her and she signed it.

"Convince them?" Nic dismissed the idea with a wave of his hand. "It would only work if you had something to hold over them, some leverage, but you don't, so forget it. The reality of the situation right now is that they can fire us at any time. You have to accept facts."

Sandra then said, sadly, "I just hope that Galt will be OK. Does anyone know what the mechanidoc said?"

Sam, trying to hide her anxiety, reported the bad news. "He has a broken back, and all four limbs were fractured in multiple places. He'll be out of work for a long time."

"Probably forever," Nic said. "Company policy is that he'll get a month of health care, and then either has to come back to work or be terminated. With wounds like that he'll never heal in a month, forget it. We'll never see him again. When he finally gets out of the hospital, he'll have to work multiple jobs just to pay back the medical fees. That's why *I'm* going for Management. That's the only way to get security. You have to reach the top! And you guys want to go on strike. Ha! You'll never make it up the corporate ladder!" The contempt in his voice made it clear that he thought all of them were idiots for not knowing the route to success.

"But not everybody can get to the top of the pyramid, Nic," said Sid, frustration in his voice. "It's mathematically impossible. Not everyone can fit on top. Only a small number can. We'll all have a better chance for a good life if we flatten the pyramid rather than try to climb up it."

"Shut up, Sid. *I'll* get there, and that's all that counts."

"Then *you'll* be the one stuffing people into Awkwards," said Sid. "Is that who you want to be?"

"What are you accusing me of, you jerk?"

All of a sudden everyone started speaking all at once, none of them listening, all of them talking past one another as the conversation descended into a quarrel.

Sam felt afraid to keep speaking, and the hopelessness and cynicism of her coworkers disheartened her. That disempowered them all. The extreme anxiety and uncertainty caused by the original situation, not to mention the endless hours of torturous aches and pains produced by the cubisizer, were also depressing. How could she climb back into an Awkward if it was possibly going to crunch her up and maim or kill her? She was anxious about defying Ellitson, to be sure, but she was downright terrified of getting back into a deathtrap. But as she thought about it, she was also quietly furious. How could Ellitson treat people that way? How could *anyone* in Management? What kind of person actually risks inflicting permanent injury or death on other people just to make money? It wasn't just the fear of physical harm to herself that was at issue; so was the disregard for the well-being of people, the basic disrespect for their humanity. The more that Sam thought about it, the more her anger slowly replaced her fear.

Sam thought her anger was warranted because it was based in fairness and justice, not irrational rage. She was beginning to understand that all of this was an outrage against her human dignity, the dignity of her fellow coworkers, and the dignity of all people in any office where Awkwards were imposed, whether Sam knew them personally or not.

In her mind something clicked. She did not deserve that. None of them did. None of them deserved the fear, the risk, the constant aching pain, the sensory-blasted minds, the broken bodies, the disrespect, the disregard. They all *deserved* better: they *deserved* to be treated with respect and dignity, even though they weren't Management. After all, before someone became either a Manager or worker, they were first and foremost a human being. They *all* deserved respect because they were *people*, and for no other reason.

The cacophony of everyone else complaining and arguing surrounded Sam. She felt something powerful in parallel with her fear. Sam stood up to get their attention and to be heard, and now, in spite of her anxiety, felt like she *had* to speak to the group.

"Excuse me! Excuse me! I have something to say!" Sam said loudly, and the hubbub died down. "I think you're all forgetting something, and you're making things seem too negative and hopeless. From what I hear, you're afraid of confronting Ellitson. Or you believe that nothing we can do will work. Or you think that you're special and going to be one of the lucky ones who escapes getting crunched. So basically: you're afraid, you feel powerless, or you're being selfish. All those feelings paralyze you. All those feelings paralyze *us*. But it doesn't have to be that way."

She took a breath and continued. "The whole reason we're here as group is to complain. To complain about work. And we are complaining because we are upset, because our working conditions have become dangerous and undignified.

"Now, sometimes people say that you shouldn't complain, that you shouldn't get upset, that you should just accept things, and that's the best you can do.

"But when you complain, when you're upset, it's often a sign of something. It's a sign that your safety and dignity are being threatened, that your physical, mental, and emotional systems know it, and are trying to express it.

"We are upset, scared, cynical, and complaining because of one reason: *we don't deserve this!* We don't deserve to go to work terrified every morning that we might be crushed and killed. But it's not just that. Even when the Awkwards work right, we don't deserve all the pain those rotten machines cause. We don't deserve all the jerks, pulled muscles, shocks, headaches. We deserve safe, healthy, pain-free, comfortable working conditions that respect our human dignity and freedom. We don't deserve to have to go in every day and plug ourselves into devices designed to restrict and control the way our bodies move, to make us conform in every motion and action to what the company wants. We don't deserve to be subjected to a machine that watches our every move in order to control us. The damn thing even tries to control where our attention lies at every second, to control what we are thinking with those shocks!

"No such system should ever be installed in a workplace. No such system should ever be imposed on a human being!"

Sam was on a roll now, and she kept going. "In fact, we didn't deserve the poor working conditions that preceded the Awkwards—stuck in cramped, sunless workplaces with old cheap furniture; working long hours, and usually overtime without pay, on temporary contracts with no job security—with our wages and benefits constantly squeezed, and routine disrespect from Management! We don't deserve to go to work every day knowing that we could potentially be fired at any time. *We* are the ones who do the work that makes the whole operation of our corporation possible.

"Why don't we deserve any of this? We don't deserve it because we are *people*. We are human beings who think and feel, who have goals and dreams in life, who want to do better in the world, who must feel some pain in life but want to avoid it when we can. We go to work, of course, to earn store credits so we can eat and have shelter and live, and to do all the other things that we want to do. But we also go to work to make a contribution, to be upstanding members of society—society wouldn't survive if nobody worked to make it all run smoothly. But there's nothing in that bargain that says we have to suffer, or give up our dignity or our safety. Nothing is more important than our safety and dignity, nothing stands above these things— not Ellitson's performance report, not the company's profit, not the convenience of some other corporate bureaucrat or Manager. The AWCRD is a threat to human safety and an outrage against human dignity. It must therefore be opposed until we have put a stop to it."

Sam looked around and added, "I've seen you all sitting here quarreling about things that are totally meaningless compared to our dignity and security. You're scared? Me too. But if we stick together and back each other up, we will give each other courage." She glanced at Nic. "You think that you can go it alone? That you can climb the social ladder, escape through a promotion or something? Well, you're not promoted yet, and you might be dead before you are! You will certainly suffer discomfort, pain, and indignity before you get that promotion, *if* you ever do. But if you stop thinking that you're better than the rest of us, and instead join with us, we will make work better for *everyone*, including you—we may even raise *all* of our working conditions to a higher level than you'd get alone if you were promoted."

Sam looked around at the others. "And some of you say that nothing can be done, that we can't succeed, that there's one way that reality is, so we have to accept the status quo. Says who? Human beings work on reality and change it all the time. Why are you so certain of failure? Do you not know that being convinced of failure is the best way to make yourself fail? It's a self-fulfilling prophecy. It stops you from even trying, and there is no chance of success if you don't try. But if we believe in ourselves and we *do* try, then we are likely to get at least *some* of what we want—and sometimes, if you are bold and courageous, when you try, things work out even better than you expected! All we need to do is to commit to sticking together *no matter what*, and make a plan, and then we will confront Ellitson and get control over our working conditions. We will find courage in our solidarity!"

"But what if we get fired? People could lose their jobs and their careers here." Nic said, his arms crossed.

"Then we will pool our resources as a group, help each other get through a period of unemployment, and help each other find new jobs. We will find strength if we act in unity."

"What if Ellitson thinks less of us? Or tries to get back at us?" Nate asked.

"He will respect us *more* if we stand up to him," Sam pointed out. "And when it's all done, we will have to watch him closely for a long time in order to make sure that he does nothing against us in the future. We should also find something to hold over his head to protect ourselves from any revenge he might think of."

"But I still don't feel like we should do this," Nate said.

"Get over the hump, people! We can do this! We are all connected as a group because we work together. We just need to recognize it and start acting like it."

There was a silence.

"Well," said Sid, "let's get to planning then."

And so the undoing of Mallworld began.

+ + +

On billions of holoscreens an advertisement is projected:

A sim-sunrise pokes through the large glass windows of a high-rise building and into a handsomely appointed office interior. The camera focuses on a sleek, modern desk; the large office is filled with expensive modern art and furniture. A woman in a maid's uniform cleans and dusts, her movements displayed in slow motion. An announcer with a deep, weighty voice says, "You're an achiever and striver, you're in command of yourself and your portfolio, you're a top decision-maker. Managing your wealth will be your greatest accomplishment." The screen depicts a couple, both attractive, middle-aged professionals, staring directly at the camera, arms crossed, with intense, unsmiling expressions on their faces. They are surrounded by their busy staffs in a slow-motion blur of constant activity.

"CGC Group has the skills and expertise to manage risk in capital gains accumulation in order to consolidate wealth." The camera, in silent slow motion, shows the two Executives giving orders to subordinates; one is yelling and screaming; the other slams a binder down on a desk, and papers go flying while subordinates go scampering. "Whether your goal is store credit optimization, maximizing earning index funds, default tranche management, or price/value deconnection, CGC is networked with the leaders and decision-makers to attain it."

The camera cuts to show the two capitalists on a golf course, the woman pointing her finger and yelling directly into the face of a caddy, while the man pounds his chest as he barks at another. "CGC is where serious investment professionals manage their credit—and where everyone else aspires to." The two attractive professionals smirk at the camera in slow motion. "CGC, the Capital Grows Capital group. How wealth is made."

+ + +

"Mr. Ellitson, what we're saying is that the AWCRDs are unsafe, prone to malfunction, threatening, painful to use, and at best uncomfortable. And so we're not going to use them. And we all agreed on that." Sam was speaking for the group.

Ellitson looked puzzled, his face set with consternation; he was obviously unsure how to handle the situation. He was used to managing the occasional problem employee, but he had never had to deal with a whole group of them. Usually his workers were docile and stayed in their place; they were so effectively socialized and trained to discipline themselves that he didn't have to deal with much trouble. The only preparation he had for a group of disgruntled workers like this had been two decades ago in a class at the Bush School of Business, where he had once copied talking points about managing employee discontent from his fraternity's cheat archive into a slide for a presentation. Ellitson thought he remembered enough to placate these employees. He would first try to project empathy, in order to gain influence over them and reestablish control.

"I understand your concerns, I really do, and so does Significorp. But our studies have shown that the AWCRDs are safe and effective workplace enhancers. We're all scared after yesterday's accident with poor Galton Johnson, but that was an isolated incident. The chance of that happening again, according to the techs, is under 3 percent. In other words, the

AWCRDs are safe. What I'll do is bring a tech in later this week to reinspect each cubisizer. In the meantime, you've all got to finish your TPR Progress Reports. So thanks for sharing your concerns with me, and I'll see your reports later this afternoon."

Ellitson turned and strode briskly back to his office, walking tall and not looking back, as he wanted to project confidence. He sat down in his plush office chair and started reading some TPR statistics.

After a few minutes, he realized that there was no noise of typing or other activity coming from the workroom floor. His gut tightened a little bit. He got up to investigate, creeping slowly and unsurely back down the hall. He poked his head around the corner into the office area.

He saw all the employees standing there doing nothing, glaring at him with their arms crossed.

"What are you doing? Why is no one working?" he said, stunned.

Sam waited for a moment. Then she said, "We are waiting for you to respect our dignity."

"What?! Respect your dignity?" Ellitson found anger welling up in him. "Get back to work, you, you . . . cubeys! Do your jobs!"

"Replace the Awkwards first, and we will go back to work then."

"I told you I'd send a tech in!"

"Not good enough. We want them *gone*. Not just because they are unsafe, but also because they cause so much pain and discomfort. And because of all the monitoring that they do."

"Get back to work or I will have no choice but to dock your credit accounts for lost hours. If this goes on, I'll have to fire you."

"Maybe we should do as he says," Nate wavered.

"See, it's not working," whispered Nic.

Sam ignored them, stepped forward, and spoke with simmering confidence directly at her Manager. "Mr. Ellitson, think of what you are saying.

You are threatening people's very livelihoods, their means of paying for food, clothes, and shelter, all to intimidate them into working in dangerous, undignified machines. Do you not know that this can be done to you, too? You are not a Mall Executive. You are a midlevel office Manager. You have bosses too, and for the sake of their profits they are as eager to squeeze you as they are to squeeze cubeys. Next year, they'll have Manager versions of Awkwards, or other ways to make your life difficult and uncomfortable, and you know it. What you let go around tends to come around; what strikes down others will strike you down, too. You can be fired at any time yourself. Would you want that? Of course not. So why would you do it to other people?"

Ellitson was steaming, his fists clenched. "Because I am your boss, that's why!" he yelled. "And you're the first to go, Sam. You're fired. Sandra, go into the admin records and terminate Samantha Gomprez's contract. You can give her the standard two days' severance. The rest of you had better get into your Awkwards right now!" He jabbed his finger toward the workroom floor.

Sandra, with her administrative pad in hand, stood there. She looked around, trembling. She looked at Ellitson. She looked at Sam. Then she set her shoulders, gulped, lifted her tablet, and with shaking fingers hit a few keys.

"No, Mr. Ellitson," Sandra said.

"What?!" he screamed the word.

"Sam, I've gone into the database and erased all his vacation, as we discussed earlier."

"What?!" Ellitson looked at them, eyes wide in a state of shock.

"Good, Sandra. Do you have Step 2 ready?"

"Yes."

"Mr. Ellitson, we have accessed your pay deposit account and are about to reduce your paycheck to zero."

"What? You can't do that to me!"

"You just threatened to do it to all of us."

"How are you doing this?"

"I'm an admin person," Sandra said, shrugging. "I can fuck up all your paperwork if I have to. It would take years to fix."

"Well, then, you're fired too!"

Sam said immediately, "Dump his credit line, Sandra." Sandra moved to hit a button.

"Wait!" screamed Ellitson. "Stop! I have to pay my mortgage!" He pleaded. Sandra paused, and there was silence for a minute.

Sam crossed her arms. "Did you want to say something, Mr. Ellitson?" she asked.

Ellitson looked like a cornered animal. "Upper Management will find out about this!"

"We can mess with your credit line any time," Sandra said. "Tell them and we'll zero it."

Sam walked up to her Manager and spoke right into his face. "Look at me, Ellitson!" she barked. He did, seeing nothing but stern determination in her eyes. "YOU WILL HAVE THE AWKWARDS REMOVED. TODAY. No negotiation. Make up whatever excuse that you need to. They malfunctioned, after all—send them back under the goddamn warranty. The same company makes nice, new-model regular work cubes that are even cheaper. Tell them you want to make an exchange. They can do twenty-four-hour delivery. We already checked all of this. We will all stay and help supervise the removal of the Awkwards today and the setup of the replacements tomorrow.

"If you cause us any trouble about this, we are all united against you, and the admin people will drive you into bankruptcy and a Time Out. Do not talk or argue further. We are *not* getting back into those deathtraps. None of us. Just go and *do the right thing* and get rid of these goddamn inhumane machines." Sam moved even closer toward Ellitson, an inch away from his face. She looked him straight in the eye, and said through clenched teeth, "And, for god's sake, from now on, respect our dignity or we *will* bring you down."

She waited. Ellitson did nothing. "Well? Go make the phone call," she spat.

Ellitson stepped back, looked first side-to-side, and then at the floor.

"Sandra . . ." Sam started to issue a sentence.

"OK, OK!" Ellitson said. "What do I have to do?"

"Call the office furniture company and return the Awkwards!"

Ellitson slumped. His shoulders fell. He meekly turned and shuffled back to his office. From it the workers heard fidgeting sounds, and a choking noise that sounded like a sob. In a few moments, the associates heard him place the call. "Hello, Customer Service? I'm calling for a warranty replacement for 127 AWCRD units . . ."

The office erupted in cheers.

+ + +

Sam leaned back in her padded ergonomic chair, having finished typing her TPR Progress Report ahead of schedule, and decided it was time for a break. It wasn't exactly an Executive chair, but it was far better than an Awkward and an improvement over her old desk chair. Her new cube was an improvement too: it was part algaewood, and she had been able to choose her own colors for the walls—she had picked a warm yellow-and-maroon combination. The cube was a regular static unit, of course, that didn't move and didn't make her body do things she didn't want it to. And she was not worried at all about its safety. It had two full walls, a three-quarter wall, and a half wall, private enough for concentration but also open enough to keep her connected to her coworkers. The important thing was that she had chosen her working conditions for herself. Someday they would all have offices, she thought. But this was an improvement for now. Sometimes you have to start with small things.

Sam felt that, in a small way, they had achieved a bit of democratic socialism in their little district office of Significorp, at least for the time being. A new spirit had entered the office. Employees were engaged. They were able to have fun at work now, which made the days good; but it also seemed like they were getting things done better, and often faster too. The situation had improved overall: Ellitson had agreed to weekly meetings with an employee representative to avoid any other "misunderstandings," and an employee council had been set up, elected by all the associates. To her own surprise, but no one else's, Sam was chosen to be its leader. She didn't know how long they could keep these improvements going; higher management would eventually find out and try to crack down. But the principle of working together, united, had led to success. She was optimistic that if they followed that principle of union, it would work again. Sam ran her hand slowly across her new desk and smiled. She spent another hour formatting her TPR report, and then gathered her things to go home for the day.

As she walked through the mallways, amid the lighted store signs and muzak, a big-screen HV at an open bar-and-grill caught her eye. It showed Jime's face, and she thought about his talk on community to the book club several weeks earlier. Sam smiled; she knew that she owed him more than he would ever know. It appeared to be some sort of press conference. Standing next to him, tall and muscular and speaking into a microphone, was Steev Tilman, a former football player and famous HV sports announcer. He covered all the sports—the Olympics, the Mallworld Series, the Megapie Contest. The caption on the screen read: "Sports Caster to Refuse to Cover Lottery: Sports and Game Show World Stunned." The screen then cut to scenes of some Wheel of Fate contestants fleeing from hunters in various exotic places around the Mall. They looked terrified. At that moment something clicked in Sam's mind, and she understood the indignity that they were being made to suffer and the danger they were going through. The Wheel of Fate was at least as dangerous and uncertain as an Awkward.

How about that, she thought. And she wondered what she could do to help.

CHAPTER 5:
BEGINNING DEMOCRACY

Dixon Cheton wrapped his fingers around his gavel with a self-satisfied smirk, raised it as though it were a personal scepter, and slammed it down with a loud crack. With this act, he opened the meeting of the Northgate Condominium Owners Association, of which he was the chair. Cheton was pasty, with dark, slicked-back hair. Beads of sweat ran down his forehead, and although he wore an expensive suit, it was out of fashion and didn't fit quite right; no suit ever seemed to fit him quite right. A dour and insecure man, Cheton was born of a saley family but had risen up through Management. He was driven by a need to prove himself to Mallworld elites, and he did this by making sure the wrong people never got in their way.

Cheton sat imperiously in his tall leather chair and began with dull bureaucratic matters such as entering the last meeting's minutes into the record. His monotone voice echoed off the wall of the large, well-appointed meeting hall, which was paneled in real wood grown in real forests decades before, and carefully preserved. The committee table at the front was made of real marble, not algaeplastic, and stood high above the rows of chairs that looked up at it from the floor of the room. There were only a few people in the hall—the board members outnumbered those in the audience. They all wore expensive business clothes. The Northgate COA handled the affairs of the Mall section just north of Mall Central, nominally representing seventy million property-owning shoppers who had, to use the Mall

Street financial jargon, borrowed credit to go long in split tranche certified triple-A funds to take out high-interest perpetual mortgages on condominiums. In so doing, they had purchased a standard shareholder's right to vote for COA committee members. Cheton droned on for fifteen minutes about administrivia, after which the discussion moved to policy.

"What if we dim the sim-sky by 12 percent or so? That would reduce energy costs and save credits," one pin-stripe-suited committee member said.

"But only in certain sections," another replied, this one in tufted silk. "If we dim it on the main concourses or in major domes, then business will suffer, and the economy will decline."

"Good point. I agree that we have to preserve a positive business climate in the pricier areas, since we need to keep the spending flowing and attract residents to those developments," said a third, wearing the latest designer one-piece suit. "But in those areas where we do dim the light, we can also cut back on landscaping to meet our budget targets."

"Yes, I think that's right," said a fourth, in a sateen dress. "Cutting the retail property tax rate by 15 percent will help retain business activity—Mallmart has threatened to close three megacenters in the section if the cost of doing business increases."

A fifth, wearing a purple silk power tie, observed, "We should also consider increasing rents and fees in other areas to improve profit margins for the Association."

Sid and Nic were sitting near the back, observing the board members from across the sea of empty chairs. Sid leaned over and whispered, "You see? There it is."

"Yes, I see what you mean."

"They sit here pompously making policies that take from everyone else and give to themselves and other rich people like them. They try to justify it by saying it's good for the economy, or creates jobs, or increases choice, or some other self-serving rationalization, as if they act for the public good. They may even talk themselves into believing it. But it's all a smokescreen."

"How do you know that they aren't acting for the public good?

"Because things keep getting worse for most of the public but keep getting better for the already-privileged rich people. A thousand facts and trends, all following the same trajectory of inequality, disprove their justifications. Every time, somehow, their proposals and policies benefit the rich—even if sometimes they have side benefits for others. Which, of course, they don't usually."

"You're really smart, Sid! You take in the big picture, which I sometimes don't see."

"Thanks. I have lots of political ideas that rattle around in my head. I never get a chance to get them out, though."

"Well maybe here's a chance to turn your ideas into action. So how do we stop them?"

"I don't think that we can stop them outright. They control the COA, and everyone who's got a condo in Northgate technically consented, legally, to the COA decision-making authority when they signed their mortgage papers. Renters do that through their leases with their landlords, who get their votes by proxy. See, here's how it works: decades ago when the Mall first went up, we shifted away from democratically elected *civic* officials like mayors and city councilors—who received their authority to govern from the body of the public that lived in a defined territory—to organizations like Condo Associations and Mall Management, who claim decision-making power based on investment and property ownership. As the ecosystem died and the Mall started to grow exponentially, anyone who wanted to get Inside had to join a COA, which basically took over public functions. They used the environmental collapse as a rationale to privatize every last thing, saying that the market was the best way to organize all social activity, even in a crisis. Condo associations started handling water, plumbing, garbage, landscaping, ventilation, sky lighting, zoning, contracting for services, and so on. So instead of providing these public services equally to all through a public authority, private enterprises supplied them, and how much you got depended on how much you could pay. Regular people, if they had invested in a condo, were able to buy into voting shares. The Old United States and other countries had been moving toward *de facto* plutocracy for decades. With the arrival of Mallworld, oligarchy became open and entrenched."

"Oligarchy—rule by the rich, right? Isn't that the same as plutocracy?" Sid nodded, and Nic continued, "But people still vote for condo board members, right? So isn't it a democracy?"

"Technically there are elections, yes," said Sid, "but in actual fact they aren't democratic. The plutocrats keep up the thinnest appearance of democracy with public meetings like this farce. It *looks* democratic, but in practice it's not—and actual, real-world practice is what matters. Sure, there's voting, but it's oligarchy because the vote is based on property, not personhood. Only actual condo owners have an individual vote. Some residents, the ones without property who rent, have no direct vote at all, and their landlords vote for them. And some landlords rent out thousands of units, so they decide thousands of votes. More fundamentally, *regardless of outward form* it's an oligarchy because influence over political decisions is unequal, biased in favor of the wealthy. When that happens, despite the superficial appearance of voting and elections, it's not democracy in actual fact."

"But *shouldn't* people who own more property have more say, even more votes? Don't they have a greater stake in how things go? They could lose more money."

"No, they don't have a greater stake in society! The measure of that isn't the amount of money one has in investments but the fact that everyone's very *life* is invested in society. The basic *trait* of being a live, conscious, experiencing being who can feel joy and suffering over a complete life, and who can reflect on those experiences thoughtfully, is fundamentally the same for everyone, whether rich or poor. The *quality* of everyone's actual, lived experience, though, is determined by political and social conditions. Therefore, each person's entire life—their quality of life—is at stake in politics, and morally speaking, *that* is far more important than the size of their bank account. In politics and government, each of us can potentially lose all that we have and end up at zero, no matter how much we start with. Politics can ruin your life, and that's true for everyone. So even when people have differences in wealth, fundamentally we all have the same share at stake in government: our total life chances and life experiences. That means that for *good* governance and democracy, each person must have a say, and each person's say must be equal. And I'm not just talking about votes! There's much more to politics than voting: there's petitioning, meeting with representatives, trying to persuade others, and much more. As much as possible, each person's political influence must be equal, and it should not vary based on money.

"I'll put it this way," Sid continued. "Money and economic resources are only *means* to quality of life and good experience. They have no inherent value apart from improving them. What's the inherent value of a piece of paper currency, or a digital bit in a bank account? Nothing. Zero. Money has value only as an instrument to acquire other things. But in oligarchies money becomes the primary value and main goal in itself. So the priority of ends and means gets flipped. This not only makes for vast inequality and suffering, as differences in money give some people fantastic life experiences and other people impoverished ones. It also hollows out experience itself, because the primary value celebrated in oligarchy, money, is inherently empty and worthless when it has become separated from the greater aim of improving human experience."

"Well, that's very philosophical," Nic said, "which is great, but I'm a practical guy, so let me ask a practical question. As things stand, politics is *not* equal, because the rich have more influence and control. They have all the power. So how can we win anything for saleys and workeys? For the common people?"

"Thankfully they don't have *all* the power," Sid replied. "There are a great many people who are individual condo owners. It's still just flat enough that we can win a majority on the COA board, although it'll be difficult to do. We can potentially win the individual condo owners and any condo complexes that don't have renters. With rental units it's harder, because the votes are all bundled and decided by landlords. But we could win the duplexes and triplexes, and many of the smaller complexes. And we can also get renters in the larger complexes to petition their owners to vote for particular candidates, which will at least have *some* impact. Eventually we have to establish the principle of 'one person, one vote,' rather than 'one dollar, one vote.'

"The whole idea that markets are democratic because you can 'vote' with your money by spending it with a firm you like rather than one you dislike—the idea of an economist named Milton Friedman, by the way—is fundamentally mistaken.[5] Those market choices are based on property, not personhood—on the possession of money, not equal consideration of individuals. Therefore, such 'voting with your money' is oligarchic voting, not democratic voting. And more fundamentally, *structurally* the commercial market is *not* a democratic election. Those two things are different social institutions, with different designs that express different aspects of social decision-making—one the considered judgment of a people, the other individual consumer choice.

"But back to your practical question: while it is necessary to achieve 'one person, one vote,' in the meantime we *can* get enough votes. The basic idea that we have to follow is that the common people *always* have numbers on their side, so they can always win—although they have to be united to do so, which means they have to be aware, smart, and organized."

"But nobody votes in condo elections," said Nic. "Turnout is always almost nothing. They just let the association sort of run itself."

---

5   Milton Friedman, *Capitalism and Freedom* (Chicago: University of Chicago Press, 1982).

"Exactly! We can win by getting as many people as possible to vote." Sid sounded enthusiastic. "The COA members have been in office for so long they think that their reelection will be automatic. They won't be expecting anyone to mobilize a popular electoral insurgency, so the first time out we'll have the advantage of surprise, if we can get people to the polls. I can't guarantee anything, of course, but if we put together a slate of candidates who are appealing, and push a platform of can't-lose, pro-middle-class policies, then we have a really good chance of winning at least some COA seats—maybe even a majority and the chair. Even if we lose, if we give it our all, then we can put *some* pressure on the board so they know people are unhappy, and maybe will change some policies for the better, or at least think twice before making them worse. Plus we'll get our ideas out there and set ourselves up for success in elections down the road. You're very good with people, you're a public relations person, and you've got management skills. You could help."

"It sounds like a lot of work."

"Yes, but it's harder for us to *not* do it." Sid felt very firm about this. "They impose policies that make our lives harder and more frustrating— policies that sometimes even harm or kill us. They raise prices and rents as they wish; they make it harder for people to find jobs, so some people are unemployed for years, and more and more jobs are temp ones without security or benefits. They make those of us with jobs work longer and longer hours, and they expect us to work overtime without asking, and even without pay. They rarely give raises, and when they do, they're tiny. We get very little vacation or sick time, and we're expected to work from home during our off time. We have to pay high prices for health insurance that denies coverage when needed. Finally, our employers nickel and dime us with extra fees or paycheck deductions for, say, tech support or admin support. If we made policy ourselves, life would be safer and easier for everyone. As hard as it is to participate in politics, it's even harder to *not* govern yourself."

136

Nic looked doubtful. "But people are so busy. Who has time for politics?"

"We have to make time. One thing that we could do to make it easier is put in place a shorter workweek in this Mall section, and a monthly civic day for public meetings. That would give people more time to be political."

"Oh, that would be great. Not everybody would use the extra time for politics, though."

"But *some* would, especially when there is a big issue getting lots of public attention, so it would help make things *better*. Having the freedom and opportunity to get political is important, and more and more people *would* get political on Civic Day if they saw others doing it. And even if they use some of the new time off for family or friends or chores or leisure, who cares? Everyone could use more time off anyway."

Nic was stroking his chin and thinking hard. He said, "I guess . . . I mean, what else am I going to do? Sit on my ass and play hologames? I know that's not the best use of my free time—especially while the jerks at the top keep taking everything away little by little, preventing people from getting ahead. They make me feel smaller and smaller all the time. I felt so much happier and more confident than normal when we won against Ellitson on the Awkwards! I felt . . . what's the right word? Dignified. Respected. I want to feel like that all the time!"

"Well then, get political!" Sid laughed. "We have to be active and take the initiative, and we need to get others to join us. The first thing we need is a slate of candidates—for chairperson and other offices."

"So, when do you announce your campaign?" Nic smiled.

"Me? No, no—I'm an intellectual, not an orator. I can do public speaking when needed, but I have limited talent for it. We need someone who combines the necessary political traits—someone who is intelligent, principled, *and* charismatic."

"Do you have anyone in mind, then?"

Sid smiled and said, "Why, indeed I do."

+ + +

On billions of holoscreens an advertisement is projected:

"New episode Thursday on *Wheel of Fate*: Which contestant will do what it takes to win?" says an announcer. The holoscreen displays reality show contestants in various undignified struggles against one another: a tug-of-war naked in the mud, crawling through a filthy pig sty to capture a flag, stuffing their faces in a worm-eating contest, dressed in clown suits and dancing on one foot in front of thousands of people in Piazza Plaza.

The announcer asks, "Who will pay the ultimate price?" Several contestants are shown sitting around a campfire talking. One asks, "Why are you here?" and another responds: "You can win a *billion* store credits! Can't do that workin' nine-to-seven every day! If I win, I can quit work, control my life, live my dreams—be free!"

"But what if your spin lands on Fat Pig?"

"Not gonna happen to me. And if it does—at least you get a year to party! I'm *so* glad they give us this opportunity!"

The screen cuts to a large, spinning prize wheel, and the announcer says, "Who will spin the Wheel and win it all?" The scene shows a previous winner jumping with joy at his good luck. "Who will lose it all?" The scene cuts to a terrified Fat Pig being hunted in the white pine forests of Grizzly Mountain, blood from a wound reddening the snow.

"The funnest reality game show of all—where everything is at stake! *WHEEL! OF! FATE!*"

+ + +

Jime banged a gavel to open the party meeting then set it down and put both hands on the table in front of him. The hubbub of the room quieted, and he began speaking. "Welcome to the first meeting of our political organization. Unfortunately, our group doesn't have a name yet—that's one of the things that we'll decide in coming weeks. Once we've figured out our principles, we can choose a name that reflects what we stand for. Tonight, we'll discuss our issue platform and start talking about how to organize ourselves." There was purpose and firmness in his voice that made people's ears perk up, and as he spoke to the attendees, he looked them in the eye to galvanize their attention.

The small room had been rented for the evening from a local Grade C charter school, and everything about it said "average." The walls were painted plainly and had algaeplastic sim-wood trim, and the committee at the front sat at a simple folding table. The people who had called the meeting were dressed for business, but not ostentatiously: Jime wore a gray suit and a tie, but no flashy jewelry; Sam was her usual self, in a sleek and professional business suit; Sid had added a blue blazer to his usual collared shirt; while Nic had toned down the glitz just a bit. On the concrete floor on which the table sat, on the same level, were rows of folding chairs occupied by the audience. The room was not crowded but was about three-quarters full—something that both surprised and pleased Nic and Sid, for although they had done their best to advertise through word-of-mouth and on the holoweb, they had feared a low turnout.

"My name is Jime Galilei, and this is Sidney Bernard, Nicolas Tattico, and Samantha Gomprez. For tonight we've volunteered to run the meeting, but one thing we're going to do at this initial organizing session is nominate people to be elected as permanent officers for the future. Of course, those of us here at the front table, who called the meeting, would like to serve in a permanent capacity, and we hope that you'll vote for us for some of the positions; but if other people want to serve and they win, we will of course go with the majority will. And in that case we'll also still volunteer for the group, because our main motivation is to contribute to improving things. We're human, but we're not power-hungry. Like you, we're just upset at the state of the world and want to help make it a better place.

"So our agenda tonight will consist of the following: a discussion of our policy platform; figuring out our core ideas for a statement of principles; and nominating officers." Sid, Sam, and Nic passed out holo-papers with the agenda to all the participants.

"We thought it would be best to kick things off with a discussion of our issues. We have six policies that we can implement here in Northgate to start with, but we're open to new ideas. So we'll tell you our ideas and then open the floor to other proposals. We have about an hour to discuss the platform, and at the end we'll vote for the different issues that are nominated. So here are our proposals."

Jime began to read from a sheet of paper: "One: Due to the recent spate of workplace accidents, in which dozens of workers have been badly injured or killed, a ban on Awkwards in the Northgate section of the Mall.

"Two: A 'Civic Day' once a month, in which business closes and the major mallways and squares are available to the public, to be used for public meetings and activities, so people have time for politics. There also could be volunteer-run street fairs, public ceremonies and celebrations, and other noncommercial activities.

"Three: A section wide pay raise for cubeys and saleys of 10 percent in annual store credit. We thought that's fair and would attract lots of new voters.

"Four: Establishment of a Northgate Public Health Insurance Option to give people an affordable choice for health care, to be funded by a surcharge on corporate profits. Eventually we'll demand fully public health insurance for everyone, and this is a step in that direction.

"Then we have two democracy-related issues. If we're going to get more people to vote in COA elections, then we believe that we need to practice democracy in other places too. What we are going to propose will be seen as unrealistic at first by both the public and the establishment, and we don't expect these two proposals to pass right away. These are mid- to long-term goals. So:

"Five: A sectional bylaw stating that businesses with eight or more employees must institute employee boards that have the power to veto major business decisions made by Management. There have been threats from Mallmart, for example, to close some megastores in the section, and we think that employees should have a say in that, since they will be adversely affected.

"And six: a rule of 'one person, one vote' for the COA election must be put in place. *All* residents of this section of the Mall must have equal voting shares on matters that affect them, whether they are condo owners or not.

"So those are our proposals. Let's talk about them. Then, if you have others, you'll be able to propose them for discussion."

A lively dialogue followed. A man who was fingering a thick moustache raised his hand, and Jime called on him. "How does this work? Can you even implement these things? Is that legal?"

Sid answered. "According to the Mallworld corporate bylaws, any business in Northgate has to get COA permission to operate in the section, and without the proper permit a business can be shut down. Corporations are chartered to provide some good or service of public use. According to my research, it's in the purview of the COA to make operating permits contingent on a variety of ordinances, such as noise restrictions, minimum profit margins, and even pay raises and worker safety rules. There's nothing in the corporate bylaws that prohibit sections from requiring workplace democracy. So a COA can legally mandate our proposals, under Mallworld's charter."

Another attendee objected, "No one wants the local Mallmart branches to close, but it's the company's property to do with as it wishes, without restraints."

Another interjected, "I don't think that your employee representation veto idea will hold up—it will be challenged by the company and the arbiters will strike it down."

Jime responded, "All sorts of property is subject to the rule of law. Business has to follow rules and laws, like any other group in society. Why should *they* be deregulated when no one else is? We all accept that society has to have rules to function—but all business does is complain and whine about regulations. Businesspeople seem to think that they, more than anyone else, should be especially exempt from the rules—all to make more profit. But we, the people, don't have to accept such exemptions. We, the people, have the *right* to make rules for organizations in our society. We legally and legitimately *can* make rules to govern commerce, so that business functions properly to meet society's needs without harming us."

After this argument for the legality and legitimacy of regulation, Jime, Sid, and Sam then advocated for laws and rules to govern business based on fairness. They contended that associates, salespartners, and even workpartners are affected by what happens at work and therefore should have a say in what goes on; indeed, they argued, working people's lives are so deeply affected by what happens at work that they should have the *predominant* say.

Sid said, "There was an ancient principle of governance that we can follow: 'what touches all should be decided by all.'[6] If something affects someone, they should have a say over it."

Sam added, "While businesses own physical property, the people that work within businesses are not *themselves* property, but are in fact conscious, reflective, thinking persons, and should therefore participate in decisions about how they are treated. They shouldn't be treated like mere things."

Jime pointed out, "Economic democracy is morally *right*. Outrages like the recent section-wide Awkward crisis can be prevented if working people are able to vote about work policies, because no one will vote to put their own lives at serious risk.

---

6   Michael Walzer, "Town Meetings and Workers' Control," *Dissent* (Summer 1978).

"The same is true about terminations," Sam said. "Remember the massive layoffs last year at the Specta corporation? If workers were in control, who would vote to end their own job? When hard times happen, it might be better to have cuts in working hours, evenly spread across the workforce, rather than firings—but that can only happen if the workers have a choice over the policies that affect them."

There was some nodding of heads among the audience at this, but some people sat with arms crossed, skeptical looks on their faces.

"Let's now shift the discussion to our proposal for 'one person, one vote,'" Jime said. "Please note that this should be understood as meaning equal votes for each person, not strictly as one vote each. In ranked-choice voting, approval voting, and other alternative systems, for example, people get more than one vote, so they can express their preference for more than one candidate or party. In those system, what matters is that everyone has an equal voting share."

"Oh, equal voting makes total sense," the man with the moustache said. "I don't know about this new 'economic democracy' stuff, but the fact that renters have to give their votes as proxies to landlords is absolutely unfair. We should have a direct say in things that affect us in our communities. 'One person, one vote' is just and fair."

Sid explained that there were few procedural issues in the way of a good electoral reform. "Landlords and condo owners have the franchise under the Mallworld charter, but we want to allow everyone's voice to count. Because rental complexes are businesses subject to certification, a workable, although not perfect, solution is for rental property business permits to mandate that landlords must vote for the COA candidate who wins a majority amongst the renters in each complex. This would, in effect, turn each complex into a small voting district."

Someone stood up and raised his hand. "I move that 'one person, one vote' be added as a platform item to be implemented in Northgate."

"I second!" the man with the moustache said. Jime then called the vote, and it was approved by a wide majority. There was also a consensus that a long-term goal for the organization should be the implementation of the principle of "one person, one vote" across the Mall, which also passed.

The Awkward ban and Civic Day proposals were nearly unanimously approved, but a majority of people didn't accept the rationale for the 10 percent pay raise. Most did not see it as fairly earned, so it didn't pass muster, even though it would directly benefit them. While many thought a sectional public health care option was desirable, there were doubts about its affordability and funding. Some people didn't think it would be politically possible to do at all. The issue was tabled for further debate at future meetings.

Participants in the audience then proposed other issues, most of which were not like the theoretical, abstract measures about democratic structures that the panel had put forward. Instead, they were more concrete, pocketbook concerns. One proposal, offered in lieu of the 10 percent credit boost, was an increase in minimum pay. There already existed a "minimum wage"—really minimum credit, since everything in Mallworld was done on credit—of 290 store credits, which would barely cover the cost of housing for a couple, much less food and other necessities, so most households needed two or more incomes just to get by. It hadn't been increased in years. Someone proposed increasing it to 600 credits, and this passed. So did a proposal for an hour cut in the working day, and for longer lunches and breaks. Other items that made it into the platform: a park with real, not fake, foliage; brightening the sim-sky in dark areas; public announcements on HV of COA meetings and decisions (with the same production quality and prominence of display as private advertising); and subsidies for children's day care. The high cost of rent was also an issue, but people couldn't agree what to do about it. As time ran short, other issues that people wanted to discuss were tabled for the next meeting.

Once the policy discussion was over, they took a short break, and people got to know each other over coffee. When the meeting resumed, Jime directed the group back toward general principles. "The next item on tonight's agenda is the one I consider most important. We need to figure out what general beliefs we stand for, for two reasons. First, and most importantly, so that we clearly understand our own moral principles and let them guide us. And second, so we can communicate our message effectively to other people.

"Here's the procedure I propose: our platform items are not just a list of preferences; they tell us something about who we are and what we are willing to fight for, politically. So what we will do now is take our list of concrete proposals and wrap them up in a package of general ideas. A conceptual package, one that can be communicated easily, and one that we ourselves understand easily too, so that it helps guide us. That package should consist of two parts.

"First, we need to lay out our two or three basic principles, things like 'justice for the people' or 'freedom from want' or something like that. I think that we can figure them out by going through the platform items we just voted on and *categorizing* them, working upward from specific policies to general principles. Some are about the economy, so that becomes one category, some are about elections, so that becomes another, and so on. That will help us clarify to ourselves what we stand for, and if it's clear to us, we can make it clear to others. Understanding our principles with clarity will help us adhere to them and avoid compromising our fundamental ideals. We don't want to get co-opted by the powerful, the way that some political parties have in the past in the name of 'centrism' or 'pragmatism.'

"Clarity about our ideals leads to the second part of our conceptual package: we should answer the question, 'What kind of people does this make us?' For *who we are*, our basic character, as individuals and as a group, is shaped by our principles—or the lack thereof. I think that our principles are going to turn out to be just and good ones, so having them clearly in focus and striving to live by them will make us better people, and will help us lead good, fulfilling lives.

"They will make us politically appealing as a group, too. Most of us in the Mall lead lives that are based primarily on consuming goods and services. Thus in character we are consumers, for consuming is what we habitually think and do. Society has even come, over time, to refer to people generally as *shoppers*, rather than as *people*! I now believe that this is an empty and unfulfilling way to live, and I think most people, deep down, feel the same way, because we all want important purposes that give our lives meaning. And capitalism, by reducing everything to money and self-interest, erodes the social sources of meaning. I think this group can offer a more satisfying and morally fuller way of life, lived in service to and in cooperation with others. A better identity, a more community-based identity. And that's something that I think a great many people will actually find enticing—in fact, it seems to me that they hunger for it."

Jime walked over to a holoboard at the front of the room and with a marker listed all the platform items the group had discussed in their first hour. He then asked what was common about them and what was different. For the next thirty minutes or so they discussed how to classify them, trying to determine what each policy was about, fundamentally. They grouped them and came up with the following categorization scheme of three general principles:

- Awkward ban, pay increase, employee boards = Justice at Work
- Shorter workday, public park, health care, day care, pay increase = Quality of Life
- Civic Day, public park, COA public announcements, equal vote = Stronger Public Sphere

It was not a long list, only three short things, easy for comprehension and mental recall: fairness in the workplace, improved quality of life, and a stronger civic sector. These were moral principles that reflected how the group genuinely thought and felt about the issues, as they had determined through their deliberations; thus the principles represented their civic selves authentically and were not products of political calculation. They were also precepts that movement members could keep in mind and could easily discuss with potential new members. The list was concise and easy to understand, not a long inventory of "policy wonkish" or excessively detailed specifics, which would only turn off people who might otherwise take an interest in the group. Those facts and details were important, but public discourse was not the time or place for them; for a political movement, public discourse was for drawing people in and getting them interested by standing for basic principles. Nearly everyone was capable of discussing moral and political principles. Policy specifics, on the other hand, could all be debated and worked out during expert discourses in working groups, academia, thinks tanks, and so on, and later included in a detailed policy platform and issue papers that the wider public could refer to on their own as needed.

Jime was pleased that people were open to this exercise in moral generalization. In his historical research he had seen videos of an earlier generation of leftist political activists who couldn't seem to help themselves from becoming incomprehensible by putting a hundred words on a protest sign, chanting slogans that were far too long, or going off on tangents and losing their main point during press interviews. Likewise, technocratic political wonks who got lost in the weeds of policy details and forgot about the moral purposes behind policies had failed at building a strong and confident left-wing political movement. Policies were important, of course, but they were really just the specific expression of more general moral principles. This exercise of classifying the specifics into broad, general categories helped the meeting attendees understand that, especially those who initially didn't think much of abstract principles. Knowing the general principles would also help everyone remember the more specific policies in each category, and it would guide them in the future when the time came to develop other policies for new problems.

"OK, finally, we should address the 'identity' issue," Jime asked. "What kind of identity or personality flows out of these principles?"

"I see a problem," someone in the audience said. "Those are things everybody obviously wants, so it's not any particular identity at all. Who *doesn't* really want better quality of life, and a better time at work? It's more a matter of being willing to *do* something about it rather than just saying the words."

"Yes!" said Jime. "Maybe that's exactly it! Instead of thinking, 'What kind of person *agrees* with these principles?'—nearly everyone does, in the abstract—maybe we should ask, 'What kind of person *supports* these principles?' I mean, *really* supports them, in their actions?"

"It would be someone who's involved in politics, involved in their community, who cares about working people, who goes to rallies and meetings and strikes," another person said. "Someone who votes, and who talks to people about the Mall's problems and political issues."

"Someone who is very active in all those things, rather than just a lump on a couch watching the holotube all day," a third person added. "Someone with energy, drive, purpose. Someone who makes something of themselves, but not in a selfish way—they make something of themselves in a way that benefits others, too."

"Somebody actively involved in the community, a community leader, or at least a participant. I think you can't have a strong community or society unless people are active in it," said someone else.

"An activist," said yet another person.

"'Active' was the word I'm thinking of too," said another.

"So," Jime said, "if we want a healthier society, we have to encourage more people to be active in it. And if we want a stronger political movement, then it will help to have activists for that, too. Sounds great!"

"But most people don't like being active. They just want to sit around and watch HV, or browse the holonet, or hang out on social media."

"Yeah, but most people are also pretty unhappy these days, and on some level they know it—and it's partly because they passively sit around and do nothing, rather than actively engage life," Jime said. "Human beings aren't built for just sitting and consuming and getting fat. Your body and your mind *want* you to exercise your abilities, your human powers. Your muscles want to move and stretch, your senses want to see and hear and smell and touch, your mind wants to solve problems and create, your voice wants to speak and be heard. Of course, *excessive* activity and busyness are bad for us, but being too passive is bad for us too. Yet capitalism imposes *both* busyness and apathy on us, for it makes us work too much on the job and induces too much passivity during free time. I think that we have to promote our group by stressing to people that we want to encourage and help them be more active in life—in their social life, their personal life, and their communal and civic life, too. And we want that because active living, not passive consumption, is really what makes life worthwhile and what makes us happy. So I think we should promote a more active, focused way of life in which regular people get in the habit of exercising their human capacities and abilities. Those abilities include their latent political powers, because while people find satisfaction in exercising their individual talents, some of our powers are social ones that we exercise jointly, such as talking and deliberating, or working together on combined projects. Furthermore, it's good political strategy: the peoples' powers grow exponentially when they combine them, so if we build our movement by fostering active civic character, our political power will eventually snowball."

The group was running out of time, so they wrapped up the discussion. They then took nominations for officers—several people volunteered for different positions—and Jime announced that at the next meeting they would solicit proposals for what to name the group and would elect officials. Jime knew there was no easy recipe for political change, but there were necessary tasks: organizing, consciousness-raising, educating, cooperating with labor and other groups, forming a political party, and campaigning for political power, among others. He was satisfied that the initial organizing work for the new political group had gone well. It was the first step of a potentially long road to try to change Mallword from within.

It also occurred to him that he didn't feel out of touch with others anymore, as he had after his first Time Out. Instead, he felt a sense of common purpose with these people, his new political companions. This might be a good community for me, Jime supposed. He paused and thought for a moment about Phoenicia. Then he hefted the chairperson's hammer, smiled wistfully, and gaveled the meeting to a close.

CHAPTER 6:
FIRST AWAKENINGS

David Sall walked down a mallway quickly and with purpose. The neon lights and store fronts did not distract or entice him as they used to. Like many young people in their early twenties, he worked as a saley in one of the millions of stores in the Mall. But now, a couple nights a week after work, he spent his evenings knocking on doors and talking to people about the new political movement. He loved it! There was nothing better than meeting new people and seeing them perk up with the idea that their lives might get better. He had even invested in a new pair of athletic shoes designed for heavy footwork.

David had been canvassing for a few weeks, and he was thinking about everything the group had been doing. Since he'd first heard about the group on the holonet he had thought that their ideas would lead to positive changes. His first meeting had been one in which the new group chose how to organize itself. During that meeting, several different possible organizational structures had been discussed, including a very democratic one in which nearly everything was voted on by everybody. After all, if the group was going to have democracy as its basic principle, then it should act like it all the time, right? The counter argument was made that too much democracy was self-defeating because it was so time-consuming that decisions couldn't actually be made. The group decided that the best way to follow democratic ideals was by deliberating and voting as a body about the most important things: the basic structure of the group, its main direction, major policy decisions, and electing officers. But they also decided that those officers, who would be elected semiannually or annually, depending on the position, would have the authority to manage the group's routine business. The whole group didn't need to vote on how many staples and paper clips to buy or how to arrange the chairs and tables in a conference room. Voting for every little thing would take too long and, what's worse, would allow contentiousness about unimportant details to burgeon, rather than active deliberation about important matters to flourish. The group therefore decided that they would be partly a direct democracy and partly a representative one.

The group had also recognized that a mixed democratic structure like that would allow two beneficial forms of knowledge to grow: the acumen of individual experts and the collective competence of the whole group. With elected officers, the knowledge of individuals with skill and expertise could be tapped into and channeled for the good of the group, those interested in taking on active leadership roles would acquire and refine skills at organizing and leading, and institutional memory would develop. On the other hand, regular deliberation of the whole body would allow everyone to contribute their knowledge to the group in a wiki-like way. No single individual, no matter how smart, was smarter than the whole body of them together, and democratic deliberation would enable them to utilize their collective knowledge. These two kinds of knowledge—individual expertise and collective wisdom—would complement each other.

In addition to running the daily business, leaders were elected to run and organize subgroups. Subgroups were established for online and social media campaigns, face-to-face canvassing and outreach, advertising, recruiting, and the other functions the movement needed. David was a naturally gregarious person, so the first time he attended he found the grass-roots outreach and organizing discussion interesting. He spoke up a few times and felt like he was making a real contribution to something important. Ever since, he had been involved in the door-to-door canvassing effort, finding his extroverted personality well-suited for it.

With a bounce in his step, David skirted the perimeter of Piazza Plaza, bypassing a crowd that was gathering for a show near the fountain. He could feel that he was part of something bigger than himself. He knew where he was going.

The canvassing subgroup focused on interpersonal outreach. While everyone recognized the importance of online and mass media in reaching large numbers of people, the movement decided that face-to-face contact was still crucial for making deeper connections with people who were otherwise turned off by politics. Face-to-face interaction allowed for interpersonal empathy that was lacking in online encounters, through the expression and reception of nontextual forms of communication—eye contact, tone of voice, facial expression, gestures, touch. It also showed that the movement was making a real, credible effort at including people and personally listening to their concerns. Face-to-face efforts would take the form of canvassing and of local meetings led by movement members and officers. David's canvassing subgroup had plenty of internal deliberation and consultation. They had met twice to lay out their canvassing plan, dividing up locations and schedules. Most volunteers were canvassing a few hours a week after work or on the weekends, going door-to-door to persuade people to come to meetings, vote in the next COA election, and get more active by volunteering if they could. They worked with the movement officers and the outreach subgroup to keep their talking points consistent with the movement's message. Furthermore, the canvassing subgroup was not only out pounding the pavement, but a special effort was being made movement-wide to identify and recruit good canvassers because the organization recognized that canvassing took a special kind of person—someone who was outgoing and positive, but not egotistical, argumentative, or combative.

The canvassing group had also met to design and memorize a rhetorical plan, which everyone was now putting into practice. It was based on the organization's basic principles of Workplace Fairness, Quality of Life, and Stronger Civic Sphere. The idea was to always start from the general principles and then apply them tactically, rather than getting lost in short-term, unguided tactical thinking that only reacted to immediate problems and circumstances but never made real progress. They figured out themes for discussion based on the party principles and platform, and they wrote scripts to use when talking to people: one for knocking on doors, one for conversations on the street, and so on. They also created a Q&A guide that anticipated common questions and set up canvassers with prepared, but principled, answers. The advertising subgroup had started to design logos and holopages, and one of the holographic artists printed up holo-fliers to hand out, all of which featured the three tenets and stressed the benefits of being an active, civic-minded person. The group also practiced together repeatedly before going out into the corridors and neighborhoods of the Mall to spread the good word.

The canvassing group had come up with slogans for meetings and rallies. One slogan, mainly for posters, was going to say simply "Get Political!" It was a way of reminding people that if they wanted their government to work for them, they had to overcome apathy and become politically active. Another slogan was a call-and-response to be used as a greeting between activists, or at the opening of meetings: one member would say, "Courage in Solidarity," and the other would respond, "Strength United!" This would be a way of boosting backbone and fortitude within the group, while reminding everyone to rely on each other. As with groups throughout history, such rituals created cohesion and *esprit de corps*. David liked one slogan so much he wished he had thought of it himself. It was a demand for greater democracy: since the movement believed that any decision that affects a person should include that person, at rallies and protests they would chant, "Nothing about us without us!"

David checked his schedule on his phone and marked off canvassing areas he had visited that day. In his first month of canvassing he had talked to people in three large condo complexes. He was actually convincing people to get out, vote, and make their world a better place! The thought of it made him smile.

The movement had little money and few resources, and so it had to rely on the efforts of volunteers. Sid pointed out that this was a good thing: it made the movement more democratic because it got many people involved and engaged, rather than putting things into the hands of political professionals or, even worse, a corrupt political machine. "You can't have a movement of the people without the people actually moving," he said.

He gave the example of the Old United States in the late twentieth and early twenty-first centuries, when liberal parties, civic groups, and labor unions deemphasized local chaptered forms of organization to do their work and spread their message. Instead of relying on members of local chapters to knock on doors, stuff envelopes, and so on, liberal organizations became dependent on professional lobbyists and expensive advertising campaigns, centrally directed from the O.U.S. capital in Washington, DC. Because they let their chapters whither, they became oriented toward the concerns of the elite and almost totally ineffective in promoting working people's interests. Eventually many such public interest groups became practically indistinguishable from corporate interest groups, leaving an ideological vacuum. With those on the political left (a term referring to those who typically support the concerns of common people) no longer arguing and fighting for working people's interests, the political right (supporters of the elite, the wealthy, and owners) swooped in to fill the vacuum and won people over by appealing to their worst instincts with populist, nativist, and racist overtures. Eventually the internet and social media allowed for more true grass-roots involvement and the self-organizing of large groups of people, but online fora could also succumb to conspiracy mongering and hate. They also became conduits used by malicious state and corporate front groups posing as grass-roots organizations that really promoted the interests of elites.

Thus the new democracy movement needed to make good use of lots of people. It couldn't rely on financial wealth or physical capital or an existing media network. Instead, it had to rely on people power and organization. If people remained active, motivated, and organized, it would be more than enough to create real social and political change. In the end, nothing could defeat the people but their own apathy.

David veered away from the plaza to a nearby food court where he knew lots of saleys hung out. He started putting fliers out on tables. A young, garishly dressed man who was sitting nearby with friends looked up from a Pizza Trough and asked him what he was doing.

"Is that for a concert or something?"

"No, it's for the Condo Association elections."

"For the what?"

"Board elections!" said a friend. "Boooooring!!"

"We're trying to win seats on the Northgate Condominium Owners Association so that we can do some good things for people."

"I've seen you guys passing stuff out. I'm starting to see you everywhere," said the first man.

"Yeah, we're out here, all over the place. It's what we do. If you join us, we can help you take charge of your life."

"Whaddya mean?"

"If you feel like you've got no control at work, we can help. You become part of a group that's making a difference. If you need help getting control of your life personally, we can help with that too." David met a blank, quizzical stare, so he elaborated. "If your working conditions are bad, we can help with legal advice. We're helping labor unions organize, and we're already helping employees negotiate with employers. On the other hand, if you just wanna lose a couple pounds, need help with your budget, or you need a babysitter, we can connect you with people who help each other out."

"Oh! Ok." The garish man thought for a moment and smiled snarkily. "I can just go on the holonet to connect with people."

"Of course, and that's totally useful, and we use online organizing just like everybody. Personal connections are still important, though. In fact, we think they're fundamental, and we help make those connections for regular people. And a lot of it is free, or low cost, because our people volunteer to help each other."

"OK, sure, face time is really important. So, I wanna learn karate, but just never got started. You gonna help me get a black belt?"

"Yep, actually we can. I bet we can find a good instructor for you who may be willing to give a discount. We also have motivational meetings where we support each other and help each other get going on the things we really want to do, and stay on track."

"Really? No kidding." The young man was impressed.

"Yeah, no strings attached. But once you get started, active, and involved, we hope you come to some other meetings, hear our message about changes we think are needed in the Mall, and think about helping out."

"Like what kinds of changes?"

"We want fairness at work—a higher minimum wage, a public option for health care, and workers' councils to veto stupid things like Awkwards."

"I hate those."

"Us too. And we want to improve the quality of life in the Mall—brighter skies, cheaper rents. We want more public goods—equal votes for renters, and a park dome with real plants, not plastic ones."

The young man thought about it, and then reached out his hand. "Alright, give me a flier and I'll think about it."

"My name's David, by the way. David Sall." He handed him a holo-flier and shook his hand, and pointed on the paper to the Mall Positioning System map that showed the movement's meeting locations and times.

David strode off, feeling good. He was surprised at how taking this action made him feel powerful. In charge. Alive. Helping out. He knew then that the movement was going to make a difference, little by little, person by person, and that he was at the forefront of that effort. He believed the movement's ideas were just and good, and in his interactions he had found that people were open to just and good ideas when presented with them. He believed that the movement was truly capable of making changes, and that changes could be made sooner rather than later. He and his people were going to change the world!

David soon arrived at the next condo complex he was supposed to canvass. His sharp knock on the first door of the evening was self-assured. The door opened, revealing a harried-looking woman, out of breath and holding a baby; other children were running around inside, one being chased naked through the living room by an equally harried-looking man. The place was as disheveled as its owners. David knew that the movement's growing network could connect these people with others who might be willing to share child-care duties.

"Wow, you guys look busy!" David declared. "Do you need help with baby sitting or day care? I know exactly who to call!"

David knew that the movement was needed, and that it could make life better for many people.

+ + +

On billions of holoscreens an advertisement is projected:

A heavily muscled man wearing a construction helmet and vest sits in a Burger Palace restaurant, hefting a huge four-patty cheeseburger, stocked high with trimmings and dripping with sauce, into his wide-open mouth. The BP logo shines steadily behind him, its golden glow reflected off the gleaming plastic walls and furniture. Jubilant trumpets flare, and a manly voiced narrator announces, "Now at BP, the new Big Belt Buster Burger, for only 499!"

The construction muscleman looks into the camera, smiling as he chews, and gives a thumb's up. The announcer bellows, "The latest thing to satisfy a tough, hard-working, hungry Mallworld shopper. Only at Burger Palace. Big Meat Tastes Great!"

Marc Hebert clicked a button on a remote and stopped the commercial. Marc was a schoolteacher in his early fifties, a little bit round in the middle and a little bit thin on top, and wore a professional shirt with a light jacket on top. His most distinguishing feature was his thick moustache, which he habitually stroked when he was thinking. Marc taught counter-advertising classes for the new political movement two nights a week. He was a teacher by temperament and enjoyed the night classes, even though volunteering took him away from his wife and two daughters. It made him feel like he was doing his part for society.

Counter-advertising classes were interactive lessons that the group started offering to volunteers and the public at large to prompt people to think more critically about what they saw on HV and the holonet. The classes involved viewing several ads with an instructor and identifying all the psychological techniques that commercial advertisers used to try to influence and even manipulate potential consumers. Counter-advertising was necessary education for people who wanted to make social change: it helped them free their minds from the thick fog of imagery, advertising, and propaganda that surrounded them every day throughout their lives.

"OK, class, we just watched a Burger Palace holovision ad," Marc said. "What did we see that was propagandist? What in it tried to trigger your emotions and subconscious reactions, and how did it bypass your considered reflection, your reason?"

An elderly woman was first to answer Marc's question. Her nametag read "Palina Newman," and she said, "The lighting and the camera angle made the Big Belt Buster Burger look better than in real life. Those things are actually really limp and greasy, and the lettuce and tomatoes are soggy, not fresh and crisp like the picture."

"Good! Anything else?"

A mechanic wearing coveralls that said "Vince Powerly," and who had come to class straight from work still wearing his tool belt, said, "The deep, throaty voice of the announcer made it seem like somebody manly and grown up wanted me to eat that burger. My dad, my teacher, my boss. The deep voice had authority. Made it seem like you were tough if you ate that thing, and a wimp if you didn't."

"Yeah, I got that impression that too," a saley named Wally Ruthers said.

"Good. What about the music?" Marc asked.

"Oh, it was all victorious and triumphant, like it was a big deal to invent this fatburger and present it to the world," said Vince.

"Yes, and that was the announcer's message, too," said Palina. "As though a hamburger is a great accomplishment. 'Look, here's this great thing, you should be the first to try it! You'll have the latest and greatest thing and be better than everyone else!'"

"So, in short, the commercial made it seem cool and awesome to eat this junk food, which packs 1,200 calories into a single sandwich and is guaranteed to make you overweight and unhealthy?" Marc asked.

"Yes," came several nods.

"And so commercials go," Marc said. "They're short, flashy productions that are junk food for the mind just as a Big Belt Buster Burger is junk food for the body. The whole point of them is different from what economists say. The traditional economic doctrine on advertisements is that they convey information about products to consumers, and are thus essential to how markets function. But notice how commercials almost never convey any substantive information about a product or service, or perhaps only a small amount, such as the price. You don't get an independent evaluation of quality, a menu of options, a list of materials or ingredients and their potential dangers, or anything like a complete description of the item. You certainly don't get informed about the industrial processes, like the location and method of manufacture, working conditions or pay of the workers, or how much profit goes to company Executives and stockholders.

"Instead, what commercials do is to associate a product with some version of the good life: freedom, wealth, luxury, sex, power, strength, or something else perceived as desirable. And that product-desirability association is impressed onto people's minds, whether it is valid or not and regardless of product quality, through tested, psychologically powerful imagery, music, and narrative. It is then repeated and repeated and repeated until it sticks. The average person is exposed to several thousand advertisements *per day*.[7] Thus, advertising does not give you more information so that you can make *rational, deliberate* choices as an *informed* consumer, as economists claim," Marc said. "Advertising's purpose is exactly the opposite: it triggers subconscious needs and drives to induce you to make *irrational, impulsive, uninformed* choices so that you will consume more and more, in order to make money for those who profit from your purchases.

"For example, showing a man wearing cologne who is surrounded by beautiful women is subconsciously, irrationally making it seem sexy and powerful to use that cologne. Same with that wristwatch ad with the skier in Alpine Dome that's getting a lot of play right now. Before the Mall, the global auto industry sold *six billion* cars, total, largely displacing public transit, by showing ad after ad of automobiles driving fast through deserts or along twisting mountain roads. They thus equated cars with freedom and fun in people's minds. Yet for most of the history of the automobile, people spent most of their car-time trapped in traffic jams during long and frustrating commutes, inching along slowly or going nowhere at all. That's hardly freedom, and nothing like zipping along a picturesque coastline. Advertisers try to trigger your subconscious in order to sell you a bill of goods and make you buy more stuff than you would ever *rationally* choose to buy. And they have honed their psychological techniques into powerful weapons. Advertisers are perhaps the greatest psychologists in history."

----

7   Caitlin Johnson, "Cutting through Advertising Clutter," CBS News, September 17, 2006, https://www.cbsnews.com/news/cutting-through-advertising-clutter/; Ron Marshall, "How Many Ads Do You See in One Day?," Red Crow Marketing, September 15, 2015, https://www.redcrowmarketing.com/2015/09/10/many-ads-see-one-day/

Marc's audience was paying close attention, with furrowed brows and some nodding of heads. They didn't like to be fooled, and they were beginning to see how advertising did exactly that.

Marc stroked his moustache and continued. "Have you noticed the use of stereotypes, too? The deep, authoritative voice makes it sound like strong, capable men eat at Burger Palace, when in fact if you lived on a diet of their food, you would turn into a big, weak, passive, obese blob. Certain voices and images are used in ads to convey a variety of traditional associations: manliness or toughness, sexy femininity, youthful fun, smartness. If you see an elderly person in a commercial, they are probably trying to convey either sympathy or trust. A deep manly voice conventionally conveys authority. Young people are shown in order to associate products with energy, novelty, and dynamism. The main strategy of advertising is not to try to tell people *what to purchase* by informing them, because no one likes being told what to do, and they resist that. Instead, advertisers portray *who to be* by creating positive images of success, wealth, sexiness, and so on, and associating their product with those images. This leads consumers to think they're creating positive identities for themselves through the mere act of consumption, when in fact making yourself a better person requires work, attention, and no small degree of self-discipline. But advertising promotes the easy, false path of trying to purchase good qualities instead of cultivating them. In that way, advertisers indirectly induce you to buy their products—or at least to think more favorably about them."

"But why would they do that?" Palina asked.

"Follow the money," said a hotel custodian named Kandy Hattee.

"Yeah, it's to make money for somebody," Vince said.

"But that's a good thing, isn't it?" Wally, the saley, asked. "It increases demand and keeps the economy going, and it creates jobs."

"That's an interesting point, and a very common rationale for advertising," said Marc. "But we think that's not a good argument, for two reasons. First, advertising creates *overwork*, not work. If we had an economy without advertising, we'd have an economy that produces for people's authentic needs, and no more. With advertising, everyone ends up working too many hours in order to produce all the things that people don't rationally need but are irrationally induced to buy. Overwork is onerous, dangerous, burns people out, and prevents them from spending time with family and friends, or volunteering, or getting educated. Overwork causes all kinds of physical, mental, emotional, and social illnesses. We could be quite happy without the many consumer goods in our society that are superfluous, and eschewing them would allow us to cut the workweek back to a rational level.

"Second, but more important, is this: if advertisers are influencing people subconsciously into buying stuff that they wouldn't otherwise rationally want, well, that is *not* freedom. That's manipulation. That's exploitation. That's a form of subliminal, subtle control; it's not democratic, and it's not self-government. It's a con job. When I think about it, it actually makes me angry that they try to beguile me like that. Who likes to be fooled and manipulated?"

Although the people in the class didn't want to admit out loud that they were susceptible to manipulation by commercials, if they were honest with themselves they knew they were, and they appreciated that Marc had shown them so.

"I think," said Vince, adjusting his tool belt, "that habitual exposure to advertising makes us more susceptible to salesmen, swindlers, and con artists. I mean, we're surrounded by advertising all the time; it repeats and repeats everywhere until its deceptions become everyone's truth. You get used to taking what it says for granted, and you don't notice the illusions and manipulation. Maybe we end up thinking according certain patterns from it, become more open to its appeals, and so are more easily moved by the tricks and frauds of people who are trying to sell us a bill of goods. We maybe even become gullible and fall for a lot of nonsense, like pseudoscience and conspiracy theories. You can lose your healthy sense of skepticism when you swim in a sea of advertising, and some people become completely bamboozled. These counter-advertising classes of yours are really helping me think about all of that." People around the room nodded their heads in agreement.

"Good, I'm glad to hear it—that's what these sessions are supposed to do, so I'm happy you find them helpful. We may not be able to physically escape the Mall, at least not yet, but we can escape it mentally by critically examining and questioning its ideological superstructure. Once we've freed our minds, we can work to transform it into something more democratic than an oligarchy."

The group then analyzed several other commercials—for clothes, home HV systems, a lottery reality show—and began to see how emotional appeals, flashy video production techniques, and simple repetition, usually associating commodities with something positive, affected how they thought, what they believed, what their preferences were, and even how they viewed themselves. Advertisements were a constant presence in their lives, endlessly repeated on HV screens in their homes, workplaces, and schools, and in stores, squares, and corridors. The group came to see how profound an effect they could have on people's consciousness and identities.

"Speaking of con artists, as someone did a minute ago," Marc Hebert said, "now let's move to a discussion of political commercials rather than economic ones." People laughed. "Notice how political ads also try to manipulate your preferences? They take candidates or issues and package them like commodities. Then they use the standard advertising techniques to associate their favored candidate or issue position with good things. Notice how political candidates are often dressed like cowboys, or wear old-fashioned bomber jackets like ancient military officers. That's supposed to make them look rugged and tough. The reality is that politicians sit at tables and desks and spend most of their time in meetings, talking. Not really tough-guy stuff. Or, notice that despite all the sex scandals in recent years, politicians are shown surrounded by good-looking, happy families, posing as responsible family men who would make good leaders. Smiling wife with perfect makeup and hair, two or three perfectly behaved children, and the family dog. I love my family, but I've never seen a real family like that in my life. I don't even think that actually exists!"

Everyone chuckled, and Marc smiled, knowing that they were starting to see through illusions more clearly than before.

+ + +

"This is Christine Kimberly reporting to you from Piazza Plaza, where a group of activists has gathered to discuss what they say are problems in the Mall—although they are using Mall property itself to make their complaints. The Plaza is usually quiet on Tuesday nights, with only a few shoppers in cafés and restaurants or peacefully window shopping. Spectas at the central fountain end early on Tuesdays, and that's why the agitators picked tonight to hold their first demonstration. Protest leaders say they want to introduce their movement and present their platform to the public, and while they've advertised extensively online and door-to-door, they confess that they didn't really expect a big turnout. Nonetheless, a crowd of several thousand curious onlookers has turned up. The mix of people reflects all walks of Mallworld life: there are parents with children, Managers in business suits, saleys on break, restaurant workers, hair stylists, condominium realtors, all curious about this strange group that has knocked on their doors or popped up in their media feeds. How will this new group entertain them? Will there be an angry debate? Will they poke fun at someone? Will they burn a heretic? Let's hear what they have to say."

The camera switched to a lectern set upon a platform, and Jime, wearing his best suit and tie, stepped forward to speak. Behind him were a few large, rented holoscreens that magnified him for the crowd. He smiled his broad, warm smile and gripped the podium with both hands before beginning to speak, almost as if to take control of the situation and steady it. He had a different purpose for the speech than the reporter assumed: he did not intend to stupefy the audience by appealing to impulses for consumption, conflict, or entertainment, but rather he wanted to inspire them with hope in the power of solidarity and remind them that they needed only the will to take that power and exercise it.

"Good evening," Jime spoke. "We have asked you here tonight to declare our belief that a better future is possible, and to persuade you that we have the strength, together, to create it. My name is Jime Galilei, and I am running for the office of Chair of the Northgate Condominium Owners Association in the upcoming election. I am here to ask you to vote for our movement, for only by working together for the good of all can we make our world one worth living in.

"Most of us are hard-working, intelligent, reasonable people; we live our lives according to the rules, having been told that we will receive our just rewards. But instead, every year, every month, every week, life gets harder. We all feel it—that uneasy sense that something is wrong, that everything is frustrating, that no one can really be trusted, that things are not going to turn out alright. Every year, every month, every week, a little more effort is demanded at work, and a little more overtime, so that in a few years we're doing twice as much as before. Every year, every month, every week, a little more is trimmed from our pay. Every year, every month, every week, the cost of living—especially rent—gets a little higher. Every year, every month, every week, the number of jobs gets smaller, and the number of people applying for them gets larger. Every year, every month, every week, more of those jobs get turned into temp work or contracting positions without protections, benefits, or security. We're not getting ahead but are struggling just to stay even. And our bosses continue to inflict indignity after indignity upon us."

The crowd seemed interested: attentive and quiet.

"So how do we respond? As things stand, we compete against each other, always trying to win a better job or a promotion; some of us to get ahead, others just to stay afloat. Or we constantly try to finagle as much as we can out of our customers, selling at an unfair price, or not being entirely truthful about our goods and services, or cutting costs by cutting corners.

"As that kind of competition becomes widespread, society becomes colder. We don't know our neighbors or our neighborhoods. There's less trust in society, and we feel that no institution can be relied on. At best, we have a circle of friends and family that we confide in, and when we can find time, we escape with them into some HV show or specta, to forget our troubles, and to forget the feeling that things have gone wrong. But then we come back to reality again, to a cold, anxious, harsh, even dangerous world, where no one is treated fairly, where it's harder and harder to maintain our livelihoods and our well-being, where there is nowhere to go to redress our grievances or to make things better. There seems to be no one to turn to, no one to put our trust in.

"Our movement aims to earn your trust and to become that group to which you can go. We are a movement of common, working people who do not come from or possess great wealth, but who earn our daily bread through our own efforts. Just like *you*. We have gathered together to elect candidates to the Northgate COA board who will be the voice of *you*, the common people of Northgate, and who will aim to protect your interests. We are the best candidates to represent you, because we *are* you: we come from the same background, we work at the same jobs, we endure the same indignities and injustices. We want to work together, all of *us*, to make the world a better place.

"Our purpose is to build a genuinely people-based movement that is capable of taking political and economic power from the oligarchs, and then wield it in the interest of all of us, not just the wealthy few. Our pur- pose is to transform society into a full democracy, through the patient, persistent, determined work of political persuasion and organizing.

"We want to help you at work by making workplaces just and fair. We want to help you outside of work to improve your quality of life, however you define it. And we want to help you in wider society through a restoration of civic life and institutions that were ruined long ago. We want to improve our neighborhoods and schools, ensure that you have the compensation and benefits that you deserve, and make your voice heard in decisions that affect you, both in your workplace and in the public space.

"We cannot, and would not, do this *for* you; we are here to do it in concert *with* you, for we can only restore democracy *together*. In solidarity. To do all this, however, and to give you courage, we will help you find your power. You cannot have hope and confidence without having power, and those who are powerless fall into diffidence and despair. Together, we will join our individual powers and make them into a power greater than the sum of their parts. We will become a social power that provides mutual support, aid, and assistance to regular people who are struggling to stay afloat in this awful oligarchy that benefits the rich at the expense of everyone else. And we will become a political power that elects representatives *of, by, and for* the common people to COA boards, for that is where the power to make change lies.

"Now, since this is about all of us cooperating together, and not about me personally, we would like you to hear from two other candidates today who will say more about what we stand for.

"First allow me to introduce a working person, just like you, who has been a leader against the use of Awkwards in our workplaces, and who is also running for office. It's my pleasure to introduce Samantha Gomprez, our director for labor justice." She stepped up to the podium, and, magnified in the holoscreens on the stage, stood straight and tall and looked nothing but confident on the outside, even though she felt nervous on the inside.

"Hello, people of Northgate!" Sam said into the microphone. "Thank you for coming to our rally! I am a data processing associate at Significorp. I am also head of the new Workers' Consultation Board at one of our regional offices, and I led a protest that stopped Significorp from using Awkwards in our branch and which has now caused a review of their use companywide. I want you to have a workers' board too, just like us. Ideally, we would all have workers' representation *with teeth* that can veto management decisions, in order to prevent abuses like Awkwards and to make sure that you have fairness at work.

"People sometimes think that progressive reformers just complain— that they're lazy whiners who want to be handed stuff for free rather than earn it. And people sometimes think that reform is about taking money from the rich to give to the poor, as if we were thieves rather than hard-working people who actually *make* the money for the corporations in the first place, with our own hands and minds. Money that the wealthy then appropriate for themselves from those who actually create value—the working people. Let me say it clearly: we *are* the corporations! Like the cells of a body, workers are the parts without which a corporation could not exist. The Executives are *dependent* on the labor of the common people for their incomes and positions, not the other way around: a company can always find a new CEO, but if it fires all the workers, it will cease to exist. It's the 1 percent at the top who take an unfair share, skimming so much that a few dozen Executives receive the same income from Mallworld's economic production as the 99 percent at the bottom—the billions of people who do the vast majority of the work. We aim to correct that unjust distribution of society's shared production. We emphatically do not want *unearned* rewards; we want the *just* rewards that we have earned through our work."

Many in the crowd, accustomed to thinking in terms of distribution according to deservingness, nodded and murmured affirmation of this.

"But while money is an important issue, it isn't the primary one. The primary one is *control*. Democracy is about who controls you, about how much control you have, and about being free from unaccountable control. It's about having a fair say over what happens to you. Money issues are important, for sure, but they are second behind the question: who is in control, the people or the elite? Because I'll tell you: right now, it ain't you."

This caused muttering among the crowd.

"We believe in both political *and* economic democracy. Just as citizens, not nobles, should be in control of government, workers, not Executives, should be in control of corporations. Why? Because what happens to us at work profoundly affects and shapes all of our lives, so ultimately we should have *full rights* of decision-making power over what happens there. We spend most of our waking hours during the best decades of our lives at work. The boss determines what we do for eight to twelve hours a day, how we do it, what tools we use and in what conditions, and who we do it with. The boss can tell us where to place our bodies, and what to do with them; what motions to make, how fast, and how many repetitions. Indeed, the boss can even tell us what to do with our very *minds*, what to think, by demanding that we focus on particular tasks like data entry or writing reports, and demanding results in a short time period. That's what the Awkwards are about: controlling our bodies and our minds.

"Workplace decisions affect us outside of work, too, in our personal lives—where we live in the Mall, whether we live Inside or Outside, who our friends are likely to be, how much time we get to spend with family, how much leisure time we have for ourselves. And of course, your company decides very important things like what your basic income is; whether you have health insurance or not; whether you get a promotion or not; what training and education you get; what shape your career and retirement take. With work taking up so much of our lives, it ought to be fair, shouldn't it?"

Some people shouted "Yeah!" at that.

"Because workplace decisions affect us all so totally," Samantha said, "our movement believes that workplaces should be run democratically by the workers. When you don't have a say over decisions that affect major parts of your life, when decisions are made for everyone by only a few elites, then you are living under an organization that is effectively a dictatorship or tyranny. Whether that organization is called a government, a corporation, or something else doesn't matter—it's the reality of the interrelationship between organization and individual that counts. Democracy belongs in both our political and our economic spheres, because it's the most moral and proper decision-making procedure for common, shared affairs of any kind. It's the *only* fair and just way. If we truly want a better world, worker veto boards are just the first step in the right direction.

"Some claim that companies are democratic because they have stockholder elections. That is wrong. Don't be fooled by it. Stockholder elections are *elite* elections that keep control in the hands of mostly rich people. They still exclude the vast majority from decision-making; they still don't put the common people in charge. Likewise, distributing some dividends or benefits to employees as profit-sharing doesn't make a company democratic. Unless workers have the final say over workplace *decisions*—for example, by voting for company officers, by vetoing decisions that negatively affect them, and by real deliberation that determines policy—then the workplace is not a democracy. It is merely a petty and venal tyranny.

"Our economic organizations should reflect the reality that the workers, not the so-called Executives, are the ones who create wealth. Executives are nothing more than over-glorified administrative employees. They do have a real, and important, economic function—organizing a company's production—and they should be rewarded with a fair salary for it, at roughly the same level as other managers. Corporate officers can provide valuable administering and coordinating services, when they're not busy destroying the economy with some irresponsible financial scheme. But the *massive* incomes they claim for themselves are entirely unjustified, and do not reflect the fact that the vast majority of the work is done by other hands. No one's value-added contribution justifies a salary or bonuses worth millions or billions of credits. When Executives take more income than is warranted by their personal labor and effort, then they are parasites on the value created by others, parasites engaged in massive, systemic, and often hidden theft. Salaries, bonuses, and other compensation that is tens, hundreds, or thousands of times the wage of the average worker neither reflects the effort in labor that Management actually exerts nor the value the Executives individually add. That value, in reality, is added collectively and jointly by workers, who are not compensated for the value of the work they do which is purloined by the Executives. Thus, the workers work for free part of the time, just as if, for part of the time, they are slaves serving a larcenous master.

"Furthermore, the Executives do not deserve *any* of the wealth that comes from using their privileged positions at the top of the corporate pyramid to skim off value from everyone else. How is it just or right that CEO compensation is determined by corporate boards that are appointed by the CEOs themselves? Their privileged positions mainly come from insider deals made in boardrooms and Executive suites, so are based on collusion, not merit. Meanwhile, those who do the work of the company, earning their way, see their earnings funneled to these insiders at the top. It's an outrage."

Loud shouts of affirmation came from the crowd.

Samantha continued: "Democratically run companies would hold these Executives accountable. Workers with the right of democratic control would share income and benefits fairly, ending an unjust system in which Executives make many times more than employees do and instead creating a fair spread of income, benefits, and work time. This can only happen if we rethink what a corporation is, stop treating it like a commodity, and start treating it like a community.

"You see, we treat corporations like articles of property, like your shirt or your computer or your condo. In our system, private individuals can own entire companies, just like they can own personal commodities. But firms are not property like personally owned items. They are *organizations*, first and foremost, not objects; and morally speaking, they are organizations primarily of *people*, configured according to rules for some particular purpose or purposes, who use tools, machines, computers, and other material goods to meet those purposes. What's morally important in a corporation is not its physical capital but the fact that it is made up of people. Since corporations are organizations of people, they are more similar to a town or city than to a shirt or computer or condo. Yet we treat corporations as property to be owned by private individuals or by other firms. Why should that be? Slavery, the ownership of people, has been forbidden for centuries. So I ask: if you can't own an individual person, why should you be able to own a group or organization of people?

"When you own an object, you control it as your tool; when you are allowed to own an organization as if it were an object, then you control all the people in it as if they were your tools. This is unacceptable. We categorically declare that corporations should not be thought of as, and are not in actual fact, property at all; because as organized groups of people they cannot morally and legitimately be owned, and certainly cannot be owned in the same way as your shirt or your condo. Why? Because people are not objects, and we must not objectify working people. Just as ownership of individual persons is one form of slavery that disrespects the dignity and moral personality of human beings and therefore is immoral and illegal, so private ownership of *groups* of people, such as corporations, is another form of slavery that disrespects the dignity and moral personality of human beings, and is therefore immoral, and should be illegal."

The people in the crowd actually started clapping at that, and Sam smiled.

"And it doesn't matter one whit if people join a group or corporation voluntarily. A company cannot by moral right be owned as property in any sense, even if people have joined intentionally, precisely and solely because the company is made up of human beings with moral personality. It has long been recognized that you cannot legitimately sell yourself into slavery: voluntary contracts in which individual persons sell themselves to be bought by others are null and void, because you cannot freely sell yourself into unfreedom; a single *act* of freedom that subverts the general *principle* of freedom is self-refuting. It disrespects human dignity and moral personality. Likewise, contracts in which *organizations of persons* sell themselves to be bought and controlled by others should be considered null and void too, for the same reasons.

"Instead, corporations must be rearranged as free and voluntary associations made up of their worker-members, who have the predominant say in how they are run. Democracy is the only form of organization that respects members' moral identity as beings who make choices, the only form that respects freedom. That principle applies to economic organizations as much as political ones, and it is why corporations cannot have the moral status of mere property. If we are to treat corporations as 'owned' in any sense, then they must, as organizations of people, be owned and controlled in concert by all the people in them and all the people affected by them. They should be governed democratically as economically productive joint communities, rather than treated as tools or implements to serve the will and whims of individual Executives. That's why our movement supports worker boards with veto powers and worker elections for executive officers as a step in the right direction, until real and deep control of companies by workers and their communities can be put in place."

More applause came from the crowd, and Sam felt a positive energy from them that she had never experienced before.

"Let me finish by telling you about our other policies to put these principles of workplace fairness and economic democracy into practice. In addition to worker boards and Executive elections, we also support better pay, cuts in working time, and better regulation of workplace safety. We will raise the minimum pay for this section, and we will cut the workweek. The average real weekly worktime, counting people working multiple jobs as well as uncompensated time, is now over fifty-five hours a week, which is too much to be a good citizen or parent, or to grow as a person. We will immediately cut it down to what it used to be, 40 hours, and over time will cut it again to thirty-five, then thirty, then twenty, and even more if we can. Finally, we will categorically prohibit workplace conditions that can cause *any* harm, injury, or death to human beings. If you elect us, no Awkwards will be permitted in *any* company in Northgate. We will create a new investigative body, fully staff it, and give it the power and authority to inspect workplaces to make sure that working conditions are not only safe but *healthy* and, yes, even *pleasant* to be in.

"In addition, we will create a Public Health Insurance Option for Northgate as an alternative to the private health insurance available on the open market. This is a transitional step to universal health insurance, suitable for the local and sectional levels. Today, private insurance is under the control of oligopoly corporations and, in some medical subsectors, under monopolies. This makes prices outrageously high and deprives many people of health care altogether. This is absolutely unacceptable in health care, for medicine is supposed to alleviate human suffering and prevent unnecessary death; making the life and health of millions subservient to profit, in the end, amounts to a human rights atrocity. Forcing these large-scale private insurance companies to compete against an affordably priced, publicly subsidized alternative, the Public Option, will help bring prices down and improve service.

"But that is only a first step to universal health care, free of charge at the point of service for everyone. We believe that is the best system because markets don't actually efficiently organize the provision of medical service, for two reasons. First, there is a disconnect between supply and demand, because there is a disconnect between the consumers of medicine and suppliers: using medical goods and services is not like an individual choosing which phone to get or which restaurant to eat at, because *doctors* make the consumption decision, not patients. The field of medicine is so complex that highly trained experts, not individual consumers, must make decisions about what medical services are needed. Thus the market mechanism breaks down, and there's only so much a public option can do to fix it. And second, we believe a universal health insurance plan is most affordable, because when it comes to insurance, the larger your insurance pool is, the more expenses fall; and because the administration of one simple program is less costly, overall, than many complicated ones.

"Finally, we will start to provide better day care for young children by mandating that primary schools extend preschool to younger ages. Day care for infants and toddlers is so expensive that it can impoverish families, but raising children well is necessary for any society to be a good and decent one. Cutting the workweek back to reasonable levels will also help make child-rearing less burdensome on parents. Our eventual goal is to provide free, high-quality education for everyone, from preschool to college.

"Thank you. We fight to put *you* in charge and to make *you* your own boss. Mallworld is a rich society, and an abundance of material goods is available for everyone. We will work toward an equal society, and eventually we *will* get it! The more people who join us, the sooner we will have it!" Sam pumped her fist in the air and people clapped and cheered as she left the podium. She felt energized and validated—and no longer nervous or insecure.

Jime stepped back up to the microphone. "I now have the pleasure of introducing a surprise guest. He is one of the Mall's leading public figures, someone who has made the health of the people of Mallworld his life's work, and we are very pleased to announce that he has decided to promote healthy well-being by endorsing our new movement and joining us in our cause. You all know him, so I will not go into long preliminaries, but will simply introduce—Dr. Davis North!"

The crowd was surprised and impressed at this announcement, and they started cheering and clapping loudly. North was only a middling physician, but he was a hologenic one: he was a grandfatherly man in his early sixties with a warm, reassuring manner, a pleasing bearded face, and an authoritative baritone. Consequently, he consistently polled as one of the most trusted public figures in Mallworld. People relied on his medical advice, which was in reality compiled by a research team of very good physicians. Jime had believed that winning him over to the movement would help lend it the respectability it needed to be taken seriously rather than dismissed as part of the lunatic fringe, and the initial reaction of the crowd suggested he was right.

Dr. Dave stepped up to the podium, appearing on the holoscreens for all to see in his usual white lab coat, which, just like his gray beard, was a bit disheveled. He waved and smiled at the audience and was met with cheers. "Greetings, and thank you for coming! My name is Davis North," he said in his pleasing, measured tone, and people cheered. "Thank you. Thank you. Many of you have seen my holovision program, 'Health and Well-Being with Dr. Dave.' I am here today to talk to you about your health, as I always do. But today, I want to talk about another kind of health: not individual health, but social health, and how social health affects personal well-being. I'm here to talk about Mallworld as a whole, and the quality of life here, and where it is lacking.

"Ms. Gomprez just spoke to you about the economics of universal health care, and why we need it. As a physician, I find nothing more heartbreaking than turning away a patient who can't afford the medical care they need. I want to talk to you about the wider economy and, as a doctor, about what makes for a healthy economy. What is an economy? Why do we have one? Why do we organize things to produce more goods and services together than we could alone as individuals? We do it, of course, to improve the quality of human life, by creating the material basis for survival, health, education, and well-being. This includes not only bodily integrity but mental health too. The best and healthiest economy is one that creates an appropriate amount of beneficial goods and shares prosperity widely, in order to meet people's needs and free them from material worry, therefore enabling them to find and pursue their deeper purposes, connect with the world around them, become active members of their communities and society, and live truly fulfilling lives. In short, the point of an economy is to satisfy human need and to increase the quality of human life. An economy is *not* supposed to whip and drive the majority of people in order to produce decadence and luxury for a few. Nor should it benumb and stupefy people by overgorging them on bread and circuses. Nor should it leave some people impoverished, abandoned by society to live in hunger and fear.

"This Mallworld, in which we are born, live our whole lives, and die, which surrounds us and from which we cannot escape, is an unhealthy economy and society. It is based on consumerism—not healthy, moderate consumption, but consumer*ism*, which are two different things. Of course, people need to consume things to survive, to be healthy, and to be happy; we need food, water, shelter, clothes, clean air; education, art, music; and much else. But consumer*ism* induces us to consume too much: it is the ceaseless absorption, use, and devouring of goods that goes beyond the satisfaction of healthy, balanced needs. It is not a system of consumption, properly speaking, but a system of *over*consumption. An economy can fail by providing too few of the goods needed by humans to live in a healthy way, but it can also fail by overproviding those goods and promoting unhealthy, excessive consumption. Overindulgence is as much an economic failure as is poverty. The first is like tuning the string of a music instrument too loose, and the second is like tuning it too tight: neither hits the right note.

"The solution, as it is for many things in life, is to find a balance or golden mean: not too little, and not too much. A healthy person, and a healthy society, will aim for neither underconsumption nor overconsumption, but for moderate consumption.

"We know from ancient studies that people need a certain level of consumption to be happy. Poor people tend to be very unhappy, of course, due to their deprivation. Happiness increases, on average, as people have more material goods, until about the upper-middle-class level of comfort and security. After that, additional wealth no longer leads to greater happiness. In the 2010 dollars of just over a century ago, happiness increased with income up until about $75,000, or around 3,000,000 of today's store credits.[8] Additional consumption above that level is unnecessary and superfluous because it doesn't increase well-being. Moderate consumption thus makes us healthy and happy, while overconsumption adds nothing to health and happiness. Thus it is a social injustice if the economy is set up to deprive many people of a moderate level of consumption merely in order to allow a few wealthy people to overconsume.

"In a crude sense, a consumerist economy does provide for people's physical needs, since there are seemingly endless supplies—of cheap, greasy, sugared food to pig out on; of fancy clothes to show off in; of shiny gadgets to use and throw away; of entertaining spectas to distract and stupefy us. We are bombarded everywhere with the bright lights and loud music of advertising until our heads hurt and our concentration fails. We are sheltered under the all-encompassing roof of the giant Mall. We have so many clothes that we have closets full of them and can throw them away after wearing them only once. We over-meet our food needs so well that we've had an obesity crisis for more than a century. In what sense, some might say, are our needs are not being met? Our needs *are* met, they would say. We have an abundance of wealth; we are victims of our success.

"Indeed, we *are* victims of our success. So much success that it overwhelms us, for humans did not evolve in circumstances of plenty. Modernity cured many diseases, but overconsumption causes all sorts of physical ills of its own, from heart disease to diabetes to dental problems to osteoarthritis to some kinds of cancer. Stress and alienation also cause or worsen mental ills, including depression, social anxiety, and narcissism. Many people end up suffering psychological emptiness in the midst of material abundance. A system of overconsumption fails to meet the needs of healthy bodies and minds just as much as the underconsumption of poverty does.

"What kind of economic system promotes drug use, tobacco use, overeating, and passively sitting around watching HV? None of these things

---

8   Daniel Kahneman and Angus Deaton, "High Income Improves Evaluation of Life but Not Emotional Well-Being," Center for Health and Well-Being, Princeton University, August 4, 2010.

make for healthy bodies or minds—which is just a way of saying that they don't meet human needs. Consumerism is unhealthy because it is consumption *beyond* the limits of human bodies to handle, and of human minds to handle, too. Unhealthy consumption that does not support or enhance human life, but actually diminishes and degrades it, is not meeting our needs, is not hitting the right note—ill health is the sign of that. Because advanced, modern economies are so productive, scarcity is solved. Therefore, the problem of modern economics is no longer one of solving underconsumption. The problem is instead that of solving overconsumption.

"Healthy, moderate consumption, on the other hand, supports our intellectual, psychological, and social needs. A healthy economy would provide not only the necessary high-quality material goods to meet people's physical needs, but also healthy communities, good schools, rich cultural institutions, and the leisure time for people to participate in and grow from these things, so that everyone could lead fulfilling social lives. In sum, the healthiest economy is *not* the most efficient one, *not* the one that produces the greatest possible amount of private consumer goods. That is not what makes us happy. A healthy economy would produce a *moderate* amount of consumer goods, about the middle-class level for everyone, as well as an abundance of high-quality public goods, so that community, family, friendship, education, and personal growth all flourish.

"Some have called me Mallworld's doctor, and many of you trust my advice. Here is my diagnosis: Mallworld is afflicted with a disease, and that disease is consumerism. Consumerism has destroyed individual health; it has destroyed social norms and decency; it has destroyed human community and fellowship; and it has destroyed the natural world. It makes us consume too much of the wrong things and not enough of the right things. And as your doctor, here is my prescription: moderate your own personal consumption, and devote more time and resources to public goods and public activities. Overcoming consumerism will require a long period of recovery and rehabilitation. We have abused our social body for so long that becoming healthy again will take a long time. Most of this new political movement's agenda goes in the right direction to overcome the disease of consumerism, and there are things that we can do right now to start down a healthy path and provide immediate relief. As your doctor, here are my instructions: Connect with other people. Vote in the COA elections next month! And vote for the movement! It will be good for you!"

The crowd whooped, cheered, and applauded. Dr. Dave smiled and waved again, and as he walked off and Jime returned to the stage, they shook hands; Jime pulled him close and thanked him, complimenting his speech and saying that he appreciated the endorsement, especially from such a trusted figure. Dr. Dave said it was an honor and that he would give his all to this new movement.

Jime stepped back to the podium to give closing remarks, grasping it with both hands, his broad, uplifting smile appearing brilliant on the large holoscreens. He paused and looked across the crowd, reconnecting with his audience. He then spoke with a serious tone appropriate to the weighty topic of politics, aiming at the same time to be positive and uplifting. "I want to thank you all for coming today, for joining us to have a frank and open discussion about the unjust state of things in our society. Dr. Dave just spoke about how consumerism deprives most people of a good and happy life merely so that a few elites can live in the lap of luxury. We believe that is unjust and that we must strive for greater equality. Making this change is a political matter, and it involves changing the systems and structures of our society.

"Consumerism turns the act of consuming into an ideology and a way of life. And it is a destructive way of life. But consumerism is not an unavoidable fact, nor is it the pinnacle of human civilization. It is just a system created by human beings, and a highly dysfunctional one. It is a system that has been imposed upon us, and it is reimposed in our daily lives, continually. Instead of consuming to live, we live to consume. We have forgotten that our lives are for other purposes. But even today, after generations of this lifestyle, consumption still may not be the primary felt purpose of most individuals: you may think of yourself, individually, as primarily a father, mother, teacher, doctor, and so on, and only think of money as a means to your deeper ends. But our *society* has consumerism as its primary purpose and imposes it on everyone, through social structures and economic institutions that make it mandatory. Consumerism is created, re-created, and continually sustained for the purpose of making profits for those who sit in the privileged positions of society. But it is more complicated than that, because we all participate in this system and impose it upon ourselves, too. We are attracted by the goods it offers, the fancy food and drink, the flashy gadgets, the posh homes. Consumerism reaches down deeply into our identities. Consumerism also, in a sense, makes us modern-day serfs or proletarians, caged in the unfulfilling jobs that the system offers and bound by chains of debt in order to pay for it all.

"We perpetuate the system because we have lost the ability to think of something different. We are convinced of its inevitability and goodness by the environment of advertising that surrounds us and promotes it. But really, when you think about it, advertising is just a form of privatized propaganda, using mass media and social media to indoctrinate and mislead us into perceiving the world in a way that works to the advantage of those in power. We are so taken in by it that too many of us shuffle off sickly to early deaths, with an empty, medicated smile on our faces as we succumb to our bodies' own protests against the abuses we heap upon them. We are miserable along the way, whining in our selfish wants. We become entitled and throw tantrums like children when our desires are not immediately met. We are so taken in by consumerism that we consume our own and other people's dignity, and even lives, as we watch human beings die in the lottery. It consumes our lives by wasting them with the pointless, meaningless activity of consumption for the sake of consumption. In the end, consumerism consumes the consumers.

"We believe that a new beginning will be found in measures to stop consuming on autopilot, to make ourselves more aware, and to pay attention to the neglected sectors of our lives, such as our civic life. Our proposals for a monthly Civic Day fair and for regular public holo-announcements are just a start. To help raise awareness, we are offering counter-advertising classes, provided by our volunteers in person and online, free of charge. We encourage you to take them. They examine common advertising techniques and demonstrate how ads manipulate people. Such education is key to understanding advertising and making sure that you aren't fooled by it. That's the first step to getting healthy again.

"In addition to awareness measures, our policies to provide public goods will directly and indirectly improve quality of life and offer alternatives to the privatized consumerist goods that the system floods us with. A brighter sim-sky and a public park with real, natural plants, not plastiflowers, will increase physical, mental, and even social health. Our proposal for subsidized day care will relieve stress on busy parents and help them take better care of their children. And our proposal for higher minimum pay will increase take-home income so that you don't have to get a second job or work as much overtime. The idea is that you will have more time for family, friends, and community, be able to restore a proper work–life balance, and revive physical and mental health. And our proposal for real, enforced workplace safety, which would outright ban Awkwards and similar machines, will prevent some corporate actions that cause harm and death. Lastly, our proposal for workers' councils with veto powers is not only a step toward workplace democracy but will provide another layer of protection to prevent harmful working conditions.

"These early proposals are just first steps in what we foresee as a long journey to our movement's ultimate goal and purpose: ending oligarchy and restoring a democratic republic—indeed, restoring it at a higher level by establishing communitarian, democratic socialism.

"And to promote these policies and this vision is why I am proud to declare today, on behalf of our members, that we are officially a political party. We are a political party that will organize itself to win Condominium Owners Association elections, for that is the route to political power in our society. When we do so win, we will organize in solidarity to pass and implement bylaws and policies that serve the interests of regular, everyday people, not the wealthy few.

"Our members have democratically considered different names for our party, and I am proud today to announce the choice we have made. Our name will be *ReBound*." The word flashed in giant letters above the stage on the holoscreens behind Jime. "Yes, it is spelled just like that, with a capital B in the middle. Through solidarity we will *rebound* from this dark age of oligarchy, with its exploitation and alienation and suffering. But our task isn't just about recovery. We are also going to *bound forward* to a morally higher plane of human society and civilization. Moreover, we are *bound together* in a shared fate, because we all live in the same society and are mutually tied with social bonds."

"All of this *can* be accomplished by us, together. There is no reason to simply perpetuate the system for the system's sake. The system is a creation of our decisions. Therefore, we have the power to change it; and if the system needs to change, then we can and should change it. All of our proposed bylaws are meant to begin restoring health and sanity to our Mall and our society. Like going on a diet or starting an exercise routine, making necessary social change may sometimes be difficult at first, and it takes attention and effort. But the economy can and should be organized to meet the full range of the human needs, physical and mental, of everyone.

"A better future depends on whether we are loyal and good to one another. The only way for the 99 percent to be strong and confident is together, through solidarity, not division. *Together*, we have the strength and common purpose to recover the rights, quality of life, and interconnection we have lost. *Together*, we have the foresight and creativity to progress to a higher stage of human existence, based on healthier, more decent, and more advanced social, economic, and political institutions. *Together*, we can and will make our world a better place. *Together*, we can and will elevate each other's lives. We ask you to rebound with us, and to bound ahead with us." A slogan appeared in holotext on the screens behind the stage: *ReBound. Bound Forward. Bound Together.*

"Thank you again for your time and attention. Please look us up on the holonet, and we hope to see you again in the near future. Thank you, and good night."

The crowd applauded and some people whistled, although they certainly weren't as raucous as at a sporting event. Jime waved at the throng and stepped off the platform.

Christine Kimberly came back into the holopicture. "Well, quite the surprise here at Piazza Plaza, as Dr. Dave comes out in support of what is really a minor, and apparently rather radical, political movement that calls itself ReBound. Will that diminish his standing as Mallworld's most trusted man? Only time will tell. This is Christine Kimberly reporting from Piazza Plaza. Next up: who has the best gourmet cupcakes in the Mall? Specialty bakeries: our food reporter digs up some hidden gems, and also finds the best deal on gelato. Back to the studio, after this commercial break!"

CHAPTER 7:
CITADELS OF DEMOCRACY

ReBound rented space in an empty office building two streets off Piazza Plaza and turned it into a campaign headquarters, using donations that had allowed the movement to make initial investments in campaign infrastructure. The building was decidedly *not* a gleaming corporate tower. It was an older, three-story, gray algaeplast building, but clean and in good repair. The ground floor was originally a medium-sized commercial space with a glass storefront, and ReBound had that floor and the basement to itself. Volunteers set to work fixing it up, knocking down some interior walls and building others to arrange the space in useful ways, creating offices, classrooms, a conference room, and a large lobby that could be used as a common space for a variety of activities. In the basement they built a communication center with donated equipment. Outside the front door, across the street, was a small square or park that could be used for small rallies and such; in its center stood a statue on a pedestal, a mechaniman simulacrum of famed investment guru Julian Coak. Larger events could be held in Piazza Plaza two blocks distant.

Sam and Jime walked through ReBound's new digs. "Having a building of our own makes this all feel so real—like we're established, like we've come into our own," Sam said. "I feel almost like we can do anything!" She grinned, and Jime smiled back.

As they walked Jime took the time to stop and chat with volunteers. Sam was impressed with his ability to connect with people; he had an open, welcoming demeanor and looked you in the eye in an attentive way when he shook your hand. He combined warmth, intelligence, and understanding in a way that uplifted and inspired people. He would be good on the campaign trail, she thought.

In the headquarters lobby, the HV was tuned to the JNN coverage of political issues. The anchor, Charles "Chuck" Anderson, a news reader and commentator who was widely respected among the punditocracy for his moderate centrism, was speaking. Chuck Anderson projected a calm and rational demeanor, despite being someone who allowed others to do his thinking for him. He was the kind of opinion maker whose opinions were conventionally retrograde: rather than believing in the value of foresight, he thought it was actually possible for someone to "be right too soon"— that is, that those with knowledge should wait for the rest of society to catch up to them before they deserved credit for being correct.

Chuck Anderson looked into the camera with his most serious face and puntificated: "What about this young upstart ReBound movement in Northgate, which hopes to challenge, if you will, the sectional Condominium Owners Association Board and its chair, the Executive Dixon Cheton?"

In the lobby, someone said, "Hey! We're on JNN!" and the ReBound volunteers excitedly gathered around the HV.

"Some say it is a radical fringe group. Some say it has no good ideas. Some say it will ruin Northgate's economy. And some say it won't win any seats and will go nowhere. Yet respected physician Dr. Dave has endorsed ReBound. Here to give in-depth analysis of recent events in Northgate is George Buckles, professor of economics at the Bush School of Business, senior fellow at the Chamber of Commerce's Laffer Research Institute, and Jackal News commentator. Impressive credentials, George. Thanks for speaking with us today."

"Thank you for having me, Chuck." Buckles wore horn-rimmed glasses and a bow tie. He fancied himself an intellectual, used the biggest words and most condescending tone he could, and was also a fan of baseball.

"What do you think the prospects are for a ReBound victory?"

"Chuck, looking at the political landscape, I don't think there is any way this radical movement can win a majority of COA seats and the chair, which is what it needs to do to change association bylaws. This group is not a serious group. None of their policies meet the approval of the business community. Neither the Chamber of Commerce nor LoanEx bank have vetted their proposals. Their policies would be a disaster, but I do not believe the people of this section will be so foolish as to vote for them in any great numbers."

"Booo!" Jime yelled out, and the volunteers moaned in frustration at the negative coverage.

"First, the group's proposals would raise taxes, which would stifle business," Buckles said. "Supply-side economics tells us that tax cuts promote business activity, which trickles down to working people in the form of jobs, wages, benefits, more and more consumer goods, and greater revenues. Second, people simply do not want their taxes going to pay for welfare for lazy, undeserving people. And why should they? Why should they pay for those who don't help themselves? They resent that. Welfare creates dependency on government, and therefore puts people under government control, and therefore steals their freedom even as it steals other people's money. These two principles have been the basis of sound economics since the Great Reagan, and are universally adhered to throughout Mallworld. It is politically impossible to go against them. The fact that people want low taxes created a demand for small government that led to the building of the Mall in the first place, entirely free from big government regulation. The Executives who manage Northgate are successful businesspeople, not wasteful bureaucrats, and it's better this way. So ReBound is unrealistic, and no one wants their radicalism.

"Our projections show that the current board will maintain a large majority, and we are officially predicting a victory by the current Executives. It looks like ReBound has to get its act together before it can seriously compete with the big boys in elections. Better luck next time, Dr. Dave and Mr. Jime."

The camera cut back to Chuck Anderson. "There you have it," he declared, matter-of-factly. "ReBound's economics won't work, and who will pay for all of it? Thanks for that cutting-edge analysis, George," he said. "We'll be right back after the break with the latest in Mall Cup football. With a new coach, can Londonshire United repeat? This is the Jackal News Network."

Jime walked up to the HV, hit the "off" button, and turned to look at the volunteers. "I'm sorry, everyone, I . . . I just can't wait to see how good it'll feel to prove these fools wrong!" He smiled and someone whooped and everyone in the room laughed.

"Courage in solidarity!" Sam called out.

"Strength united!" they all shouted back.

+   +   +

"OK, Mr. Galilei, your lease looks to be in order." Jime was sitting in the conference room with a Mall Management lawyer from the Customer Service division, and he was on edge. No one liked to deal with Customer Service—people who crossed them had a tendency to wind up Outside. The man was tall but thin, and he was impeccably groomed and wore a perfectly pressed bespoke Bergendale's silk suit. He had come to inspect the files for the building rental. Sam and Nic were also there, and the lawyer had brought three assistants.

There were also two muscular Mall Security bodyguards, in plainclothes but armed, hovering vigilantly around the fringes of the conference room. When the group of inspectors had arrived Nic pointed out that armed guards weren't necessary, but was told in no uncertain terms that security was absolutely essential when financial matters were discussed. He objected that this was a mundane review of leases, contracts, and utilities; that he had attended many such meetings; and had never seen a police presence at any of them. The lead lawyer pointedly did not respond but jumped right into a rigorous point-by-point review of ReBound's legal paperwork.

They had been there for two hours already but had only gotten through the rental contract.

"Shall we discuss utilities now?" asked Jime.

"Before that, next on the agenda is establishing your business's main purpose," the lawyer said.

"OK, but we are not a business."

"Oh? A chamber of commerce then? A cartel?"

"We are officially registering as a lobby group, class 502c-4bs-12a."

"A 502c-4bs-12a? I'm not familiar with that category."

"We are a nonprofit advocacy group."

"Nonprofit?" The lawyer looked puzzled. "I haven't seen an application for anything like that in . . . I was going to say years, but I don't think ever. Only in law school."

"I'm sure. Here's the form." Jime passed it over, and the lawyer begin reading it.

"Let's see here now," he said. "Er . . . if you're not operating as a for-profit corporation . . . I'm not sure I understand the group's purpose."

"We're an advocacy group for working people, and we're organizing to win COA elections to put representatives of the common people into decision-making positions."

"To then use those positions to make money?"

"No! To represent in the interest of regular working people."

"That's not necessary. The interest of condo owners are represented on COAs. Hence the name: Condo Owners Association."

"Yet many people are renters, whose interests are not formally represented on the boards. And the actual people on COA boards mostly represent the interests of the wealthy and Mall Management, not condo owners themselves."

"Mall Management represents the interests of all of Mallworld shoppers. There are contracts that say so, and a mission statement."

"We do not feel that's how it works in practice. Only the people themselves, or representatives chosen by the people, can speak for their interests."

"COA board members are chosen in elections by people. I see no purpose to your group."

"Almost no one votes in those elections, and one of our purposes is to mobilize them to vote. Another is to organize their representatives to win those elections."

"You said you were a nonprofit advocacy group, but that's not advocacy. Why should Mall Management approve your application?"

"We are advocating that people cast a vote in COA elections. And we are advocating that they vote for us," Jime said.

"Ah, I see." That seem to make sense to the man. One of his aides leaned in and spoke into his ear. The lawyer then said, "That seems to fulfill the definition of organizational purpose as required by the Mallworld, Inc. corporate bylaws." The man electronically stamped the form on the tablet with his thumb.

"Great!" said Jime. He, Sam, and Nic were visibly relieved.

"Now let's talk about utility services." The discussion continued about the details of that for another ninety minutes, as Jime and the group chose different levels of services—water, sewage, electricity, holonet—based on what they were able to pay. For each category there were different packages, with more service the more money you were willing to spend. In all cases, they chose a basic level of service for ReBound.

"Well, that about does it for today. It looks like everything is in order." The lawyer closed his tablet and put it in his pleather bag. "I'll have to take your files back to Customer Service to double-check them, report the group to the Central Office, and file them for our records. You know," he continued, "there are legal servicing companies that offer paperwork processing and administrative services, for a fee of course, so that you don't have to personally sit through long sessions like this one. I highly recommend a company called LawForSale.hnet—I used to work there and know they do good work. Their Platinum and Gold executive packages include full-service paperwork processing. You never see a form, and you get perks like champagne and flower deliveries when, say, a permit or license has been approved."

"Sounds like that's affordable only for wealthy people and corporations," said Sam. "It's quite the advantage," she said sarcastically.

"Oh, indeed it is!" said the lawyer, oblivious. "If it's a question of available means, there are more basic packages that provide helpful services as well."

"No, thanks," said Jime. "We want to handle administrative matters in-house."

"As you wish," the lawyer said. He stood up to leave.

"One more thing," Jime said, and the lawyer turned to look at him. "What did it mean when you said 'report the group to the Central Office'?"

The man paused, then looked Jime in the eye and said, "Well, Mall Central is going to be very interested in any group that tries to put together a coalition to win shareholder elections. They want to avoid any . . . hostile takeovers." He stepped toward the door, even as Jime's eyes went wide.

The lawyer paused, and looked back over his shoulder. "But you knew that, right?"

Then he turned and left, dutifully followed by his Mallcop escorts.

+ + +

On billions of holoscreens an advertisement is projected:

A middle-aged, middle-class couple sit at their kitchen table eating Cake and reading their tablets, which are marked with Significorp insignia. The man, slightly overweight, is dressed in a red LoanEx sweater; the woman, also slightly overweight, in a coral pink blouse prominently labeled "Bergendale's." They are the epitome of decent, hard-working, responsible shoppers.

The wife pulls her store credit card out of her tablet, sets both down, and says to her husband, "Isn't it nice that Harriet got into the Bush School of Business? I'm so proud of her."

"Me too. BSOB," he intones each letter, "the best education money can buy."

"She's all grown up into a confident, beautiful young woman, dear."

"And our little rascal Louis wants to follow his big sister's example!" They both chuckle.

"You know, honey," the woman says, "I keep hearing about this new movement of protestors. They seem to me to be causing a lot of trouble. When I think of them, I worry about our children's future."

"I know. The radicals secretly work their way into free enterprises, interfering with contracts and business operations. Will they worm their way into our schools next?"

"They could be anywhere, darling. They might even be our neighbors!"

"They're do-gooders just making trouble!"

The woman looks directly into the camera, her face filled with worry. "I hope that Harriet and Louis have enough sense to work hard and stay away from the radicals."

The scene cuts to the BSOB logo, and a low voice speaks. "Bush School of Business. We help you make money the old-fashioned way: we *invest* it. Accounting, management, and finance degrees now on sale. First semester half-off. Contact our associates for thirty, forty, and fifty-year academic mortgages. Brought to you by Educorp."

+ + +

There was a consensus around the ReBound headquarters that the group should be more representative and more deliberative than political parties of the past, so they sought out new methods of democratic organization. Sidney, a voracious reader of history and politics, took the initiative to promote an inclusive, thick form of democracy for both ReBound and the wider political system. It was called "deliberative democracy," a practice he had learned about during his research in political theory. It involved deliberative, reflective discussion among citizens. Sid was often frustrated when people didn't think critically, didn't take in the big picture, didn't think about the long term. He wanted to live in a world where good reasoning and well-thought-out principles would win out more often than empty, flashy rhetoric, impulsiveness, shortsightedness, and narrow-mindedness. Promoting more serious deliberation was necessary to bringing that kind of world about. He started talking to people individually about it, then, at Jime's urging, he held several seminars for members to explain deliberative democracy, and put up a video of his presentation on the group's holonet site for everyone's benefit.

Deliberative democracy, Sid explained, involves bringing citizens together to deliberate about proposals, policies, and candidates to help the citizens become better informed about political matters and to refine their opinions through discussion and debate. This would occur in a refereed, structured setting to prevent discourse from descending into contention and vitriol. In such a setting, deliberation would enable people to educate each other through discourse. They would learn to listen to other's needs and perspectives on issues instead of attending only to their own, and they would work together to find common solutions and compromises. Sid described one proposal for something called Deliberation Day by two

O.U.S. scholars,[9] in which people would meet two weeks ahead of an election in local schools and community centers to deliberate, both in small groups and large ones, about proposals put forward by the major political parties. Citizens would begin the day in small groups of fifteen to formulate questions, then move into larger citizen assemblies consisting of hundreds of people from their neighborhood, where political party representatives would be respond to those questions; then the deliberators would return to their small groups to discuss and debate the answers. After a communal lunch, the process would repeat itself in the afternoon. It was expected that the political discussions generated by Deliberation Day would continue around offices, lunchrooms, and dining tables until the election two weeks later. Although Deliberation Day was intended to enhance and deepen citizens' political participation, there was no voting at the end of the day; the deliberative process was only meant to inform citizens' votes in the actual election.[10]

Although Sidney didn't consider himself to be a scintillating speaker in front of crowds, he was proficient at speaking to small groups of people, and his earnest advocacy persuaded many people of the value of incorporating deliberation into the new movement. Sid thought this was important to do at its founding, when practices and norms would be established that would endure for a long time. With his interest and erudition in social and political theory, Sid had many ideas in his head about the best way to organize a society, just as, say, a composer has ideas for a symphony or a carpenter ideas for a beautiful house. Unlike other practitioners of a craft, however, a social theorist can see his or her ideas realized in the world only by persuading others of them. Sid was naturally introverted and knew that while he had some persuasive abilities, they had limits, and he was often quite frustrated when people who were more charismatic, but clearly less intelligent or politically educated, managed to get bad ideas put into practice through the force of charm. He was worried that his advocacy for

9   Bruce Ackerman and James Fishkin, *Deliberation Day* (Yale University Press, 2004).

10   For Sidney's presentation about deliberative democracy, see Appendix 3.

deliberative democracy wouldn't be enough. So he was deeply pleased when, at one monthly meeting, ReBound voted to include a plank for Deliberation Day for Mallworld into its political platform.

ReBound was already putting deliberation into practice by holding structured consultations with members on various issues. Since ReBound had started to grow and now needed to buy space, materials, and some services, one of those issues was funding. A proposal had been made to raise funds through a *political tithe*, where each member would donate 10 percent of their income. A schedule for small groups of members to discuss the question in the classrooms and conference rooms of the new headquarters was made. Each group had a moderator who would adjudicate disputes, maintain fair and open discussion, make sure that no one dominated the floor by talking for too long, and cool tempers if needed. It was also the moderator's job to introduce the question at hand and to present different expert points of view for the deliberators to consider.

One day Sid was acting as moderator for a group in the main conference room. He had already introduced the topic of the tithe and given the preliminary background information, and some of the deliberators were questioning how much money ReBound needed.

Vince Powerly, the mechanic, was there and asked, "How much does it take to organize protests, anyway? Most of it can be done by volunteers online, very inexpensively."

Sid said, "Street politics alone won't do the job, even though protests are sometimes good tactics."

"I don't understand why I should have to pay a certain percentage of my income to ReBound, though," said Palina Newman, the elderly retiree.

"Because the movement can't just be protests and demonstrations. It has to actually take *power* in order to change the Mall's bylaws and regulations and other rules. That's necessary to have social change. Even if change must involve a shift in peoples' opinions and attitudes, it must also involve changes in laws, policies, and institutions."

"OK, I see your point, but so?"

"So you have to be organized, institutionalized. You have to organize a campaign to take political power, or your movement will always remain incomplete and unfulfilled. Basically, you have to do what political parties do. So you have to *be* a political party, one that is of, by, and for the working class."

"So what?"

"Being a political party takes time and resources, which requires volunteers. But they can't do it *all*, so it also requires some money. And it can't all be done online, especially when we're trying to build interpersonal connections. You need a physical infrastructure, so you have to pay rent and utility bills, buy supplies, and so on, even if volunteers are doing most of ReBound's work."

Palina thought about it and nodded. "I see. That makes sense."

Kandy Hattee spoke up. "So why can't you just have an annual fee, like two or three kilocredits or whatever? I work cleaning at resorts, and I'll tell you, I just don't make that much."

"That would hardly be enough, unfortunately! That's maybe what a nice dinner costs."

"That's right! And I can't afford a nice dinner! So being asked to give *10 percent* of a paycheck is out of the question—and every payday? And mandatory?"

Vince shrugged and looked over. "The movement needs it."

Wally Ruthers chimed in. "I still don't understand why. Why does ReBound need so much? Why not just an annual fee?"

Palina said, "The moderator guy explained, it's because the movement of the working class . . . blah blah blah." People laughed.

Sid smiled. "I know, it gets very theoretical and abstract. But the theory is still important to understand: it gives us purpose and helps us keep our direction. So, let me repeat what I said before. The reason that the wealthy control everything is that they have economic power. They control the corporations, so they make lots of surplus money, which historically has allowed them to control, or at least have predominant influence over, society's other major institutions. They own the banks, financial funds, and stock markets. They sit on the boards of the large corporations, directly running them. They exert control over cultural institutions, since they own the media, fund the universities, pay for scientific research, patronize the arts, and so on. Most importantly, they pay a lot of money to lobby politicians, most of whom are members of the wealthy elite themselves; and the upper class has long funded political campaigns, and they funded the political parties too, when those still existed."

"Wasn't there a democratic party?" Wally asked.

"Yes, but because it didn't have something like a tithe to provide it with its own economic resources, it eventually got bought off and co-opted, so that on economic issues it stopped representing regular working people and instead promoted the interests of the wealthy almost as much as the pro-oligarchy party did. It still often tried to improve the fortunes of minorities, women, and other marginalized people, but in a limited way, mostly by making sure some of them could try to climb up the ladder of wealth, rather than by knocking that ladder down and building a society of people living in equal circumstances."

"Ok, we get that, but with the rich taking all of the money, we don't have much left to give to causes," said Kandy. "Yet you want to take more."

"Our democratic, anti-oligarchy movement needs an independent economic base," said Sid. "Working peoples' parties in the past got co-opted because they took rich people's money to fund themselves, and they became dependent on those donors. This also happened to civil society organizations—issue groups, associations, charities, environmental groups, and so on. In the end they couldn't bring about real change, at least on economic and class issues, because of their dependence on wealthy and corporate donors. Communitarianism didn't lead to systemic change because it didn't have an economic base. And protest movements couldn't achieve real change because they didn't have much money or organization at all. Social identity movements, street politics, party politics, at least when there was no labor party—none of these displaced the oligarchy. They didn't have a large enough source of economic funding that they could draw on for the activities, actions, resources, and organizing needed to win and exercise political power as representatives of working people. Thus no one could end exploitation of labor by putting economic democracy into place.

"So you have to find an economic source for the movement, one that makes ReBound *independent of the wealthy* and *dependent on the common people.* We aren't going to be able to start our own corporations or fund ourselves on the stock market; we don't have the startup capital to even begin to do that, and that would just turn us into the capitalists that we're opposing. We already rely on donations, but that's not enough to actually beat the wealthy and fulfill our mission. So the leadership committee came up with the idea of tithing, or members giving a mandatory 10 percent of their income to ReBound, like religions used to. Why? First, it would give us the minimum amount of money needed to be effective. Second, all the funding will come from working people. The proposal includes the stipulation that tithes will be the *only* source of income for the organization. Once those are coming in, we won't even accept donations that members might offer over and above the 10 percent, because we want support for the group to be equal; we don't want even a hint of unequal monetary influence. Tithing is a way of planting our economic roots in the people, so that we will never be bought off by the wealthy elite.

"So the leadership committee has put tithing before ReBound for its consideration, and now we're talking about it using the deliberative democracy principle. That way we can all discuss it and think about it before voting on it in a few weeks."

"Why aren't donations enough?" Kandy asked. "We could just make tithing voluntary—like a goal to shoot for. Everybody give what they can, but try to give 10 percent. It would be a standard, a goal, an ethical norm, but informal, not a requirement. Why wouldn't that work?"

Palina looked over and answered. "Because of the free rider problem. If it's voluntary, most people will tend to be partial to themselves and not give what they actually can, because they'll think that someone else will cover it. Or they'll think that their own contribution is so small that it doesn't matter if they give less, or nothing at all."

"Okay, but what I'm worried about is that poorer volunteers really won't be able to afford it." People thought about that silently for a moment.

"It's like a flat tax," Wally added.

"Yeah right, good point," said Palina.

"Well, it's not a tax," said Vince.

"I know, but if you want to be part of the group, it's mandatory. And it's like the 15 percent flat tax idea that libertarians always seem to love. It's unequal."

"Whaddya mean unequal? It's the same percent of income for everybody!"

"Because of what economists call the 'diminishing marginal utility of income,'" explained Wally. "Basically, every dollar is more valuable to a poor person than to a middle-class person, and more valuable to a middle-class person than to a rich one, because they have fewer of them. When you're poor and you get some money, you first spend it on the basics of life—food, shelter, clothes. If you have a lower-middle-class income, then you might have some money over and above those basics to buy things that are optional, strictly speaking, like HV, or movies, or healthier food. Upper-middle-class people have that plus some luxuries like nicer clothes, bigger condos, and vacations. Rich people have all their needs and desires met easily, and they have money to spare.

"So if you take a 15 percent tax from a poor working saley you might be taking money they would've spent on health care or transit to work, things of relatively high value in life. Take 15 percent from an office associate and you're not taking anything strictly necessary, but it might be from their kid's college fund or their own retirement account. Take it from a rich person and it won't impact their lifestyle at all. The 15 percent flat tax is equal in *number*, but not equal in its *effect* on people with different incomes. Same holds for a 10 percent tithe."

Vince said, "If money is rarer and more valuable to poorer people, maybe they shouldn't be required to tithe at all." Other people nodded their heads at this.

"What about tithing by a sliding scale according to income?" Kandy proposed. Others thought that would be a good idea, and they agreed that to be truly equal in reality, tithes and taxes had to be progressive, meaning higher rates for those with higher incomes and wealth. The group then spent time discussing accountability in the spending of the money, with everyone insisting that good practices of monitoring and evaluating the movement's books were essential.

The debate continued until Sid announced that the time allotted for discussion was up. Before the volunteers left, he administered a brief post-deliberation review to assess how valuable the deliberation had been to them, if at all. This was done with an anonymous survey, which asked multiple-choice questions about the quality of the discussion and left room for comments. These were some of the statements:

"I thought the deliberation was good—it wasn't just yelling and screaming, but a useful discussion. The moderator did a good job."

"I learned a lot about the tithe that I didn't know before."

"This will definitely affect my vote."

"I didn't like the discussion. It took too long and was boring."

"I felt a real connection to everyone in the group. I learned how important it is for a political party that tries to protect the people to have a good amount of funding."

"It made me feel like ReBound cares about my opinion."

"We really need a reliable source of funds not controlled by corporations. This is good."

"We liked the tithing idea, but with some changes—hopefully they will be considered."

A few weeks later the tithe passed, in modified form: the poorest volunteers, those who made below one-third of average Mallworld income, were exempt from the tithe, and a sliding scale ranging from 3 to 12 percent based on income was adopted for the rest. Exemptions were also included for those who fell on hard times or had extraordinary expenses in a given month, and the tithe was to be mandatory for only nine of every twelve months. These changes came out of the deliberation sessions ReBound had held, which had been put onto the ballot as variations on the original proposal. The tithe would help ensure that ReBound would represent the common people and not the elite, since it was funded by the former, not the latter. Furthermore, it could invest in their growing numbers of volunteers and their political activities, making use of their collective skills and networks in order to remain a people-based movement.

Soon, as ReBound started raising funds from the tithe, they were able to conduct a major recruitment drive: they expanded their presence on the holonet, paid for thousands of holo-flyers for canvassing, and funded a spray-poster campaign on the date that was once called Labor Day to celebrate the dignity of working people. They plastered their three principles of "Justice at Work, Better Quality of Life, and a Stronger Civic Sphere" everywhere and were able to introduce the idea of the active political life to more people as they drew increasing numbers of volunteers. It was ground-up, democratic cooperation aimed at connecting with each other and with as many other people as they could.

CHAPTER 8:
VALIANT CAMPAIGN

I t was a week until the Northgate board elections, and Jime felt electricity in the air. He and Sam were returning from meeting a labor group about union organizing, and as they entered ReBound's headquarters they stopped short at what they saw—a multitude of volunteers doing the work of politics: making phone calls, sending h-mail, chatting online, organizing postering teams, printing holo-flyers, and planning the next rally. They walked through the lobby, down the hallway of classrooms and offices, past the conference room, and then down the stairs and through the phone bank and communications center, tarrying as they went to observe the activities that their colleagues and fellow citizens were undertaking. All around them were people who had long been waiting for a group to act on their many problems and who had joined up to do their part. Regular people—homemakers, electricians, teachers, salespeople, secretaries, students—were getting political because they wanted to make the world a better place. All it had taken to inspire them was a little leadership from people who shared their hopes and fears.

As they walked, Sam said, "We've got really dedicated volunteers, who are making good arguments to the public and giving people real hope and direction. That kind of leadership is needed to inspire and mobilize people." Her words were optimistic, but she was concerned as well. "Jime, I'm worried that it won't be enough. We're not going to get enough votes to win a majority of seats on the board, are we? We're so new, how could we?"

"I'm entirely confident that we will, actually. And even if we don't, we'll win some seats and build an opposition presence that *can* one day become a majority. We may have to lose before we can win. We've also built an activist base and campaign movement to push for future change. We have many reasons for optimism and confidence. We're offering new ideas and consequently mobilizing large numbers of people. We have a positive vision that will carry us through. And we will get at least *some* of what we want, which will give us momentum in the future. Don't worry too much, Sam. If we stick to our purpose, we *will* get there. If not this election, then in the future."

She felt buoyed by him and reached out to take his hand. Surprise flashed across his face. Then he smiled.

+   +   +

"This is Christine Kimberly with JNN. For the first time in decades, the incumbents on the Condo Association Board in Northgate are facing a competitive election. The insurgent ReBound movement is campaigning hard and holding rallies across the section on a platform of republican, communitarian, democratic socialist reform. It is calling for justice in the workplace, a renewed civic culture, and a better quality of life for all. ReBound is proposing higher worker's compensation, a ban on Awkwards and other workplace dangers, programs for health care and day care, and a large public park stocked with real plants. Here at JNN, we wanted to know how many people support ReBound, so we hired a commercial polling firm that surveys shoppers' brand preferences to assess the popular opinion of the ReBound 'brand.' They found that 87 percent of Northgate shoppers have heard of ReBound, and that a surprisingly high 47 percent say they will, quote, 'buy the ReBound brand on election day.' What does the current COA board think of all this? With me tonight is Dick Cheton, chair of the Northgate association. Welcome, Mr. Cheton."

"Thank you, Christine, good to be here." Cheton's words, while technically polite, were taut and curt. His shoulders were tense, and his face was a pasty frown, as if he was irked or in pain. Watching him, you suspected he might scold the reporter. He certainly wasn't going to approve of anything she said.

"ReBound is pushing a long list of changes to deal with what they say are many problems that have built up over the years. What are *your* plans to deal with these issues?"

"Christine, we think the current Management of Mallworld, Inc. has done a very good job of creating a good customer experience. Mallworld shoppers in general are satisfied with the direction of the Mall: economic growth is strong, the Mall Street average is up, and there are goods and entertainment galore. Of course, there are some things we need to improve—we need to get shoppers more health options and a better childcare experience, and we are working on that. Shoppers can always take their complaints to Customer Service at Mall Central, which I think lives up to its motto, 'We make problems disappear.'

"I think those who don't recognize how good we have it in the Mall are really being unpatriotic. Some people just complain for the sake of complaining. But the danger is that they will get into positions of authority and make all the bad decisions that they're promising to make. With no experience running a business, they will take away the good things that real Mallworld shoppers have. Do we want to risk that? I think it's better to have experienced adults on the Northgate board who can manage things well."

Christine Kimberly pressed him further. "All that may be so, but the popularity of ReBound's proposals suggests that Customer Service isn't keeping pace with people's problems. Why *shouldn't* we make the changes that ReBound is proposing to make? Aren't they right that there's too much inequality, too much injustice?"

"Christine, too many changes that come too quickly cause all kinds of chaos and dysfunction. You can't make all these reforms all at once. As association chair, I have a responsibility to uphold law and order. What we need is a good business climate so corporations can continue to create jobs and shopping and spectas. We don't need radicals coming in from outside with crazy ideas, who don't respect success, who don't know what real Mallworlders want, who take money from hard-working Mallworlders for social programs. ReBound isn't like us. If you let them run Northgate, all you will see will be empty shelves, unemployment, and crime."

"Mr. Cheton, would you be willing to come on the air and discuss your differences with Jime Galilei face-to-face?"

"Yes, Christine, I welcome the chance to debate these issues for your viewers."

"Thank you. That was Dixon Cheton, chairman of the board for the Northgate COA. Up next: what's the most successful security system for your home? Chuck Anderson compares the top products in burglary prevention."

As the segment ended, a man who had been watching the interview at a bar took a mug handed to him by the mechanibarman, swiped his card to open its lid, and took a long pull. He set the mug down, wiped foam from his lips, and scoffed, "Y'know, sometimes I can't believe what I see. It just makes no sense. How do those loudmouth protestors think they're gonna improve things? By having a love-in? Yay, let's all dance and sing kumbaya! What good's that gonna do?" He shook his head. "What shoppers need are jobs. But no one ever thinks of that." He took another drink from his mug.

He was talking to no one in particular, as he was sitting by himself, although there were plenty of other people around him. One of them was David Sall, seated a few barstools down, taking a break after a long afternoon of canvassing. He looked over and said, "I guess you don't like this new ReBound movement, then."

"No way! Buncha hippies who want to take money from shoppers who earn it and give it to lazy fuckers, y'know? Outta love or whatever. Better to stick with who we've got."

"I didn't know they were hippies, I thought they're just regular people. People sick of the rich taking as profits the money earned by working people."

The man scoffed. "Yeah, right. It's like Dick Cheton says, ReBound doesn't know how to run anything or make more jobs."

David extended his hand and introduced himself. The other man's name was Patrick Sygaard, and he had recently been laid off from his job as an accounts processing specialist.

"See, that's the thing," said Pat, "the economy is tough, we can't afford to just give people stuff! Everybody's gotta get ahead on their own. But no one ever thinks of that, I tell ya. You gotta man up. Be tough in tough times. You'll learn this as you get older."

"Isn't the economy always tough, though?" David asked. "Because the rich have corrupted everything and channel all the profits their way. It's tough for most of us because it's unequal. If we made things more equal and had policies that benefit middle-class and poor people, then things wouldn't be tough. They'd be easy, in fact."

"That's BS. If you start taxing and regulating the wealthy, they'll stop creating jobs. But no one ever thinks of that."

"Then why should we let the wealthy be in control of creating jobs? Why shouldn't we do that ourselves?" David asked, with genuine curiosity. "Let's run all our corporations democratically rather than let a tiny minority of the filthy rich own and control them. That way we can stop them from taking unearned millions for themselves and from sending our jobs to other sections whenever it makes money for *them*. With economic democracy, we can hold them accountable."

Pat Sygaard thought about that for a minute. He sipped his beer.

"Let's have the workers of each company vote for their management," David continued, his words filled with youthful enthusiasm. "That way we can make the economy work for the many, not the few. What workers will vote for Managers and Executives who are gonna fire them, or ship their jobs somewhere else? If management is accountable to us they will have to keep people working. Let the workers be in control, and a lot of our problems would be solved, or at least get better."

Pat stared at David. After a moment he shook his head in astonishment, as if he were talking to a child in a grown man's body. "You live in a fantasy land, young man. That will never happen."

"No, I'm serious. It's true that if we *try* to change things, we may fail. But we may also succeed. If we don't try, then we'll fail for sure."

Pat turned back to his beer. He took a sip, and then turned to David and raised the glass to him. "Good luck to the hippies," he said.

"Thanks," said David. "Here's my holocard. It lists my h-mail address and our holonet site—maybe we can help you find a job. I really mean it."

+ + +

On billions of holoscreens an advertisement is projected:

A beautiful woman in an haute couture dress and elegant jewelry sits in the marbled lobby of an upscale condominium building, sipping a spritzer while lounging on a designer sofa. A muscular young man, ruggedly handsome but disheveled, walks through the glass entry doors, carrying moving boxes. He is dressed in a white T-shirt and off-white worker's trousers, both grubby and threadbare. He flashes the woman a smile, but she looks away, her slight frown suggesting contempt.

A deep-voiced announcer says, "Some say the clothes make the man. At Lyceum, we go more than skin deep."

Up in his new opulent condo, furniture disarranged and moving boxes everywhere, the man looks at himself in a full-length mirror, hand scratching his chin thoughtfully. He walks over to the bed, picks up a garment bag labeled "Lyceum Habit and Accessories," and smiles. The narrator says, "In some circles appearance is important, but assumptions don't always reflect the man."

The handsome man soon strides into the lobby adorned in a stylish black suit, red tie, and green pocket square, his attire a flag signaling who he is. He approaches the woman and once again flashes her a smile. Her eyes widen in surprise, and she looks down with an embarrassed grin, shaking her head at her own foolishness. She looks up at him longingly and invites him to sit. The narrator asks, "Why did you assume who he was?" The Lyceum logo appears on the screen with the words, "Assumptions can be misleading."

+ + +

"This is Chuck Anderson with JNN at Piazza Plaza, where several weeks ago we reported on a rally of the new political movement ReBound, attended by several thousand people. Mallworld's most trusted physician, Dr. Davis North, spoke then, and after going viral on social media and by word of mouth, the radical movement appears to have tapped into long-hidden discontent about the economy. The group has organized door-to-door canvassers and set up tables in squares and markets across the section in order to talk to shoppers face-to-face about their problems and frustrations. They've called this a 'listening tour,' in which they say they're trying to understand people's experiences and needs, and listen to their ideas for how to fix them. The group also has ideas of its own. People seem excited by the promises this new group is making for political and economic reforms, which they say are better than the wealth and prosperity we currently have. Critics say these are dubious claims and utopian fantasies. Today, with a week to go before the election, ReBound has filled Piazza Plaza and other squares across Northgate for a major demonstration." The camera panned across the crowd, showing an enthusiastic but well-ordered audience attending intently to the proceedings. Many held homemade signs constructed with thought and care; the most common slogan was "This Is What Democracy Looks Like." Chuck Anderson continued:

"Right now, the crowd is quietly listening to the words of the ReBound leader. Jime has already spoken about ReBound's principles of fairness at work and better quality of life, and he is now discussing the public sector. Let's listen in."

Jime stood on a stage in the plaza, with both hands, as usual, gripping the lectern in front of him. He was already speaking, in his characteristic tone of optimistic sincerity: ". . . The ancient philosopher Aristotle said that human beings are social animals, and he was right. Our society has told us for a long time that we are just individuals. It has held up as our ideal of freedom the independent, self-interested individual who, deep down, thinks he doesn't need the rest of society. The pioneer cowboy, the action hero, the sports star, the entrepreneur tycoon—they are all examples of this figment of strength and confidence. This mythical individual hero is taken for granted as admirable, and those who seem to live up to this ideal are rewarded. We have a long tradition of respect for the rights of the individual. That tradition needs to be valued, and this movement does value it: freedom and rights of the individual are important political principles that must be honored, and we all rightly assert individualism against authoritarianism and conformity. But the question of whether the individual or society has primacy is not an either–or proposition, not a matter of conflict between the two, because while we are individuals, we are *social* individuals. Individuals are born into a society, learn from it, and are shaped by it. From society we learn our language, our culture, our skills, our habits of thought; from it we gain our knowledge, our decency, our morality, our identity. We owe society much. Furthermore, without the help of others, we limited, flawed humans cannot find happiness, achieve our life-plans, or even survive. It takes real strength to admit our imperfections and limits, to admit that none of us can do it alone. None of us truly lives up to the heroic independence of a holovision action star.

"And that's why ReBound advocates for stronger communities and public deliberation; for workplace democracy and a higher minimum wage; for public health care, day care, and pensions. We must understand that we are not independent but are *inter*dependent. Even the most confident person depends on others in society to provide him with food, clothes, shelter, and all the other good things of life, and even the most successful capitalist depends on others to work for her profit. Thus we are interdependent materially. We also have emotional needs for relationships with other people, and we are uplifted by our connections with them and find satisfaction from their affirmation. Thus we are interdependent psychologically. While suppressing the individual leads to authoritarianism or totalitarianism, it is also the case that suppressing our mutual social connections leads to alienation, isolation, loneliness, and all sorts of social ills. The individualist ideal is a fiction. We are not isolated individuals; we are social beings. Our society should recognize this and foster neither excessive independence nor excessive dependence, but healthy, mutual *inter*dependence.

"We are interdependent because we are interconnected. I'm not talking about some mystical, spiritual sense of interconnection in which all things are imagined to be a transcendental unity—a benevolent oneness that somehow attends to and cares for us all. You can believe that if you want, of course, but in my opinion, that is rather sentimentalist. While we do need to restore our connections to the natural world, the universe can actually be a cold and indifferent place: things interact and affect each other, but that doesn't mean nature won't hit you with a falling boulder and kill you. When I say interconnection, I'm talking about the fact of our *social* and *material* interconnection: we live together, sharing a culture and an economy, and therefore we affect one another. The main social problem with Mallworld is that it doesn't *acknowledge* and *value* our interconnectedness. It isolates us socially and makes us compete against each other economically. In so doing, it makes life as uncertain as a lottery game show rather than making life more predictable and secure, the way that mutual social connections and support should. Furthermore, our disconnected worldview too often makes us think of other people *instrumentally,* as only means or tools to be used to satisfy our wants. In contrast, ReBound wants to promote an *ethic of interconnection* that makes us think and act differently toward our fellow human beings, other animals, and even the natural environment. This ethic of interconnection requires a *recognition* of each other, in thought and in action, that overcomes alienation and encourages us to *exalt* one another rather than exploit one another.

"To be sure, not all interconnections, not all loyalties, are of the same kind or strength. People obviously feel more connected to those who are closer to them. The way I think of it is that we are social beings inside nested circles of interconnection and identity. We have a small circle of close family and friends; then wider circles of neighbors, coworkers, and acquaintances; then wider-still circles of our corporations and municipal sections; then the widest circle of Mallworldian society as a whole. Different people will have different sets of circles, and they overlap and interpenetrate, depending on relationships, social and economic roles, and other factors.

"Only the smallest point in these circles involves our private, individual selves alone; most of our concerns and interests are inescapably social. We are embedded within the larger circles that help shape and sustain us and that affect us continuously. These circles overlap and intertwine in complex ways, helping to determine how things go for us—and we must *never* make the mistake of thinking that only the closest circles affect us, because the big political circles deeply and profoundly shape our lives too. We are, and ought to be, by right, fully empowered members, with a fully equal measure of decision-making authority, in *all* of these circles.

"We in ReBound believe that we should have social and political structures that, as their first principle and primary purpose, acknowledge, value, promote, and sustain healthy social interconnection, both materially and psychologically. Yet that is not our current situation. The Mall privatizes everything, leaving only the illusion of interconnection. It eliminates public things and treats everything as if it belongs to the sphere of the personal, until we have lost to privatization all sense, and all reality, of a shared public life. We have no shared spaces or institutions truly held in common. We only have privatized versions of the long-lost public sphere that attempt to substitute for it, but which are just poor imitations. Instead of main streets and public squares, we have market bazaars that are owned by the Executives and policed by Mallcops. Instead of public schools, we have Educorp charter schools. Instead of healthy public discourse, we have shallow, impulsive, uninformed, and unprincipled punditry, propagated by Specta and other media companies out to maximize profit. Instead of public elections with 'one person, one vote,' we have condo association election with political status based on property. These things appear *on the surface* to be public, because people can go to bazaars and schools if they can afford to, and many people may have a nominal permission to vote. But that public countenance is an illusion, because they are all *private property*, not public property, and therefore the public does not have democratic decision-making power over them. Privatized institutions are mere simulations of public things. These facsimiles can appeal to our *feelings* of interconnection, our nostalgia for less alienating times, our deep desires to belong. But they are, in the end, simulations that deceptively give the appearance, but not the reality, of deep social bonds and a shared civic life, in order to sustain a system of privatized profit that sets us against one another and exploits us. As deceptions, they deny a critical and necessary part of human life because they fail to acknowledge our social interconnectedness. Privatization and market competition kill our civic spirit, our sense of common connection with one another.

"ReBound aims to make manifest our interconnectedness through a vision of joint ethical and political action that aspires to the mutual *coexaltation* of all human beings. By that I mean we must make the goal of all our social interactions to have *good and healthy* relations with others. We must lift each other up rather than tear each other down—help each other grow into our best selves while recognizing that we are all on this great journey of life together. Our social relations should be aimed at mutual elevation rather than domination or exploitation, at interconnection not instrumentalism, so that each and every person can develop their individual genius and social talents. If we focus on mutual uplift, we can all achieve our human potential. We want to restore a 'middle-class' society of strong communities and social bonds, where individuals have the leisure, and therefore the freedom, to pursue their dreams and become who they are meant to be. A society where regular people are active in politics and society and therefore democratically control their lives, where their material needs are met as a guarantee by right, where they have reestablished political trust and feel safe, secure, respected, and validated. That requires strong political and economic democracy, strong communities, and strong social provisions like free public health care and free public education at all levels.

"We hope to gather people in an organized movement that brings us together in a common effort, an effort to define and improve our lives for ourselves. In doing so we will rebuild a shared social spirit and identity, restore our public life, and create conditions for the happiness of all. Such solidarity is our only hope for rebounding from the crisis of alienation that has afflicted capitalist society for centuries. We will ReBound from inequality's dark emptiness and build a society that serves the interest of all.

"We are not utopians. No human society can ever be perfect, for humans are imperfect, limited, and mortal. No society will bring an end to all argument and conflict, to all pain and fear, to all disease and injury, or to death and the mourning of loss. Yet we know from history that some societies are organized to permit the few to dominate, exploit, and oppress the many, while some societies are organized to allow the many to govern themselves responsibly and to flourish. We believe that there is a path to that better world. And we believe that we can build that world together, and build it solidly and well. With modern technology we can create an egalitarian, free society where the material needs of *everyone* are met, where *everyone* is able to develop their personal talents and creative abilities, and where healthy social bonds flourish.

"When we come to power, we will pass laws to ensure there is full, thick political democracy, and that all the corporations are run democratically too, with workers voting for their management and deliberating about their own pay, benefits, hours of work, and working conditions. Education and medicine will be free of charge and available to all, and generous public programs will be available to care for the poor, the unemployed, the disabled, and the elderly—as the best societies of the past once had. Civic institutions will be built, from public squares, museums, and meeting houses to playgrounds, schools, and hospitals. And policies will be put in place to encourage genuine local communities to grow. You can read more about our platform and plans for change on our holonet site.

"We believe that a better way of living is possible, but we also believe that you can start living better right now. ReBound is already building a more interconnected world, starting within our party, by lifting each other up. We are a different political party from those of the past, which only sought political office. We have an interconnective political philosophy and think of ourselves as an 'interconnective party.' When a libertarian government won't provide needed social services, the political opposition must organize to do so as best they can. ReBound volunteers are building interpersonal networks to meet each others' needs and promote stronger connections. We offer our time and effort to help each other with child care, home repair, assistance to the elderly and disabled, and more. If you join us, we will help you, too. We can help you become the person you most want to be, through creative writing workshops, music lessons, support to overcome addiction, and other kinds of self-improvement. We can help you overcome procrastination, face fear, and achieve your goals and dreams. Your natural talents and abilities *want* to be expressed, and we will help you realize them. We will encourage you, lift you up when you fall, and cheer you on when you succeed. We will help you when you need it. And thus we will reconnect.

"The Mall only offers us a passive life of shopping and spectas, of bread and circuses. It is unfortunately the case that people with apathetic habits in their personal lives, whose only behavior is passive consumption, generally don't make good democratic citizens who can keep the wealthy and powerful in check. The wealthy know this, and they *want* to keep us fat and happy and politically passive so we'll keep working for them without question, like sheep being led to the slaughter. People are *made* into passive characters by an oligarchy that benefits from having a herd to exploit. The Mall passivizes and pacifies us with entertainment and consumerism so that we will work for the profit of others.

"Democracy is the wielding of power by us, the people, for our own good governance. A society full of passive people who do not actively participate in their own governance is not a democracy, not even if it calls itself one and follows the empty forms of elections. An election in which too few people bother to vote is not a real election, and unfortunately, that is what we have now. I believe that that is the abdication of freedom. Democracy is not just about personal freedom. Freedom is not merely the ability to buy or sell without restriction, nor is it the opportunity to attend whatever specta one wants. Freedom is not merely the individual exercise of choice in consumption. Because we all live together, share our space, and bump into each other in our lives, we need to have common rules. And to protect freedom for all, we need to have fair enforcement of those rules. Since we are social beings, freedom entails participating in making the rules by which we will live, mutually, together with others. And we only have a *full* measure of freedom when we *fully* participate in making those rules. Having the right to do so and not exercising that right is freedom on paper only, not freedom in practice—that is, it is not freedom actualized in reality, and it is therefore not freedom at all. If we aren't actively helping to make the rules, then someone else will make them for us, and they are likely to make them against us. And that is the very definition of tyranny.

"We can help you improve your life—but the deal is that you must be an active citizen, because that's the only way democracy works. Freedom for the common people only comes through equality, solidarity, and democratic socialism. I believe that democracy is a joint project, and that means we have duties to one another. I remarked before how our society sets up the fictions of the cowboy, the action star, the athlete, and the tycoon as our models of strength. To my mind, the real hero is the active *citizen* who accepts the responsibilities of public service by volunteering, has the courage to speak their point of view to others, invests the time and energy to become informed about issues, possesses the self-discipline to avoid impulsive choices, has the judgment and open-mindedness to make wise decisions, stands resolutely for good principles, and has the backbone to vote their conscience. It is through the exercise of *duty* that we gain strength and purpose. Democracy, the *rule* of the people, demands an active and engaged public, and being the best citizen you can be is your democratic duty. It is an honorable one, and we praise you if you choose it.

"ReBound is actually making moral demands of you: demands to vote, demands to vote with knowledge and awareness, and demands to be an active part of the movement, as much as your circumstances allow. ReBound is not a service industry. We are not here to do it *for* you, as if you are merely a political consumer and we are merely political salespeople. Instead, we are calling you to *active* citizenship. That is a very different thing. We are calling you to *service*, to a higher goal than mere pleasure. We are calling you to take your attention and effort out of your private life, at least sometimes, and give it to society. There is no other way forward.

"In contrast to consumerism, we offer you the interconnection, purpose, confidence, and fulfillment that come from an active existence, through that path of public service and citizenship. For it is in service to causes greater than ourselves, in particular the great cause of society, that we restore the mutual interconnection that we have lost and so recover meaning in our lives. In our time, here and now, that means service to a democratic movement that opposes an alienation-creating oligarchy. In our time, here and now, democratic socialism is the means to freedom.

"You might think that next week's board elections aren't important, but they are. Although I've criticized our current elections for being based on property and wealth, Condo Owners Associations make major decisions that affect us all. The COA board is where decisions about rents and mortgages are made, about how much light and water we get, whether we have parks or not, what gets repaired and what doesn't, who can build what and where, what the quality of our schools is. These days condo boards implement the Mall regulations for local business, so they help determine how long we work, what our pay scale is, whether Awkwards are permitted or not. If we are to take the first steps to a new and better world together, those steps will be taken there. *You*—regular, common people—deserve to control your section board, and you can do it by having your own representatives on it as a majority. ReBound is your way to do that. Our movement is your movement; we are you.

"We thank you for listening. We are humbled by the attention you have given us, and we are grateful for it. We now ask you not just to listen, but to act. We invite you to join ReBound, for a better life. Please vote for ReBound in the Condo Owners Association elections next week. Some say we define ourselves in *opposition* to an outside Other. And it is true, we can define ourselves that way. But I say we define ourselves best when we define ourselves in terms of our *connection* to each other. *Bound together*, we will *bound forward*, to a better, more democratic world."

+   +   +

In the weeks that followed, ReBound executed in a full-blown political campaign the likes of which Northgate hadn't seen since before the Mall was built, when it was still Milwaukee. ReBound spray-posters appeared virtually everywhere, and many supporters put them up in their condo windows. Canvassers blanketed the section. Jime, Sam, Nic, and even Sid gave talks at local schools, clubhouses, and private homes, and they made holonet videos explaining ReBound's vision. Sid enjoyed the latter so much that he decided to start a regular holocast to discuss political ideas. Meanwhile, the other three did interviews on local media. Small rallies were held in markets and bazaars across Northgate. All of this got ReBound's name out and spread their message.

One day Jime walked up to a rally where he was supposed to meet Sam. It was at an old, decrepit library and community center across from an abandoned strip mall that was about to be razed. The crowd was loud and excited, cheering and shouting at intervals. As Jime approached he could hear Dr. Dave from the stage: "Let me tell you why you should vote for ReBound in next week's election," intoned his deep and sonorous voice. "Because it'll be good for you! Healthy in a psychological sense. Psychologists say we have less stress when we take responsibility for the course of our lives. Don't you want to feel in control of your own life? To be self-actualizing? To make decisions for yourself? Of course you do. But remember, it's not just about *you*, because *political* decisions affect how your life goes too, and that's why it's important to get political . . ." Jime thought that was a great message and that Dr. Dave was the perfect person to deliver it. He had become indispensable to the movement.

Jime heard Sam yell "Over here!" and saw her waving at him. Sid was with her but was reading something on his phone. Jime worked his way through the throng to them and asked, "How's it going?" and just at that moment the crowd erupted in cheers and drowned him out.

"What?" Sam yelled, cupping her ear.

"How's it going?' Jime yelled back.

"Great! The rally's going great!" she yelled. "I've been to five rallies in five days, and every one of them was as enthusiastic as this one."

"Really? So people are getting this excited everywhere?"

"Yes!" Sam yelled. "People are into our message!"

Charmed by her spirit, Jime gave her a huge smile.

Sid stepped in and interrupted. "Hey Jime, have you heard about the JNN survey?" He held up his phone's screen.

Jime sighed, turned to look at him, and said that he hadn't.

"It's not good. We've dropped to 42 percent in the latest poll."

Jime and Sam both grimaced. Just then the crowd cheered. "Only 42 percent?" Jime exclaimed. "What happened? We were doing so well!"

"The Executives started a new advertising campaign a few days ago," said Sid. "I think it might be having an effect."

+ + +

On billions of holoscreens an advertisement is projected:

A portly middle-aged man in a golf shirt and cardigan is standing in a SuperShop convenience store. Evidence of a break-in is all around: shelves tipped over, packages of Cake and other food products strewn about, graffiti on the walls, a saley in an apron sweeping up broken glass.

The man looks into the camera solemnly. "They ransacked my store. *My* store, my life's work. Low-life elements, probably Outsiders and their friends, broke in, took hard-earned credits from the till, and vandalized everything. They didn't even take any goods—they just trashed it all. What kind of animals do such a thing?"

A saley walks up and says, "I think this belonged to your daughter, sir," and hands her boss a teddy bear, its arm torn off and one eye missing.

"Thank you," the capitalist sighs as he takes it. "You know, I've been hearing about people demanding change in Northgate—some say it would be better to share the wealth, to take from hard-working shoppers who earn their pay and give it to those who don't. Some say it would be better to let just anybody be in charge. But I say that wouldn't be fair to real Mallworlders, the hard workers, the forgotten shoppers, who want to keep what they've earned."

Dixon Cheton walks into view, wearing a golf shirt and cardigan too, but also a cowboy hat, and shakes the owner's hand. "You know, I couldn't agree more. We need to maintain law and order to prevent property crime. Anarchy doesn't just disturb peace and quiet; it costs jobs. Socialists don't know how to uphold the law—they aren't respecters of property. Good order makes a good climate for business and for jobs. As your board chair,

I have the strength to keep the peace." Cheton looks around the store and puts his arm around the owner's shoulder. "We *must* prevent a future like this."

"Thanks, Dick," the shopkeeper says with a smile and a thumb's up.

Cheton looks into the camera and says, "I'm Dick Cheton, and I approve this message."

+ + +

A condominium door opened, and inside stood a woman with a shock of white hair and a slight stoop. "Hello," Nic said to her. "My name is Nicholas Tattico, and I'm from ReBound. I'd like to talk with you about the solutions we're proposing for people's problems, and ask you to vote for us in the Condo Owners Association elections next week." Nic was spending considerable time personally knocking on doors in order to get the ReBound message out during the final week of the campaign, and tonight he had accompanied David Sall's team as they canvassed a working-class neighborhood of saleys and cubeys. The development consisted of large, plain buildings of single-family condos, each building with a courtyard that contained a playset for children. The sim-sky was fairly dim in this section.

"Oh yes," the elderly woman said, "I've heard of your group. My daughter said you have a day care plan, and I thought that might help her with my grandchildren."

"Yes, we know day care can eat up the entire paycheck of one member of a working couple. It's so difficult. We want to add early child-care services and preschool to existing primary schools, and give people subsidies to reduce costs for private-sector day care."

"Oh, gosh, that would be good. Children are so important. They are the future, you know."

"I know," Nic nodded in agreement. "It's important to us to take good care of children. We want to build a better world for them, by improving quality of life for everyone, making sure their parents have good jobs and are treated fairly at work, and making politics more about regular people. You know, we're a highly advanced society, we have the resources, and it's time to make sure enough of those resources go to working people and their families."

"Yes," the woman nodded in agreement. "It's all about posterity."

The woman's husband, an elderly man in a polo and a cardigan, walked up to the door with a limp. "Who is it, Emma?"

"It's a man from the ReBound, dear."

"Oh, the group that wants to regulate everything," the man said with a frown. "The last thing we need is more laws. We don't even enforce the ones we've got."

"Now, dear . . ."

Nic shook the man's hand and replied, "I actually agree with you, sir. Our laws are certainly not enforced. At least not in a way that benefits everyone, for the public good. We aim to change that."

"And how are you going to do that?"

"One of our most important planks, sir, is to give everyone the vote, so that regular people have more control over their government. Things today are run for the rich, so eventually we want to take the money out of politics by publicly funding elections, too."

"All of that will just raise taxes and put people out of work. Businesses won't stay in the section with all these rules and taxes. They'll move away or just shut down."

"That is a big worry. That's called 'capital strike,' and we feel it is a form of extortion: businesses threaten to turn off productive investment unless they get special treatment. It's a sense of entitlement. That's why we want economic democracy: if workers can vote for their Managers and Executives, they won't vote for ones that will shut down their companies and cost them their jobs."

"Dear," Emma interjected, "ReBound also has a program for health insurance. Dr. Dave supports it. It could help buy you the new hip you need."

"That's right, sir," said Nic. "And as our volunteer base has grown, we've built up networks of people with skills in every field who help each other out. We can probably get you in to see a specialist this week, at a discount."

"Well, that might be helpful," the man said, "But public health care is too much! We can't afford it!"

"You know, I used to think that too. But study after study shows that it would cost *less* than our current for-profit system. You see, our insurance industry is an oligopoly, economically speaking, so prices are higher and services lower than they should be. A huge layer of expense is foisted onto consumers, and many are denied care, just to give Executives profits."

"I don't see how a medical system can work without the profit motive. It's just not doable."

"A lot of people feel that way, I understand. Yet history shows many good working examples—in old Canada, France, Scandinavia . . ."

"We'll never agree on this, young man. Your social engineering and experiments are going to ruin the Mall. It's just too much change. I'd rather keep things as they are, keep Mallworld as Mallworld. Emma, you can do what you want, but this isn't for me." He turned with a dismissive wave of his hand and limped away.

Emma looked at Nic and wrung her hands. "I'm sorry about that," she said. "He's set in his ways."

"It's quite alright, ma'am," said Nic. "People have a right to think for themselves, and to disagree with us. But I'd still like to ask you for your vote in the board elections next month."

"Oh, yes, I want a better world for my grandchildren. For posterity."

"Thank you, ma'am."

"Before you go, why don't you give me some info about those medical specialists you mentioned," she whispered at him conspiratorially, with a wink and a smile, glancing in the direction her husband had taken.

Nic gladly obliged and then made his way next door to talk to the family there. He visited several more homes to fulfill his canvassing quota, and in the end he felt energized. He was an extrovert and had many positive interactions with people that evening, but more importantly, he was certain that talking to people would ensure a ReBound election victory.

Nic was supposed to meet the other members of the team at a mallway junction nearby. He walked through the corridors with a light step, digital ads flashing all around him, muzak singing everywhere. The sim-sky was dimming from dusk to dark.

As he neared the junction, Nic heard shouting and saw the flashing red and blue lights of Mallcop squad carts. He saw a crowd gathered where the team was supposed to meet and pushed his way through to see what was happening. What he saw shocked him.

David and the other canvassers were kneeling on the ground, forced into submissive positions by a pack of Mallcops. One policeman was on his radio, and another was putting restraints on the volunteers. A few other Mallcops loitered around, glaring. The canvassers were angrily protesting their treatment, and David stood up to confront a policeman: "You can't do this!" The Mallcop barked at him to get down, and when David hesitated to do so the officer pulled out his burn spray and blasted him in the face. David hit the ground screaming, his face feeling like it was on fire.

Nic, in a panic, pushed through and confronted the officer who was on the radio. "What is going on here?"

"Sir, back away," said the officer, holding one hand up palm outward, while reaching back to put his other hand on his burner.

Nic stood his ground. "I'm a senior ReBound representative and these people are with me. What possible justification can there be for this treatment?"

"These youths were seen to be disturbing the peace and commerce. They are going to be taken to the precinct for booking, will be held overnight, and will face a hearing tomorrow." David lay prone, writhing. "They'll probably get a fine. Maybe a short Time Out."

"What do you mean, disturbing the peace and commerce? What did they do, exactly?"

"They were seen knocking on shoppers' doors and disturbing their privacy."

"There's nothing wrong or illegal about that. Cake and Pizza Trough do door-to-door advertising all the time."

"We received some complaints from shoppers, sir." The Mallcop was still in his militaristic stance.

"I will be bringing ReBound's lawyers into this. There had better not be any more burners pulled on my people, or I will make sure each of you is *personally* sued. Which precinct are you taking them to?"

"Sir, do not threaten me."

"I am bringing in our lawyers, which is our legal right." Nic was a naturally amiable person, but fierce when he felt his own people were threatened. He stared the Mallcop right in the eyes and repeated himself slowly and forcefully. "*There had better not be any more burners, or I will make sure each of you is personally sued, as is my legal right.* If you spray me, I'll sue you so bad you'll owe me half your store credits for life. We have done nothing wrong, and you know it. And they have the right to legal representation." Nic kept his gaze fixed on the man. "Which precinct?"

The policeman clenched his jaw, squinted in anger at Nic, tightened his grip on his burner, and seethed for long seconds. When he spoke it was through clenched teeth. "My name is Sergeant Harris, and we'll be going to the main Northgate Mall Security Headquarters in the vicinity of Piazza Plaza." Nic accepted that answer and turned away to make phone calls. Harris didn't change his stance until Nic was some distance away.

Nic stayed to ensure that David received medical care and that the group was treated properly. He contacted ReBound members who were lawyers to go to the precinct station in advance. When the Mallcops took the team away in their police golf carts, he headed back to the ReBound building to write up the incident.

The process had taken time, it had gotten late, and it was dark. When Nic first spotted the ReBound headquarters in the distance something looked odd about the building, and he noticed there was a journalist and cameraman out front delivering a news report. As he got closer, he could see that the front facade was covered in graffiti. It was all meant to be insulting. "Communists!" "Criminals!" "Mallworld: Love it or leave it!"

The reporter was speaking into the camera. ". . . with someone so easily pranking the new political party, Northgate shoppers will be asking, 'Can we trust ReBound to keep us safe?'"

Nic clenched his fist in anger, and then looked down at the ground. This had not been a good night.

+ + +

On billions of holoscreens, an advertisement is projected:

The holopanel depicts a middle-aged, middle-class couple sitting at their kitchen table drinking coffee and reading their tablets, apparently fretting over bills.

"What are we going to do?" the woman asks. "Now that I've lost my job, there's no way that we can spend our Shopper's Quota."

"And downsizing at work means a pay cut for me, work speed-up, and longer hours," mutters her husband.

"Why don't we have a say over business decisions—hiring, firing, pay, working conditions? It's so important in our lives."

"Rich people who don't have to worry about money make all those choices, dear."

"They choose . . . we lose," she laments.

The couple looks up from the table and turns their gaze to an HV panel nearby in their living room. The camera slowly zooms in on that screen, where a man in a construction helmet says, "Times always seem tough, and we never get ahead."

A blonde woman in a saley apron appears and says, "We're all in this together."

Then an Asian grandfather: "We need to stick together to get ahead."

Next, Samantha came on screen: "ReBound brings people together."

A man with Mediterranean European features—it was Nic—then says, "We're just like you. Regular working people."

Finally, a handsome black man with dark skin, short black hair, and a warm smile appears, both hands on the desk in front of him. "We *are* you—ReBounding upward together, to make a better world for all." He pauses, and the ReBound principles appear on the screen: *Fairness at Work. Quality of Life. Strong Public Sphere.* The man says, "I'm Jime Galilei, and I approve this message."

+ + +

"Good evening. This is Chuck Anderson with Christine Kimberly here at JNN. On Tuesday, Northgate will hold its regularly scheduled Condominium Owner's Association election, an event that normally passes by unnoticed. This year, however, is different. Problems have been festering in the Mall, despite the appearance of comfort and convenience. People are working too much, they're working multiple jobs, their pay is squeezed, health care and day care are too expensive, and bankruptcy Time Outs are on the rise. There is a general sense of alienation and malaise across Mallworld. Yet Mall Management, while respected by many, is often seen as unresponsive to the needs of everyday shoppers."

The camera turned to Christine Kimberly. "Out of this situation, a new political party, ReBound, has arisen here in Northgate to challenge the sitting Executives. ReBound has a democratic socialist vision, but, it says, a practical and workable one. It claims to have an agenda of significant but achievable reforms. With us tonight are Dixon Cheton, chair of the Northgate COA, and Jime Galilei, leader of ReBound." Both men nodded and said hello. Jime, wearing a green and red tie and a dark suit that complemented his dark skin, looked calmly confident, while Cheton was pale and sweating in his usual ill-fitting suit. "Jime, first tell us why socialism is OK now, when it was defeated a century and a half ago?"

"Thanks, Christine, for having me here tonight to talk about these important issues. Fundamentally, we need democratic socialism because our society needs more equality. ReBound believes that all people are morally equal and thus should be politically equal. The Mall may be legally chartered as a corporation, but because it makes all the decisions about how our lives are run, it is, *de facto*, a government. And because we are all equal human beings, that government should be a democracy, in which all of us has an equal say. 'What touches all should be decided by all,' as we say in ReBound.[11] But instead of equal democracy, what has evolved in practice is a very unequal oligarchy. We have had the empty forms of elections but not the substance. We have had no choice over our way of life except to choose oligarchy capitalism. But now, our party, ReBound, has stood up to give people a real choice."

"But that doesn't answer my question," Christine said. "*Why* choose democratic socialism?"

"We offer a better way of life than the Executives do. This is not your ancestors' socialism. We're not talking about a centralized command economy and a police state—no one thinks that's a good idea. What we are talking about is, first, revitalizing democracy in the political sphere, and second, extending democracy to the economic sphere. Meanwhile, we also

---

11   Michael Walzer, "Town Meetings and Workers' Control," *Dissent*, Summer 1978.

want to guarantee that the people have the material and social means to be good, self-governing citizens: free, high-quality education; affordable, guaranteed health care; enough pay and leisure time to be politically active, effective citizens; and stronger civic institutions with opportunities to deliberate. Furthermore, we hope to revive the psychological and social benefits of community, in order to give people something greater than themselves to belong to. Ultimately, our vision is rooted in a civic republicanism that aims to ensure that the people can be truly self-governing in the face of predations by a rich faction who have garnered too much power for themselves. ReBound has a vision of a better, more equal world of prosperity, full freedom, meaning, and flourishing for all."

Chuck Anderson then addressed the other candidate. "Chairman Cheton, how do you respond? What do you see in the ReBound vision that's objectionable, and why should Northgate shoppers keep the status quo?"

Cheton spoke with an undercurrent of irritation, as if he shouldn't have to be there explaining this to anyone. "Chuck, I just can't agree with any of that. I think Mallworld's traditional, official philosophy of libertarianism is best, because it is based on giving people what they *earn*, not on some fancy academic idea of equality. The Executives stand up for the quiet, hard-working shopper, the forgotten man and woman who go to work, raise their kids, take personal responsibility for themselves, and spend and enjoy their Shopping Quota. Libertarianism has always stood for minimal government, the only kind of government that stays out of the way, that lets mom and pop run the store and keep what they earn, that doesn't burden job creators with regulations or taxes. A minimal state that keeps law and order with strong police so that normal people can go about their business and not have the fruit of their hard work stolen.

"This new, radical movement wants to sink our ship of state—this magnificent, opulent cruise ship that we all enjoy. They want to make life chaotic and unstable. As I've said before, of course problems exist in Northgate, because there are always some problems everywhere. The Executives are not utopian dreamers, but we are good managers, and we take care of problems when they pop up. We think Northgate is a very well-run section of the Mall: shoppers have access to stores and entertainment, there are so many jobs that everyone can have two or three, and profits for Northgate corporations are at record highs. Now is not the time for change. Too much radical change just makes it harder for the hard-working, forgotten shoppers to live in peace. It's the road to anarchy."

Chuck Anderson then turned to Jime. "I take it ReBound wouldn't agree with what Mr. Cheton believes, Jime Galilei?"

"ReBound absolutely respects hard-working people and the work they do—which is why we oppose libertarian capitalism, because the corporate oligarchs at the top cheat everyone out of what they earn. They do it by taking the lion's share of the fruits of everyone's hard work for themselves. We have to be clear about this. Libertarianism doesn't 'give people what they earn.' It ensures that a large fraction of working peoples' earnings is channeled to the rich. Capitalism, by keeping ownership and control over society's productive capital in the hands of private, profit-seeking individuals, by deregulating and privatizing everything, allows companies to suppress workers' incomes while maximizing Executive profit. It does this in many ways, most effectively by threatening to move jobs away."

"You call that capital flight, right?" Chuck Anderson asked.

"That's right, Chuck. And it's why we want worker representatives on corporate boards with the power of the veto, to prevent that; and eventually we aim to convert corporations into cooperatives that workers control by electing their management and deciding company policy.

"ReBound believes libertarianism does *not* protect people and what they have. It protects the ability of capitalists to claim unearned riches for themselves. It is a regressive philosophy at a time when we need experimentation and progress. Mr. Cheton calls us anarchists, but our world is already very chaotic, with jobs moving back and forth, repeated recessions, and millions of lives and entire communities consequently ruined. People need hope for a better future, or they just become selfish, trying to protect what little they have from oligarchs who try to extract every last penny from them.

"Without equality, without political and economic democracy, people will continue to live the difficult lives the oligarchy imposes on us all. The Executives have no vision for a better life. They just want to keep making money off the current system—which isn't working for most people. ReBound aims to enhance social interconnection, strengthen fairness and justice, and improve quality of life for working Mallworlders."

Dixon Cheton then spoke up. "The kind of equality that my opponent wants is just taking rewards from the successful and giving them to those who've failed. That just promotes failure. It's communism, no matter how you look at it, and that's not how most shoppers want to live. My opponent wants income equality. Soon he will want workeys to be equal to saleys, and saleys equal to Managers. Then the whole system will break down, order will weaken, nothing will get done, jobs will disappear, and crime and chaos will be the result."

"And what you just said is why our society needs more equality," said Jime. "The Great Synergy Campaign helped us get over the idea that people are inferior or superior based on race, sex, gender, nationality, and other factors. Humanity couldn't live together under one roof if we were still afflicted with such prejudices. Yet you still want inequality of economic class.

"My own race is an example. For the entire history of the O.U.S., people with skin like mine were thought to be inferior. It's true that over time explicit doctrines of racial supremacy diminished to be held only by a minority of crackpot racists—although they could be a vocal and violent. But *implicit* biases continued to be widespread, causing much oppression and social division, until Mallworld was built and implemented the Synergy advertising effort. Inequality remained in the O.U.S. because of residual ideas about unequal personhood: the O.U.S. was a majority white society, so its people tended to associate full personhood with whiteness, and they associated good things with white people and bad things with brown and black people. I did my MBA thesis on depictions of black men as criminals in O.U.S. popular culture, and you would be stunned at how easily they assumed an entire race of people had criminal tendencies. The policies that resulted, such as mass incarceration and police shootings of black men, were horrific.

"Now, I am an educated, perceptive, lucid person with, I think, good social skills, and as a Manager I've held positions of leadership. In today's society, if we were talking on the phone and you didn't know me, but you imagined who I was, you wouldn't associate my intelligence or articulacy with any specific skin color or racial or ethnic background, any more than you would associate it with eye color, hair color, sexual orientation, or any other extraneous factors. You wouldn't automatically assume a well-spoken person on the phone was white, Asian, black, or anything else. But in the O.U.S., not knowing my skin color, most people most of the time would have *assumed* that I was a white person, even though I am black. The norm for 'person' was 'white person' and was the keystone of implicit racism. The Synergy campaign put a stop to thinking like that by getting people into the habit of asking themselves questions like 'Why did I think Jime was white?' It made people question their implicit positive and negative associations, allowing us today to think of all persons as equal regardless of factors like race and sex that are morally arbitrary when assessing personhood. It taught us that when we are thinking about equal personhood, we have to make a conscious effort to think of those who are *not* like us in addition to those who are. This helped equalized how we treat each other, reducing social division."

"Well, I am certainly not a racist," Cheton flared, "and I resent the impli-cation. I am definitely not assuming anyone is less of a person based on race, ethnicity, sex, or anything else. The Great Synergy was the biggest public relations campaign there ever was, and we just don't think in those terms anymore. We're all equals here, and I represent everyone in Northgate, regardless of identity."

"But when you talk about workeys being unequal to saleys, and both unequal to Managers, as you just did a moment ago, well, I say *clearly* inequality and its accomplice, division, are being reproduced in another way," Jime said. "You are implicitly assuming that Executives, Managers, and the consuming classes are superior, by matter of degrees, than the poor, laboring cubeys, saleys, and workeys. *That* kind of inequality Mallworld has yet to overcome, and that is what ReBound aims to do. But in some ways that is *harder* to change than mere identity inequality, which is fundamentally about extending the same social respect to all persons. You can do that, as the Great Synergy did, by changing attitudes, which will also change behaviors, and can even change the proportion of unequal economic treatment that is associated with identity. The kind of inequality you just expressed, however, is based on economic *class* all the way down, and it justifies treating some people as better or lesser *materially*, in their economic circumstances, all the way down. Mallworld still has that kind of inequality because it has capitalism, and material, class inequality is built right into every crevice of the system. Changing it isn't a mere matter of changing the culture—of altering beliefs, attitudes, and practices. It is a matter of changing the basic economic structure by getting rid of economic class and extending roughly equal economic circumstances to everyone. That involves changing material institutions, which is even harder than cultural change."

Cheton shook his head with a frown and said, "See, the good shoppers of Mallworld don't *want* to change that kind of inequality. They are comfortable with what they've got, with their homes and shopping and spectas, and don't want to risk losing it for some pie-in-the-sky professors' utopia. Economic inequality is what makes a market system work, what makes it productive. It rewards the talented and hard-working and innovative. It gives the entrepreneurs all the rewards they need to make new inventions and new jobs. People aren't equal in their talents, and that is why we don't want the communist equality you and your radical friends want."

"That's mostly a myth," Jime said. "Markets reward talent to some degree, but most inequality is based on inheritance, connections, cronyism, and corruption. That's always been the case when an economy is dominated by large corporations—it becomes an unequal, corrupt oligarchy that only sees inequalities of dollars and doesn't respect equality of persons. Inequality, as history shows, is dangerous when pushed to extreme limits: it ultimately leads to the dehumanization and oppression of some groups, and eventually division that threatens to tear society apart. The practical reforms that we offer aren't utopian communism. They are pragmatic ways to reduce the share of unearned wealth that goes to the oligarchs and keep it in the hands of the people who create it and deserve it."

"The current management of Northgate hasn't seen that division happen at all, but it will if you come into power," Cheton said. "We've maintained a well-ordered society, with everyone in their proper place: Executives and Managers leading with their experience, cubeys and saleys executing and implementing with their administrative and sales skills, and workeys doing the physical grunt work. This is a sound, successful business model that we want to conserve, and as COA chair, I will use law and order to preserve it."

"That's all the time we have tonight," Christine Kimberly said. "Thank you, Chairman Dixon Cheton of the Northgate Executives and Jime Galilei of ReBound." Both men nodded and said good night.

+ + +

It was three o'clock in the afternoon on election day, and Jime had been running around managing last-minute get-out-the-vote efforts. He had also been personally driving one of the shuttle carts ReBound had rented or borrowed to get voters to and from polling terminals. People had begun to recognize him on the streets, which he found disconcerting. Some came up and shook his hand and wanted to talk about ReBound, but just as many gave him angry looks. He was dog-tired, but there were only a few more hours to go.

He sorely needed an energy boost, so he stopped at a SuperShop to get a plastic cup of coffee. As Jime approached the convenience store, he took a moment to observe how everything about it was designed to persuade, encourage, and guide human beings to buy things. Its bright neon lights were meant to make the store noticeable and lure people in, like moths to a flame, and turn them into consumers. Advertising posters had been sprayed all over the building's orange and pink plastic facade in order to promote consumption of the fatty foods, sugared drinks, and cheap baubles sold inside. They displayed animated pictures of dancing double-pound hamburgers, buckets of soda, tubs of fries, and quintuple-scoop ice cream cones. Each advertisement sent a message: "You want this." No attention whatsoever had been paid in the architectural design to any aesthetic other than salesmanship, which seemed to Jime to be an utterly inadequate standard of beauty. Inside, glowing neon, gaudily colored walls, blinking digital signs, flashing digital product packages, the tang of fried food, and the relentless beat of pop music all assaulted Jime's senses. This fusillade of sensory overload prevented deep thinking or reflection: the store was a place where stimuli were meant to provoke direct and immediate responses, unrestrained by deliberative consideration—and the intended stimulus response was: "purchase this product." The entire environment was designed to *prevent* deliberate choice.

Jime found the coffee vending machine and pushed "giganti." It started to brew his go-juice from its internal algae reservoir, digitally simulating the hiss of a barista's milk-steamer.

Jime's mind wandered back to the evening before, at the ReBound headquarters. He had been feeling pleased with what the movement had already accomplished, despite their recent drop in the polls. Their organizing efforts had succeeded to a degree that he hadn't expected. Initially, he had been afraid that ReBound would end up being a basement-room political organization—tiny, ignored, staffed by a few conspiracy-theory cranks. Instead, he and the other leaders had found that ReBound's principled, optimistic, and confident message of interconnectedness, coexaltation, attending to the public good, and economic justice had resonated with many people. So many people felt disconnected, disaffected, and disempowered that they grabbed onto these ideas, which though very old, were new to them. To people raised and socialized in a neoliberal world that preached a doctrine of acquisitive individualism, ReBound's message of justice, fairness, and solidarity was profoundly fresh and appealing.

Jime had grown so pleased with the process of organizational growth that he had become blasé about actually winning the election. He did *want* to win. He was doing all he could to ensure victory, and he thought ReBound still had a realistic chance of winning. But he knew they had made so much progress already that, even if they didn't win this time, they would in the near future. Furthermore, they had already changed the public discourse. People were now talking about equality, the public sphere, and economic democracy, which they hadn't before.

Jime, who was supposed to be a leader, had forgotten that those who followed him were not so sanguine. They weren't as focused on the long-term process but were anxious to have a successful result today. He wasn't full of hubris, but the people around him were worried about the immediate consequences of winning or losing. It hadn't registered for him how close and uncertain the race was until he overheard some volunteers expressing their fears at one of the water coolers the day before. Jime had had his head stuck in an office supply locker looking for staples when he overheard one clearly tired canvasser ask another, "How many doors did you knock on this past week?"

"Too many to count," the other replied. "My feet are killing me."

"Mine too. I hope it's all worth it."

"I don't know. It's so close. I don't know if it will be. We did all this work. I know that we have to have patience and fortitude . . ."

"Yes, we have to stick with it, persist, and try, try again until we succeed."

"I know, but it helps when you're getting positive responses, so you can get energy from other people. At first it seemed like people were interested in change, but the last couple of weeks most people at the doors I knocked on got pretty cool to our ideas."

"They've been seeing all the HV ads against us, I think."

"Yeah, support has really dropped. I don't feel like we'll win now."

"That would be really depressing." The canvasser then slumped down into a nearby chair.

Jime had felt his own shoulders slump, too, from his hidden spot in the equipment locker. The other volunteer said, "As with anything in life, there are natural ups and downs; don't give in to despair. Despair is not a virtue. Confidence and persistence are. We will be up again. Sticking with our principles will win us through to the end."

That seemed like good advice to Jime, but it was sometimes hard to feel it. He reached out and took his coffee from the machine and sipped it. A pro-establishment, anti-ReBound ad came on one of the store's overhead HV panels. "Day care?" asked a sweet elderly grandmother, sitting with her grandchildren. "How can we afford it? I raised my own children, like all parents should. Who knows what they will teach them in *day care*." Granny practically spat the words as ominous music began to play in the background. On the holoscreen, darkness fell, the picture froze, and blood dripped down the screen to cover her and her grandkids. A deep, alarming voice announced, "*Do you support a movement that will go after your children?*" Jime shook his head as he paid the mechaniman behind the sales counter for the coffee.

Walking back to the shuttle cart, he thought everyone he encountered was giving him disapproving glances, as if he was a black man walking a twenty-first-century American street rather than a professional member of the Management class in post-Synergy Mallworld. As he drove back to headquarters, he couldn't get the thought out of his head that ReBound might fail, and everything they had worked for would come to naught.

He tried to keep his head high and his expression confident as he walked into headquarters to get directions to his next load of passengers. He saw Sam sitting in front of the HV with nearly everyone else, watching the election returns, and they all looked worried.

On JNN Christine Kimberly and Chuck Anderson were discussing the interview between Jime and Cheton. Chuck Anderson was saying, "What we saw from the two men was two competing visions of the future. One is libertarian, based on a market system, with its inequalities and rewards as the engine of endless economic growth. This is a vision that accepts the status quo and doesn't want change. The other is a socialist vision that promises equality and a better life for everyone through political innovation. Historically such visions have never worked out, however."

"Well, hold on a minute, Chuck," Christine said. "ReBound isn't proposing anything that hasn't worked somewhere, historically. Public health care, higher minimum wages, even workers' cooperatives have all been tried in different places, and worked."

"Yes, but never on such a scale as large as Mallworld," he replied.

"But consumerism itself, or construction a giant complex of buildings, was never tried on so large a scale before either."

"True, but it's the traditional way of life. Will Mallworld shoppers be willing to accept change?"

"That's the real question," said Christine. "Can ReBound convince enough people that change is necessary and achievable?"

"Our final poll going into the election does show a very tight race. ReBound is doing very well for a new party—46 percent of likely voters in our latest survey said they would vote for them. However, Northgate shoppers appear to prefer the status quo: 52 percent say they will cast their ballot for the Executives today."

The crowd in the ReBound lobby groaned in disappointment.

"Ah, it's all been for nothing," someone complained and threw his clipboard down on a table.

"What a waste," someone else said.

"Hold on, hold on now," Jime said. "We haven't lost yet—it's not over until the votes are counted, and every vote counts. The only poll that really matters is the final vote."

"Yes," said a volunteer, "but opinion polls are very good at predicting that."

"Well, I, for one, believe that we are headed for victory," Jime tried to show a confidence he wasn't feeling. "But you know what else? Even if we lose today, we've already achieved much—a year ago, no one would have predicted that a brand-new political party could even get 4 percent, much less 46 percent. We've done really well and should be proud of ourselves."

"We know," someone sighed. "But JNN is right. We won't win the election." Many of the people standing there just shuffled listlessly away.

Sam's shoulders sagged and she seemed to sink a few inches into the floor. "Everything we've worked for is going to go to waste," she said.

Jime smiled. "Look, I've only got two more runs of voters to make before the polls close. Whaddya say after we go get dinner somewhere nice and quiet, and leave the holovision off for the rest of the night?"

Sam brushed a strand of hair from her face. "Sounds great," she said as she forced a smile. "That will make a nice consolation prize."

+ + +

"Good evening. This is Christine Kimberly reporting to you from outside the ReBound headquarters, here with Chuck Anderson. Today's sectional elections are underway, and surprisingly, in Northgate turnout is reportedly larger than anticipated, and *much* larger than in all other section of Mallworld. At some polling stations, long lines of eager voters have election administrators scrambling to add voting capacity at the last minute to ensure that all those who want to vote can do so. Chuck Anderson, have you ever seen anything like it?"

"I haven't, Christine, it's really unprecedented. Usually turnout is very low for COA elections. To see all these people lining up to vote is amazing. That a new, upstart group could inspire so many people to vote is impressive."

"It is quite stunning to see. The message of the upstart ReBound party, which claims to represent regular working people, seems to have attracted a lot of support."

"Yes. Some are attributing increased interest in the elections to ReBound's active campaign of knocking on doors and holding political rallies, others to their holovision ads and social media outreach, and others to the mutual aid and services ReBound members offer each other, such as babysitting and home improvement. They certainly have attracted people's interest with their vision of social change. However, others say ReBound fuels division and resentment, and disrespects the values of hard work and entrepreneurship. Election officials say they won't have the votes tabulated tonight but will have to announce the winners tomorrow morning."

"Wow, Mallworld hasn't had an election this close since . . . well, ever! How exciting! We'll have to wait overnight to see what happens," Christine said. She looked back at the camera. "Next up: Are you ready for retirement? How to take advantage of a new financial tool to expand your Personal Retirement Account with asset swaps from your Family College Fund, while still ensuring your kids get their degrees virtually through holouniversity. That and more at eleven."

+ + +

Jime banged his gavel to open the meeting. The hubbub in the room quieted. The room was large and well-appointed, paneled in real wood grown in real forests decades before and carefully preserved. Jime had already had the COA committee table lowered to be even with the audience on the floor, so the elected board members were on the same level as their constituents. A buzz of excitement bounced off walls of the room, which was filled with people, standing-room only. Sam and Nic, as elected representatives, also sat at the front table, their faces beaming. The ReBound victory created the possibility to do great things in the future. Jime looked at them and smiled.

Sid leaned against a wall on one side, though, his arms crossed, looking worried. He was pleased ReBound won, but he also had some qualms. The only path to social change, he knew, was through the striving of committed, active people. ReBound had set the ball rolling to claw back power from the oligarchs in Northgate and eventually make broader change in Mallworld. He knew, however, that they had taken the Executives by surprise and that they would face more resistance in future political contests. Their victory in Northgate would certainly prompt a backlash. Sid was truly hopeful for his society for the first time in his life, but he knew the future was as uncertain as a spin of the Wheel of Fate.

Jime began speaking, and with purpose.

"Welcome to this year's opening meeting of the Northgate Sectional Condominium Association Board. In the days and weeks ahead, we will use the legislative power that the citizens of Northgate have granted us to begin building a new and better world. We will start to form an interconnective republic dedicated to coexaltation, a polity that elevates our social bonds in word and deed. We will work to restore the civic virtues by encouraging people to participate in self-government, regardless of wealth or elite connections. We will follow the principles of communitarian, democratic socialism. We will implement policies of coexaltation rather than exploitation—policies that bring neighbors and communities together in fellowship, so that our cooperative interconnections are strengthened and our sense of social purpose revitalized. And we will begin to establish economic equality in order to weaken the stranglehold that concentrations of corporate wealth and power have on us all. We will begin to build a world where we are all empowered to achieve our life-plans, manifest the full measure of freedom in our lives, and become who we were meant to be."

Jime paused and felt the gavel in his hand. He hefted it; it was weighty and substantial, not a thing to be held lightly. Much like the responsibilities he now shouldered, he thought.

But he didn't shoulder them alone. He reminded himself that everyone in the room cared about their society and its future, and they were all here to work, bound together, to bound forward and create a society fit for human habitation. He looked up at the crowd of citizens gathered there because they, too, held out hope of a better world.

"As board chair, I now introduce a platform of policy proposals put forward by the majority leader, Samantha Gomprez, to restore our public sphere, achieve justice in the workplace, and improve quality of life. As you know, if passed by a majority of the board, these measures will have all the force of bylaw and go into immediate effect, and any monies voted by the board for implementation are to be withdrawn from the appropriate Association, Sectional, and Mall accounts. Mall offices and agencies are legally obligated to enforce board bylaws with their full vigor, according to the Mallworld charter.

"Let us pledge that, as long as we are here, we will govern Northgate section not in the interests of its corporations, but in the interests of its people."

Jime slammed the gavel onto its pedestal, and the common people who filled the room clapped, hollered, and cheered in honor of their victory for democracy.

APPENDIX 1:
CLASSICAL REPUBLICANISM

J ime downloaded a decades-old holovideo and, with a little effort, got it playing on his holoscreen. An anonymous resistance activist from Mallworld's early years spoke; he called himself MachiavelliX and didn't show his own face but presented himself as an avatar of Niccolo Machiavelli. He took his guise from the famous portrait of the Renaissance political theorist by Santi di Tito, except that MachiavelliX wore a modern revolutionary beret atop his computer-animated head.

"I have made this video because I oppose the privatization that led the United States of America to sell itself to a real estate company to be turned into a giant shopping mall. I and my fellow activists hope to reverse this barbaric catastrophe. Capitalism, with its aggressive, competitive individualism and overconsumption, has destroyed the earth and our civic bonds. We, on the other hand, hold the conviction that collective interests exist and that the point of living in society is to promote the public good. These convictions can be traced back to an ancient school of thought called *classical republicanism*.

"The term 'republic' comes from the Latin term *res publica,* which meant 'public thing' or 'public business,' and refers to what people have in common, the activities and affairs that they share together. Some activities, concerns, and interests are necessarily shared by virtue of the fact that human beings live together in groups. I agree with Aristotle's contention that humans are *zoon politikon* or political animals: just as birds fly in flocks, horses run in bands, lions prowl in prides, and wolves hunt in packs, humans live in societies. To be sure, it is not entirely clear what human nature is. There are many valid perspectives on it, and claims about human nature are always debatable; but whatever other attributes humans might naturally have, I believe that science, history, and plain observation show that people are naturally social. Humans developed social interconnection as a matter of evolutionary adaptability because language, culture, and morality all helped the species survive and adapt in competition with other species. Social interconnection led humans to form communities that eventually grew into larger political societies. For the ancient Greeks and Romans, the shared social unit was a village, town, or—ideally, for them—a city-state; later forms included empires, kingdoms, nation-states, and continental politico-economic unions.

"The tradition of civic republicanism is rich and varied, as any tradition extending across many centuries necessarily must be," MachiavelliX continued. "Nonetheless, there are certain basic notions that run throughout its history and hold it together conceptually. These are the *public good, civic virtue, liberty* and its antipode *tyranny,* and *corruption.*

"First and foremost, republicanism takes the concept of the *public good* seriously. This is the idea that a group of people have shared, common interests distinct from their individual self-interest, which cannot always be reduced to the mere sum of individual interests. Republicanism identifies the matters that people share, by virtue of living in propinquity and socially, as *civic* concerns, not strictly individual concerns.

"We can think of many examples. For instance, it is in everyone's interest to have clean water and air, because physically humans need these things to survive. However, it might be in the individual interests of manufacturers, and even of consumers (considered in their role as consumers rather than as whole persons), to produce and consume goods cheaply in a way that pollutes and poisons the air and water. It is in the public good to provide high-quality education to everyone so that citizens are well informed, think critically, and govern themselves competently, as well as obtain the priceless benefits of knowledge, growth, and creativity. However, when many people feel that their immediate monetary interests are not served by paying taxes for schools, especially if they don't themselves have school-age children, education is under-provided. Leisure time also could be deemed a public good, necessary for healthy social relations, physical and mental health, personal development, and to give citizens time for politics. However, due to market competition employers have an interest in pressuring employees to work long hours, and employees find it in their interest to comply. Greater deliberation, too, is a public good that improves the quality of political discourse and governance. However, individuals might enjoy private pursuits and entertainments too much and neglect public meetings. Freedom of conscience and religion are also public goods, yet advocates of different philosophies and religions can believe it is in their interest for the state to promote their doctrine and discourage or suppress others. Erecting and maintaining the physical infrastructure of a republic—its buildings, meeting halls, courts, administrative agencies, roads, power systems, communication networks, social insurance programs, regulatory bodies, and many other things—is also a shared, common concern. However, many short-sighted, self-oriented people won't want to pay for it. These and many other things constitute the public good."

Jime found it inspiring that republicanism emphasized the good of the whole and did not reduce everything to the mere self-interest of individuals, as Mallworld and its free-market ideologies did. MachiavelliX continued:

"To perceive the public good, one must step back from looking only at the parts, and also look at the whole along with the parts that make it up. A clean environment, education, leisure, deliberation, freedom, public works—these and many other things, such as justice, equality, and solidarity, are certainly of benefit to individual persons; yet they are conceptually distinct from the *particular* interests of individuals, such as personal happiness, private prosperity, or individual pleasures. Living in a just society with high levels of social trust is a happy experience, yet a different kind of happy experience than, say, eating a piece of cake or otherwise enjoying personal consumption. They are both goods, but qualitatively different in kind: one creates conditions for good living, while the other is merely a pleasurable sensory stimulus. Furthermore, while the public good, when properly identified and actualized in law and public policy, should be in accord with the interests of individual members of the republic (whose well-being is affected by the situation of the larger group), sometimes it does come into conflict with the more immediate, particular interests of some people. In those cases, the *moral good* of the whole outweighs the *interests* of the particular individual or group (although not their basic *rights*). For example, the public good of clean air outweighs the interest in profit of a polluting factory's owners, but ending pollution doesn't extend to depriving the factory owners of their basic right to life. Pursuit of *individual* self-interest, and cost-benefit calculations of the kind advocated by utilitarianism, can often lead to negative or even destructive *collective* results that must be corrected. Indeed, the public good in many situations is not even quantifiable or subject to calculation at all but must be determined through the exercise of *qualitative* judgment. For these reasons the public good is *distinct from* the self-interest of individuals and smaller groups, even in cases when the interests of a part and of the whole directly align.

"Perceiving and attending to the public good takes special effort and the development of the appropriate mental and social skills and habits, which leads to the second key republican concept. To protect and promote the public good, civic republicans hold that it is necessary for the citizens of a republic to exercise *civic virtue*. "Virtue" here does not refer to Christian charity or chastity but goes back to ancient conceptions of the qualities of character—the excellences or *virtues*—that human beings must cultivate in order to be good citizens. These virtues include things like moral courage, frankness, and rhetorical skill when speaking in citizen assemblies; education, especially in political matters; and in ancient times, military training and physical courage to defend the polity. To be virtuous one must be an active citizen who participates in assemblies, juries, and other public institutions; becomes knowledgeable about public affairs; and votes. Virtuous citizens should vigilantly guard the rights and liberties of the people from elites—whether aristocratic, economic, or military—who are ambitious to acquire and wield power.

"*Above all, civic virtue means, at least at times, setting aside one's own self-interest, and any narrow factional, partisan, sectarian, or class interest that one might have, to attend to and promote the good of the polity.* One must be willing, as a mature adult, to give up getting everything that one wants, to let go of demands to have all one's desires met, in order to make sure that that the equal demands of others in the community are also met. One must, as a member of a society, recognize and embrace the duties one has to others. Civic virtue does not always come automatically and easily, of course. The public interest can conflict with other interests we as individuals might have—familial, professional, etc.—and so the motivation to follow the public good can compete with other motivations. In practice, these different motivations and drives have to be balanced. Moreover, people must learn to temper their self-interest and cultivate civic virtue through moral education and practice, which takes self-discipline and persistence. Economists often contrast assertive self-interest with altruism and hold the latter to be sentimental, unrealistic, and undependable as a motive upon which to base social institutions. For classical republicans, however, the opposite of self-interest is not selfless 'bleeding-heart' sympathy, but rather muscular, mature, and confident self-control—civic virtue—in the exercise of public duty.

"Civic republicans presuppose that civic virtue is psychologically real and significant. The idea that human motivations can be entirely reduced to self-interest, or even that self-interest is naturally predominant in human psychology, is entirely inaccurate. The psychology of modern economics and of much modern liberal political thought, as had often been pointed out, is very simplistic in over-emphasizing self-interest—almost a superficial 'folk psychology' that should be rejected by academics, researchers, and serious social thinkers of all stripes.

"It is, of course, the case that people are self-interested in that they jump out of the way of a fast-moving vehicle, drink and eat when they are thirsty and hungry, and do many other things to survive and to promote their well-being. But is that actually the same motivation as the unbridled 'self-interest' of a profit-maximizing billionaire? Of course not. While people may desire a certain moderate level of comfort and security, is that the same, psychologically, as a wealthy person accumulating riches without limit, wallowing in luxury, eating gluttonously, filling a huge mansion with bright, useless baubles, being waited on hand and foot, and demanding never to be bored? Of course not. And while people might desire to have control over their lives, to autonomously choose a life-plan and live according to it, is that the same as a person who is ambitious for power and indulges impulses to dominate and control others? Of course not. For anyone with eyes to see, these are all distinct and distinguishable psychological phenomena. The extreme cases are not healthy self-regard or sane moderation but unbalanced greed and self-indulgence.

"Yet all of these tend to get lumped into the category of 'self-interest.' Capitalism, with its highly competitive institutions and its emphasis on consumption, takes certain natural and healthy propensities of human self-regard, magnifies them into self-promoting acquisitiveness, and calls it self-interest. Capitalism elevated the competitive and aggressive traits of humanity to predominance in society, while minimizing other natural human propensities such as compassion, self-restraint, patience, moderation, and fairness. Human beings really do have many psychological motivations other than self-interest, and different forms of social organization bring them out. Whether engaged in an art, science, sport, or intellectual pursuit, people cultivate an interest, an engrossment or immersion, in various activities over the long term that goes beyond mere calculation of self-interest and that is not described accurately or well by the narrow political psychology of the self-interest model. People take an interest in various activities—football, painting, writing, medicine, music, astronomy, political philosophy, what have you—and pursue them out of pleasure, for mastery of skills, for creative expression, or for their own sake. We also have a drive to be active, not passive: humans are motivated to exercise their creative drives and abilities, and they become frustrated and feel alienated when expressing them is denied. But hierarchical systems of power, including capitalism, encourage passivity so that elites might more easily rule the people."

Most importantly, Jime thought, people are motivated by their social interconnections. Jime found civic virtue appealing because it spoke to his desire to belong to something bigger than himself and to make the world a better place. Republican virtue only means identifying with and promoting the good of a social group, which is entirely within the possibility of human psychology—in fact, people routinely form an identity with others to whom they feel connected. Historically, before the Mall and before modernity, republicanism's focal point was the city-state, because that was the traditional model of the polity. But as modern nation-states emerged, civic virtue became applicable to larger forms of polity, like the nation-state. Indeed, Jime thought, civic virtue could be applied to any form of association or society. Individuals identify both with other individuals and with groups—their families, friends, communities, associations, cities, and nations. They even identify with that largest of groups, humanity as a whole. As part of these groups, and through identification with them, the group interest becomes part of the individual's interest too, and the individual becomes motivated to advance the interests and causes of the group. Anyone who is skeptical that group interest is weak compared to self-interest should consider just how powerful forces such as nationalism have been in human history, for good and for ill. Such social identities in human psychology preclude boiling everything down to self-interest. Group identity and the civic virtue that can come from it are *real* phenomena, based on people's material, social, and psychological connections to one another.

MachiavelliX moved on to the next concept.

"*Liberty* is another basic idea in republicanism. The fact that people live closely together in society necessarily means that they must make rules to define shared interests, organize their public life, adjudicate disagreements, and prevent conflict from getting out of hand or even destroying the group. Self-determination is possible among social animals only by making those rules *together*. Consequently, liberty for civic republicans does *not* mean the freedom of individuals to do whatever they want without rules or restraints. Republicans define such unrestrained freedom as license. Republican liberty, rather, means *participating in making the rules by which one must live*. Republican liberty is an *active concept* and *active practice*: the people must be involved in *making* their own collective rules, *deciding* public matters, and vigilantly *guarding* their rights, privileges, and benefits. Thus liberty cannot be achieved simply with words written down in a law or constitution; nor can it rightly be thought of as a state or condition that one can passively enjoy, such as a putative state of nonconstraint or nondomination. Liberty is inherently about taking *action*; self-government is a positive activity that requires the active, repeated, practiced exercise of civic virtues. Technocracy—the rule by elite experts preferred by business schools and political scientists—is inconsistent with this active concept of freedom, even when well-intentioned. This is because technocracy treats people instrumentally as passive objects to be managed and manipulated, not as active participants in their own self-government. Knowledge is certainly valuable, but technical expertise must *serve* the public good, rather than experts *subjecting* the public to their impersonal, undemocratic rule. For classical republicans, if the common people exercise civic virtue by attending assemblies and town halls, keeping abreast of public affairs, and voting in order to exercise democratic political power and hold elites accountable, then they are self-governing—that is, exercising and actualizing their political liberty.

"If the people fail to make the public rules for themselves, then someone else will move into the vacuum and do it for them—and eventually will do so *against* them. When the people do not actively participate in politics, then some individual or faction, whether a single dictator, a class of oligarchs, a military junta, a religious sect, or other group, will acquire power and govern arbitrarily and against the good of the wider public. This is the very definition of *tyranny*, another key republican concept. Some people are politically *ambitious*, meaning they have a desire to possess power and privilege and to wield it over others. Although many political philosophers throughout history feared the common people (or *demos* in Greek) because of their overwhelming strength *en masse*, ambitious individuals and groups actually have the advantage over the *demos* because, being smaller in number and sharing common purposes, they are usually more organized, united, and nimble in protecting their faction's interests.[12] If the people are not united and vigilant in protecting their liberties through the active practice of participating in public affairs, then, tragically, ambitious individuals or groups *will* take power, either quickly or gradually, and wield that power in their own interests to the detriment of the public good. That is why cultivating civic virtue is critically important for republicans—so that the people will actively exercise their liberty in order to stave off tyranny.

"Tyranny inevitably comes about when a polity loses too much virtue and becomes corrupt. The republican concept of *corruption* does not mean merely bribery, graft, or embezzlement—although such venality is certainly part of it. Corruption, rather, is a broader concept which means that people are focused too much on their self-interest and neglect the public good. The word 'corruption' shares the same root as the word 'rupture': both come from the Latin *rumpere*, which means 'to break.' For civic republicans, corruption is the breaking of the social bonds needed by a people to organize their affairs through discourse rather than through coercion and violence. Corruption takes hold if the people are too absorbed in private affairs such as business or consumption, or if they are distracted by opulence, spectacles, and entertainment. Corruption can also occur when *factions* develop within a polity that set different parts of it fundamentally at

---

12   Adam Smith, "Of the Wages of Labour," chap. 8 in *The Wealth of Nations*, Book 1 (1776).

odds with each other; for example, when a religion or ideology induces a group to believe doctrines that make it feel as if it is apart from, above, or against the larger community or polity. To many civic republicans, factionalism, or as we call it today *polarization*, means the inevitable death of a republic. Therefore, factions must either be prevented or be allowed to proliferate so they can check and balance each other.

"In the long course of history," MachiavelliX went on, "civic republicans have proposed many methods for promoting civic virtue and holding corruption and tyranny at bay. To be sure, they recognized that no human constitution could last forever, for humans are imperfect beings who can build no permanent thing; even the great pyramids crumbled to dust. With time, corrupting decay is inevitable in any republic. But by dispersing power throughout different institutions, groups, and classes, and by properly arranging the polity to create institutions and a general environment that fosters habits of civic virtue, constitutional designers can make a republic that endures for many centuries before corruption takes hold and poisons it from within. Classical republicans used a combination of *institutional* and *educational* restraints on corruption and tyranny. These included the rule of law, separation of powers, rotation in office, public assemblies, transparency, prohibitions against standing armies, 'ward' systems, and political education.

"Many republican institutional designs became widely accepted as principles of good governance: the rule of law and limited terms of office are two examples. The idea of *mixed government* has been central to the republican program. When the power to rule was given to only one individual or group—whether a single ruler as in monarchy, an elite few as in oligarchy, or the *demos* as in direct democracy—that group would tend to wield it in its own interest rather than for the good of all. Classical republicans hold that both elites and the *demos* should therefore have a share in governing, in order to avoid consolidations of power that represent only partial interests. This eventually evolved into the idea of checks and balances—the division of governmental powers among executive, legislative, and judicial branches, so that each branch could stand watch over the others and block abuses.

"Early republicans included in their constitutions some form of citizen assemblies where the people as a whole met face-to-face to make public decisions, so that the common people would have an adequate voice in governing themselves. This originally meant the size of the republic was limited to a small community or city state, so that the assembly could meet in person. Small size also, for early republicans, helped to ensure the uniformity of moral norms and perspectives that republicans felt was necessary to avoid factions. Later republicans, such as James Madison, adapted republicanism to the larger modern nation-state by using the mechanism of *representation*: instead of the people *en masse* deciding policy themselves in assemblies, they elected a subgroup of representatives to do it. This allowed for a greater territory and population, and also admitted a larger and more diverse number of interests and factions that could proliferate and check each other, reducing the chance of one faction consolidating power and dominating the rest.[13] In this way representative democracy became a crucial component of modern republican government.

"Other republican institutions were not designed to check and disperse power but to instill the habits of civic virtue through good *civic* education of the citizens. Formal schooling was part of this, because book learning was deemed necessary to develop the mind. But republicans recognized that the general *social conditions* of a polity also shaped the mindset and character of its people, through daily experience that formed habits. A polity's social environment—the common practices and experiences of regular life—socializes people to the norms and mores of a way of life, and therefore provides training in how to relate to others. In short, a republic's social environment gives people a moral education (or, in a poorly designed polity, fails to do so). To maintain liberty, it is imperative that a republic educate citizens to habits of self-governance through experience and practice.

---

13   *The Federalist Papers*, no. 10 (James Madison, 1787).

"One idea along these lines was Thomas Jefferson's proposal for a 'ward system.' In the ward system, local communities and neighborhoods, with small populations of some dozens of people, would have responsibility for local affairs: they would run a primary school, maintain local roads and pathways, supply a constable, and so on. They would meet to discuss and decide about local issues and so would, through regular practice, learn how to take others' points of view and interests into account, to compromise, and to attend to their local collective good. The wards would be 'little republics,' Jefferson said, believing they could be the schools of the then-young American democracy."[14]

Jime thought that communitarian neighborhoods could serve a similar purpose. People in healthy local communities would learn to listen to each other, take in different perspectives, weigh different solutions to problems, consider the long-term good of the community, and take reciprocal, mutual action. In weekly and monthly meetings, and in carrying out the business of maintaining their communities, they would learn basic republican habits at the local level that they would also apply when considering larger questions of state, whether as regular voting citizens or, for some, as holders of public offices. Jime returned to the holovideo.

"Let us now consider economics. Many republicans over the centuries have argued for *moderation* of both wealth inequality and of consumption in order to maintain a republic. Aristotle pointed out that a city with great inequality was a house divided: the experiences and interests of the wealthy and the poor were so different that the society would become, in essence, two cities within the same walls, and those two cities would be at war with one another—a colorful way of describing factional civil conflict. Better to arrange things so that the polity is dominated by a middle class in which most people have a moderate level of wealth, Aristotle thought, so that people generally have similar experiences, develop similar outlooks, and share common interests.

---

14 Thomas Jefferson, "To Samuel Kercheval."

"Other republicans pointed out the negative effects of great wealth inequality on personal moral development. In addition to the sheer material injustice of some people being condemned to poverty and misery while others live in luxury and privilege, people in different classes become socialized to behave in certain ways. The wealthy become used to having their whims and desires met with little effort, and to treating other humans as servants, as mere instruments to their own satisfaction. Thus they learned habits of impulsiveness and domination. Meanwhile, the poor become accustomed to poverty, deprivation, and bad health. They also become habituated, out of necessity, to servility and obsequiousness. Worst of all, they eventually lose all hope of moral and material progress and so give up on attaining a better life, often falling into cynicism. On the other hand, in a polity where inequality is kept within a certain narrow range and all people are roughly of the same material and economic circumstances, people see each other as equals—because there they in fact are—and learn the moral habits of mutual respect, reciprocity, interdependence, and social trust—all of which facilitate carrying out public affairs.

"One example: where schools are private, or where they are public but of superior quality for those with money, such as in the American Ivy League system, education for a small elite is not only better for the rich but creates festering, nepotistic networks of contacts who give each other opportunities and access, and who develop a worldview from within their elitist bubble that makes them think they are superior to everyone else. Meanwhile, the poor receive inadequate schooling and develop no privileged networks. In contrast, in countries where education is public, schools are of equal quality, and the rich are compelled to send their children to school with everyone else, all parents, rich included, have an interest in ensuring that public education remains of the highest possible quality. Furthermore, in such societies the children of rich parents attend school with children of all classes and develop friendships with them, sometimes for life. That helps to pry open networking, instill norms of fairness, spread empathy, and prevent superiority complexes.

"One problematic development in the political economy of republicanism occurred in the eighteenth century, when a new capitalist economy of trade and manufactures emerged to replace the old agricultural economy. At the time there were various proposals for what was called 'commercial republicanism' to adapt the republican tradition to capitalism. However, there is a fundamental, fatal contradiction within commercial republicanism, because commerce is based on self-interest, but republicanism is based on setting aside self-interest and attending to the public good. The basic motive of any capitalist enterprise is the maximization of profit, and the basic motive of commercial consumerism is the maximization of personal pleasure. Meanwhile, the basic motive that makes republics work is civic virtue; indeed, intemperate pursuit of self-interest was traditionally defined as corruption that eventually led to a republic's downfall. Because commercial societies are based on markets, and markets involve the competitive pursuit of profits, wealth, status, and consumer goods, there are strong *structural pressures* in capitalism for people to unleash desires and indulge self-interest at the expense of the public good. Furthermore, a commercial, mercantile way of life develops *cultural norms* that promote the pursuit of self-interest as normal and natural, and indeed proclaim it the primary or even sole psychological motive of human beings. In short, the commercial side of a commercial republic has many powerful forces to promote corrupting self-aggrandizement. Meanwhile, forces to promote the civic virtues are weakened or entirely missing in commercial societies. Thus the balance of forces is weighted in favor of commercial self-interest winning out over the public good. There is nothing there by way of moral education to sustain a healthy polity. A commercial republic is no republic at all; it is only commerce.

"Some proponents of systems based on self-interest, however, argued that self-interest is in fact a virtue, saying that many people competing in the pursuit of their own interest improves the polity as a whole. This was the eighteenth-century philosopher Bernard Mandeville's famous argument in 'The Fable of the Bees' and the contention of many versions of liberalism, including libertarianism. The idea was to try to channel self-interest to the public good by arranging economic or political institutions to prevent concentrations of power and to produce collectively good results, such as lowered commodity prices or more representative government. It is an attempt to relocate civic virtue from individual citizens to institutions. Using self-interest to check self-interest is the main argument for market competition; it is also the argument for competition between political parties to win voter support and for dividing government powers between different competing branches so they check and balance each other.

"These can be good principles of institutional design, in that they can act as a backstop to hinder self-interest from producing bad outcomes—for example, when checks and balances stop a government leader from abusing power. But the idea that self-interested competition can produce *positive good* is a questionable proposition. Checks and balances have an inherently negating quality, in that they help *prevent or delay* bad government and tyranny, but don't by themselves *positively produce* good government. For that you still need civic virtue. A polity relying on checks and balances alone, but otherwise permeated with self-interest, might hold back the worst evils in government for a time before collapsing; but a polity that added civic virtue to the mix would be governed *well* and could rise to great accomplishments.

"Competition in politics, economics, and social life always takes place in the context of a set of rules that institute boundaries, procedures, and measures to limit the conflict. The only unlimited competition is open war, and even that normally has rules—but war is not a state of society; it is rather a negation of social relationships. Rules that set the terms for competition within a society *presuppose* cooperation in establishing those rules, and they presuppose some individual or group with enough collective virtue to safeguard and maintain the rules and to act as referee. Clearly, competition does not always result in social benefits but is sometimes very destructive.

"For example, economic competition can ruin entire communities and cities, sometimes to the same degree as war, when companies engage in what is called 'capital flight' or 'capital strike'—moving productive factories and other enterprises from one locale or country to another in order to get tax breaks, services, and favorable labor laws from communities willing to lower their standards. Capital strike is one of the main levers of power that capitalists have over the common people in their class war—perhaps the main lever. Allowing private individuals to have control over when and where society's capital is invested gives them a power like the sword of Damocles to hold over everyone else. Because people depend on their jobs for income to buy food, housing, and all the other goods of life, and because their jobs depend on capital investment, people become dependent on capitalists for their lives and for the lives of their communities. Consequently, capitalists use the threat of moving jobs away to extort tax breaks, subsidies, and other unearned benefits from communities.

"However, good economic policy that subjects capital to the rule of law and that provides education, infrastructure, and quality public services can create conditions for economic growth widely shared by all. Well-thought-out laws and regulations, established by those with civic virtue for the public good, can and should be used to prevent destructive competition and to create a growing, egalitarian economy.

"With capitalism's advanced physical and managerial technology, its promotion of limitless consumption and competitive profiteering has completely overwhelmed the public good. Awareness that we live in a common, shared society has all but disappeared under the pressure of self-interest; and our life-sustaining natural environment, surely a public good, lies in ruins. Capitalism took the self-governing republic of the United States and turned it into a giant shopping mall, where everything is commodified, natural resources are carelessly depleted, and all institutions, to the last, are twisted, by design, to make profits for oligarchs. These oligarchs now deem themselves entitled to make decisions for all of us, so democracy lies in ruins, too. It is necessary to have civic virtue in order to have good governance, a fair economy, a just society, and a healthy environment. We must halt the devolution of our civilization into a mere marketplace and restore a democratic republic that is governed in the interests of all. We hope you will join our cause before it is too late."

APPENDIX 2:
DEMOCRATIC SOCIALISM

The text Samantha read on her tablet, *Socialism and Democracy*, was a booklet that Jime had found in a holonet archive of O.U.S. political campaign literature from the early twenty-first century. Apparently there had been a surge of interest in democratic socialism in that country in the first decades of the century, before Mallworld was built. The text was a primer written to introduce socialism to those unfamiliar with it.

It began by identifying the group that it aimed to benefit:

"Because most common people have to work for a living, *economically* they have similar experiences and interests, regardless of whatever race, religious, or gender identity they might have. They therefore make up a group, or class, of people—the working class. Democratic socialists argue that the economy should work for the benefit of everyone, not the profit of the few; and this should be accomplished peacefully through social transformation that puts control of economic decisions in the hands of the working class. While there is always debate over the meaning of 'socialism,' as there is for most political ideals, today democratic socialists generally advocate for three institutions: 1) *community and workers' cooperatives* to replace privately owned corporations (this is the critical component); 2) *participatory economics*, or *parecon* for short, which involves democratic councils at the local, regional, and social levels to democratically coordinate economic activity; and 3) *social democracy*, that is, a traditional regulatory welfare state, democratically elected, transparent, and accountable.

"First, democratic socialists believe that economic enterprises should be run and controlled democratically by workers, either directly themselves or by choosing their officers, managers, executives, and others in positions of authority in free and fair elections. Community and consumer representatives, as affected stakeholders, should also be represented in enterprise governance. Democratic socialism is not fundamentally about income or wealth; it is about who has economic decision-making power. It primarily and categorically means that the principle of democracy has to be carried over from the political sphere to the economic sphere. This is because, just as people have a right to determine how their political enterprises are run, so they have a right to determine how their economic enterprises are run. Government affects every citizen and therefore should be democratic, while economic institutions affect every worker and therefore should be democratic too. A democratically run firm is called a *workers' cooperative*, in contrast to a private corporation, which is run by an elite board of executives hired to manage the enterprise in the interest of its (mostly absentee) shareholder owners. The details of the democratic arrangements might differ for different cooperatives, depending on their size, the nature of the production and work process in different sectors, and so on. But in principle, workers must regularly participate in discussions about company policy, procedures, production methods, investment decisions, and so on, and workers must have proportionate representation on company boards; they must also choose executives and managers at all levels. Representatives of local communities can and should also be included when communities are affected by what economic firms do, or when mutually beneficial interconnections between cooperatives and community institutions, such as hospitals, universities, or local governments, can be made. In some cases, workers own the firm directly; in others, communities can own the businesses and workers can be licensed to manage them.

"For workers to truly control their own cooperative firms and run them democratically, they need to have their own banks so they can accumulate capital for investment to maintain and expand the business operations. These workers' banks would make loans to cooperative firms. Co-ops could not and should not have to be dependent on private capital to make investments, because whoever controls capital investment decisions controls business. And so far, that's always been the wealthy, who have spare money accumulated that they can invest. Making the economic sphere democratic thus requires a source of capital other than private banks and stock markets. Workers would need cooperative, public banks, capitalized with their own funds and from the earnings of cooperative enterprises that workers control.

"In democratic socialism there would be no stock market: business enterprises, those all-important organizations that produce society's goods and generate people's incomes, would no longer be thought of as mere commodities, like a head of lettuce or a bolt of cloth, to be bought and sold by private, unaccountable, and mostly wealthy persons. Instead, firms would be recognized as what they are: organizations of free and equal persons cooperating in joint labor for economic production. They would be under the control of those most affected by their activities: the workers who make the company run, the consumers who depend on their goods and services, and the wider society that supports them within the economy generally by connecting them to roads, communications, and other infrastructure, and thus to customers, markets, and suppliers.

"Real-life examples of cooperative corporations exist and work quite well; this is not a utopian fantasy. The most famous is the Mondragon cooperative in the Basque region of Spain, which began in the mid-twentieth century as a small industrial workers' cooperative making electrical appliances, and eventually expanded into a multinational conglomerate and workers' federation with divisions in manufacturing, retail, finance, and knowledge. Here in the early twenty-first century, the conglomerate has grown to more than 250 companies employing nearly 75,000 people with over $15 billion in revenue. The scope of Mondragon's activities is broad: it manufactures consumer goods, electronics, home appliances, industrial components, automobile parts, construction products, machine tools, bicycles, camping equipment, exercise equipment, and more. It provides business services from architecture, design, and engineering to research, innovation, and business consulting. It operates retail supermarkets and hypermarkets (combination department and grocery stores) in Spain and France, as well as gas stations, sporting goods stores, and other enterprises. Its financial wing is not focused, like Wall Street, on appropriating wealth for the already wealthy but on supplementing social welfare benefits for its workers' retirement and disability, in order to complement the public benefits provided by the government of Spain. It also provides loans to households and small and medium-sized enterprises. Its knowledge division provides training, mainly through its own cooperative Mondragon University, which has schools of engineering, business studies, and humanities spread across more than a half dozen campuses. Mondragon also conducts research and development at over two dozen technology centers.

"Mondragon has a business culture rooted in the humanist values of its founder, the Catholic priest José María Arizmendiarrieta, which includes solidarity and shared participation. It embodies the democratic socialist principle of worker self-government, as far as any enterprise can in the wider context of the globalized, neoliberal capitalism of the time. Workers who are members in the cooperative each own a share of the company. They participate in major decisions and elect their managers and executives, both in the cooperative as a whole and in each subsidiary. General assemblies are held regularly. Mondragon has its own investment bank. Crucially, Mondragon limits inequalities of income within a narrow range by using maximum wage ratios between the highest- and lowest-paid

workers. These range from 3-to-1 through 9-to-1 in the different cooperative companies, and average 5-to-1; that is, in most cases, top executives
make no more than five times as much as the lowest paid worker. Since
most workers make more than the minimum, the difference in pay between
executives and average workers is even smaller than that. The ratios are
decided democratically by the workers themselves, periodically though a
vote. These ratios compare very favorably to the extreme pay ratios in privately owned capitalist firms, where executives might arrange to be paid as
much as 200 or 300 times the wage of the average worker.

"Mondragon is not entirely free from problems, of course; it is not a
utopian enterprise. As globalization proceeded, Mondragon's worker-owners in some subsidiaries found it necessary to expand the pay ratios somewhat, although these have not exceeded 9-to-1. Mondragon also found it
necessary to expand operations to other countries where subsidiary businesses paid workers wages or salaries but without democratic rights, as in
a standard capitalist firm. In the early twenty-first century, a situation arose
in which only a minority of employees in Mondragon supermarket chains,
less than a third, were worker-owners, which created a two-tiered system.
In 2008 members held a general assembly and approved a multiyear process to transform these subsidiaries into cooperatives and thus make worker-owners out of the wage workers. Another example: in the wake of the
2008 Great Recession, one of Mondragon's subsidiaries (which produced
home appliances) failed, showing that the cooperative wasn't immune from
market conditions. Mondragon's response was quite different from that of
a privately capitalized business, however: it first lent the company almost
$800 million to try to save it, but when that proved to be impossible, it
relocated the company's 600 workers to other companies in the conglomerate. Worker solidarity thus helped reduce the negative impact of poor
economic conditions on the lives of workers and their families.

"There are other examples of working cooperatives in many countries,
including Cooperative Home Care Associates, New Era Windows and
Doors, and others in the United States; Enspiral in New Zealand; Suma

wholesaler in the United Kingdom; and many more. Like capitalist businesses, some co-ops succeed while others do not, for various reasons. For instance, co-ops that start when employees try to take over a failing capitalist business often have a rough go of it. However, the existence and success of cooperatives for many decades, even under conditions of neoliberal capitalism, show the workability of the model. It can be generalized to the entire economy: all that's necessary is to change the law to establish workplace elections and workers' banks, and then implement the law in corporate practices. Not a simple or easy task, but also not unrealistic. There is nothing impractical or utopian about cooperatives to prevent them from being put in place; the only thing that stands in the way is the power of the class of wealthy capitalists who profit from the existing arrangements.

"Second, let's discuss economic democracy outside the individual firm. Democratic workers' control of economic enterprises is the definition and foundation of any truly democratic socialist order. If you don't have that, it's not socialism. But democracy in individual firms, while critically important, is not the sum of the economic life of society. Individual enterprises operate in a context of local, regional, and society-wide economic activity that also requires some measure of democratic coordination. Unrestrained and unregulated markets are excessively competitive, *always* lead to inordinate wealth inequality, and have very destructive outcomes for people, communities, and the natural environment. Rules, administration, and coordination are necessary to make a complex, modern, technical economy work. Decisions must be made about regional allocation of resources, rules of competition, market structure, legal requirements, certification of expertise, communications, utilities, transportation networks, financial infrastructure, matching of production to available labor, and many other considerations. These wider decisions about the economy outside the firm ought to be made democratically. Here are a few examples. Broadcast frequencies in a region need to be divided up and assigned; how will that be handled? A proposal to build a new shopping megastore is tabled; how this will affect a municipality's shopping habits, business activity, traffic patterns, and so on? A university proposes to buy up several blocks around campus, which will affect local living and business activities; how will both the community and the school deal with the changes? A new rail transit network for a city is proposed; where should the stations be, and where will the lines go? Questions like these need to be answered to make an economy work. Leaving them to private corporations or markets to decide is oligarchic, so how should a democratic socialist society make them?

"One proposal is *participatory economics*, or *parecon*, which advocates for multilevel, overlapping, elected representative councils to discuss and decide such matters. These councils would exist at the local, regional, and societal levels, and would be composed of representatives from cooperatives in the various economic sectors, as well as political representatives from the appropriate level. They would deliberate and determine policy about economic matters following the principle of *subsidiarity*, that is, making decisions and carrying out functions at the *appropriate* level of governance, with functions that are performed effectively by subordinate or local organizations handled by them, and those most effectively performed by the central government handled there.

"Thirdly, let's turn to *social democracy*, which is not quite the same thing as *democratic socialism*, despite the similarity of names. In a nutshell, democratic socialism is voting for your boss, while social democracy is the welfare state. Whereas democratic socialism focuses on *putting the people in control of economic life,* social democracy focuses on *economic well-being and equality.* Social democracy is a concept of government in which the state is a key instrument of promoting the economic and social welfare, or well-being, of the people. The term 'welfare' long ago took on a negative color, but in reality it only refers to the well-being, or well-faring, of people. In the social democracy model, the state funds and organizes programs and services that improve well-being, such as health care, education, pensions, public infrastructure, housing assistance, disability aid, unemployment insurance, child-care assistance, and others. It also creates agencies and programs that increase well-being by regulating health and safety, environmental pollution, and so on. These programs are funded through progressive taxation, or taxes that are larger for people with higher incomes. This not only helps fund the welfare state but also narrows the gap between the rich and poor.

"Social democratic taxation is often derided as 'redistribution,' the taking of wealth from those who have supposedly earned it fairly, and deserve it, to those who haven't. But that's a misnomer: that way of framing the issue assumes that the unequal income distribution of the unregulated market, in which the rich take the lion's share, is natural, justified, and deserved. In reality, however, the rich have *already redistributed* wealth to themselves, at the point of the paycheck, from the workers who actually produce goods and services and thus who truly earned and deserve it. The rich call this 'profit,' which is a kind of upward redistribution that had gone on for so long that it seems normal and natural. But profit is merely a social convention, one that convinces workers to accept the redistributing of much of the value that they create with their own hands and minds to those who haven't created and earned it. Thus, progressive taxation is not actually a *redistribution*, but a *restoration* of commonly produced wealth and value to its rightful, deserving owners and creators, the working people."

Sam had always thought that paychecks should not only show how much is deducted in taxes from workers' income, but how much is deducted in *profit* from the total value in goods and services that each worker produced. Perhaps no other single thing would create a workers' revolution faster than that!

"In any event, the fact that social democracy creates a *different* distribution of wealth and income from that of the uncontrolled market does not make it a *wrong* distribution," the book continued. "The rightness or wrongness of an economic distribution must be determined by moral standards that come from outside the market and are independent of it, just like the moral rightness or wrongness of a CEO's pay package must be determined by someone other than the CEO, or his or her toadies.

"Historically, the social democratic welfare state corrected for the inequalities, bad working conditions, and environmental destruction caused by capitalism's unregulated pursuit of profit. But even in a future after capitalism, a social democratic state will still be necessary to ensure a good quality of life, help administer economic affairs, and be a single point of authority to make, interpret, and enforce law on economic matters for society as a whole.

"Social democracy, additionally, holds that the government should provide certain things, like public goods and social insurance, that markets are bad at providing. For example, infrastructure—roads, bridges, ports, public transit, communications networks, education, electricity, water, sewerage, and other shared goods—is widely recognized as a government responsibility, even by conservative economists, although there are differences over specifics. Adam Smith himself, considered the father of capitalism, argued for a strong government role in providing infrastructure. Democratic socialists believe that such public goods should be funded at a very high level and be of very high quality, so good that there will be no need for people to look to private enterprise for such services.

"Because markets have inequalities built in, government must step in to provide goods and services that are needed for a good quality of life but that capitalism often fails to provide (or fails to provide in sufficient quantities) equally to all persons. There is no magical market system that can furnish all the goods and services needed in a society, myths of the 'invisible hand' notwithstanding. Education, health care, unemployment insurance, pensions, a basic income for the poor, leisure time, vacation time, parental leave, workplace safety and health, and decent working conditions are all things needed by people, but which capitalism does not adequately supply. Some public authority, whether local, regional, or central, has to step in to ensure delivery of these goods and services, either through direct provision, public programs, or mandating that nonstate providers do so. *Every* economy the world had ever seen was a *mixed* economy, involving both markets and state administration: under communist command economies, black markets arose to provide goods the *state* could not, while under capitalist economies that attempted 'minimal government,' state action was ultimately needed to provide goods that *markets* could not.

"The objection that public welfare makes recipients lazy and creates a 'culture of dependency' is often raised. So-called welfare dependence of course sometimes happens, because no program is perfect. But it is not a systemic problem: historically, the vast majority of people on welfare have also worked, and eventually they got off public assistance—using it as intended, as temporary help to get back on their feet. This objection is considerably overblown, mostly a myth, and pales in comparison to the amount of corporate welfare that occurs in capitalism.

"Social democracy also insists on the rule of law in the economic sphere. Whereas libertarians, conservatives, and orthodox economists rail against regulation as burdensome to business, social democracy holds that public regulation of business is not only necessary but is legitimate and *positive*. The state, as a public entity, has the *right* to make laws that economic firms *must* follow; it is necessary to regulate market activity so that it remains consistent with, and subservient to, the public good. Such laws include workplace safety and health laws, rules for competition, and rules to control pollution, among others. The arrival of modernity and industry brought with it vast, complex social machines in the form of large organizations: corporations especially, but also universities, churches, subnational governments, and others. These complex bodies make modern life extremely complex and systemically dangerous in many ways to individuals and groups: pollution or unsafe workplaces, for example, can injure, poison, traumatize, and kill when unregulated. It is therefore necessary for the publics of modern societies to have a vast social machine of their own, democratically accountable to the people, to protect their well-being. This is the modern regulatory welfare state.

"Social democracy mandates a much bigger role for government in managing the economy and providing certain goods than capitalism, with its outdated and dysfunctional faith in minimal government. The theory that the best government is that which governs least, that government should get out of the way and just let business do its own thing, was already invalidated in the nineteenth century by the horrors of the industrial revolution: child labor; sweatshops; filthy, crowded, disease-ridden cities; unsafe housing; inequality and poverty; industrial pollution of the air and water. Government was needed to step in to make capitalism consistent with human well-being, and *no* other institution could do it. *Only* government has the capacity to set rules that prevent and correct such massive failures of the market system, which permeates modern society. Markets still exist in a democratic socialist model because their pricing signals allow individuals and groups to coordinate complex production, distribution, and consumption activity that can't be done in any other way yet discovered. But under democratic socialism markets operate in an entirely new context, one that is democratic and not oligarchic. Instead of being attuned to the priorities and imperatives of a small class of people who have accumulated large amounts of financial capital, and who are accountable to no one, markets are set within a context of democratically decided and egalitarian laws, regulations, and administrative decisions made by workers, cooperatives, communities, and public authorities. The people would make decisions for themselves about pay, hours, working conditions, investment, production, and distribution. Workers making these decisions would end systemic exploitation, both by definition and in actual practice: they would no longer be working for the profit of the wealthy but for the benefit of themselves.

"The democratic socialist combination of social democracy, cooperative companies, and parecon would increase worker quality of life, improve working conditions, and enhance job security. Even more importantly, by putting the people in control, democratic socialism would respect worker humanity, autonomy, and self-governance, providing the material means for common people to be truly be self-governing republican citizens."

APPENDIX 3:
DELIBERATIVE DEMOCRACY

id had given his talk on deliberative democracy to ReBound supporters about ten times, and he was presenting it again to two dozen activists in the ReBound conference room. He always began his seminars by contrasting *deliberative* democracy with *representative* democracy.

"After the seventeenth and eighteenth centuries," Sid said, "representative democracy became the main way of doing politics in the modern world, and by the late twentieth century it had replaced older, nobility-based systems and also defeated most modern dictatorial challengers. But, as was commonly noted by political theorists, representative democracy was different from direct democracy. Direct democracy arranged things so that citizens governed themselves by gathering face-to-face in an assembly to make laws and public decisions directly, as in some ancient Greek city-states. In modern democracy, on the other hand, the people's political role was limited to electing representatives and other officials who would act in their stead as the makers and executors of laws.

"This was done partly for practical reasons, since in large modern nation-states, unlike in small ancient communities, it was impossible to gather all the citizens into one place—and even if one could, such an assembly would be too large to discuss anything. But direct democracy was also rejected out of deeper fears: it was traditionally believed that the common people were too uninformed and impulsive to govern well, that they were vulnerable to the emotional appeals of demagogues, and that direct democracy was too unstable. Modern political theorists generally preferred to filter people's desires through representatives who, they believed, would slow the process down and temper decision-making with wisdom and expertise.

"However, as the modern era progressed it became clear that representative democracy was still vulnerable to demagoguery and ignorance. Furthermore, it created new problems of its own making. Representative democracy was not usually very representative, actually: it tended to underrepresent or exclude major social groups, such as women, people of color, and the poor—often enough, groups that made up the majority of the populace. Such groups were marginalized in every modern 'representative' democracy; thus experience showed that underrepresentation/exclusion was a feature, not a bug. Additionally, and most critically, among large populations of modern societies, candidates for office needed to mount large, costly, media-based political campaigns in order to be elected. Consequently, money-driven political campaigning and lobbying processes evolved that, over time, tilted law and policy making in favor of those who had the most wealth. Eventually, representative democracy evolved into *representative oligarchy*, in which governments represented the interest of the wealthy few rather than the interests of everyone.

"Importantly, the emergence of oligarchy was made possible by a feature of representative democracy that bred habits of political apathy in the common people, rather than habits of political participation. Political philosophers as early as Jean-Jacques Rousseau in the eighteenth century pointed out that representative democracies did not ask much of citizens and only rarely made space for them to participate in politics: once every few years, during elections, citizens were prompted to choose from a limited menu of candidates, and for most people, that was the sum total of their political activity, if they even did that much.[15] The real action of governing was otherwise done by political and economic elites. By demanding

---

15 Jean-Jacques Rousseau, *On the Social Contract*, Book 3, chap. 15 (1762).

so little in the way of political obligation, the basic structure of representative democracy thus did not induce much political participation, and consequently the people did not develop habits of active participation but instead became habituated to apathy, leaving the political field uncontested for oligarchs to dominate. Representation caused a separation between the people and governing. It was no wonder that people *felt* alienated from politics—they *were* alienated, as a matter of fact.

"Thus representative democracy contains within itself a fatal contradiction: it needs the people's participation in order produce accurate representation, but because actual governing is reserved for a few representatives, in both theory and practice, the people participate only infrequently. Consequently, their habits of participation degrade over time, and representation ceases to accurately reflect the will of the people and becomes biased toward an elite. In that way, representative democracy is destined to commit slow suicide."

Sid paused and sipped some water before continuing. "By the late twentieth century, some democratic thinkers began to argue that one solution to these problems would be to create frequent opportunities in the political system for conscious, structured, joint *deliberation* by everyday people. This would give them more of a voice, increasing the representativeness of representative democracy and reducing political apathy. Deliberation would be a way for citizens to critically examine political issues in concert with each other, sharing information and refining their opinions, and it would reconnect them to political life and help restore government legitimacy.

"Let me introduce a conceptual distinction that was made in the eighteenth century by the Irish statesman Edmund Burke between reason and what he called 'prejudice.' By prejudice Burke didn't mean only racial or ethnic prejudice, but was using the term in an older sense to refer to thinking off the top of one's head: prejudice meant taking the first thought that pops to mind as the true one, leaping from thought to thought haphazardly, indulging streams of consciousness, or jumping to impulsive conclusions, all without adequate critical examination. The Latin root of the word prejudice was *judicium*, or judging; the word could be read as 'pre-judgment.' Prejudice could, to be sure, refer to unreflective bigotry against particular groups of people, but it could also more widely refer to any belief that had not been subjected to reasoned reflection. Prejudice in this sense, strictly speaking, was not entirely a bad thing, for most of the assumptions people in any given culture develop about the world are accurate enough and enable them to operate and function successfully, but are usually taken for granted and not usually exposed to reasoned scrutiny. The philosopher Edmund Husserl in the 1930s introduced the concept of the "lifeworld" to describe the universe of self-evident, given beliefs and conventions that people in a culture share and experience together, and which is the starting point for any rational inquiry. It seems clear to me that the existence of a shared lifeworld makes social life possible and smooth," Sid opined. "Yet, the taken-for-granted ideas of the lifeworld—what Burke had called prejudices—must not remain immune from critique, for sometimes they became outdated, outmoded, and obsolete as conditions change but assumptions do not. That causes social problems or even grave injustice and oppression, and those who over-valorize their own culture or folk can get into ethical trouble. While the whole of the lifeworld cannot be subject to rational examination all at once, parts of it can be, and should be, regularly. Yet, all too often modern mass society has encouraged people to operate merely according to unreflective prejudice, and has had too few institutions to promote reflective reasoning.

"Critics of democracy had historically blamed turbulence and instability on the passions and irrationality of the *demos*," Sid went on. "But in advanced societies where the main channels of communication and information dissemination are technological media networks, people are constantly bombarded by advertising from interest groups and political parties, and by the ideas of 'opinion makers' and 'thought leaders.' Furthermore, in modern societies the media is not a democratic institution but is largely owned and controlled by capitalists, and therefore the media mainly follows the capitalist logic of profit. Overall, information in the wider media environment is propagated by political and economic elites, who have vested interests in manufacturing support for their self-serving programs and agendas. Thus, mediated political 'information' is almost always misleading rather than informative, and furthermore is designed to overstimulate people's emotional responses—for example, by agitating racism or xenophobia to win political support. Thus, elite-steered media is a prime source of the ignorance and emotionalism among the common people that is condemned as a flaw of democracy by the very elites who propagate that low-quality content. The *demos* can't be blamed when it is the victim of propaganda and emotional manipulation. You can't have demagoguery without demagogues: it is invariably a member of the *elite* who is actively distorting information and misleading the people, and it is the perpetrator, not the victims, who must bear the blame for such a crime against freedom and self-government.

"Modern mass media, guided by the elites who control it, distorts consciousness and misleads people in a systemic way. Most turmoil and division in political discourse is a media production, caused by media outlets, sometimes owned by or under the sway of factions with political agendas, that compete to gain attention, ratings, and cash by making the most noise, by saying the most shocking things, and by encouraging tension and conflict. In short, conflict sells: higher ratings bring in more advertising revenue. In fostering turbulence and conflict, media help to divide people into separate perspectival communities, in which people develop different worldviews and forget what beliefs they share. Eventually people become polarized into perspectival *factions* that share nothing but mutual hatred and contempt. I'll remind you that the classical republicans considered factions to be a threat to the existence of republics, because if one faction gains the upper hand it can tyrannize over others. In modern, mediated societies, factions led by demagogues have turned democracies into dictatorships more than once.

"Deliberative democracy, I believe, would help ameliorate the problem of perspectival factions, facilitate the overcoming of prejudice, and help get around the problem of elite-mediated political disinformation. It would do so by allowing people, in face-to-face interactions, to directly inform each other and engage in conscious consideration and discussion of what they learn, in face-to-face interactions. It is not meant to be a mob melee of yelling and shouting about politics, as has all too often been the case on social media and on commercial mass-media 'talk' shows—which more often resemble the antidemocratic stereotype of chaotic, argumentative mob politics than does actual democratic deliberation by regular people. Polarized civic discourse is a symptom of a *lack* of deliberation, not a surfeit of it.

"Deliberative democratic theory, rather, advocates structured, bounded, refereed discussion by citizens with each other, for the purpose of reconsidering their prejudices and developing more considered opinions about politics, which should then inform their voting choices. Such structured deliberation, by its very nature, counters short-term, impulsive, tweet-like thinking in politics, because it is a practice of examining issues in a slow, reflective way. I believe that deliberation could act as a countervailing social force to the power of the media. In a highly mediated society, the media have a certain influence or force over people, regardless of any partisan considerations. Deliberative democracy would provide a space and opportunity to circumnavigate that media force by allowing citizens to interact on a face-to-face basis and learn from each other, thereby getting around the media filters. Deliberation has the potential to be a democratic counterweight to the institutions of the media, both the elite framings of mass media and the impulsive free-for-all of social media."

Sid then presented a proposal for Deliberation Day, an idea described by Bruce Ackerman and James Fishkin in the early twenty-first century.[16] "Ackerman and Fishkin were O.U.S. scholars who approached deliberation

---

16 Bruce Ackerman and James Fishkin, *Deliberation Day* (New Haven: Yale University Press, 2004).

from a starting point of political opinion polling," he began. "They found that polling usually only measured what they called voters' 'raw preferences' or off-the-cuff responses—that is, their prejudices—not their considered opinions. In fact, they found that when people didn't know an answer to a survey question, often they just made one up so they wouldn't be embarrassed by admitting ignorance. Ackerman and Fishkin concluded that standard political polls couldn't tell what an informed, considered opinion of the people might be. That would require measuring their 'refined preferences,' or their thoughts after a period of deliberation.

"So they introduced the idea of a 'deliberative opinion poll,'" Sid continued, "which combined small-group deliberation meetings with larger samples of public opinion in order to determine what an *informed* public opinion might look like. People participating in a deliberative poll were selected randomly and offered some incentive to participate, usually a small cash stipend. Then they went to a research center and spent a weekend learning basic knowledge about certain issues and discussing and debating amongst themselves. They filled out questionnaires before and after the deliberations, and it was often the case that their opinions changed through the deliberative process. Learning and deliberation helped them refine their preferences and change their minds.

"Ackerman and Fishkin took this finding and turned it into an idea for a national holiday that they called Deliberation Day. In their proposal, a holiday was set aside for deliberation two weeks before an election—actually, deliberations were split over two days, so that emergency service workers could participate. Citizens would gather at local venues—schools, mostly—to deliberate in a structured, refereed setting about the current issues being discussed by political candidates. People could choose to go or not; if someone did participate, he or she would receive a stipend of $150 in Old United States dollars, or 6,000 Mallworld store credits, for the day's work. Participants would spend the day in both small-group deliberations of about fifteen people and large-group deliberations of about five hundred people. The schedule would go like this:

"About a month before Deliberation Day, the political parties would propose two major issues each to be on the agenda.

"Deliberation Day would start at nine o'clock a.m. The first event would see everyone gathered in a school, public auditorium, or similar space to watch a live televised political debate between presidential candidates.

"At ten fifteen, after the debate, people would be randomly assigned to small groups of fifteen people. Each group would choose its foreperson randomly. Then they would have the task of sitting down together to deliberate, with a goal of coming up with questions to be proposed in a later, larger group debate. Each person would get ninety seconds to talk, a time limit enforced by the foreperson. Vulgar, obnoxious, or rude participants could be ejected by a supermajority vote of the small group, or twelve out of fifteen people; two ejections meant that the person couldn't come to Deliberation Day anymore.

"At about eleven o'clock, everyone would move into an auditorium for the citizen assembly, a larger debate in front of a live audience. This debate would be between local representatives of the major parties—local politicians, officeholders, etc.—and would be moderated by local community leaders, such as heads of charities. They would be asked the questions submitted by the small groups.

"After that would be a lunch break, served in the local facility, if possible.

"Around two o'clock in the afternoon, the process is repeated as a follow-up to the morning's deliberations. People again would deliberate in small groups, then move into another citizen assembly at three o'clock. The goal here is to clarify matters from the morning or to raise issues that didn't get covered but that are important to someone.

"At four fifteen, people return to their small group for a very important concluding session. Here they sum up their impressions and discuss matters that have been left hanging. For example, what concerns were not answered? Which party did a better job? Did the deliberations change anyone's mind about anything?

"At five o'clock, the foreman signs everybody's certificate of attendance and turns them in so that everyone will get paid.

"One key feature is that there is *no voting* at the end of Deliberation Day itself. It is *not* direct democracy. Voting for representatives would come two weeks later during the regular election. With deliberation, however, that voting would occur in a different context—one in which people had seriously discussed political issues in a way that they would not have otherwise. During the next two weeks, the discussions that started on Deliberation Day would continue at breakfast tables, around office coolers, in lunchrooms, and elsewhere, raising the level of political debate to a higher plane in the run-up to Election Day.

"Ackerman and Fishkin estimated the costs for Deliberation Day in the early 2000s for the Old United States, and while it would not be cheap, it also would not be a budget-buster. The O.U.S. electorate then consisted of about one hundred million people, and if seventy million showed up to deliberate, the cost, including stipends and administrative costs, would be $14.98 billion; for fifty million participants, $11.96 billion; for thirty million participants, $7.37 billion. This was pennies on the dollar compared to the total O.U.S. budget of $3.65 *trillion* and total economic production of $18.56 *trillion*—a sound investment in democracy."[17]

Sid wrapped up by explaining some of the more theoretical justifications for deliberative democracy that had been offered by political philosophers.

"As Ackerman and Fishkin noted, deliberation allows citizens to transform their opinions and preferences from a raw to a refined state; deliberation is *educational* for citizens, because it allows them to share information, perspectives, and ideas with each other. As the political theorist Bernard

---

17   All figures in 2017 USD. Original data from Ackerman and Fishkin (2004). Administrative costs taken from Appendix A, Table A, p. 227; stipend totals estimated for a $150 stipend, adjusted for inflation. US budget estimate for 2017; US GDP estimate for 2016.

Manin said of citizens deliberating together, 'They spread light.'[18] During deliberation, people share their expertise and knowledge in an informal way, unmediated by elites and undistorted by the fog of media advertising and propaganda, so people's judgment would improve by becoming more clearly informed.

"People are also educated in a moral sense by being exposed to the concerns and needs of others. Deliberation is to be done face-to-face, not in the anonymous, impulsive, impersonal way of holonet social media, where virtually every expression is an expression of a prejudice. Consequently, debate is less likely to become vitriolic—although nothing can *completely* eliminate contentious periods of debate on certain issues, and it's probably not even desirable to do so. During the process of deliberation, people hear the concerns of others, learn about what matters to them, and often discover that issues they believed trivial could actually be of vital importance to other people. And since politics is not just about common, shared problems, but also about common, shared solutions, deliberators have to consider and negotiate policies that will work not only for them but for other people, too. Deliberation is thus transformative in a moral way by expanding citizens' moral horizons, as they come to more deliberately consider the needs of others. This isn't *moralizing* in the sense that it imposes a moral code, for it does not; that's for the deliberators to figure out for themselves. But it's *morally expansive* in that it extends citizens' considerations to include not just themselves and their own concerns, but also those of others and of the public as a whole.

"ReBound hopes to one day introduce Deliberation Day to the Mall. But in the meantime, we're putting it into practice within our organization by using it in advance of our elections for ReBound officers, as well as periodically when a significant policy is proposed for the group. We believe in democracy, and we practice what we preach."

---

18   Bernard Manin, "On Legitimacy and Political Deliberation," trans. Elly Stein and Jane Mansbridge, *Political Theory* 15, no. 3 (August 1987).

ABOUT THE AUTHOR

Jeffery Zavadil is an author and political theorist interested in democratic socialism, classical republicanism, environmentalism, liberalism, and communitarianism. He lives and works in Washington, D.C., where he has done policy work on democracy and human rights as well as analysis of global political extremism. He has taught college courses on ideologies, democratic theory, and political metaphor. He is an activist with progressive political groups and helps organize the best philosophy book club in D.C. He lives with his long-term girlfriend and their cat, and when not reading, writing, or discussing philosophy and politics, he enjoys jazz, modern art, and modern architecture, and travels when he can. This is his first book.

Books coming soon:

Mallworld, Inc.: Bound Together, forthcoming Summer 2020

Mallworld, Inc.: Bound Forward, forthcoming Fall 2020

Connect with me:

Website: www.coexalt.com

Facebook: https://www.facebook.com/MallworldInc/

Twitter: https://twitter.com/JefferyZavadil